CEREMONY OF DARKNESS

She was jolted out of the reverie by a strange sensation—Enrique knelt in front of her, a clay pot beside him and a paintbrush in his hand, applying blue paint to her body. He smeared the cool liquid over both her feet and then up her leg, dipping the brush in the large pot after each two or three strokes.

"Spread your legs," he said, as he swabbed her inner thighs, almost to her pubic hair.

When he was done, he led her to the mat, and they sat down facing each other as they had the time before. He handed her a large golden goblet with bas-reliefs of Mayan deities covering its outer surface. "Drink," he commanded—and she did.

POWERPOINT

John Selby Smith

WARNER BOOKS

A Warner Communications Company

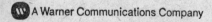

Itzam'na
The cross-eyed god of the heavens
Pierced the backbone of the mountain
And all the vastness of eternity
Shuddered.

(from the ancient Mayan *Chilam Balam*)

When a child is born in the Quitapul tribe of highland Guatemala, the midwife attending the birth is a "bruja," a Mayan sorceress. She can divine immediately if the infant is a normal Indian, or destined to be a member of the cult of witch doctors and sorcerers who rule over the tribe's destiny.

There are three levels of sorcerers among the Quitapul. First there are the witch doctors who deal in white and black magic. Then there are the fortune-tellers and mystics who prophesy forthcoming events. Finally, and rarely, there are superior sorcerers who can commune directly with the gods. These sorcerers are born cross-eyed, and are by this token recognized to possess immense occult powers.

Since the conquest of Guatemala by the Spaniards, the Catholic Church has tried to eradicate the influence of the ancient Mayan deities among the Indians. However, certain isolated tribes such as the Quitapul have successfully resisted European attempts to destroy the power of the pagan gods. Even to this day, the thin veneer of Christianity imperfectly conceals the true grain of the ancient Mayan civilization.

According to Mayan tradition and the Quitapul calendar, a great sorcerer is destined to be born during the present era, who will lead the Quitapul into a new age of dominance and glory. History awaits the appearance of this special being.

POWERPOINT

chapter 1

In the early afternoon the glassy stillness of the lake begins to give way to a subtle movement of air coming from the west, a wind called the Xocomil by the local Indians. The Xocomil starts as a slight cooling breeze but quickly picks up to a strong head of wind. By three o'clock the waves are treacherous on the lake, and the fishermen in their dugout cayucos are gone from sight back to their village. As sunset approaches the wind dies down again for the night, and the waves are large but well formed as they crash against the low breakwater of the hot springs pool.

An American in his late thirties sat cross-legged with his friend in the small hot pool at the foot of the hot springs cliff. His eyes were closed; the warm glow of the setting sun sent twisting, glowing snake-shapes across the inside of his eyelids. He sighed with contentment, listening to the splashing of the waves intermingled with the cacophony of birds singing in the trees up above the cliff.

With the wind reduced to a mere sigh of air, Chris could savor the heady scent of orchids, begonias, and jacaranda flowers, with hints of orange and pine. The lake, at five thousand feet above sea level, was a combination of the tropics and the mountains. Ah, Guatemala! he thought. After two weeks here at the hot springs house which he

11

had rented from a local Ladino, he was finally feeling completely relaxed, as if for the first time in his life he was at the right place at the right time, ready for anything. San Francisco seemed so distant that his life there was no more real than any of the vivid dreams he had been having. Only the anticipated arrival of his daughter in a week gave him reason to think of things in the States. As the days rolled by, he was more and more considering the possibility of never returning home.

"Chris, look," the woman beside him said suddenly, her voice pulling him out of his reverie. "There's someone swimming around the point, heading this way."

He opened his eyes slowly, allowing the panorama in front of him to manifest itself. There was the shimmering expanse of the lake, ten miles across, reflecting the rays of the low-sloping sun to the west. And towering above the lake, the volcano. Chris still hadn't lost his sense of awe at the sight of the giant, cone-shaped mountain.

But at this time of day, with the sun almost touching its south side, the volcano somehow instilled in Chris, as it always did, an inexplicable anxiety. All day long he would be overjoyed at finding himself at this magnificent lake, the sun warm, the Indians open-hearted toward him, his immediate world at peace; but when sunset approached, a sense of foreboding crept across the lake from the opposite side, and the volcano itself took on a somehow ominous stance.

"It's a woman," Wendy said, sitting with the top of her bathing suit off, her breasts catching the last sloping rays of the sun. "I wish she'd turn around and swim away. I don't really feel like socializing."

Chris gazed at the swimmer stroking powerfully through the waves, then turned and looked at Wendy. They were fellow teachers at Marin Junior College; he had known her for several years, and they had been lovers for the last six months. He had enjoyed the relationship in the States, but somehow, down here in this primitive, vital Mayan

12

world, she seemed two-dimensional, lacking something Chris could not define but knew he was hungry for. "Relax," he said. "There's always room for one more."

"You're so generous with your hot water."

"It isn't my hot water," he said, looking again across the rippling lake to the deep greens of the volcano's lower slopes, where coffee plantations grew up the bottom half of the mountain. "This is really Indian property; the Spanish stole it from them. I was talking with one of the fishermen earlier today; he rowed over and we chatted. He wouldn't elaborate, but he told me that this hot spring used to be a powerpoint of the Quitapul tribe that lives over there under the volcano."

"A powerpoint?" Wendy asked, not really interested, watching the approaching swimmer with a mixture of impatience and anxiety.

"That's what he called it in Spanish. He had a Indian name for it but I forget what it was."

Wendy took a sharp breath of surprise and sat upright in the hot water. "My God, Chris, it's that damned Indian woman again!"

Chris tried to make out the features of the swimmer squinting to sharpen his slightly myopic vision. Her long black hair trailed in the water like a horse's mane, and her arms were strong as they stroked through the waves. "It can't be her," he said, feeling a flutter of excitement in his stomach. "Indian women aren't even allowed to swim in the lake at all after they have their first period. There's a taboo against it."

"Well, it's her, I *know* it is," Wendy said, biting her lower lip. "Goddamnit, I don't like it at all! She was there staring at us at the bus stop when we arrived here, and she's been tailing us ever since."

"You don't even know if it's her," Chris retorted. "I can't tell from this distance."

But as the swimmer approached, Chris felt a dry sensation gripping at his throat, half anxiety, half excitement. It

13

was the woman, he couldn't forget that face, the dominating broadness of the Mayan forehead, the high beauty of her cheekbones, and the incongruously Caucasian nose.

And the eyes—he could see those penetrating crossed eyes of hers glancing up at him now as the woman raised her head to look toward the pool. He had encountered those same eyes at least a dozen times since he and Wendy had arrived at the lake—staring at him as he walked down the bustling main street of Panahachel; watching him as he bought vegetables at the outdoor marketplace; and just yesterday, eyeing him at the public beach by the Hotel del Lago. That same woman, standing taller than any of the other Indians, and yet definitely an Indian, wearing the traditional native costume of one of the tribes on the lake.

She raised her head again and Chris found himself looking directly into her eyes, into the one eye that focused on him while the other drifted. It was not an uncommon visual disorder—his daughter Michelle had it, though in a milder form, never quite obviously enough to warrant the surgery that might correct it, but there was the uncanny feeling about this Indian woman's divergent gaze that it might be her natural, ordained state, and not a bodily malfunction. Chris felt acutely uneasy as he met her stare. Just the night before, he had dreamed in vivid detail of a sexual encounter with this woman, and now, she was actually swimming toward him and Wendy, with the obvious intent of joining them in the hot pool.

"I don't like it one bit," Wendy said, her voice nasal with anxiety. She shrugged into her bikini top. "She's spooky and I don't want her here."

"She must be Ladino." Chris pondered. "Indians don't wear bathing suits and—"

"I want you to tell her to leave, Chris. You speak Spanish. Tell her this is a private beach, and we don't want company."

The woman reached the low breakwater that separated

14

the hot springs pool from the cool water of the lake. Without hesitating, she climbed quickly up the slippery rocks, as if she had made the climb many times before. Chris watched the movement of her sensual body, displayed rather than truly concealed by the one-piece bathing suit; he registered fleetingly that it had the air of being in the latest fashion. A rush of sexual energy shot through him, an energy that had been missing with Wendy ever since they had come to Guatemala two weeks ago.

The woman paused on top of the breakwater, ten feet away from where Chris and Wendy sat. Her crossed eyes gave her poised, assured presence a disturbing edge.

"Hola," she said in a low, melodic voice, while she casually squeezed water from her long black hair. And then in precise city Spanish, not the guttural Mayan accent that Chris had become familiar with in the lake communities: "Might I perhaps join you?"

Captivated, and ignoring Wendy's plea for solitude, Chris responded with proper Spanish formality: "Por supuesto." He gave Wendy a determined stare.

The woman walked the three steps across the rocks of the breakwater and then touched her toe into the water of the pool. Chris watched her graceful gesture, glad finally to be this close on a personal basis to an Indian. Many times in the last two weeks, he had looked into a Mayan woman's eyes in passing her on the road to town or in the marketplace, and experienced a feeling of immediate heart contact, a warmth and an openess almost never found in his own world. But they were fleeting moments only.

This woman was somehow both Indian and *not* Indian at the same time. She stepped into the water and walked across the knee-deep pool, her grace primitive but the calculated sexual candor of her maillot quite contemporary. She sat down beside Chris, sending ripples across the pool. "Ay, perfecto," she said.

For some moments, nobody spoke, and the conversation void was filled by the sound of the waves breaking

15

against the rocks, and the lilting, chirping of small birds in the trees above them. Chris knew that Wendy was upset, but did not care. He was tired of catering to her shallow alarms and irritations; he wanted to relax and flow with whatever might be happening, to experience every minute as it came and went.

A blue heron was flying over the lake a hundred yards out, its neck pulled back against its chest, its legs sticking straight out behind it, its great wings stroking through the air, as the woman beside him had stroked through the waves minutes ago. How remarkable she is, Chris mused. Ever since seeing her at the bus stop when he had arrived in Panahachel, he had had her on his mind, the image of her rough gracefulness and athletic sensuality remaining in his mind's deeper recesses like an ongoing dream, reinforced each time she had appeared. How old is she? he wondered. Her lips with their full flush of youth, her skin with its soft, slender almost adolescent, tautness, were belied by a somberness in her eyes, and a mature sense of purpose in her bearing. She was at least five, maybe even ten years younger than his own thirty-four years, Chris estimated.

"The sunset," she said suddenly, as the sun neared the southern edge of the conical mountain. "It is so powerful, seen from this side of the lake. Over where I am from, in Zacapula, the sun goes down so abruptly behind the volcano."

Wendy, at a loss with Spanish, asked Chris what the woman had said. Chris told her in a low, half-mesmerized voice as he stared at the setting sun and felt the Indian's radiating presence.

"She barely got into that bathing suit," Wendy said. "The way it fits and what she's showing, she must have gone to the Junior Miss department. Ask her who the hell she is and why she's been following us."

"I'm sure it's been pure coincidence that we've seen her so often," Chris said curtly.

"Well if she's from the other side of the lake like she

16

just said she is, what has she been doing over on *this* side for the last two weeks?"

"That's her privilege."

"She *spooks* me with those damned crossed eyes," Wendy went on, nervous and needing to talk. "I wish we could leave tomorrow; I've had enough of this lake. We could fly to Puerto Vallarta and have Michelle meet us there. *Please,* Chris."

He looked at her with impatience. "You know Michelle's been waiting for months to come down here to Guatemala. She's the one who put the Guatemala bug in my ear in the first place."

"Well the reality of this place is completely different from those mystic Mayan tourist books she's been reading."

"And just what *is* the reality down here?" Chris asked. "Here we are in paradise, with fresh papayas and mangos for five cents apiece at the marketplace; this entire virgin lake to enjoy; hundreds of friendly Indians—"

"Indians who used to cut out girl's hearts, who probably still would if the Catholics hadn't taken over and stopped the sacrifices."

"The Indians would be a lot better off if the Church had left them alone," Chris said.

"The Church taught them that God can be loving, that he doesn't require human sacrifice to appease him."

"The Church taught them that their culture is inferior to the white man's culture," Chris said heavily, "that their Mayan tradition is of no value, that they're all sinners who have to bow down to the white man's God or else—"

"Well you just stay here with your Mayan princess, then," Wendy snapped. "I'm going up to the house."

She leaned forward and glanced angrily at the other woman. Then she sat back against the wall with a sharp exhalation. "Well!" she muttered. "God, how could I have been so *dense?*"

"What're you talking about?"

"You two've been eyeing each other all *along*. It hasn't

been just her, you're *both* in on this. You want to make it with a Mayan beauty and I'm in the way. Well I'll just make my exit and leave you two alone."

"Get off it, Wendy!"

She stood up and stared at him, then at the woman. "Enjoy the sunset," she said tersely, and quickly climbed up the boulder to where her thongs and towel were. Chris wanted to deny her accusations, but remained silent, no words coming to mind.

Wendy disappeared up the trail to the house. Chris had for some time been expecting a confrontation with her. He knew that she sensed his recent dissatisfaction with her, that he had hurt her deeply. He should follow her up to the house now, he told himself, make peace, try to help her work through her erupting emotions. He remained where he was.

"She should return north," the woman beside him said suddenly in Spanish. "She is out of place here."

The words had the weight of a verdict. Chris said nothing. He became aware of an acute tension in his stomach and, with that recognition, could feel the heat of the water starting to relax his muscles.

A gust of wind blew over the waves a hundred feet out from shore, tossing golden crests of spray into the sunset air. The sun, hanging just above the side of the volcano, seemed to finally give in to the pull of the mountain. The distance between the globe of fire and the solid edge of the volcano was bridged and the sun merged with the earth.

"Our tradition tells us what happened here a thousand years ago," the woman said, her low voice almost in harmony with the lapping of the waves. "The earth shuddered, the top of the volcano blew off, ash filled the sky and hid the sun. Lava flowed from the volcano, destroying the old town of Zacapula on its slopes."

Her words stopped as abruptly as they had started. The sun disappeared behind the volcano and was gone. The breeze seemed suddenly much cooler. Without warning,

18

the woman brought the palm of her hand down with a slap against the smooth surface of the pool. "Like that!" she said. "Itzam'na cracked open the volcano."

"Itzam'na?"

"And at the same moment, an earthquake opened up this side of the lake and hot water started running out of this cliff. A child was conceived in the womb of a bruja, and nine months later he was born. His power lasted for five hundred years."

She seemed to have ended her story. "Then what happened?" Chris asked.

She did not respond. Chris looked away from the volcano and at her face. Both eyes, the normal one and the wanderer, had a common focus now, his face, and they pierced into him. "You know as well as I do," she said in a harsh dry tone. "The Spanish came. Itzam'na sent them as punishment for the Quitapuls' sins; they killed the priests and destroyed the new city of Zacapula. Evil striking out at evil. And in the midst of the conquest, do you know what happened?"

"No."

"An earthquake hit, the worst ever to strike the lake. The Quitapul temples collapsed, the sacred tunnel was sealed off, and all the gold of the Quitapul, an immense treasure, was buried."

"Why are you telling me this?" Chris asked, his eyes unable to leave hers.

"Because you are sitting in a shrine of my people."

"I don't see any shrine."

"Of course not," she said hotly. "The Spanish destroyed it all. They know the Mayan gods had hidden the Quitapul treasure from them, and they were very angry. They destroyed everything. But there are some things that can never be destroyed."

She stood up suddenly.

'Wait!" Chris said.

"It is too hot for me to stay in the pool long," she said. "I am going for a swim in the lake. Will you join me?"

19

She extended her hand. She was staring at him again, with her stable right eye focused on him while the wandering left one stared off to the side. He found himself thinking again of his daughter back in California, reminded of her as much by the intensity this Indian woman shared with her as by their common physical anomaly.

He reached up and took the offered hand, feeling the contact of their skin, palm to palm. Her fingers maintained the touch after he was on his feet, and she looked him up and down appraisingly. He had recently brought his body back into shape with a jogging schedule every morning and evening, and she smiled approvingly as her eyes met his again. They were once more both focused on him; he reacted with a shudder throughout his body, as if she could project an unseen beam of energy at him when her eyes were working in unison.

"My eyes, do they bother you?" she said softly.

"A little," he said. "My daughter's cross-eyed too; strabismus, they call it; it's a serious problem."

Her fingers gripped his hand tightly. "Your daughter," she said. "Is that Michelle, whom you were talking about, who is coming down soon?"

"How did you know that?"

"I speak some English," she said. Her left eye slowly abandoned its focus and drifted away from Chris's face.

"I wish you wouldn't play with your eyes like that," he said impatiently.

"I am not playing," she said hotly. "Only an ignorant gringo could possibly say such a thing to a Quitapul."

"You're not Quitapul," he challenged her. "You're a Ladina."

"Please, I have no Spanish blood in me so I am definitely not Ladina. I am a Quitapul, from Zacapula." She gestured with a sweep of her free hand toward the volcano.

"You're pure Indian?" Chris pressed.

She was staring out across the lake. The sky behind the volcano looked as if it had caught fire from the sunset glow. "My mother, she was Quitapul," she said. "My father, he is the same as you, a gringo. I think he said once he was part English, part French. I don't remember and we don't talk to each other now, so perhaps I will never know. It doesn't matter. Tell me, Christopher—"

"You know my name."

"I have heard it."

"From whom?"

"Around town."

"And you are called . . . ?" he asked, still aware that she was holding his hand, aware that there was a consciousness independent of their talking minds, aware of the physical contact and the bridge it made between their two bodies.

"I am called Magdalena in Spanish," she said.

"And in Quitapul, what?"

"Caban does not allow a gringo to know the Quitapul name of one of his people."

"Who's Caban?" Chris asked.

"You don't even know who Caban is?"

"I've only been here two weeks."

She dropped his hand and raised hers to point at the volcano. "That is Caban!" she stated proudly. "The god of the Quitapul. Zacapula has been under the rule of the Catholics for five centuries, but Caban is still the god of the Quitapul. The Catholic priests call Caban the Devil. I call the priests of the Catholic Church the Devil!"

She turned and started running along the breakwater, jumping from rock to rock. Chris watched for a moment, impelled to join her, but somehow also reluctant, almost fearful. In a way, this strange woman stood for what he had come here to seek, the mysterious directness of life lived at the basic human level, without the soulless plastic trappings of modern civilization; but now, confronted with her vital force, he sensed the danger as well as the attraction of that force.

In the early 1960's, the hunt for the paths to Truth— which could be chemical, spiritual, emotional, or political —had seemed to Chris Barker the only worthwhile goal

21

in life. Early marriage and fatherhood had cut him off from that quest—and, it seemed to him, looking back on the time, saved him from becoming a perpetual dropout or burnout. But now, with the marriage ended these five years, and fatherhood only a part-time job, the undemanding life of a tenured college teacher did not provide the bite that he felt life ought to have. It seemed to him that he was stagnating in a quiet academic backwater while the civilization around him lashed itself into a frenzy of self-destruction, with the numbed consent of the whole population.

There had to be something more, he had thought, with increasing dissatisfaction; and, curiously enough, it had been his daughter who suggested what it might be. Michelle, for some reason, had lately taken a strong interest in the history and culture of the Maya, and urged him, when he spoke tentatively of a vacation, to go to Guatemala, where the old ways might still survive. The prospect of ferreting out the remnants of an ancient culture so different from the industrial one that dominated the planet had fascinated him. He was experienced enough to know that the Rousseauesque ideal of the Noble Savage was nonsense, but cherished the idea that, all the same, a different approach to human relations and the mysteries of the universe would be worthwhile. Once his decision had been taken, it had been almost inevitable that he would invite Michelle to join him for part of his stay; and he had the wry conviction that her initial enthusiasm had been intended to bring about just that result. Well, he thought, if I'm going to be manipulated, I'd sooner it be by Michelle than anybody else.

So far, the trip had been a couple of weeks of pleasurable idleness. Now, the obscure but obvious invitation this woman was extending to him promised something more significant. Would he take her up or not? With an inward twinge of uncertainty, he made his choice.

By the time he caught up with the Indian woman, she was standing on a tall boulder overlooking the lake. She

22

seemed now to be in a completely different mood, and was smiling slightly. "Hola, gringo," she said as he approached her.

"Hola yourself," he said, grinning back. She was about half-crazy, he figured. But there was a sense of overall control to her sudden shifts of mood, to her almost schizophrenic jumps from one topic to another.

"You Americans," she shot at him with a playful look of disdain, once again surveying his body with obvious sexual interest.

"What about us?" he bantered back.

"You come to Lago Atitlán, you buy at the gringo market, sit in the hot springs, dine at the Hotel del Lago—and then you return home and claim you have seen Guatemala. Have you been across the lake to Zacapula?"

"Not yet," he said.

"Well you must go to Zacapula before you return home."

"The tourist boats haven't been running since I got here, there was trouble over there and—"

"You don't have to tell me there was trouble, seven of my friends were killed last month!" she said harshly, her anger momentarily directed at him. Then she relaxed. "But that is how life goes. You are not afraid of dying, are you, gringo?"

"I have my daughter to take care of."

"Ah yes. Your daughter," she said.

"Why were your friends killed?" Chris remembered vaguely some distorted talk of intratribal conflict among the Quitapul, of sabotage of some building project in the village, of savage reprisals. There had never been any clear account of it; somehow, in Panahachel, there was a sense that it was best to leave the Indians of Zacapula to themselves and not take too close an interest in their affairs.

"Politics," the woman said shortly. "It is nothing you have to worry about. The mailboat leaves tomorrow at noon. You should come over with me."

"Tell me something," he insisted.

She smiled at his seriousness. "Anything," she said softly.

"Tell me why you've been following us all this time."

"Why do you think? It is a crime for a woman to be attracted to a man?"

Before he could think of an answer, she dove off the high boulder fifteen feet down into the water. Chris hesitated a moment, stunned by her candor. Then he dove in after her. She was twenty feet ahead of him. As he stroked through the waves his mind was racing. For ten years he had been teaching literature classes, he had written dozens of stories and read thousands. Finally, he thought, he was living out a story, not merely reading or writing it. He swam after this Mayan woman with a great surge of energy, as if he could swim all the way across the lake if that was what she was doing.

But she stopped, treading water, and waited for him, a hundred yards out from shore. When he caught up with her they were silent a moment. Her gaze was again unified and intently upon him, as they rose and fell in the waves.

"Your daughter," she said finally. "Is she beautiful?"

"Michelle? A princess."

"Blonde hair?"

"Halfway down her back."

"How old?"

"Fourteen."

"The woman in the hot springs is not her mother?"

"No."

"And her name is Michelle."

"Yes."

"We have a goddess, the goddess of fertility. We call her Ix Chel. It is almost the same, yes?"

"Almost."

"And she is coming down soon?"

"In a week."

"Well then. Come with me to Zacapula tomorrow."

"Maybe," he said.

She removed a necklace from around her neck and

placed it over Chris's head with a swift motion. "Wear this until we meet tomorrow," she said.

"No, don't—"

"Meet me at the mailboat at noon, and please, whatever you do, don't lose the necklace."

Before he could protest, she was swimming away toward the point. He shouted after her, "Wait, have dinner with us, take this back!" She did not respond. He started swimming after her. But he was tired, she was outpacing him, it was hopeless. All he could do was turn around and start swimming back to shore.

It was getting dark. The lake took on an eerie quality at night. Chris could almost feel the nibbling of imaginary sea monsters at his toes. The fisherman he talked with that morning had told him about a giant snake that lived in the depths of the lake and came up to feast on unsuspecting swimmers at the time of the full moon.

But there was the moon, only a bare sliver in the sky. It would be full at Easter, he realized. He would keep away from the lake at night then, keep Michelle away too. He wasn't a believer in fairy tales, he wasn't much of a believer in anything he hadn't experienced directly himself. But down here, myths seemed to be ready to turn into reality at any moment.

He swam as fast as he could and arrived at the hot springs pool breathless and chilled. As he sat down in the hot water, his mind was racing. Madgalena—she had been like a ghost, the way she had appeared and then vanished. But he had the necklace around his neck, with its jade figure hanging from a silver chain. She had been real, all right. He was surprised to realize how fervently he was hoping that she would be real tomorrow.

Her eyes. So much like Michelle's eyes. Michelle wore corrective glasses usually, but when she didn't have them on, she had that strange wandering eye also. Chris could see her pretty face in his mind's eye; he yearned to have her down here with him. She would love Guatemala as much as he did, he was sure of that.

Fifteen minutes later he was walking slowly up the steep trail toward the house. The heavy daytime scents were gone now, as a cooling breeze blew softly off the lake with nighttime odors; closed petals, damp grass, sweet pine. The tall mango trees towered above the small cottage, shadowing it even from the light of the stars and the new moon. As Chris approached the house, feeling Wendy's presence inside where kerosene lamps were burning, he realized that he wished she would return home without him, leave him to explore the lake by himself.

"What's that?" she said immediately as he entered.

"Necklace."

"I'm sorry I got so upset," she said.

"It's okay."

"I'm frightened down here, Christopher."

"I know. Maybe you should go."

"I'm going tomorrow. I've decided."

"I'm going to stay and wait for Michelle."

"She gave you the necklace?"

"The Indian woman, yes. Her name's Magdalena."

"I wish you wouldn't wear it. I wish you would come with me tomorrow. I feel you're in danger down here, Chris."

"I don't think so," he said.

"She gave me such spooky feelings. You shouldn't wear that necklace. It could have a curse on it."

"I don't believe in curses, you know that," he said, and went to pour himself a cup of coffee.

chapter 2

Except for a glowing redness nearby, everything was dark, obscure. She struggled to move, but she was being held down by both her arms and her legs, pressed against a cold smooth surface. Her naked back was slippery with the sweat of extreme exertion. She screamed out one final time, the sound of her own voice echoing back at her menacingly.

Then something inside her yielded, and she relaxed against the stone under her body. The iron grip of hands around her wrists and ankles held her in position on the altar when she went limp. A sense of euphoria flooded her, her heart was beating with powerful, pumping thrusts; her temples pulsated as the blood rushed through her veins.

Then she heard a sound—a high-pitched animal sound. It was definitely the cry of a small animal in extreme distress, but it seemed to be almost the same sound she had been making just a moment before as she cried out for mercy.

Her eyes snapped open. The dream disappeared instantly when she saw the early-morning light coming through her bedroom window, and heard the agonized cry coming from just outside. She cocked her head and listened, her eyes peering at the door that led out into the backyard.

Her eyes were doing that strange thing they sometimes

27

did when she didn't have on her corrective lenses. Usually her strong right eye predominated and she wasn't even aware of what her crossed left eye was seeing. But sometimes, like now, she could feel the left eye registering images, strange images, perceiving a different reality from what her right eye could see. She felt dizzy. She knew she could look right through the wall and see what was making the tiny, frightened squeaking sound if only—

The sound stopped. There was a frozen silence. Michelle jumped out of bed, ran to the door and without hesitation opened it wide.

The cat was crouched on the doorstep, with a mouse between its paws. The mouse was covered with cat slobber but not bleeding. It stood normally with its hind feet, but the front feet splayed out limply, so that it seemed to be prostrating itself in a gesture of total acquiescence. This wasn't the first time that the cat had brought its kill to Michelle's doorstep, but never before had she come in so early on the cat-and-mouse game. Usually she awoke with a jolt at the sound of the crunching of bones, and opened the door to find the cat devouring the mouse, slowly, methodically, with a complete lack of guilt.

The mouse was breathing with rapid vibrations of its tiny heaving chest, looking vaguely into the eyes of the cat. From where she was standing, Michelle couldn't see the cat's eyes, so she quickly walked out into the cool dewy morning, and crouched down with her feet flat on the ground and her knees to her chin, the dew-wet grass cold against her buttocks.

The cat was half-Siamese and half-tabby. Its eyes were crossed as Siameses' eyes usually are, and were of different colors, just like Michelle's—one blue, the other green. The cat had appeared one morning a month ago, startling Michelle when she looked up from a book on the Mayan culture she was reading and found it staring at her.

The mouse made its move. Not a move of determined escape, but rather one designed to complete the action of the life-and-death drama. It made a little leap into the air

28

to one side, and the cat, as if on cue, responded. Michelle's eyes followed the motion, her right eye seeing the cat's mouth open wide and crunch the head of the mouse —and her left eye, suddenly back in her dream, looking up at a face staring down at her, a horrible blue-painted face with matted, blood-colored hair. It was a man, holding an obsidian knife and—a shudder ran through Michelle's body like an electric shock. Her eyes fused, brought the image of the man and the image of the cat together. The cat growled. Michelle felt herself losing consciousness and she watched the shining obsidian knife raised high above her bare breasts.

She fell backwards, rolling onto the wet grass. Multiple images existed in her mind's eye; the cat staring at her with the half-consumed mouse in its mouth; the Indian staring down at her with the sacrificial knife—and the sky above her, with the first rays of sunlight striking the upper limbs of the oak tree overhead.

She lay there, legs spread and arms wide on the grass, listening to the crunching, the snarling, the rapid consumption of the mouse. She closed her eyes and imagined being the mouse, imagined what it would be like to experience death, to be consumed. The wetness of the grass under her body felt like her own blood. She felt the mundane reality of being a human being in Mill Valley all behind her—no more school, boyfriend, church, family, all just a dream passing away; she was floating free, shining, fulfilled.

"Michelle! What in God's name are you doing out there!" Her mother came running across the lawn toward her daughter carrying a terry-cloth robe. The cat took the remains of the mouse and disappeared into the shrubs beside the house. At the sound of her mother's voice, Michelle started to regain consciousness. She sat up, dazed, unsure of where she was.

Her mother was upon her, pulling her up onto her feet, looking at her nakedness with shock, with fear, then roughly shrouding her in the robe. "This is too much!" the woman shouted, her voice shaky. "I can't stand this. George would have died if he'd seen you; I thought you'd been killed!"

"Mom, please, everything's okay. I just wanted to see what it felt like to lie in the dew and stare up at the sky; it was beautiful. Please, everything's all right."

Her mother's hand, gripping Michelle's forearm, relaxed a little. "Well I don't want to ever find you out here naked again. You're a mature girl now and you do *not* lie naked in the grass; it's disgusting and I won't stand for it!"

"You're just afraid of what George would think. You wouldn't have minded back when you were living with Daddy."

"I'm *not* afraid of what George would think. And that's exactly why I'm not living with Christopher any longer— he has no sense of morals at all."

"Please, Mom, don't be angry with me. But really, it felt good to lie in the grass and watch the sun rise on the oak tree. You should try it sometime."

Her mother sighed, relaxed another notch, and they started walking toward the house. "Well, church is in two hours. I suggest that you get showered and dressed for breakfast before we go."

Michelle stopped, remembering how her vision had fused. But it was cross-eyed again; only her right eye was seeing. "Something happened," she said.

"Yes?"

"My eyes came into focus."

"Without your glasses?"

"Yes. But it only lasted a few seconds."

"That's wonderful. What was it like?"

"It was . . ." Michelle hesitated. She wanted badly to tell her mother what had happened. They used to be confidantes, before the divorce and her marriage to George; but now she felt she mustn't talk about those things that happened to her anymore, or her mother would tell George and it would be off to the psychiatrist for her again, and that had been *so* humiliating last year. So she just shrugged her shoulders. "It was like seeing when I have my glasses on, kind of," she said.

They approached the house. Her mother went up the steps first, stepped on something underfoot, and screamed. She jumped back off the steps, her bare foot raised and her scream continuing.

Michelle looked at the step, and her eyes suddenly came into fused focus again! There was a small bloody lump on the step. The cat had left the heart for Michelle, as it had done with those of several earlier kills.

George appeared in the doorway, with shaving cream on his face. "What's going on?" he said, seeing Michelle in a skimpy robe and her mother near hysterics.

"Nothing," Michelle said, her voice becoming instantly harsh and flat at George's appearance. "Mom just stepped on a mouse; the cat was eating it on the doorstep I guess."

"God, how repulsive," her mother managed to say.

"I'll throw it away," Michelle said, her eyes crossed once more.

"We should call the pound for that cat," George said.

"No, don't do that," Michelle pleaded. "He's a nice cat."

Michelle could smell bacon cooking in the kitchen as she stepped out of the shower and reached for a towel. As she dried herself off, she found herself thinking of Barry, her boyfriend. The sensation of the towel against her skin was pleasurable, and she gave herself to the feeling that was building inside her. Whenever the sexual energy hit her like this, she had the distinct feeling that her body was being taken over by another being, a being without a physical body, but who desired intensely to experience the pleasures of the human sexual response through Michelle's body. She rather liked the feeling of being overwhelmed, obliterated by the sexual experience. She had spent enough time at her father's when he had his

31

girlfriends over to know that her mother's and George's inhibited uptightness wasn't the only way to approach the experience.

As she slipped on a simple white dress and sandals, she could hear the morning news blaring on the kitchen radio. There had been a minor earthquake in southern California and the ongoing debate about the safety of the nuclear reactors down there was continuing. And two women had been raped and stabbed to death in San Francisco. The Russians had a new weapon that could destroy the entire East Coast with one nuclear blast. Starvation figures for Cambodia had relief organizations hurrying to offer more help. The usual horrible news. Michelle was so sick of the news. Her father had thrown his television set out the second-story window two years ago after watching the evening news, and she sided with him. She yearned for spring vacation to be here, for the next week to fly by so that she could be on her way to Guatemala.

George was standing at the kitchen counter with a knife, bringing a momentary flash of memory back to Michelle as she walked in, a memory from her dream, a man with a knife. The image faded though; her dreams almost always faded quickly after she woke up, leaving her with stirred emotions but little recall. George inserted the knife into the cantaloupe as Michelle watched, fascinated. He made a circle cut and the melon fell open, its innards exposed. He emptied the seeds into the skin and glanced at Michelle.

"Valery!" he shouted. "Look at your daughter!"

Valery turned her head and looked. All three of them knew what was being looked at. The material of Michelle's dress just slightly showed the outline of the maturing girl's small, firm breasts, unhampered by a bra. "You march right back into your bedroom and put on a bra or you won't go out for a month, do you hear!" Valery ordered.

"But nobody'll notice and I don't like those things."

"Do as you're told," George insisted.

Michelle turned angrily and stamped out of the kitchen.

In her bedroom she slipped off the dress and stood in just her underpants looking at herself in the mirror. Her body was soft but athletic, a tennis player's body, already tanned by the springtime sun. Her father had lectured her against the influence of her mother and stepfather. You've got to love your body, he had told her. Don't believe a thing they tell you. The most important thing about being a human being is the fact that we can experience things through the body. It's a gift from God. You should respect it. But whatever you do, enjoy it.

She opened a drawer and took out a bra. For some reason, she had woken up hypersensitive this morning, and just the touch of the material of the bra against her nipples aroused them, gave her a rush of pleasure. She stood looking at herself in the mirror again, hating the sanitary look of the bra and underpants. A grin came across her face. She wasn't about to be ordered around without getting even. She quickly slipped off her pants and then put on the dress. In the mirror, she made sure her pubic hair wasn't noticeable under the dress.

Behing her, reflected in the mirror, was a poster of a temple in Guatemala, a mammoth stone pyramid, overgrown by jungle plants, with a stone altar at its top. She suddenly found her eyes fusing again as she looked at the reflection in the mirror. The dream she had woken up from almost surfaced; she felt a cold sweat growing over her body. A tingling sensation rose up from her legs into her sexual parts, a strange sensation that made her dizzy.

"Michelle, breakfast!"

They were almost late getting to the Presbyterian church in San Rafael. As they hurried up the steps and then walked down the hushed aisle to a pew, Michelle felt her airy nakedness underneath her dress and grinned to herself. She felt light-headed as they sat down, still hypersensitive sexually, riding the tingling energy which spread throughout her body.

The organ boomed out in Christian fervor for the first

hymn, shaking the building with deep vibrations. Michelle stood up, holding the hymnal in one hand, pressing secretly against her groin with the other. Staring blankly up at the great stained-glass windows at the front of the church, and then at the minister, she felt her dream starting to overwhelm her again. Her right eye continued looking at the minister, but her left eye wandered off and gazed at the sunlight streaming through one of the windows, showing Jesus illuminated on the cross, his head hanging, his body limp.

The mouse, she found herself thinking. The mouse! Jesus was sacrificed just as the mouse was, in order to save the world, to bring the gods power to servive on earth. It all made sense at last. Communion was a sacrifice, these people in this church ate Jesus' body, they drank his blood, this was no different from the cat-and-mouse game, this was like the books on the Maya she was reading—this was sacrifice!

The service droned on, monotonously, but Michelle was ecstatic. Why did everybody here miss the point? Why didn't the minister explain to them that sacrifice was the heart of the Christian religion? Jesus had sacrificed his life just as the Mayan virgins had, just as the mouse had, laying down his life for God, for the people, to bring a union between the mortals and the gods.

Communion was being served. Stale Wonder bread was passed, and Michelle took her tiny cube and gazed up at Jesus on the cross. "Take, eat, this is my body, sacrificed so that you might have eternal life," the minister intoned. Michelle popped the bread into her mouth, thinking of the cat eating the mouse.

Then the tiny glasses of Welch's grape juice. Michelle held hers reverently. "This is my blood. Drink ye all of it." Michelle felt the cool liquid as it ran down her throat. The cat and its blood, the heart on the doorstep. The hearts of young Mayan virgins offered up to the gods— the ultimate sacrifice, like Jesus' sacrifice on the cross.

34

How could these people sit here in church and not realize what it is all about!

The tingling sensation spread suddenly like a rocket taking off in her body, exploding up through her head and then taking her with it, expanding in a flash of light, filling the church, then bursting free of the church and outside in the air, looking down, the warmth of the sun filling her—

"Michelle, sit up straight this *instant!*" her mother hissed, puncturing the transcendent moment.

"It simply isn't safe," George was saying at the lunch table. The formal Sunday dinner in the dining room was laid out on the lace tablecloth. A copy of the Sunday paper was spread out as evidence in front of Michelle. George stuck a piece of rare roast beef, dripping juice, into his mouth. With her strong eye, Michelle watched him chewing. "And put on your glasses," George insisted uncomfortably. "The doctor said you should wear them all the time."

Michelle put them back on. She had set the rimless glasses down on the table a moment before when she had become so angry that she didn't want to see straight. "It's just not *fair,*" she cried. "You promised, you both promised me I could go for at least Spring vacation; you promised Daddy."

"But that was before we knew what was going on down there," Valery insisted.

"All the papers have said is that there was a little trouble last month in one single *village,* not the whole county. And it says right here that the trouble was over in three days; it's perfectly peaceful down there now. Daddy said in his letter that it's the most peaceful place he's ever known."

"There were seven people murdered in that village, Michelle," George went on. "Read the article. It says there is general unrest in Guatemala this Easter, that tourist

35

boats have been canceled on the very lake Christopher is staying at."

"But it was just in one town and—"

"All we're concerned about is your safety."

"I think Daddy's an adequate judge of whether or not it's safe for me down there," Michelle retorted. "Besides, I'd think you'd want me to see where some of my ancestors—and yours, Mama—came from."

"Great-grandmother Reyes was a member of a fine old California family," Valery said frostily, "and of the purest Spanish blood. There is no question of any connection with a savage place like Guatemala or the half-breeds who live there, let alone the Indians."

"If you say so," Michelle said grudgingly. But she had seen the faded tintypes of her great-great-grandmother, and it had seemed to her that there was something a good deal more Mayan than Castilian in the Roman-nosed, strong-jawed profile. In the five centuries since the Spanish Conquest, there had to have been a lot of intermarrying and moving around, and it seemed to her more likely than not that a "fine old California family" would carry at least a few drops of the blood of the ancient inhabitants of the hemisphere in its veins. Anyhow, it was nice to think so.

"And besides," her mother went on, "there's such a lot happening here this Easter, it'd be a shame to miss—"

"I'm going and that's my final word, I'll run away from home, I'll do *anything*, but I'm going," she said, and started to cry. "You know I've been wanting to go to Guatemala for a long time; you can't take it away from me now!"

"Please dear," Valery said. "Don't get upset."

"Then don't say I can't go."

"All right, you can go—as long as we don't hear of any more trouble, and as long as you phone us."

"There aren't any phones where Daddy is."

"Why?" Valery sighed. "Why do you want to go down there in the first place? You think the Indians are so

36

romantic, you idealize them, just like your father. But you were with us in New Mexico last year, you saw the squalor Indians live in, you saw them drunken, brawling, degenerate."

"It's not their fault; we did that to them," Michelle fought back. "And besides, it's different in Guatemala, that's why I want to go there. The Indians haven't lost their traditions, they live like they always have, and they're happy. I showed you that *National Geographic* article, and Daddy says that it's pure paradise. I've just got to go, please?"

Valery and George looked at each other, frowning in concern. "All right then," Valery conceded tersely.

The afternoon was warm and Michelle spent it in the backyard, reading through one of her Mayan books while she waited for the phone to ring. When it finally did, she jumped up and ran into the house, yelling "I'll get it!" It was Barry, and he did have the car tonight, and he could pick her up to go to the youth-group meeting.

Valery checked her out before she left after dinner, noting the bra in place under her light blouse but unable to detect the lack of underpants under her long Guatemalan wool skirt. "And come home right after the youth group, I don't like the idea of a fourteen-year-old girl—"

"I'm almost fifteen, Moms."

"I still think you're too young to be going out alone in the car with a boy, it's simply not proper."

"We're only going to the youth group—you make it sound like we're going off to an *orgy* or something!"

Valery exhaled in exasperation; the argument was a variation on a theme that had been going on for five years now, ever since she had separated from Christopher and started to regain her conservative stature in the community after her fiasco of a marriage with a radical. Every weekend, Michelle would go to Christopher's house and pick up his ongoing immoral ideas, and then Valery would have to work all week trying to guide Michelle in the other direction.

"Hey, you look great," Barry said as Michelle slid across the big Buick's front seat.

"Except this dumb bra Mom made me wear."

"Well take it off."

"The youth minister would notice and report me, it's all Secret Service everywhere," she said.

They drove through town toward the church. Barry was a junior in high school; he was really popular and she was lucky to have him as a boyfriend. But sometimes, when he touched her as he was now, running his fingers along the material of the skirt up her thigh, she felt he was just another dumb smart aleck who shouldn't even touch her at all. But at the same time, she loved the sensation.

The youth group was boring except for a couple of kids who started arguing with the youth minister and got him all confused and upset about Adam and Eve. Michelle sat and listened absent-mindedly, running through her mind the creation myths of the Mayas, with the four cycles of creation-devastation which had happened thus far. The Christian stories were dry and uninteresting to Michelle, compared with the myths of the Mayas. When she had tried to talk with the youth minister about Mayan gods, he had been offended at her attitude, explaining to her that Christ had come to set the world free from such barbarous myths and religions.

Now, as the argument in the youth group droned on, Michelle took off her glasses and let her eyes play their games. When she had her glasses off, people related to her so differently; she had known this ever since she was very young. No one seemed able to meet her stare for a prolonged period when it was just her single right eye staring at them; they became acutely uncomfortable and looked away.

Even Barry couldn't meet her eyes now when she

looked at him across the room. She knew she had power over him, over everyone, it she wanted to use it. And sometimes she did, especially at school, when she didn't want to be called on in class. All she had to do was take off her glasses, and the teacher never looked at her.

Finally the meeting was over. She and Barry didn't stay for refreshments, but left when the minister was on the phone in his office. Barry drove up Fourth Street to the end, where an alleyway emerged high above the town. He turned off the engine and sighed contentedly, then went immediately for her, knowing they didn't have much time.

She took off her glasses so their kissing would be unhindered. He considered himself a great lover, starting out with soft tentative touches and kisses, then slipping his hand under her blouse and popping her bra up off a breast so he could feel her. The sensation was like fire inside Michelle; she felt that possession coming over her, the hot glowing light flashing through her body, the ecstatic drifting-away feeling in her head. She relaxed and let him explore her body with his fingers, and the energy continued to build. But this time instead of touching her where she had told him she liked it, he suddenly was poking at her, trying to push his finger inside her—and she reacted with the swiftness of a cat, scratching at him, pulling his hand away from her.

"Hey, what's the matter, what's wrong with you?" he cried out.

"Don't you *ever* do that again," she said breathlessly.

"Why not? You'd like it."

"I just don't want it, do you understand?"

"Hey, come on, I thought you—"

"Well you thought wrong!" she shouted at him, surprising herself by her vehemence. "Take me home."

"Well, I don't give a damn anyway," he said hotly. "You're just a little girl, afraid to do it."

"Well maybe I am."

"So you want to run home to Mommy now?"

"Yes."

An hour later, she lay in bed. She could hear the television going in the living room. She got up from bed and walked outside into the dark backyard. The moon was a sliver high in the starry sky.

She walked out through the grass in her bare feet and stood in the center of the lawn. Slowly, she started turning around, her hands and arms outstretched, her body spinning, spinning. The dizziness increased, the sensation welled up in her breasts and genitals. Guttural sounds started coming out of her mouth, a chant that came from nowhere as it always did, and then filled her with a rushing sense of power.

She danced until she was silly with dizziness, and then fell onto the grass, outstretched, hugging the earth with a manic lust for contact with something beyond everything up here. Guatemala, she thought. I'm coming, I'm coming.

chapter 3

They came walking up the dirt road from the hot springs house. The sun was warm and their backpacks heavy. There didn't seem to be anything left to say. The necklace was still around Christopher's neck even though Wendy was convinced that it was a bad-luck piece. And he was determined to stay.

Several Indians approached them on the road, headed with their own crude backpacks toward the small town of Santa Catarina three miles to the south of Panahachel. The first Indian was a boy of perhaps ten, carrying a sack of sugar that weighed at least fifty pounds. He was straining under the load. A single rope that went from under the sack up around his forehead held the load in place, and his hands were underneath the sack to take some weight off his forehead. This was the traditional way of carrying loads for Guatemalan men. Chris smiled encouragingly, but the boy was so taxed by the load on his back that he could hardly muster a grimace in response.

The next man carried twice the load of the boy, at least a hundred pounds. Chris felt anger welling up in him at seeing the Indians being pushed so far beyond normal limits of endurance. Ever since the Spanish Conquest, the Indians had been the work horses for the Ladinos, and it wasn't fair. Chris greeted the straining man with a 'Hola" but the Indian did not respond at all.

The woman who brought up the rear, wtih a giant bundle of clothing on her head that she had probably been trying to sell up at the Hotel del Lago to the tourists, did greet Chris, with a friendly smile and warm eyes.

"Amazing people," he said to Wendy, hoping to escape the heavy silence between them.

"It breaks my heart to see them working that hard," she said. "That's another reason I'm leaving here, Chris. I just can't stand to see all this injustice, all this suffering."

"But through it all, they're still ten times happier than we are in the States."

"You romanticize it; you're *blind*. You haven't noticed how deeply unhappy they are. And I'll tell you another thing, since you're staying and I'm going. You'd better start seeing the other side of the Indians, not just their big hearts and beautiful smiles. You seem to ignore completely the fact that most of them are crafty—they're only nice to you because you've got money; they're conditioned to treat you nicely to see what they can get from you, and—"

"That's not true and you know it!" he retorted.

"And that mystic Mayan lover of yours. She's out to take advantage of you one way or the other; they hate us down here, the white man is the Devil. They hate you, Chris, under all their surface love they *hate* you. You're acting like a teenager in love, blind to what's really going on down here."

Chris walked in silence, looking out to his left at the lake, the volcano. He felt angry at Wendy, but he tried to stay open to her words, in case there was any validity to what she was saying; she was a pretty smart person; he should trust her opinion. But this time, he concluded, she was out of her element and completely off base. She was, in fact, jealous of the Mayans for their ability to be open

42

and loving in spite of their persecution. "I just hope one thing," he said.

"What's that?"

He paused, and she paused beside him. They looked at each other intently. "I just hope that all this isn't going to do in our friendship in the long run," he said.

"Well I just hope that all this isn't going to do *you* in completely," she responded somberly.

"Hey, please, stop worrying about me, okay? We all have different needs. This lake isn't the right place for you. But it is for me."

"But what about Michelle, she's liable to be frightened down here. Don't you feel the negative energy in the air?"

"It's pure positive. You're really contracted, Wendy."

"Please, stay on this side of the lake at least. Don't go off chasing that Mayan woman. I'm not jealous, Chris. I'm frightened for you."

"Well don't be."

"What time is it?" she asked.

He glanced at his watch. "Half an hour before your bus leaves."

"We'd better keep moving them. I don't want to miss it."

They walked quickly through the small town. Panahachel was the only tourist-centered town on the lake. A curious mixture of youthful hip travelers and older tourists dressed in polyester ambled along the narrow streets amidst the indigenous Indians and an occasional Ladino. There was only one paved road and few vehicles. But everywhere, people: handsome Mayan women in their traditional wipile blouses and long foot-loomed skirts; Mayan men either dressed in the long shorts of their tribe or in western trousers, and the children; Chris was constantly charmed by the children, the ragamuffins in their faded wipiles or patched shorts, hanging onto Mamacita as she did the shopping, or playing games in the street—such happy, innocent children, almost always

43

ready with a warm friendly smile in response to the slightest show of interest from a foreigner.

Chris wanted again to point out to Wendy the pure, spontaneous joy in the faces of the Indians they were passing. But she was walking with resolute footsteps toward the outdoor bus stop where they had arrived two weeks ago. It was definitely best that she left, he found himself thinking—for her *and* for him. And at the same time, he was scanning the passing Mayans, looking for a pair of crossed eyes watching him and Wendy as they headed for the bus stop.

"You'll write me as soon as Michelle arrives, and tell me how she's doing?" Wendy said as they approached the small crowd waiting for the morning bus.

"Sure," he said, knowing that Wendy felt close to Michelle, almost like a second mother to her. "And give her a call tomorrow when you get home, will you? Tell her I can't wait for her to get here."

"I will."

"And don't paint a negative picture of this place for her, okay?"

Wendy, standing five inches shorter than his five foot ten, stared up at him with intent, anxious eyes. "I feel very strange about this," she said.

"More of your occult visions breaking through?" he said with forced lightness.

"I hope not."

"What does that mean?"

"Please, I want to ask you a big favor."

"Fire away."

"Don't go across the lake today."

"Oh come on now!"

"I sense danger for you, Chris. Listen to me. You don't have to go over there. I feel I'm deserting you to that woman—and she's trouble."

The bus came roaring down the steep grade into town. Chris was angry again at Wendy, for being so negative, for giving in to jealousy. She sighed, stepped close to him,

44

and put her arms around him. "I love you, you know that," she said. "I can't help it if I'm afraid for you." She was starting to cry. Chris had hoped she wouldn't cry. "Write me, please, and stay on this side of the lake, promise?"

He stared into her eyes. "I can't promise anything," he said.

The bus was waiting. The driver had the side storage doors open and Chris stuffed Wendy's backpack into the hold. She kissed him, with a soft overflowing of passion and anguish. Then she was up inside the giant coach and out of sight. Chris stood there a moment, numbly. The bus took off with a high-pitched whine. The smell of diesel fuel lingered in the clear mountain air for several minutes. In the aftermath of the goodbye, Chris felt Wendy's absence acutely now that she was irrevocably gone.

Then the warm bustle of the town brought him back into the present. He turned and walked down the side road that went half a mile to Hotel del Lago and the lake. He had almost an hour before noon. The breakfast café that served yogurt and papaya crêpes for the tourists was on his way, so he stopped there and took an outdoor table.

The café was very simple, as were the other five in town. An influx of hippies ten years ago had brought the concept of vegetarian cooking to interested Indians, along with the perception that here was a way to make money from the less-than-wealthy young international travelers who were coming to the town with more and more regularity, and who didn't want to eat at the expensive restaurant at the Hotel del Lago. This café, Mario's, was a gathering place for hip tourists who wanted to exchange travel notes and strike up new friendships.

"Hey, where'd you get the necklace?"

Chris glanced over to the table beside him. A young man with his hair back in a ponytail and a small gold ring through his left nostril was addressing him. He seemed friendly enough, and Chris returned his smile. "A friend of mine gave it to me," he said.

"Down here?"

"Right."

"Be careful trying to take it out of the country. They'll confiscate it for sure, maybe fine you too, you can't export Mayan artifacts you know. But just stick it in your pocket, they don't usually body-search you unless they've got you tagged."

"Thanks, I'll remember that."

"Can I see that?"

Chris hesitated, then took the necklace off over his head, handing the ancient work of sculpture to the man, who studied it quickly, and then looked up. "Quitapul," he concluded. "Better be careful wearing this around here."

"Why?"

He handed Chris the necklace. "Put it in your pocket," he said in a low voice.

"It's against the law to wear this around here?"

"Quitapul stuff is off limits; they don't like gringos wearing their artifacts. Where'd you get it, over in Zacapula?"

"Kind of."

"There aren't many of them over on this side of the lake, but if one was over here on a buying trip and saw you with that around your neck, he'd give you a pretty rough time."

The waitress, a ten-year-old girl, the daughter of the owner of the café, appeared to take Chris's order. She smiled, recognizing him from his previous visits. The man at the adjoining table put his hand over the necklace, hiding the Mayan figure from the girl's view. Chris ordered orange juice and a crêpe, with a side order of yogurt and fruit.

A young woman came running in from the street, a pretty blonde-haired girl of about seventeen. She came and sat down breathlessly at the man's table, leaning for-

46

ward and whispering to him. "Have you heard?" she said.

"Heard what?"

"About the two French chicks."

"What French chicks?"

"They drowned in the lake yesterday afternoon."

"Did I know them?"

"I don't think so, but—"

"So what's the excitement? People get drowned in the lake down here like people get killed in car wrecks up north."

"They'd been over to the sacred island."

"Oh?" the man said, his interest instantly alerted.

"A squall came up out of nowhere, before the Xocomil was blowing at all, and capsized their boat. People are saying they were digging for artifacts at the temple."

"Well, people will say that kind of thing."

"What's that?" she said, noticing a part of the necklace showing from under his hand.

The man lifted his hand and the girl gasped. "What're you doing with that?" she said hotly, with a touch of fear in her voice.

"It isn't mine, it's his," the man said, nodding at Chris.

"You're stupid to get involved with something like that," she said. "You'll never get it out. They put a curse on people trying to steal them."

"I'm not stealing it."

"You got it in Zacapula?"

"Maybe."

"So you've been over there?"

"I'm headed there right now," Chris said.

"Why?"

"To return this necklace."

"Well don't go. It's a bad time to go to Zacapula. We were over there a week ago and the vibes were bad for gringos, especially ones fooling around with artifacts. You flash that piece over there and they'll kill you."

"Hey, cut the melodramatics," the man said to the excited girl. "Let people do what they want to do; it's none of your business." He handed the artifact back to Chris. Chris put it around his neck, then slipped it inside his shirt where it wouldn't show. The man smiled approval. "So you're off to Zacapula?" he asked Chris.

"Just for a day or two."

"I'll buy that necklace from you."

"What's it worth?" Chris asked.

"I'll give you ten for it."

"No, it's not for sale."

"Thirty then."

"No, can't do it."

"Fifty, that's my last offer."

"Sorry, but it belongs to a friend."

"A hundred," the man said, reaching into his pocket for his wallet. "You probably got it for ten but I haven't seen any of those around for a long time; I'll give you a hundred for it." He handed him a hundred-quetzal note, worth its equivalent in American dollars.

"No, really, it belongs to someone else."

"Who, if you don't mind my asking?"

"I'd rather not say."

"Well whoever your friend is, he's crazy to let you wear that thing around like you were. You be careful in Zacapula, like Lisa was saying. It's a rugged place right now if you dip into the wrong circles. Stay away from the ruins and don't get involved in any local politics. See you later, I've got to run."

Chris watched the two head off up the street. The girl attracted him a great deal. With Wendy gone, he felt an emptiness, but also a readiness to open up to new experiences, to new people. He could stay here in Panahachel this week, and certainly meet someone he'd enjoy spending time with. He didn't have to go across the lake and take a chance with Magdalena at all. But he knew he would.

The crêpes arrived. Chris fell to eating, feeling suddenly famished. He wolfed down the crêpes and then started in on his yogurt-and-fruit plate. He could feel the weight of the artifact around his neck. Magdalena had let him wear the necklace, knowing that he could get into trouble with it. Why had she done that? He glanced at the Indians walking by, looking to see if he could pick out any members of the Quitapul tribe from the other Indians by their costumes.

On this side of the lake, the Cakchiquel and Quiche tribes predominated, along with the Tzutuhil, most of whom lived a good distance away in Santiago. Most of the women wore their hair on the top of their heads, held in place by orange scarfs. Bright-colored wipiles moved past him in a constantly changing collage of colors.

There was a woman wearing a wipile with horizontally striped colors, with light blue, soft green, white, brown, and yellow stripes. Her hair was down, and she had on the traditional headdress of the Quitapul, an inch-wide red belt that was wrapped around and around the head until it stood out like a halo. She stood a good six inches taller than most of the other women. She walked up to his table, even though Indians never ate at Mario's, and sat down opposite him.

"Hello, gringo," she said.

Chris stared at her crossed eyes, his heart racing. "Hello."

"Where is your woman?" She spoke in English, with only a slight accent. Chris registered a flicker of surprise, then realized that he was not truly surprised.

"She left."

"That is for the best."

Chris felt tense and uneasy as she continued to look at him with her strong right eye, while her left seemed to be watching people passing on the street.

"So are you coming to Zacapula with me today?" she asked.

"I haven't decided yet."

"Please come. I assure you it won't be dangerous."

"Why did you let me walk around with this necklace

49

on, when it could have gotten me into trouble with your people?" he insisted.

"Who told you such a thing? A gringo?"

"Maybe. But he knew what he was talking about."

"He knew nothing! No Indian would dare confront you about that necklace. You do have it, don't you?"

"No, I gave it to Wendy to take back to the States, in memory of you."

"You're joking."

Chris smiled. They both relaxed. She sat back in her chair. The embroidered birds on her intricate wipile rose and fell over her breasts. Chris remembered her in the bathing suit yesterday, and felt slightly weak in the knees, realizing that he could go off with this Mayan beauty to her village.

"Are you hungry?" he said.

"No, I have eaten."

"Where do you stay in town?"

"I have friends among the Cakchiquel."

'So you don't think it is dangerous for me to go to Zacapula?"

She raised her head high. "Life is dangerous for those of us who are chosen."

"I'm sorry, but I'm not one of the chosen ones."

"You are wrong."

"I've made it a point to keep clear of people who think they've got destiny on their shoulders," he said.

She brought her chin down, sighed, and relaxed into a posture that somehow conveyed intimacy. "Let's not argue," she said softly. "You are chosen in that I have chosen to spend time with you. And do you not suspect that spending time with me could be a little dangerous for someone like you?"

"Well I don't want to end up like those two women who drowned in the lake yesterday. Did you hear about them?"

"Of course. They asked to die, and they died. You should not be so stupid."

"What did they do?"

"They were digging for artifacts on the sacred island."

"And where did you get this?" He tapped the jade figure concealed under his shirt.

"It was given to me."

"Nobody dug it up?"

"The artifacts are all in graves of brujos, and you do not dig up a brujo's grave without great cause and sacrifice, and the blessing of the gods."

"What kind of sacrifice?"

"May I have the necklace now?"

"What if I decided not to give it to you?" he said.

She smiled a slow, even smile and spoke in a very friendly tone of voice. "I would kill you."

"Sacrifice me to the corn god, perhaps?"

"Oh no, you're much too special to go to the corn god."

"I thought you only sacrificed virgins, anyway?"

"In your own way, gringo, you are definitely a virgin."

He was looking at her right eye, and then suddenly became aware of her left eye focused on him also. At the same time, a searing heat seemed to radiate from deep in his stomach, as if her eyes were activating a furnace inside him. Then the left eye wandered off again and he felt the heat dissipating. She stood up. "It is time we started for the boat," she said. "We should not miss it."

He paid the bill and walked out into the street with her, feeling somewhat self-conscious walking with an Indian. Two young men, talking in emphatic German as they passed, eyed them, obviously envying Chris Magdalena's company.

"Oh, the necklace—I should have it before we get on the boat," she said.

They paused and he brought the necklace up over his head. As he handed it to her their fingers touched, and he was sharply aware of the contact. They continued walking down the nearly deserted street. No cars had gone by since Chris had sat down at the café, it was a dead-end

51

road to the lake and only foot traffic, and an occasional bicycle, used the wide path, except for vehicles going to and from the Hotel del Lago.

He felt her fingers come to rest lightly on his arm as they walked side by side. Her touch excited him, but not so much with direct lust as with a sort of dreamy fantasy. He imagined himself falling in love with this strange woman, coming to penetrate and share her strangeness and share himself with her. What was there, after all, back home for him, but growing insanity and alienation all around? Nothing, really, but Michelle—and she could join them, why not? She had her education to complete, but with Christopher Barker on hand as parent and teacher, she'd get better schooling than the Mickey Mouse place she was going to now offered. Loving, teaching, relaxing—that would be what that prospect offered, and what more was there that a man could want out of life? And doubtless he'd find time to set about writing that novel.

He shook the dream off irritably. Get hold of yourself, Barker. You thought about what you and the Mayan princess and Michelle would live on? You qualified to rake in the big bucks by catching fish or raising mangos? Perhaps you'd like to hire Louis Nizer to pry Michelle loose from Valery? You are down here on a visit, man, and don't forget it.

But it could be a hell of an interesting visit, no doubt about that. He quickened his pace toward the mailboat, with Magdalena matching his stride.

chapter 4

The lake was still calm, the Xocomil had not yet risen. Chris glanced at the deep-blue silent vastness of the water, surrounded by steep cliffs, with occasional inlets where streams made their way down from the mountains—and the volcano, of course, staring down on its domain.

The mailboat was waiting at the pier, a small launch that carried up to twelve passengers. Magdalena paused a hundred yards from the beach. "It is best that we do not seem to know each other," she said. "We'll board separately. Sit up in front, and I'll join you in a while."

"Why the secrecy?" he asked.

"Quitapul women do not associate with gringos."

"No?"

"Not openly. The driver of the boat would notice, be sure of that, and you don't want him talking in Zacapula tonight about how you came across the lake with Magdalena."

She walked ahead of him, the poised stride of her lithe body entrancing Chris as he watched. He followed her slowly across the gravel beach to the rickety dock where the boat rocked placidly in the noon sunlight. The driver was a Quitapul, dressed in the bright embroidered shorts of his tribe. He eyed Chris suspiciously, took a quetzal note for the fare, and let him aboard.

Several Quitapul men, and two women, were sitting in the cabin along with Magdalena. There was a tense silence, and Chris noticed that Magdalena was being overtly ignored and isolated physically from the rest of the passengers. He went through the cabin and up to the bow of the boat. The roof seemed a good place to sit, so he climbed up to it and sat cross-legged, his backpack beside him and the world of the Quitapul ahead of him across the lake.

A few minutes later they were off, putt-putting away from shore. Chris turned and watched Panahachel recede into the distance. The massive modernity of the Hotel del Lago, with its private swimming pool and tennis courts, was a violation of the lakeside scene. On either side of the hotel were the sumptuous homes of rich Ladinos who made the four-hour drive from Guatemala City three or four times a year for a brief vacation of the lake. Their estates were also out of harmony with the natural feeling of the area, but they were smaller and already coming to terms with the landscape, overgrown with trees and hedges, and so did not collectively form a eyesore like the hotel.

The vibrating of the boat's engine was soothing, and a warm breeze was picking up, scented with a heady mixture of splashing spray and local flowers. Chris turned his head and surveyed the panorama of the lake. Most of the shoreline consisted of escarpments rising sheer, reaching from the water for hundreds of feet and then continuing somewhat less precipitously for several thousand feet to the genuine highlands of Guatemala. It was obvious to Chris that the only practical route from Panahachel to Zacapula was by water. There was no road around the lake, and to hike over the rugged terrain would take days.

Here and there, small rivers had cut their way down to the lake, and for every isthmus there was a small, isolated village delineated by thatched-roof huts and small rectangular plots of farmland. Chris had heard in town that some of the villages on the lake had had almost no contact with westerners at all, that they were frightened and hostile to intruders into their communities. He found himself hoping that the mailboat wouldn't suddenly stop running, and leave him stranded in Zacapula when it was time to go get Michelle in Guatemala City. Perhaps he should write her right away and have her come up to Panahachel on the bus from the airport, rather than him having to go all the way down. She was a big girl; she could manage.

The boat was heading directly across the lake, toward the ever-dominant presence of Caban. Chris felt slightly dizzy looking up at its towering heights. The bottom half of the volcano was covered with coffee trees, and mango and orange groves. But the top half was uncultivated and very steep. Cypress and pine stood for some distance up the inhospitable slopes toward the top, but finally, nothing could grow in the lava flows, and a barren hood of grays and blacks covered the head of the once-omnipotent god Magdalena had told him about the day before.

Magdalena's head appeared from below. She gave him a soft, relaxed smile, and Chris noticed the smooth, sensual texture of her skin as she climbed up to join him on the boat's roof. She pulled her long skirt up and sat cross-legged beside him, her knee touching his.

"Ah, much better," she said contentedly. "I love the feeling of being out in the middle of the lake. By the way, the women down below think you are very handsome." She rested her hand on his knee. "So do I."

"I don't know what to think about you," he said.

"I am not pretty?"

"You're certainly that. But you seem to like to play games all the time, I never know when you're serious or joking."

Her expression clouded. "We all have games we must play."

Chris looked around the panorama once again, allowing his eyes to take in the Indian woman's body along with the terrain. "Beautiful place, this lake," he said after a few moments' silence.

"The most beautiful in the world."

"You've been elsewhere?"

"My father sent me to the city to study. And then I spent a year in Madrid, half a year in Paris. A few months in your country. But this is home. Do you have a picture of your daughter with you?"

"Picture? Uh, sure," he said. He drew his passport wallet from his jacket and extracted a school photo of Michelle.

Magdalena took it carefully, staring at it for a long time. "Her eyes," she said finally.

"What about them?"

"You said they were crossed. But they look normal."

"She wears corrective lenses," he explained.

"Ah yes. My father wanted me to wear those."

"Why don't you?"

"I see much better without such things. Tell me, what do you know about the Quitapul?"

The rocking of the boat, the steady drone of the engine, the feel of sunlight on his face, and Magdalena's hand on his knee, all combined to create a sense of perfect satisfaction inside Chris, and he sighed contentedly. "I don't know much," he said. "Just what I've heard about them the last couple of weeks. I've studied a lot of anthropology, but I never came across any articles on the Quitapul."

"Then I shall educate you."

"I'd appreciate that."

"The Quitapul are the only tribe in this area who have not yielded to the foreign invasion."

"But you said the Spanish conquered them."

"They never broke their spirit!"

"Ah."

"You see the volcano there?"

"Yes."

"What you are looking at is the physical manifestation of the godhead, of Itzam'na. A spiritual force emanates from Caban. Do you believe in such things, gringo?"

"I believe what I see. I see a volcano."

"You see the heart of the Quitapul!" she said emphatically, pounding her fist down on his knee. "And you see that small island just below the volcano, to the right of the town?"

"Now I do, yeah, I see it," Chris said, noticing a small, overgrown island at the foot of Caban.

"That island is the sacred island. It is the powerpoint of the entire planet."

"Wait a minute," Chris said skeptically. "You've traveled, you can't be so provincial as to think that your tribe's god is the God of the whole planet. Every primitive tribe believes the same myth."

"What everyone believes may have some truth behind it," she answered. "Your tribe believes that something that happened on an insignificant hill in the Middle East two thousand years ago changed the destiny of the world. Golgotha was your powerpoint, and I will not deny that truth. But I tell you know that in this age there is a new powerpoint, and that it is here, on this lake."

Chris didn't respond. He had expected her to be more worldly, less caught up in her tribe's superstitions. But now he knew that, regardless of her ability to put on well-educated airs, she was definitely still caught up in the Quitabul tradition. He didn't know if that was positive or negative, but it would certainly make it more difficult to relate deeply with her.

"Is that island the one where the two French girls were digging?" he asked.

"Yes."

"And, uh, is that where the treasure of the Quitapul is supposed to have been buried when the Spanish arrived?"

"That is where the treasure is buried, yes."

"So why doesn't somebody just start digging until they find it?"

"To set foot on the sacred island except to perform the ordained ceremonies is forbidden."

"Forbidden by whom?" Chris asked.

"By Caban."

"And what would Caban do if you dug there?"

"Ask the two drowned women."

The only sensible answer to this was "You're kidding." Chris did not make it, as it seemed to him that Magdalena was deadly serious.

She looked at him gravely, as if appreciating that he had not made the obvious gringo response, and said, "I want to take you to the sacred island."

Chris considered this with some unease. It showed a willingness to treat him as a person to be trusted, almost an honorary Quitapul, which was good; on the other hand, it could be seen as setting him up to join the two French girls in their watery grave. "I thought you said no one could go there," he ventured.

"I will perform the proper ceremony."

"What kind of ceremony?"

"I will ask Caban for permission."

"Well, I'd like to go there, sure," he said. "As long as nobody would mind."

"No one will know. No one but Caban, and he can be persuaded to accept you."

"Well don't go wasting a chicken or anything like that, sacrificing it for me," he said.

"I have already sacrificed a chicken for you."

"You're kidding!"

"I am not kidding, gringo."

"When did you do that?"

"Three days ago."

"Why?"

"I needed to know something."

"What?"

58

"If it would be safe for you to come to Zacapula."
She smiled at him, signaling a change to a lighter mood.
"I have worked a spell on you," she said. "You will be
well protected in my home town. And Caban approves of
you. For a gringo, you are not so bad a person."

"Well, tell Caban thanks for the good word."

"You tell him yourself. He is listening."

"Come on, now, I really don't enjoy all these fantasies
you have going. I feel you're hiding what you really feel
behind a bunch of romantic notions."

She turned her head from Caban and looked at him.
Her eyes weren't crossed; she was looking directly at him
with both of them, and the burning sensation flared again
in his gut.

"No one chooses the lot that falls upon him," she said
quietly, with no hint of frivolity in her voice. "All we
choose is whether or not to respond to opportunities as
they open up to us."

"Like what?"

"Look, there is the volcano in front of you. What do
you see?"

"I see a volcano. What do you expect me to see, this
Caban character grinning down at me?"

"You could if you were open, yes."

"Well I'm open to anything. I just don't see anything
but a volcano, that's all. There's nothing else there."

"Close your eyes a moment," she ordered.

"Okay, why not?" he said, and shut them.

"Focus your attention on the volcano and hold it
there."

"Whatever you say," he agreed.

"I am going to count to twenty, and while I count, I
want you to see what experiences come to you from
Caban."

"Start counting."

She took a deep breath, and muttered something in her
native tongue. Then Chris heard her start. "One . . . two
. . . three . . ."

As she counted, Chris found he could visualize the volcano quite easily. There was the immense mass of igneous rock, covered with groves down below, then the struggle of trees higher up, and finally bare rock for the last precipitous fourth of the ascent.

"... four ... five ..."

A gust of warm wind hit Chris in the face, the first touch of the Xocomil for the day. For an instant he fancied it was Caban himself blowing on him, then pushed the thought away. Magdalena was clearly a fair amateur hypnotist, and he was aware that he was already in a light trance state.

As Magdalena's voice droned on past the count eight, something completely unexpected happened. His visualization of the volcano suddenly came to life, and smoke started coming out of its top—magnificent, billowing smoke, issuing triumphantly from the giant mountain.

A low rumble reached Chris, vibrating his bones as well as pounding at his ears. The sound was like a jet taking off, and it startled him so much that he opened his eyes to pull himself out of the trance. But with his eyes wide open, he saw the same thing he had seen with them closed. And the rumbling of the volcano became even louder.

He grabbed Magdalena's arm. "Keep watching Caban!" she shouted at him. "Don't look away, whatever you do. Eighteen ... nineteen ... twenty!"

Her counting stopped, and so, impossibly, did the rumbling. As Chris watched, spellbound, the smoke issuing from the top of the volcano stopped also. The Xocomil attacked the remaining smoke in the air and disintegrated it almost instantly, whipping it into nothingness.

Chris was still gripping Magdalena's arm with fingers frozen in fright. "My God," he whispered.

"Exactly," she whispered back.

"But I was told the volcano had been dormant for hundreds of years."

"It has been. But at your bidding it responded. Now you see, you *are* a chosen person."

Chris let go of her arm. "No," he said emphatically.

"Yes!" she responded.

"So you know how to do hypnosis. You talked me into a trance. You do have power, enough to project the image of the smoke and the sound into my mind. But that is all that happened, nothing more."

She looked at him. Her eyes were crossed and once again she had become suddenly light hearted, smiling coyly. "You are a clever man," she said.

"I'm no fool."

Her mood shifted again in reaction to his words. "You are a clever man," she said. "But you are most certainly a fool. Consider, O fool, that the volcano smoked and rumbled when you focused your attention on it, when you and I together focused out attention on it. I have never known this to happen before with Caban. Brujos for centuries have been calling upon Caban for a sign, without success."

"I just don't buy it."

"No, you must take it as a gift."

"Witchcraft maybe. Nothing more."

"Ah yes," she said. "Witchcraft. So you have come under my spell. Poor, poor gringo. Kiss me at least."

"What?"

She leaned forward and kissed him on the lips, catching him so off guard that he neither resisted nor responded. She pressed her lips against his with an astonishing tenderness that touched him piercingly.

"Whatever else comes about," she said softly, "I want you to know that it is special between us."

"Why?"

"Because Caban has decreed it! No one knows what is happening to the Quitapul this Easter, but now I know that I am not alone. You have come, and you and your culture, and me and mine; we will make the difference."

"You're talking riddles again," he protested.

"I must go down now, or they will see us from shore. Enjoy Zacapula, relax tomorrow. Don't have anything to do with the gringos in town. That is important! And, the day after tomorrow I will come to the hotel, at dawn, and take you to the sacred island. Kiss me again."

She leaned forward to him and kissed him, her lips pressing against his with an energy he had known before only from avid lovers in the heat of passion. He felt himself falling under her sensual spell. She sighed, then brought her lips away from his before he had truly started to respond. Her eyes, staring at his, searching him for something beyond them both, were acutely in focus. "Think of me," she whispered. "I will be thinking of you."

She kissed him one final time on the lips, and then quickly got down off the roof and disappeared into the cabin below.

chapter 5

The boat slowly approached an old rough-hewn plank dock that extended forty feet out into the shallow water of the lake. Another boat was tied to the dock, a sleek Chris-craft inboard with the classic all-wood hull and half-canopy cabin. Chris wondered if the boat belonged to a wealthy Quitapul Indian, or if there were Ladinos, or even gringos living over here. He glanced along the shore but saw nothing except primitive Indian signs of habitation. Fifteen, maybe twenty cayucos were pulled up onto the reed-lined shore to the left. An expanse of grassy meadow lined the beach, and several men had their fishing nets laid out for mending. Farther over to the left and up the slope, small patches of garden land were being worked by men wearing the traditional purple-and-white shorts of the Quitapul, embroidered with birds like those on Magdalena's wipile.

There was a small welcoming party waiting at the end of the dock, where it met the shore. The women were colorful in their native costumes, standing and talking with water jugs on their heads. Down the beach to the right, twenty or thirty women were washing clothes on the rocks, their long skirts tucked up into their belts as they stood knee-deep in water. Many of them had babies on their backs, wrapped tightly in wide shawls. Chris was enchanted by the scene.

The boat banged gently against the dock. The engine was cut and ropes tossed to an Indian helper who tied the boat securely. The Xocomil was just starting to pick up on this side of the lake, blowing down from the volcano which loomed over to the right across a bay. The town itself sat on the hill that climbed steeply from the lake. Chris could see an outer wall of volcanic stone, and the thatched tops of perhaps a hundred huts. And dominating the scene, high above the town, was an adobe church, its whiteness contrasting sharply with the gray and black stones of the Quitapul village.

Magdalena was the first passenger to hop up onto the dock and walk its rickety length to shore. Chris watched, his mind dreaming of pleasurable things to come with her. But when she reached the beach an ugly scene developed. A small group of women surrounded Magdalena, shouting angrily at her in Quitapul. The overt animosity seemed nothing new to her; she just walked past them ignoring the hostility completely.

The other passengers made their way along the pier to solid ground, and were greeted by the women who had just hurled abuse at Magdalena. There was another person standing near them, a tall, gaunt man in the black garb of a priest, apparently in his fifties, who eyed Chris as he approached. Chris felt dimly uneasy; he was not especially anticlerical, but in this country, so strongly imbued with the Indian way of life, the Roman Catholic clergy seemed like forbidding and ill-omened aliens.

"Welcome to Zacapula," the priest said in Spanish-accented English, extending his hand in greeting. "I do not recall seeing you here before."

Chris, with half his attention still on Magdalena, who was now walking alone up the steep path to the town walls, shook hands. "My first time over," he said.

"I am Father Morales; I meet the boat and distribute

the mail," he said, nodding to the bag being brought down the pier by the boat driver.

"Tell me something, did you see the smoke coming from the volcano just a little while back?" Chris asked, as Magdalena disappeared into the stone maze of the village.

"Smoke? No, no smoke," Morales said, taking the bag from the driver. "It must have been a cloud. The volcano hasn't smoked in many years."

"It rumbled, did you hear that?"

The priest looked at him oddly. "I've been here by the dock for an hour talking with the women. There was no rumble, I assure you. It must have been the engine of the boat you heard.

Chris was not sure whether he was disappointed to have this confirmation of what he had suspected, that the whole experience of the volcano's sudden activity had been an illusion. It would certainly have been terrifying to have to admit that somehow his and Magdalena's energies had united to arouse Caban; but was a little galling to acknowledge that he had been so easily and convincingly deluded. "Perhaps," he said to Father Morales. "Did you notice that tall Indian woman who came over on the boat?"

The priest's eyes hardened as he frowned. "Of course; Magdalena. Did you have anything to do with her?"

"What can you tell me about her?" Chris asked.

"What do you want to know?" Morales said uneasily, as if talking about her bothered him a great deal. "She is certainly beautiful, the most beautiful woman of the Quitapul. Her father is an American, Richard McGrabbin. He lives here also. But I must warn you strongly, she is a woman to be avoided, no matter how beautiful she is. Come, shall we walk to town? I assume you will be spending the night at least. I'll show you the hotel. We don't get many visitors over here, I hope you will come up to the church so we can talk."

65

They started walking up the path. Quitapul women passed them and eyed Chris with both suspicion and curiosity. He was aware immediately that the Indians in this town were quite different from those across the lake. Here, they were less willing to make eye contact; instead, they shot him quick glances and then looked away. "Tell me," Chris said, "what's so upsetting about Magdalena?"

The priest sighed. "I don't enjoy such talk as this, but there are times when even a man of God must be blunt, Mr.—What is your name, please? I don't think you told me."

"Chris Barker."

"Christopher, a good Christian name. In any case, I feel it my duty to speak to you about Magdalena, since you have come into contact with her. You see, Christopher, the Devil is very much alive here in Zacapula. You have perhaps heard of the killings a month ago. Magdalena was responsible for them."

Chris stared at the priest, shocked, and protested, "But she told me the people who were killed were friends of hers!"

"I do not think that one has any friends," Morales said heavily. "Those unfortunate men, I would have to call them her followers. She deluded them, persuaded them that they could seize control of the tribal government here, and force a return to the old ways. She even stirred them up to try to sabotage a project of the utmost importance to this village and the whole tribe. But they did not succeed, thank the Lord."

"They were killed in some kind of fighting?" Chris asked uneasily.

"Most were taken alive," the priest said. "The Quitapul, even those who are not opposed to progress, and who acknowledge the Church, do not care to have the politicians and police of Guatemala City involved in their business. They settled the matter according to tribal law." He sighed. "Those foolish men paid for their error, but the one who led them into it, Magdalena, she is beyond

66

the reach of government law or tribal law. You see, she is a bruja, and in addition is known to have been from birth a Chosen One. She is a woman of great powers, I assure you. Such people emerge among the Quitapul from time to time. The Devil is by no means gone from this planet, and especially not from this part of it."

They had reached the top of the path and entered the village. A narrow cobblestone road led up the steep hill toward the church, and a side road went off to the right. The priest led Chris down the side road, past the few adobe buildings of the town, to a primitive hotel that extended down the lakeside of the town. Chris was half listening to his companion and half watching the procession of Indians ambling along the street. There was a strong feeling in the air, a consciousness of a proud people. Chris found himself thinking, This Catholic priest is out of his element here. He sounds scared.

Four beautiful little girls, their big, shy eyes blinking with eagerness, held up Quitapul backstrap-loomed wipiles and shawls for the gringo to consider buying. Chris smiled to them, but wasn't in the mood to buy anything. "No ahorita," he said. "Posible mas tarde, pero no tengo mucho dinero."

The girls, their smiles uncertain, not understanding Spanish at all, stared with hopeful looks. The priest spoke to them severely in Quitapul, his voice sounding like a parody of the true guttural language as Chris heard it all around him from the Indians. They dropped their smiles and sadly walked away, rebuked too harshly, Chris felt, by the priest. "Beautiful girls," Chris said. "There's so much love down here, compared with up in the States."

"Yes," Morales said, "the primitive, communal life does foster such emotions." There was a bitterness in his tone that surprised Chris. "This tribe, you see," he went on, "still adheres to its pagan beliefs, though nominally converted to Christianity. I have been here eight years now, and in Guatemala twenty-two. The Quitapul are my specialty; I have been in and out of Zacapula for twenty

67

years; and I am sorry to say that I have not seen much progress here. Richard McGrabbin, he has spent his lifetime trying to raise living standards and improve health care in the town. We have worked side by side. I have sometimes come to believe that we were achieving something of what we hoped, to bring the Quitapul to the light of God and at the same time lift their burden of disease, ignorance, unending toil and early death. But they shun the light and cling to their burdens." Morales gave Chris an intent glance, almost a glare. "You see love in these people; yes, it's there. But I will tell you, Christopher, something your flabby culture does not seem to realize— love is not a good in itself. The object of love is what is important. And for me, it is a horror past your imagining to learn, as I have been learning lately, that the Quitapul love their old, wild ways more deeply than they love God. For me, for the Church I serve, Easter, which is coming so soon, is a supreme moment of joy and renewal. But for too many of my—" His lips twisted in an ironic, bitter smile. "—flock, this Easter is a time foretold in their heathern Mayan calendar, when their filthy idols will regain the power they lost five hundred years ago. Zacapula is, at the moment, not the ideal place for tourism." He glanced sharply, inquiringly, at Chris.

Chris answered the implied question. "I'm staying a few days only," he said, grinning inwardly at the thought of Morales' reaction if he were to mention that one of those days was scheduled to be spent going to the sacred island with Magdalena.

"A few days will be all right. But take my advice, if you will. Shun that woman you met on the boat. These are trying times in Zacapula. The Devil is at work, and Magdalena is most certainly helping him to—"

"Wait a minute!" Chris interrupted. "I think you're way off base, accusing people of working for the Devil— that's inquisition talk. This is the twentieth century, you don't go around accusing people of being witches and—"

"Listen, she *is* of the Devil!" Morales said hotly. "She

68

has power, the kind of power that can come only from Satan. I have seen it with my own eyes! I am just a priest, I cannot match her unless Christ acts through me. But I pray to God, He will this Easter." He crossed himself. "That woman and her followers, they are out to destroy this town, just when the Quitapul are making a great stride into the twentieth century."

"What great stride is that?" Chris asked irritably.

"Magdalena's father, Richard McGrabbin, is building a resort over on the bay across from the volcano—it will mean jobs, money, a new kind of life for the tribe. This hotel here is his also, by the way. He's a fine man, respected by the Indians. It is such a shame that his own daughter would be born to assume leadership of the tribe, and then reject her responsibility and work to undermine the progress her father has struggled so hard to bring to the Quitapul."

"And just what is she doing?" Chris asked, beginning to feel quite angry at the priest's narrow-minded attitude.

"The Devil's work," the priest said bitterly. "And I don't mean that symbolically. There is black magic, and worse, in what Magdalena is doing. That volcano you see there—" He gestured to his left. "—is the old Mayan god the Quitapul worship, and Magdalena has a pact with it. It would be very comforting to think that the Quitapul are no more than poor, deluded souls, wasting their time giving reverence to a dead manifestation of geology. Patient instruction and continued disappointment could in time deal with that. But there is something in that mountain that feeds on the worship of these people and gains power from it. They will say it is Caban; *I* say it is Satan. And Magdalena serves it. This Easter is in their calendar Ilum K'inal, the *sacred* time as they believe, the time of abominations and desolation as I see it."

Chris was both repelled and impressed by Morales' fervor. "What's, uh, supposed to happen at this sacred time?"

"Scripture tells us of the final struggle, Armageddon,"

69

Morales said. "The ultimate battle between the forces of good and of evil. God will not lose that fight, Christopher, but those who are on his side may well fall. Jesus redeemed us, but it is in our power to forfeit redemption—I am not a fool, Christopher!" he said suddenly, glancing at his companion. "You think, I can see it in your face, that I am, what would you say, feeding you a line of priest's talk. But I tell you that what I am saying is as real and important as any intelligence report your President gets from his CIA, and the antagonist I am talking of is far more formidable than the petty politicians and warlords who prefer a German pedant for their Messiah to a Galilean carpenter!"

"I, uh, thought Armageddon had to do with some place in the Middle East," Chris said. "The Plain of Megiddo or something like that?"

Father Morales said quietly, "It is Satan who will choose the ground and open the battle. With a whole planet to choose from, I do not believe he will confine himself to the Holy Land. I have seen and felt the gathering of his forces, and they are here. We are almost at the hotel, I see."

Chris looked up and found that they had arrived at a long stone building, two stories high, distinguished by a wide flight of steps that led up to a large front door. As he studied the hotel, two women, obviously tourists, approached the steps. They were young, dressed in jeans and blouses, and Chris felt cheered at seeing them; they were a note of normality in this intense town, and a welcome contrast to the fervent Father Morales. One, with blonde hair pulled tight back from her face into a ponytail, gave him a sour glance and then walked on; her companion, prettier, and crowned with a nest of frizzed brown hair, smiled at him as she and the blonde walked up the steps.

"Interesting talking to you, Father," he said. "I expect I'll be seeing you."

"Indeed you will, Christopher," the priest answered.

"God be with you." Chris sketched a farewell wave in the air as the priest turned and strode down the street. He stared after Morales for a moment, puzzled and uneasy. Whatever romantic or sexual fantasies he had entertained about this trip to Zacapula, he was getting a bit more than he'd bargained for so far, with that weird business out on the lake and then Morales' crack brained discourse. They were both too intense, that was it. Intensity, of course, was a good thing, and part of the reason for his leaving the States so eagerly had been to escape from its shallow casualness toward life. But maybe the laid-back, take-it-as-it-comes attitude had its uses after all.

He walked into the hotel. The two women he had noticed in the street were at the other end of the lobby, ascending the stairs that led to the second floor. He watched them as they vanished, making an instant appraisal of their sexual potential—the blonde uptight, the frizzy-haired one jouncing gently under her thin dress in a way that suggested she enjoyed her body and its motions. If there was anything doing with either of them, she was the one.

He could almost hear Wendy berating him for the thought. "Visual rape, that's all it is," she had said angrily, when he had once commented on a striking woman they had passed. "That's a *person* you're talking about, not a skin-mag centerfold. And you look at her and wonder if she'd be fun in the sack! Can you *imagine* how demeaning that is? Damn, it, Chris, you ought to know a woman, have an idea of what she's like and where she's coming from before you *dare* to dream about taking her to bed!"

"Senor?" the young Ladino woman at the desk said to him.

"Uno, por favor," he said.

"Tres quetzales," she responded, greeting him with the most relaxed, friendly smile he'd encountered since arriving in Zacapula.

" 'Sta bueno," he said, and handed her three bills.

71

"Para un dia o mas?"

"No estoy seguro, probable mas."

"No hay problema. Numero trece arriba."

"Gracias."

He took his key and headed up the stairs and down the hallway. His backpack was heavy and it would be good to relax. The second floor was a rectangle with an open patio in the middle. At the far end was a view of the lake, picturesque in all its native richness. Chris paused a moment, watching the Xocomil blowing the water into small waves, the waves that grow in their passage across the lake and crash fiercely against the hot-springs breakwater. For a moment he wished he was back on the other side of the lake, where everything was somehow more sedate, relaxed, controlled.

He went into his room, closed the door behind him, and opened the shutters. Out the window he could see north toward the volcano which towered beyond the edge of the town and the small bay beyond. He could also see the sacred island to the right. His mind was still unsettled by the priest's accusations, and by the uncanny experience with Magdelena on the boat. The entire day had been a flood of new feelings, and new realms opening up to him.

The room was very simple, reflecting the atmosphere of the town. A wooden chair with a reed-woven seat, a bed in either corner of the room on each side of the window, a bare bulb hanging from the ceiling, and a couple of candles on a small table under the window, indicating that the light bulb might not work from time to time.

Chris sat down on one of the beds, letting his backpack drop to the floor. As he glanced again at the volcano, he suddenly visualized Magdalena with acute clarity, looking at him with her eyes fused. His vision of her was so strong that he felt intruded upon, as if she must be thinking of him at that moment. He didn't believe in such things as ESP—he was a pragmatic man who didn't believe in something unless he experienced it directly. But what was this feeling now, of her presence somehow in the room with him?

He lay down on the bed and closed his eyes. The image remained, and to his irritation but also to his enjoyment, he found himself directing the obscure but strong energy coming from her into sexual channel, thinking of her in her bathing suit with her firm breasts held in place by the tight material of the suit, her tall slender legs walking across the breakwater—

The priest's words clutched at him and threw the erotic images into confusion. That nonsense about her being in league with the Devil, when there wasn't even a Devil in the first place! The woman was obviously being persecuted in this town, the priest was very likely jealous of her power and beauty, and with fanatic zeal was trying to turn the natives against their own leaders so that the Church would gain more and more control. What had Magdalena said about the Church and the Devil, back at the hot-springs last night? She had mentioned that Caban was the god of the Quitapul. And then said, "The Catholic priests call Caban the Devil. I call the priests of the Catholic Church the Devil."

Chris could remember her hot expression as she had spoken those words, burning them into his memory through her intensity of feeling. Again he felt the erotic tension building inside him as he remembered her in her bathing suit, running off across the rocks. He had spent two years in Reichian therapy and knew that the Devil image was repressed sexual energy, nothing more. He had also written a paper in college on the psychological causus of so-called witchcraft and the insane, murderous energy of the Inquisition, which had put more than a hundred thousand men and women to the stake.

He rolled over onto his stomach, not wanting to think about Magdalena as a witch, refusing to entertain such sick ideas. The priest was a typical repressed celibate who was probably secretly lusting after her sexual favors but who, putting such feelings out of his conscious mind, was instead determined to see her as a witch.

It was unsettling that Magdalena also seemed to see herself in that light, though. She and Morales might be enemies, but they shared the same credulity toward the supernatural.

Well, if he had to participate in someone's lunacy, it might as well be Magdalena's.

chapter 6

Michelle tossed the tennis ball into the air and slammed a serve into the fifteen-love court. An April breeze was blowing, immediately evaporating the sweat as it appeared on her skin from the strenuous exertion. Barry scrambled for the serve, but it was an ace right down the center, hitting the white line and zipping past him. He scowled and walked angrily to the other side of the court for the next serve.

This time her serve went out on the first try, and when she hit the second serve with less velocity and then ran to net on him, Barry powered his return past her with a grim smile of revenge. She walked to the back of the court to get the ball. High in the sky a hawk was circling and she glanced up at it, wondering how Mill Valley looked from that high up. She was in the middle of reading a book called *The Flight of the Feathered Serpent,* about the Mayan god Kulkulcan, and she had birds on her mind. That one up there certainly had the grace and awesome sense of freedom and power to be a god, looking down at her playing this silly game, wondering how it was that humans spent so much time doing things that didn't really matter in life.

"Hey, come on, I'm late!" Barry shouted at her. "Serve

and let me whip you one more game; I've got a biology lab at two-thirty."

Michelle pulled her thoughts back to the game, and walked up to the serving line, staring across the court to where Barry was hunched over with his racket, ready to attack her serve. He usually beat her two or three games to one. He was so strong he overpowered her with his serve, and he had such a fierce determination to win that she was hardly his match. Besides that, he got so upset when she took a set from him that she usually didn't try to defeat him.

But the way he had just yelled at her angered her. She felt a familiar energy well inside her, an energy that seemed to pulse from her belly into her shoulders and then out her arms and hands, as if she could raise her arms at him and destroy him with a blast of a demonic power. She immediately pushed the impulse out of her mind. But she did ace him again with her next serve, and went on to beat him, first with a passing shot when he came to net, and then through a well-placed lob after a long rally.

In the locker room, while she was showering, Judy came in, her naked body ruddy with exercise, and stood in the adjoining shower. They were very close and at the same time, defensive with one another. Last year they had been best friends, spending most of their free time together rather than hanging out with boys. But one night last summer they had found themselves attracted to each other so strongly that, when they gave in to the attraction, they found themselves holding each other, kissing with a passion they had never experienced before with boys, fondling each other's breasts, and melting into an exquisite euphoria.

Ever since that night, Judy had been distant emotionally from Michelle, frightened that they might do it again and become caught up in it, when both of them knew it wasn't right, that they weren't supposed to feel that way toward each other. Now, as they stood in the shower room, Michelle glanced at Judy and found her friend looking at her with eyes that betrayed a sexual desire. But Judy instantly averted her gaze.

"So, are you still planning on going down to Venezuela for Easter?" Judy asked with forced casualness.

"Guatemala," Michelle corrected her. "Definitely."

"But you're going to miss the dance."

"I don't care."

"Isn't Barry upset that you're going?"

"Yes. But that's his problem, I want to go more than anything."

"You've been such a nut about that place, all those books you read."

"It's interesting," Michelle said.

"I suppose."

"I was just reading about the creation myths of the Mayas. They believe that there have been five different creations, that the first four were destroyed because people didn't live right. Now, this fifth one is liable to be destroyed too, if we don't change the way we are."

"It sounds like Holy Roller stuff to me," Judy said.

"No, it's really interesting. It's all about being balanced, of having the four elements balanced. There's spirit, and mind, emotions, and the body. And this fifth creation, we're supposed to be balancing all those together or we'll be destroyed and have to start all over again."

"You're too much of a philosopher for me," Judy said, turning off her shower. "You think too much."

"But it's really worth thinking about. There are a lot of people who take the Mayan myths seriously these days. They're the real Americans, you know. We're living on their continent, and we'd better learn how things are."

"Well the Mayans have been extinct for five hundred years. They were horrible; they sacrificed girls to the gods, and God punished them for worshipping idols," Judy said, rubbing her tanned, slender body with a white gym towel.

"Who told you that?" Michelle challenged her, turning off her own shower and grabbing a towel.

"My father," Judy retorted. "And he should know; he's teaching the course in anthropology that your dad dropped to run off with his new girlfriend."

"He didn't run off with her; they've been good friends for years."

Judy was rubbing her dark head of hair vigorously. "So do you think he'll come back? My dad hopes he stays in Guatemala so he can take over his program at the college."

Michelle didn't answer. Judy's attitude was bothering her. They had hardly talked at all for quite a while, and now that they found themselves alone again, there was a harshness to Judy's voice that had not used to be there. Michelle rubbed herself dry and tossed the towel in the towel bin. She sat at her locker bench, momentarily lost in thought about Guatemala, wondering where her father might be at that moment—sometimes she slipped into states when she felt his presence with her, when she picked up feelings that she knew were his. Right now, she was aware of a crystal-clear, relaxed feeling, with a high-energy sense of anticipation, welling in her body. Four more days! she thought. Just four more days and then she'd be on the plane heading for Guatemala.

"So are you and Barry doing it?"

Michelle opened her eyes. Judy was standing in front of her, her pubic hair curly in its golden dampness. "Oh," Michelle said, caught off guard, looking up into Judy's brown eyes and noticing how the girl was looking at her, with eyes that moved quickly over her body and back to her eyes, communicating something that Michelle withdrew from and yet responded to. "Uh, no."

Judy cocked a naked hip. "So why not? You're certainly buddy-buddy all the time. I figured you'd be on the pill by now and going to it, the way you act."

"Well I'm not."

"Why not?"

"That's my business."

"Want to get stoned?"

Michelle stared up at her. There was a sexy come-on quality to Judy's voice, a mature, experienced tone that seemed somehow offensive to her. Judy passed a hand casually over a breast. Michelle felt that ongoing conflict inside her. She was certainly an overtly sexy girl, liking to get the boys' attention whenever she could, enjoying the rush of excitement that came with the games she was learning about relating sexually. But at the same time, there was something in her that was revolted by her own actions, a deep childhood sense of reverence, a religious feeling almost.

"Why, you have some grass?" she asked. She had the same feelings about drugs. They were the hip thing in school, and she really loved the effects of a few hits, that euphoric rush of energy through her body, with its sexual overtones. But at the same time, she felt she was violating herself with the stuff, just as she felt Barry violated her sexually with his probing fingers and his intense animal desire to get inside her.

"Got a joint of Maui Wowie, as a matter of fact. We could take off, I've got my car."

"Oh—well, I don't know."

"Please?"

"No thanks. I want to finish reading this Mayan book this afternoon."

"Come on, we could have fun. You're always off dreaming of that Venezuelan nonsense, take a break."

"No, I want to finish the book."

chapter 7

The wind banged the shutter outside Chris's room and woke him up. He opened his eyes, his mind foggy from a fleeting dream during his nap. His mouth was dry and there was an acute sensation of anxiety in his body. He rolled over onto his side and looked out the window. All he could see was sky, and the top of the volcano. As he looked, darkness suddenly replaced the brightness of the sunlight outside. A cloud was rolling past the volcano, an ominous black thundercloud coming from the warm Pacific a hundred crow-miles to the west.

The Xocomil banged the shutter again. Chris sat up. The anxiety receded slightly. He felt as he used to feel as a child, waking up from a nightmare dream. Something was after him, something in another dimension which he couldn't see or even suspect, but which was there nonetheless, below the level of consciousness, lurking menacingly.

He got to his feet. The dry sensation in his mouth seemed to be related to something sexual. He felt tension in his groin and at the same instant found three women on his mind. Wendy: She would be in Guatemala City now, at the airport. Magdalena: Where was she? Out in that Indian world. And there was Michelle, lingering like a sweet childhood fantasy, her long blonde hair and strange crossed eyes, her sexually enticing body—she had better not be making it with her boyfriend, he found himself thinking. Surprised at the intensity of the last thought, he firmly told himself that it was only a father's natural protective reaction.

He noticed the light increase dramatically as the clouds opened up and the sunlight regained its dominance over the day. He put on his shoes and emerged from his room. The brunette girl with the frizzy hair was sitting on the veranda. She had a book in her lap, and was staring across the lake to where the Xocomil was whipping up the waves into a small frenzy. She glanced at Chris and smiled. He walked over to her. There was no one else on the veranda.

"Hello," she said.

"What're you reading?" he asked.

"Nothing. A mystery novel they had downstairs." Her English was tinged with an accent he could not place.

"Where's your friend?"

"In the room. She has the turistas."

"Too bad."

"Have you just arrived in Zacapula?" she asked, her eyes showing obvious interest in him.

"Came in on the mailboat today," he said. "How about you?"

"Yesterday," she said.

"Seen much of the town?"

"Not really. What's your name?"

"Chris."

"I'm Anita."

"Where are you from?"

"Holland. And you're an American."

"Sticks out like a sore thumb?"

"I rather like it. My last boyfriend was from New York."

"So how do you like Zacapula?" he asked, leaning against the handrail of the balcony, warming to her quickly. She was no more than twenty, at the most. She re-

82

minded him of college girls he had had affairs with when his marriage had broken up several years ago.

"It's kind of scary, actually."

"Scary?"

"My friend, Cathleen, knows a lot about the town. But she's been too sick to do anything but lay in bed or sit on the toilet down the hall. We were just out walking for the first time, and she started feeling sick again. She's taking pills for the runs. I'm afraid she might be getting hepatitis or something, she's feeling so weak."

"Well. I guess I'll go walk around the town. Want to come with me?"

She definitely was eager. "I'll have to check in on Cathleen and see how she's doing first."

"Fine."

She stood up. She had changed from her dress and was now wearing shorts and a light blue blouse—and, fairly obviously, little else. As before, the sexy bounce to her gait immediately aroused Christopher's genital interest, and with a fleeting recollection of Wendy's acid comments, his self-reproach. But it was true, he felt a deep need for physical contact right then. He missed Wendy acutely and hoped something might develop with Anita.

Once they were out walking along the ancient cobblestone street, however, surrounded by the Indians and their town, Chris found himself in a different mood. The sexual impulse had come from his need to dissipate the anxiety he had awakened with; now, out in the afternoon sunlight, with occasional clouds blowing by overhead, he felt the tension subside inside him. Anita walked by his side with comfortable familiarity, and talked easily about herself.

"We were in Egypt last month," she was saying as they turned onto the main street that ran up toward the church a quarter mile up the hill. "Cathleen's grandfather was with Howard Carter when he discovered Tutankhamen's tomb in the Valley of the Kings."

"You were there? I've read about that dig."

"When her grandfather died last year, he left Cathleen a trust to be used in traveling to visit all the sites that he explored. This is one of them; so here we are."

"He did archeological work here in Zacapula?" Chris asked, excited at the thought.

"I wish Cathleen wasn't so sick; she could tell you all about it. I glanced over the manuscript of his 1947 trip here, but I have to admit I don't remember much. It was rather stuffy."

"Do you have the manuscript?"

"No, it's locked up in Cathleen's family archives. But I do remember something in it about the sacred island. We saw just one island as we arrived yesterday, so I assume that's the one where he said the temples were."

"That's right. Let's go down this way; I think it'll take us to the bay where we can get a good view of the island." He led the way down a narrow path, lined on both sides with six-foot-tall walls of the rugged volcanic stone. Every fifth foot or so there was an opening in the wall, and Chris could see dusty courtyards and stone-walled houses inside; children playing naked with chickens; dogs and pigs everywhere; women sitting grinding corn or weaving on backstrap looms; men doing chores or sitting chatting. The atmosphere seemed charged with an energy that Chris found thrilling, as if he were exploring the living quarters of beings on a different planet. The Indians looked out and noticed the gringos walking by staring, and stared back with equal interest at the strangely clothed outsiders.

"Tell me, did Cathleen's grandfather write anything about a tunnel under the sacred island?" Chris asked.

"How did you hear about that?"

"An Indian told me," he said.

A small group of women and children passed them, coming up from the lake with jugs of water on their heads. Chris scanned the women, looking for a tall figure that might appear at any moment, but seeing only strangers' faces as the women went by.

84

"I was under the impression that the Indians wouldn't talk at all about the island," Anita said. "Cathleen's grandfather got nowhere questioning them, and finally gave up and went on down to Peru to another site."

"What else do you remember from the manuscript?"

"Well, he talked about an earthquake that destroyed everything just when the Spanish conquered the town. It buried the entrance to the tunnel. The Spanish were certain that there was a vast Quitapul treasure buried in the tunnel, but they never got any of it. Cathleen's grandfather was naturally interested in discovering the treasure, after what he had helped unearth in Egypt in King Tut's tomb. I want to go across to the island tomorrow, even if Cathleen isn't well enough for it."

They walked out into an open meadow that ran along the bay. In front of them, across a mile of water, was the volcano. Just as they emerged into the open sunlight, a cloud covered the sun and a cool, stronger wind hit them. In the shadow of the cloud, the volcano looked ominous. The greens of the coffee trees down low were dark, seeming to absorb what light there was rather than reflecting it. The cedars and pines higher up stood defiantly rooted in the steep volcanic rock. And higher up where clouds were swirling around the top of Caban, the bleak lava flows, hardened into a black mass, seemed a perfect cap for a god of darkness.

Hostile Quitapul voices broke the silence. A group of women were shouting at a lone figure who was dipping her jug into the water and balancing it on her head. Chris felt his heart catch, his breathing stop. It was Magdalena, standing tall with her skirt tucked into her belt and her long legs slender in the knee-deep water. She turned around and walked out of the lake with perfect balance, the large gourd on her head. The women were shouting harsh-sounding phrases at her, but standing away, making no signs of physical aggression, as if they were both angry and frightened at the same time.

She came walking up toward Chris and Anita, her skirt

still tucked in and her appearance striking in its primitive beauty. Chris found himself wanting to disappear, to run and hide. He certainly didn't want her to see him with another woman; but beyond that, a sudden panic seemed to have gripped him. It was too late, though, to do anything but stand there as she approached.

Her eyes left the ground in front of her and looked directly into Chris's eyes. Her wandering eye slowly came into focus with the good right eye and she paused a few feet in front of Chris and the girl, staring intently at him.

"Hello, gringo," she said strongly but in a low, even-toned voice. "We meet again."

Chris didn't know what to say back. "Uh, this is a girl who's staying at the hotel," he said awkwardly.

Magdalena did not look at the girl, but continued to search Chris's face. "Why are you nervous?" she said.

"Why are those women so angry at you? What did you do to make them shout at you like that?" Chris asked.

"I refuse to be who they want me to be," she said. "It is Ilum K'inal and they are angry with me. But they cannot touch me; it is nothing. I told you, this town is in turmoil and you cannot expect everything to be calm at times like this. I will see you the day after tomorrow, at dawn. What is your room number?"

"Thirteen," Chris said.

"Good. Until then; I have much work to do. Adios."

She walked past them quickly and on up the path. Chris turned and watched her walking away, her tall slender body graceful and her very presence magnetic. But then she was gone and he suddenly felt an acute loneliness. He almost went running after her. The time span between now and the day after tomorrow seemed like forever to him; he wanted at least to walk with her, talk with her, this afternoon. But he resisted the urge. It was obvious she felt the need to be distant. He did not dare break into her other world unless invited. Perhaps she would appear again; she was so good at her sudden appearances.

"You know that woman?" Anita said, an acid tone in

her voice indicating surprise at the encounter and a ripple of jealousy.

"She was on the mailboat today."

"She's the tallest Indian I've seen down here."

"She's part American."

"Really?"

Chris started walking down the beach along the bay to the west. Anita caught up with him and he stopped, suddenly feeling the need to be alone. "I think I'll just go down to the rocks there and meditate awhile," he said. "Can you find your way back to the hotel?"

"I should probably get back and see how Cathleen is doing," she said. "Will you knock when you're back at the hotel?"

"Sure."

"Maybe we can do something tonight," she suggested, her eagerness betraying an anxiety, a need to be with another of her kind down here. "I want to talk some more with you about the ruins over there."

"Me, too. I'm just feeling that I have to be alone right now."

"Later, then?"

"Definitely."

She stepped up to him and gave him a tentative hug, then walked back up the path. Chris watched her, this time without any sexual appraisal. Magdalena had blown him into very deep spaces inside himself. He didn't want Anita, he wanted Magdalena. Yet Magdalena was displaying such ominous aspects that he feared what would happen if he pursued her. His anticipation of being with her had nothing to do with his usual desire for intimacy. She seemed to promise him something; her eyes spoke of a deep need she craved to have fulfilled. But what was it?

He walked across the rocky outcropping a hundred yards farther down. When he reached the tip he could see the next expanse of beach along the bay. He was amazed. There was a giant edifice, like a European castle, built of volcanic stone. It was half-finished, and at first he thought it was a Quitapul ruin. But there were men working, building it. And the speedboat that had been at the dock was there now. That must be the new hotel the priest had mentioned, he guessed.

chapter 8

When he knocked on Anita's door at the hotel several hours later, Chris felt much more at ease than he had when he'd left her over at the bay. He had sat on a giant, flat-topped boulder that looked across at the volcano and the sacred island, and watched Caban go through several different moods as the storm clouds massed with the threat of a thunderstorm, then blew over and were gone. For half an hour, the sun had been warm and bright and Caban had seemed drenched in a radiant calm. Then after the sunset, with the Xocomil dying and the air fresh and cool, Chris had felt an immense sense of peace come over him. He had expected Magdalena to appear then, to take him and lead him into her private world of sensual beauty and primitive intimacy. But as it grew dark, and she had not appeared, he found the volcano staring down at him with an immense, brooding presence. A chill seemed to come into his bones from the lake, and he rose on stiff legs to hurry back through the darkness to the hotel.

The door opened. Anita stepped through it and closed it softly behind her. She looked somehow very frail to Chris, and the feeling emanating from her room seemed to suck at his vitality. There was a sexual energy about her, but it was rather desperate clinging that Chris withdrew from. "I'm heading over to the restaurant for dinner," he said. "Want to come?"

"I'd love to, but Cathleen's really sick, she's running a fever. I gave her a sleeping pill and she's dozing off. But I don't think I should leave her for that long. I've been nibbling some nuts and raisins anyway, I'm not very hungry. But stop by when you get back, please?"

"Sure."

"Hold me a minute, would you? I feel shaky, something has me frightened."

She stepped up against him, her arms going around him and pressing his body against hers. The contact felt good to Chris. Anita melted into all the women who had held him to their breasts and given themselves to him. After the walk through the dark town, with candles and fires flickering eerily from doorways and dogs barking threateningly as he walked by, it was like finding a haven to sense Anita's warm presence against him.

"I'm so happy you're here at the hotel tonight," she whispered. "We're the only three here. And this town, it is such a strange place. I've been in dozens of primitive villages, but this one, it feels different, threatening."

"Hey, there's nothing to worry about," Chris assured her. "I'll be back in an hour or so."

As he stepped back to go she leaned up to him and kissed him. The kiss lingered. Chris felt his penis growing against her, but his lips felt nothing emotional, her hunger activated his sexual response but not his heart. Still, as he walked down the hallway to the street outside, it felt good knowing he could return to her after dinner.

There was no electricity in town; he had noticed that as he walked back to the hotel. Kerosene lamps lit the lobby of the hotel, and an old Indian woman sat in one of the easy chairs. She stared at Chris as he walked through. To his relief, she smiled and nodded, saying something in Quitapul.

Outside, the street was dark. A scented breeze blew gently, and Chris detected the odor of many cooking fires mixed with the smell of flowers and the lake. He relaxed into the nighttime atmosphere of the town center. The townspeople were mostly inside their homes. It was the wealthy Indians who lived on this street, with genuine adobe houses and even cassette players blaring Mexican music into the night. An old Indian passed by Chris and greeted him with a formal but friendly "Buenas noches," to which Chris eagerly responded.

In stark contrast to the Mexican music coming from one of the houses down the street, Mick Jagger was blasting "Beast of Burden" from the open door of the only cafe in town as Chris approached it. He paused where he could hear both strains of music. A feeling had been welling up in him as he walked along the street, looking in at the happy family scenes, listening to the gay music of the children, feeling the charm of the evening—he was admitting that the town itself wasn't ominous or threatening to him. It was his own reaction to the foreign culture that made him feel uneasy here. This town, outside of the strange vibrations he had picked up from Father Morales and Magdalena, was an amazingly beautiful place. Mick Jagger seemed plastic, inauthentic in comparison with the reality Chris was walking through. There was a vitality here, a sense of an entire village being one living organism.

The restaurant, in spite of a few superficial gringo touches—the music, a giant Budweiser wall hanging, a Kiss poster, and a reproduction of a winter scene with a sleigh and horses coming down a snowy trail—had much the same atmosphere of unhurried, genuine warmth. It reminded him of places where he'd eaten up in Mexico years ago, when he had been doing anthropological field work in Chiapas.

As he entered the restaurant and stepped into the soft glow of the hurricane lamps that illuminated it, the Jagger song came to an end; no one bothered to start another tape. Faces stared at him as he walked over to a far table. There was a general atmosphere of alcohol in the room. Two tables were occupied with what must have been the wealthy Quitapul residents. Four men of various ages at each, both groups cheerfully confronting a number of beer bottles in the middle of their tables.

A large table with perhaps ten people seemed to provide the main activity in the room. At it, several gringos were sitting with Indians. Spanish was being spoken and Chris could pick up phrases as he sat waiting to order: carpentry talk, construction talk, mason talk.

Chris guessed they were from the crew building the resort he had seen in the distance on the bay. They were all young, so Richard McGrabbin probably wasn't among them. They were fairly drunk, laughing and joking with the coarse but comradely energy of men who have worked a hard day and want to lose themselves in their beers for a while. One of them kept eying Chris. He was a young man with long hair; Chris had known a number of similar men back home who were working part-time in construction to put themselves through college. They weren't a bad sort, in his experience.

A pretty Ladino woman dressed in disco clothes came over to Chris's table and gave him a menu. She was an energetic girl who went from table to table, joking with the customers who all appeared to know her well. Her low laugh reminded him of Wendy. He wished she was with him. But even as he admitted that desire, he knew he didn't really mean it, that whatever might happen with Magdalena would not happen if Wendy were here. And he didn't want to get involved with Anita either, for the same reason. There was something happening in Zacapula, and with Magdalena, and he felt compelled to find out what it was.

He ordered a chicken dinner and a beer and hoped for the best. As the waitress returned with his beer, a tall man in Levi's and a cowboy shirt walked in, took off his Stetson, and hung it on a nail. The different groups of people in the restaurant all shouted out greetings to him and he gestured a general greeting to everyone with a wave of his hand in the air. He appeared about forty-five or fifty to Chris. His hair was of medium length, and was turning gray. Slightly pudgy, his stocky body was a little over muscled and his reddish face was marked with the heavy drinker's burst veins.

He looked directly at Chris before sitting down at the big table with the construction crew. His eyes were alert and sensitive, in contrast to the other men in the room whose gazes were blurred by alcohol. Chris met his stare and nodded slightly. The man's presence in the room gave it a solid, dynamic atmosphere that Chris appreciated. He was so used to encountering the usual gringo malaise of expatriot lethargy south of the Rio Grande that this man's energetic positiveness was a relief.

As he sat down, the men started relating the problems of the day, talking about a plumbing difficulty they had struggled with all afternoon while he was gone. He listened, an obvious authority figure, his sense of command evident in the casual control of his voice, his attitude of relaxed attention. When he gave a brief response to the report, everyone seemed content to let business drop and get on with the drinking.

"So who's the new gringo?" Chris heard him ask the young, long-haired American in English.

"Got in on the mailboat today," the man responded without much interest, as if newcomers weren't easily welcomed into the small tight circle of gringos in the town.

"You talked to him yet?"

"Nope, he just came in."

"Well I might as well check him out," the older man said, and stood up, walked over to Chris's table, and sat down without hesitation. "Howdy." He extended his stubby, muscled hand, with hair thick on its back. "Name's McGrabbin. Ricardo down here."

"Chris, Chris Barker."

"Welcome to Zacapula. You ever do carpentry?"

"No. Not one of my strong points."

93

"Damn, I'm needing a good carpenter."

"Sorry."

"So how do you like our fine city?"

"I like it a lot."

"Going to be a hundred percent, thousand percent better in a year or two, just you watch. Got a resort going in up the bay a ways, landing strip, golf course, the works. Going to fly people in directly from the airport in Guatemala City. Give this town a great leap forward economically. Finally bring some vitality to the place."

"Town looks pretty healthy the way it is," Chris found himself saying defensively.

"About half the kids are brain-damaged because of poor nutrition. Half of them die before they're twenty. Three-fourths of them can't read or write. Sorry, but it's a short-lived fantasy of newly arrived tourists, thinking this town is healthy."

The waitress brought Ricardo a mixed drink and he took a welcome gulp. "These Indians need jobs; they need money to care for their children just like people do anywhere. And that's what I've been trying to do for them for almost thirty years."

"So I've heard," Chris said.

"I came down here just like you, romantic as all shit about the Indians. I'd had it with the States, so I bought a house here, settled in. My wife left me, so I married the prettiest girl in town and had a bunch of kids by her."

"I've met Magdalena," Chris said evenly.

Ricardo blinked and peered at Chris. "Magdalena?" he said, his voice hesitant.

"Your daughter."

"Not hardly. I've disowned her."

"Why? She seems, uh, quite a nice person," Chris said. He flushed a little as he realized how feeble the term was —and that Ricardo was not fooled by it.

"So, she's got another gringo under her spell, has she? Well listen to me, Barker, she's pure poison. Bad medicine. Get my point? You go after her and she'll ruin you. And you won't be the first."

"I'm not after her. I just met her on the mailboat."

"Well leave it at that. I'd heard she was back in town. How long are you staying, by the way?"

"Depends."

"On what?"

"I'm writing an article on the Quitapul," Chris lied. Ricardo's hectoring manner and assumption of authority irritated him; it would be fun to give the older man a little jolt. "On the earthquake, the volcano, the buried treasure."

"The hell you are," Ricardo said flatly.

"The hell I'm not."

"For what magazine?"

"A local one in San Francisco."

"And just how come you chose the Quitapul for your article?"

"I read about the buried treasure and it sounded like a good story."

"It's just a fairy tale," Ricardo said hotly. "Just another old-time Indian yarn."

Chris's dinner came. It looked good. He ordered another beer, enjoying the buzz he was getting from the alcohol. "I want to go over to the island tomorrow," he said. "Do you know anybody with a boat who would hire out for the morning?"

"Tourists aren't allowed on the island," Ricardo said.

"I'm not a tourist, I'm researching an article."

"Nobody goes to the island without permission."

"Permission from whom?" Chris pressed.

"I own the island."

"Come on now, the Indians wouldn't sell their sacred powerspot."

"Powerspot?"

"Isn't that what it's called?"

"Magdalena told you that?"

"You don't really own it, do you?"

"Just trespass and find out."

"What are you going to do, shoot me?"

Chris's beer came, along with another mixed drink for Ricardo, who held up his glass for a toast. "To your audacity," Ricardo said. "May it not get you into trouble down here."

They clicked glasses. "To your island," Chris said. "May the volcano not erupt and bury it in molten lava."

"So you have been talking to Magdalena."

"We came over on the boat together, like I told you."

A man walked into the restaurant; Ricardo noticed immediately, shouting to him in Quitapul. He was obviously an Indian, wearing the traditional embroidered shorts and the long sash tied in front. But on his head was a cowboy hat like Ricardo's, only brand-new. He was a solid but agile young man of perhaps twenty-five, very handsome, almost strikingly so, and quite aware of it.

He sauntered over to the table, looked at Chris, and suddenly seemed startled—shocked, even. Ricardo, watching this, asked the young man something in Quitapul. They talked for a moment in rapid guttural phrases. Chris drank the rest of his beer, feeling suddenly unnerved by the young Indian's reaction to seeing his face.

"Barker, this is my right-hand man, Enrique," Ricardo said, slapping the young man on the back affectionately as he sat down to join them at the table. "You want something done in the realms of the occult, and senor brujo here can do it!"

"Does he know anything about the treasure of the Quitapul, on the sacred island?"

"You're a determined man, Barker."

"Just doing my job."

"What do you say?" Ricardo asked Enrique in English. "Do you want to tell this gringo anything about your sacred island?"

Enrique looked at Chris with hard, penetrating eyes. Chris felt the full power of the man hit him head-on, with a force that reminded him of Magdalena. Somehow there was some quality the two had in common. "I will take you to the island tomorrow," Enrique said, speaking English with a strong native accent.

Chris wasn't sure how to respond. Magdalena would be taking him there the day after tomorrow. But it couldn't hurt to go there twice. "Hey, thanks," he said.

"So now, tell me about your family."

"What about my family?"

"You have children?"

"One."

"A daughter?"

"Yes."

"Blonde hair?" Enrique went on.

"As a matter fact, yes."

"Perhaps she is thirteen, fourteen years old."

"You guessed it again," Chris said.

"Yes," Enrique said. "Just as I thought."

"How'd you know?" Chris insisted, feeling edgy with the young man's guesses.

Ricardo broke in. "Like I told you, he's a brujo. They have powers. Humor him," he went on, slapping Enrique on the shoulder again. "He's half-loco, but the other half is clear as a bell."

"I will tell you one more thing," Enrique said, as if he was concentrating to receive word from some inner source. "Ah, there it is now. Yes. Your daughter, she is coming down soon."

Chris stared at him, defensive.

"Is he right?" Ricardo asked.

"Maybe."

"Hey, amigo, don't be bothered by Enrique's psychic powers. He likes you; he wants to help with your article. I personally think he's just guessing, you know. I don't really put much stock in the psychic world. But regardless, he picks up good vibes from you, as the hippies used to say. You can help us with our work."

"All I'm doing is writing an article," Chris said.

97

Enrique leaned forward intently and whispered. "We are needing help; my people are very poor; we have been through much suffering."

"But what can I do?"

"You can write an article about what we are doing here, about our new resort. You can write about this year's Ilum K'inal celebration. We are beginning a new era, and you can tell your people about us. This will help bring people to the resort, and all of Zacapula will be thankful to you."

"Well, maybe," Chris said, feeling it might be a good idea anyway actually to write the article.

"Good," Enrique said, and reached over to grip Chris's arm emphatically.

Ricardo slapped his hands together. "Well then, we've got PR taken care of, just like that! You'll need a place to stay for Easter. I have a house over on the volcano that's empty right now; you can have that for a week or two. Is your daughter really coming down, or is Enrique here not always accurate with his guessing?"

"She's coming down," Chris said.

"Excellent, she'll love it here, I'm sure."

"Sounds good," Chris admitted.

"Have another beer, amigo!"

Sometime later, Chris made his way out of the restaurant, not quite drunk but fairly high on four beers. The street was asleep, most of the candles out in the houses and the radios silent. He made his way into the hotel and up the steps, then paused at Anita's door and knocked. She opened the door and stepped out onto the veranda, wearing a t-shirt and underpants.

"She's sleeping," she whispered. "Can we go to your room?"

Chris fumbled with his key and finally opened the door. "Too many beers," he said.

They both felt around in the darkness for matches. Their fingers came into contact, reminding him of the touch of Magdalena's hand and his when he had given her back the necklace that morning. That moment in Panahachel seemed like so long ago.

In the candlelight they sat on his bed and made small talk. But the talking quickly stopped as she leaned against him, sighed, and rested her head on his shoulder. Her hand came to rest on his leg and when he turned his head to her, she kissed him. It seemed to him dimly that he had not meant for this to happen, but with the alcohol fogging his resolution, he received the kiss and opened up to her, his fingers touching her bare knee and drifting sensuously up her thigh.

She was hungry for him, hungry in a way Wendy had never been, reaching under his shirt with warm fingers, unbuckling his belt as her lips probed his mouth, wanting him right then, with no questions asked, with no hesitation. Her breasts were firm and her sighs passionate, and Chris came alive inside with desire for her, pushing her gently back on the bed while he took off his boots and pants.

When he turned around to her, she was naked, smiling up to him, extending her arms. But for a moment something inside him went numb. He felt Magdalena suddenly, as if she had just focused her energy on him, intruding on his awareness with her presence. He looked down at Anita and knew that he didn't feel love for her. But she sat up and the contact of skin against skin was too much for him. His erection was obvious and she reached for it, and with her body leaning over and her mouth taking him with eagerness deep into her throat, he lost Magdalena's image and floated into the euphoria of the immediate moment.

They were under the covers quickly, body against body, her fingers everywhere, stimulating him until he caught fire and took the initiative, his weight on her, feeling her breasts pressed against his chest, her legs apart under him, and that magnetic pull of her insides waiting for his penis to make its move, push into her.

99

The energy surged through his system as he let go of everything and gave himself to the rush of adrenaline through his body, the superlative sensation of entering the female warmth. He felt himself losing consciousness except in his genitals as he pumped inside her faster and faster, and then suddenly he felt he was the volcano, ready to erupt inside her, the earth rumbling, shuddering under him triumphantly.

And as he came, it wasn't Anita under at all, it was Magdalena, he could feel her, coming with him, exploding!

Then he was lying on his back, silent.

"What's the matter?" Anita said softly beside him.

"Nothing."

"You're thinking of another woman."

"No."

"I think I should go back to my room."

Chris knew he was supposed to ask her to stay. But now that he was exhausted sexually, all he could think of was Magdalena. Would he see her tomorrow? Would she be angry with him if he went with Enrique to the island a day before going there with her?

Anita got out of bed.

"I'm sorry," Chris said. "I'm kind of drunk and drifting away."

She didn't say anything. She left quietly. Chris watched her naked body disappear out the door. He blew the candle out.

chapter 9

A knocking at his door. Chris opened his eyes. The morning was already bright outside, with sunlight shining on the top of the volcano. He rolled out of bed, mumbling "Momento, momento," and put on his Levi's.

When he opened the door, there stood Enrique, beaming a self-satisfied macho smile, looking dashing in his cowboy shirt and hat, juxtaposed with his brilliant Quitapul shorts and sandals. "A little hung over?" the young Indian said, grinning.

"A little," Chris conceded.

"And what is that?" Enrique said, walking into his room while Chris sat down on the bed to put on his boots. "Is that the underwear men wear in the United States?"

Anita's underwear was on the floor in plain sight. "Uh, no," Chris said, "those belong to a friend of mine."

Enrique picked them up eagerly, his sexual interest instantly aroused. "So you are hiding a girlfriend?" he said.

"She's back in her room."

"This is what I like, an American with the proper spirit about women. Tell me about your daughter."

"Michelle?" Chris said, standing up and starting to put on his backpack.

"She is very beautiful? Does she have a boyfriend?"

"Yeah, she has a guy she likes a lot."

"Do they do it?"

"What?"

"You know what I mean."

"No, not that I've heard."

"Well, would she tell you?"

Chris was standing, ready to depart. He paused and reflected a moment. "Yeah," he said. "She'd tell me."

"So she doesn't do it, then."

"No," Chris said, beginning to be irritated by the conversation.

'Well good. She is too young. Your girlfriend, does she want to come with us?"

"Oh. Well, we can ask."

"Women, gringa women that is, they are like nothing else in the world," Enrique said, with a tone of male gloating that Chris found almost ugly.

Chris knocked on Anita's door, after a moment it opened a crack. "It's me," he said.

She stepped out into the hallway in just her shirt and immediately put her arms around his neck in an embrace, not even noticing the Indian who stood to the side and watched her firm, tanned legs and buttocks tauten as she stretched up to kiss Chris. "I have to go to Guatemala City today with Cathleen," she said softly, reluctantly. "I think she has hepatitis again; she had it awhile back and she's been drinking so much, I think she has a relapse. Anyway, I have to go. Would you want to come with us?"

"Uh, no, my daughter's coming in soon; I need to be here."

"Won't you need to go to the city anyway to meet her at the airport?"

"I'm going to have her take the bus up here from the airport."

"Oh. Well." She suddenly felt Enrique's presence and realized her half-nudity; she stepped back into her doorway. "So maybe I won't even seen you again," she said.

"Come back up, I'll be here through Easter."

"Do you want me to?"

"Sure. I'll be over in a house on the volcano, just ask for Enrique here and he'll take you across."

"My pleasure," he said, grinning his way into the conversation. "Do come back!"

"Well—I don't know what will happen. Cathleen pays my bills, you see, I have to stay with her. But I'll try."

"Oh, your underwear's in my room; the door's unlocked."

She looked into his eyes, but he was not there for her, and it was painful to both of them. "Well," she said, and extended her hand formally. "Thank you."

Chris took her hand but didn't find any words in reply. He had been in this situation before and had sworn never to get in it again, but here he was. "I hope Cathleen gets well quickly," he said.

"Yes," she said. "Me too."

She turned and went back in her room, closing the door behind her.

Knowing he would not see her again, he felt oddly desolate. Not because he would miss her—he wouldn't. But what should have been a pleasant adventure and a little comfort for them both had turned out so very differently: for him, an experience of almost ferocious intensity that had almost nothing to do with Anita—it had been the fantasy of Magdalena that he had responded to —and for her. . . ? It couldn't have been very pleasant down here, it seemed; nothing was casual. I wanted to escape from triviality, he thought, but it'd be damned upsetting not to be *able* to be trivial anymore.

The morning was magnificent outside. There was a heady fragrance to the air, an expansive feeling among the townspeople. Chris watched the Indians going about their routines of carrying laundry to the lake, or bringing water up to their homes. Men walked by with large hoes on their shoulders, headed for their garden patches. Women were returning from the gardens with baskets of produce to sell at the daily market up by the church. Chil-

103

dren's voices shouted out to one another, their guttural language vibrating in unison with the many birdcalls scattering song across the morning.

"Padre Morales is meeting us for breakfast," Enrique said.

"Oh?"

"He would like to talk with you."

"Fine with me, I guess," Chris said as they turned into the café. "Tell me, are you Catholic?"

Enrique gave a mocking laugh. "Of course," he said. "We are all Catholics. But we are also Quitapul. There has been a merging of the two traditions."

"And Padre Morales doesn't mind your holding on to your Mayan religion?"

"Oh, he minds. But he has accepted our need to worship in the old ways, as long as he thinks we hold Christ above all else. He represents the government, you understand. He is in charge here. He can order in the troups if he wanted to. But that is all changing; our tribal government is gaining respect and power. Still, the padre is very important."

At the restaurant they found Father Morales at a far table, sipping orange juice. There were ten people in the place having breakfast, mostly well-to-do Indians, but they did not include the padre in their jovialities; he sat apart, solemn in his black attire. He stood up formally in greeting. Chris looked into his small, beady eyes but was unable to penetrate the exterior glint of friendship.

"I understand you're off this morning to the sacred island," Morales said as they sat down.

"Enrique's been good enough to offer to take me."

"The ruins are quite beautiful." The priest and Enrique glanced at each other, and Chris detected an underlying conflict between them.

An Indian girl came to take orders. While they were talking with her, a young man came hurrying into the café and spoke quickly to Enrique, who excused himself for a minute to go outside and talk.

104

"How are you liking Zacapula?" Morales asked once the girl was gone.

"Just fine. No signs of the Devil yet," Chris said lightly, then wished he hadn't. Morales' obsession yesterday had been both tiresome and troubling, and it was stupid to give him an opening to start airing it again. He suppressed the uneasy, vagrant thought that his loveless mating with Anita had been a little like one of the punishments in Dante—sinning lovers condemned to copulate without passion forever. If so, he told himself firmly, it was only confirmation that the Devil was no more than a mistaken embodiment of all-too-human emotions and conditions.

"They are there, but you do not read them," Morales said. "You are a stranger in a strange land, Christopher, a land stranger than you imagine, however well you may feel you know it from books. The signs I talk of are not as simple as international traffic symbols by any means. When the scales fall from your eyes and you understand them, you will be a wiser man, and I fear, a much sadder one."

Orange juice arrived for Chris and he sipped it, eyeing the priest warily. "I told you yesterday, Father, that I don't go along with what you were saying. If you want to look at your try at imposing your church and your beliefs on these people as some sort of cosmic war, fine, do that. But I'm out of it. As far as I'm concerned, this Caban stuff is what's true for the Quitapul, your church is what's true for you, and my . . . well, the way I see things, that's what's true for me. I'm not going to argue with other people's truth, but I'm not going to share them, either."

"Ay de mi," the priest said, shaking his head. "It is no wonder things have come to this pass, when educated men can speak seriously of truths that change from man to man! Christopher, truth is one and unchanging, or else it is not truth. And I tell you that it is the plainest of truths that the Devil is loose in this world. It is the truth—my truth, if you insist—that when the priests of my church

105

came here three centuries ago, they met the Devil, face to face, in the guise of Caban. They were too blind, or perhaps too faint-hearted, to see that truth fully and pursue it, and were content to suppress the worship of Caban and compromise with the Quitapul so as to get them to accept the Church. Itzam'na, the son of the sun, was remote enough so that he could be explained as an imperfect understanding of the True God, and an accommodation could be made. But now the seeds of that compromise have borne their fruit, and the harvest is near. The Mayan tradition has it that Caban was punished and rendered powerless by Itzam'na, but that at the end of a thousand years that term of punishment would end and Caban would be given his chance to exercise power once again. It is at this Easter that the thousand years will be fulfilled."

"I hate to seem like an arrogant gringo," Chris said, "but I don't see how a Guatemalteco volcano god getting out on parole, or whatever, affects the whole world. Away from his own turf, I would say Caban is pretty small potatoes."

Morales blinked. "Potatoes? Ah, I see, an idiom new to me, but I understand its import. Christopher, you mistake me. I do not credit the theology of the Mayas or their descendants. I do credit the fact that they have had experiences which have led them to construct that theology in, so to speak, good faith. Satan is the Father of Lies, and he and his legions had countless ages to perfect their lies with these poor people before the Church, working through its human instruments, arrived to combat them. Caban is no other than an arch-demon, directed by Satan himself; and all that is needed to bring on the final struggle for the entire community of human souls is that such a being be freely and with full consent accorded supreme power by any one of the peoples or nations of the world. The Quitapul, or those among them who seek to placate and restore Caban, are not many in number; but if Caban has them, the rest of us will be in short order facing his power and the unleashed malice of his Master."

Chris's stomach rumbled, and he wondered gloomily when his breakfast would come. "So McGrabbin's daughter, that Magdalena, she's committed to this Caban?"

"Possessed by him," Morales said.

"But you seem to be on pretty good terms with Enrique, and he's a brujo as well."

Morales scowled. "Enrique is working for the things—the material things—that we want for the Quitapul and for Zacapula. It helps with that that he is a brujo, that the Quitapul—that side of them that is unchurched and clings secretly to the old ways—respect him as a man of power. I see him as one who wishes to keep one foot in each camp, a dangerous position indeed. But I trust and believe that he is coming my way."

"And so he is," Chris said heartily, "right through the door and toward us. Hola, Enrique."

Father Morales glanced dourly at Chris. "Think about what I have been saying," he said. "As I told you, you can find me at the church." He nodded a curt farewell to Enrique and stalked from the restaurant.

Food came. Chris gobbled at his eggs, his stomach tight from the confrontation and needing some food to stop his shaking. He had never liked ministers; they always conveyed a massive superiority complex under their aura of humbleness. His parents had been stern Presbyterians, and it had taken him years to shake that world of sin and devils from his life. He wasn't about to take any of that hocus-pocus on again. Still, the priest's words had shaken him in some way.

Fifteen minutes later they were back outside in the morning sunlight, and Chris felt his spirits once again rising. No more talks with Father Morales, he promised himself. He didn't need conversations like that; there was no need to focus on the negative in life. All around him, he saw happy Indians, and not a hint of the horrors that

Morales kept harping on. Those Catholics, he mused to himself as he followed Enrique down the path to the lake, they're always trying to frighten people into being religious. It should be just the opposite, though. Religion should be a celebration of this joyous feeling in the air.

The cayuco, a well-shaped but still somewhat awkward hollowed-log canoe, responded to Enrique's strong strokes of the paddle and headed out from shore. Chris was an experienced whitewater canoer and had offered to row, but Enrique insisted on handling the job.

The sun was now fully risen, and Chris pulled the brim of his cap down. They were rowing along the shore a hundred yards out. Ahead, dead on, was the island, a couple of miles away. To the left was the volcano, looking benign this morning, with a lingering touch of mist at its top. And farther to the left, the bay was appearing, although Chris still couldn't see the resort.

"Rain tonight," Enrique said. "The rain is early this year. The men will be out planting corn and beans right after Easter."

"Do you farm?" Chris asked him.

"Of course not. I work with Ricardo. I am a partner in the resort; we do everything together. I am his son."

"Son?"

"His most important son because I am a brujo."

"You have powers?"

"Of course. When I was born, they knew I would grow up to lead my people."

"If you're Ricardo's son, then Magdalena is your sister," Chris said, turning around in his seat to where he was facing backwards watching this young half-Indian.

"Magdalena is no longer part of our family," Enrique said. "Ricardo did all he could for her; she was his favorite. He sent her off to school, spent a great deal of money on her in the hopes that she would alter her course. But nothing helped. She has sold her soul to the Devil and we would be better off if she was dead!"

"You really believe that?"

"Gringos know nothing of the workings of power. When there is an evil element, it must be eliminated for the sake of the tribe."

"But she is your sister."

"She is the enemy! She is trying to stop the Quitapul from regaining their power. If it wasn't for my presence and my counter-curses against her, she would have the entire tribe in her power right now. I have worked very hard to stop her."

"To stop her from doing what?" Chris pressed.

Enrique gestured toward the resort project that they could see on the shore of the bay. "To stop her from sabotaging the resort first of all," he said angrily. "The fighting a month ago took place there one night, when her men tried to dynamite the main building. But that is not all; that is secondary to the main battle."

"Which is?"

"Listen, I'll tell you. See the island there? That is the sacred island of our forefathers, the powerpoint!"

"I know that already."

"You know of the tunnel?"

"Yes."

"She told you!"

"Maybe."

"Well, this Easter is to be the day when the tunnel opens up."

"You're going to dynamite the cave?"

Enrique shot Chris a hostile glance, as if such an idea was blasphemy. "Of course not. The tunnel will open of itself. Caban will open his heart and his treasures will once again be ours. For centuries, prophecies have foretold it, and this Easter coincides with Ilum K'inal on our calendar—the great awakening!"

Enrique was rowing with manic strokes, his voice intense, and his eyes cold, demonic, frightening. He had that same look of madness which Magdalena had at times, and Chris shrank from it, sensing a pagan, uncontrolled energy ready to break loose.

109

"Nothing can stop the prophecies," Enrique went on, "not even Magdalena. She wants us to remain starving, poor, powerless, when in that tunnel is enough treasure to make us the power of the planet."

"So how is the tunnel going to open up?" Chris asked.

"There is a way to get Caban to open his heart, the way has been known for generations. It is all a matter of timing, and of performing the proper ceremonies."

"What kind of ceremonies?"

Enrique stared at him, and Chris realized that the Indian really did have a crazy element to his personality, one which scared Chris so much he wished he'd never come out to the island with him. "Perhaps you will see the ceremonies," Enrique said. "You must write down everything that happens; it must be written for the world to know."

"Well I certainly want to be around when the tunnel opens up."

At this comment, Enrique seemed to drop his crazily elated mood slightly, as if suddenly he had forgotten the role he was performing. It was a tall tale the Indian was telling, designed to impress an ignorant gringo. Chris laughed quickly, but Enrique's expression reacted to the laugh, and Chris quickly changed his outward emotion. "So," he said, "soon you'll have the riches of the Quitapul and will be so powerful—"

"It is not the riches, it is the opening of Caban's heart to his people that will give us power, that will return us to our rightful dominance."

"And who will be the leaders with the power?"

"The elected officials, of course."

"Are you one of them?"

"Of course."

"And your father?"

"He was long ago granted a Quitapul birthright; he is my partner. Look, there is the house which you can use."

On the volcano's shore, across from the island and a little toward the bay and town, was a Spanish-style adobe

110

house, large and well landscaped, nestled under a stand of mango and avocado trees.

"It's beautiful," Chris said.

"It is the home Ricardo built for a woman he loved. But she left and has not returned for two years now. Ricardo has been broken-hearted. Magdalena put a curse on the woman and drove her away."

Chris decided not to comment on this, and turned to face forward. The island was approaching, a beautiful little island, thick with vegetation, with lush little canyons and rugged rock outcroppings. It was about a mile offshore from the volcano, and perhaps a quarter-mile long. Enrique rowed to the east side of the island, heading toward a sandy beach. Chris took a deep breath, and gazed with anticipation at the approaching shore.

The cayuco ran aground with a sudden grating sound. Enrique jumped out into the knee-deep water and pushed the boat farther onto shore, so that Chris wouldn't have to get his boots wet.

"It will take us half an hour to row over to the house when we leave here," Enrique calculated. "And then I need another half-hour to get to the resort before the Xocomil picks up. If we leave here no later than noon we will do all right. By one-thirty it is dangerous on the lake, by two-thirty impossible. Not even I can row a cayuco through the Xocomil. Even Ricardo's launch doesn't venture out after one o'clock. He lost a boat two years ago."

Chris put on his backpack and started walking up toward the trees and hill, eager to explore the island. "No one lives here?" he asked.

Enrique had taken the lead toward an overgrown trail. "No one but Ricardo and me, and our guests, are allowed on this island. It is death for an Indian to step foot here unless the proper ceremonies are performed."

"You mean he'd just drop dead?"

"You don't understand such things. But I assure you, no Indians come here. In the old days, brujos lived on the

111

island. A hundred years ago there was the mightiest of the brujos, my great-grandfather. He almost succeeded in working the spell to open the tunnel. But he was missing the essential element."

"What was that?"

Enrique paused and grinned. "The proper virgin of course," he said in a joking tone of voice.

Just then the sound of a whining engine cut through the morning air. Both men stopped talking and stared down at the boat that had appeared around the point of the island at a rapid speed, its propeller overrevving as it made a sharp turn and headed to shore.

"Ricardo," Enrique said anxiously, and headed quickly back down to the shore.

Chris stood a moment watching the Indian hurrying toward the approaching boat. He had an urge to push on up the trail alone, to let Enrique catch up with him. It would be an extra thrill to come upon the ruins by himself. But Ricardo stood in the boat and waved him to come down, and he obeyed. Enrique caught a rope and pulled the boat onto the sand, and father and son talked emphatically in Quitapul, pointedly leaving Chris out of the conversation. Ricardo was upset, angry, and he seemed to be berating Enrique. Then he turned his attention to Chris.

"Hey Barker, hop in, let's go. I need Enrique, something's come up at the resort he needs to take care of. I'll drop you off at the house."

Chris felt acutely disappointedly in the change of plans, and then had an idea. "I'll row over in an hour or so in the cayuco," he said. "I'm good with a canoe and I'd like to look around."

"Nope, can't do that," Ricardo said. Then he let the idea sink in and changed his mind. "Well, I guess there's nothing wrong with that. It's not allowed, of course, but no one will know. Just hike up that trail and down to the ruins, and then get off the island, no more than half an hour at the most, okay?"

"Sounds good," Chris said.

"But don't go to the other side of the island, that's the sacred burial ground of the brujos. Okay, we've got to get going. I'll see you tomorrow. There's food and everything you need in the house. Just don't get caught in the Xocomil or you're a goner, you understand?"

"Right."

Ricardo put the engine in reverse and backed away from shore with Enrique standing beside him. They had a quick conversation and Enrique took over the controls. Chris stood and watched the powerful boat zoom off and out of sight around the point. As he turned and started back up the trail, he found himself wondering what kind of a relationship Ricardo had with such a headstrong son. It would be a father's nightmare, Chris decided. Old Ricardo really ended up with more than he could handle, a brujo son with a crazy craving for power, and a bruja daughter who fought his every move.

He recalled his brief fantasy of the day before, of genuinely falling in love with Magdalena and marrying her and settling here. The thought of her was as powerfully attractive as ever, but—after her rantings about Caban and the eerie hypnosis demonstration, followed by his meeting with batty Father Morales and weird Enrique —she and her associates and family didn't seem to fit into any kind of marriage he could be comfortable with. Have I got a girl for you, Barker, he told himself wryly. A little argument over who gets the car or whatever, and she'd call down a couple tons of molten lava on you.

Yet, despite his determinedly flip attitude, the thought of Magdalena obsessed him, until it seemed that he could almost sense her presence near him—or within him.

A small animal broke and ran crashing through the undergrowth, making Chris jump. The deep-throated croak of a hidden bird high in a mango tree ahead of him announced his approach to the top of the ridge. An almost foreboding awareness of solitude warred with his excitement as he reached the high point of the trail.

113

He could see down into a small, overgrown canyon. His eyes scanned the area for signs of the ruins, but the vegetation was so thick and the canyon so deep that all he could see was a green mat of trees and vines. Chris followed the trail down into the canyon.

For the first few minutes he could still see the tip of the volcano towering ahead beyond the island, but then he was in the thick of the forest and a dark canopy of trees blocked his view. A tiny stream joined the trail and ran down the steep canyon side, pausing to form little pools and waterfalls. The trail was evidently not much used, and seemed a natural part of the landscape.

He paused a moment to catch his breath. It was cool in the shadows. With the coolness Chris felt a touch of uneasiness, as if he were being watched, as if Ricardo and Enrique had returned to stalk him in the canyon, perhaps with some weird sacrificial plan for the lone gringo. . . . He shook off the notion and pushed on down the trail.

A few minutes later the canyon opened up into a welcome meadow of sunlight and swaying grass. Chris thought he saw a glistening of gold flecks in the sunlit water of the stream, and he watched it with intense curiosity as he walked. Suddenly the stream itself disappeared, falling with a low rumble down a hole in the ground, beside a giant, overgrown . . . Chris stared up in disbelief.

Right in front of him was a thirty- to forty-foot-high ruined structure, barely discernible at first glance from the other mounds of . . . This was the spot! Chris felt a chill run up his spine as he gazed up at the temple. He had been to many ruins in Mexico, and these were similar, so overgrown with shrubs and moss that at first they looked like natural formations, except for their steep, regular sides and pyramidal shapes.

Chris took off his pack excitedly, feeling as if he were the first discoverer of this ancient Mayan site.

He started climbing the ruin which from its size he took to be that of the main temple; its mossy steps were soft under his boots. By the time he was halfway up and had counted thirty-five steps, he was out of breath. Turning around, he looked back down. The height was not all that great, but it felt so, giving Chris a cliff-hanging sensation in his gut, as if forces were pulling at him to lose his balance. The slope was very steep, and he knew he would roll all the way down if he fell.

As he gazed up the rest of the steps of the temple, Magdalena suddenly flashed into his mind again. This was her haunt, Chris found himself thinking. But no, not if her father wouldn't allow her here, and he most certainly wouldn't if what Enrique had said was true.

A thought struck Chris so strongly he stumbled and would have lost his balance if he hadn't sat down. What if this was all a game? he found himself wondering. What if Magdalena was in cahoots with Ricardo and Enrique? There was obviously something in the air, something going on that he didn't know about.

He shrugged and forced himself to dismiss the idea, then stood up. He focused his attention on the climb, wanting to reach the top before his courage gave out. He half-ran up the steep steps; then he was there, standing on a ten-foot-square flat surface of mossy stone. In the middle was a sacrificial altar much the same as Chris had seen on many other temples, where the victim, animal or human, would be held down while his heart was cut out. While *her* heart was cut out, he corrected himself automatically, then wondered uneasily why.

He approached the altar and touched it, rubbing his fingers along the smooth surface. An anger grew in him which he always felt at places like this. The priestly cult, in the Old World and the New, had ruled and manipulated the human race for at least eight thousand years, using fear to gain dominance over the primitive mind. The thousands of gods the human race had worshiped, and the hundreds it still worshiped, were, Chris's studies had convinced him, only manifestations of mankind's need to know the unknowable, to gain some control over

115

a hostile and dangerous world by creating gods who in some measure could be swayed by absolute obedience, propitiation, and sacrifice. The cosmic irony was that the few men smart enough to see the fallacy of this had used their intelligence to become "servants" of the gods and gain control over their credulous worshipers.

The worst of it was that power had bred perversion and atrocity. From the unrecorded victims of Cro-Magnon shamans, the infants fed to the furnaces of Moloch, the ghastly "blood eagle" ritual of northern Europe, the skull pyramids of Genghis Khan, to the hecatombs of the Inquisition and the Puritan witch-hunters, the priestly caste the world over had killed and tortured—with, worst horror of all, the consent and approval of their cowed communicants.

A few hundred miles to the north, Aztec priests had dressed themselves in the freshly flayed skins of their victims, and had whipped children as they walked to their deaths so that their tears would bring rain. And here— very likely on this spot, among many others—the gentler Mayans had sliced the beating hearts from countless girls . . . girls even younger than Michelle . . .

In the middle of his racing thoughts, Chris noticed something sticky on the stone. He withdrew his finger as if he had touched fire. The blood was fresh, only a few hours old. Someone had come over to the island early this morning and performed a sacrifice! Chris noticed chicken dung on the stone below the altar. At least it had been just a chicken, he told himself, relieved. Nothing, maybe, to be shocked by. Of course Indians would sneak over here now and then to perform secret rites. Ricardo wouldn't be able to patrol the island. And why would he want to, anyway? Let the peasants continue to worship the gods, to live in fear of their wrath if the proper ceremonies were not performed. It would keep them from wondering too much about what Ricardo was getting for his efforts.

The volcano stared down at him. Chris felt his attention suddenly leaving the altar and rising up to the towering magnificence of Caban. So, is it you that they kill chickens for? Chris asked the volcano. Is this blood spilled for you?

As he stared at the giant cone, he realized with an intuitive flash that Caban himself had his own blood that once in a great while was spilled, when the lava flowed with its red-hot eruption down Caban's slopes. Lava was the blood of the earth. What greater god, then, caused Caban to give his blood from time to time?

Chris felt suddenly vulnerable as he never had before, as he sensed his own blood pulsing through his veins, his own heart pumping excitedly. He felt pulled toward the volcano, could not take his eyes from it; and in an instant his imagination had him lying on the altar with a Mayan priest leaning over him with an obsidian knife, ripping into his chest between two ribs, and yanking his still-beating heart out as an offering to Caban.

He blinked his eyes, shook his head to free himself of the image, and then turned and started running down the steps. Only when he reached the bottom and was on the ground again did he start to regain his composure, to get control of his imagination and start thinking rationally again. He knelt at the stream and drank quick gulps of the water, glancing over his shoulder around him as if he expected to be surrounded by . . .

But this was all so foolish, he chided himself. He had seen too many scary movies, he was just letting his imagination get the better of him. He walked out into the middle of the little clearing. It was obviously the overgrown central court of the ruined complex. The main temple was to the west, facing Caban. Two secondary temples were on either side, and the fourth side was a sheer cliff of reddish igneous rock. An earthquake seemed to have cracked and shuddered the cliff badly, and Chris stared at the massive hundred-foot wall of stone with a sudden conviction that it might at that moment be hit by another quake and come tumbling down on him.

With an effort, he pushed the fantasy away. He was embarrassed that he had slipped so completely into his daydream up on the temple that he had come running down in fear. He was grateful that no one had been around to see him.

He put on his backpack, not wanting to linger here at the ruins. Still, he didn't feel like leaving the island yet, and felt a pull to go over the next hill and see what was there. Going ahead with the exploration of the island made him feel better about himself. He wasn't used to fantasies taking over and he wanted to show himself that it had been just an isolated occurrence, that he could march over and look at a few brujo graves without freaking out. He had, after all, spent three summers in southern Mexico excavating temples; this was nothing new to him.

When he topped the ridge five minutes later, breathing heavily but feeling confident and stable again, he saw the other shore of the island, with the volcano standing across the mile of water and off to the left, the house he would be staying at. Boy, he told himself jokingly, that volcano better not erupt while I'm staying right there under it, or I'm going to have to do some quick rowing.

A magnificent little bay was nestled along the shoreline down below him. A perfect place for a boat to put in at, he thought, as he remembered sailing trips he'd been on down the western coast of Mexico. But here there were no boats, no rich Americans on vacation. This highland lake was its own world, and that little cove down there, unseen by the occasional tourist to Zacapula and off limits for the Indians, was an enchanted dream spot.

Chris hurried down the trail toward the cove, certain that he wouldn't get caught if he violated orders and visited this side of the lake. Ricardo and Enrique were at the resort with problems of their own; they wouldn't be checking up on him. As long as he made it back to the cayuco in an hour or so, the Xocomil would be no problem for him either.

The trail was overgrown, and twice Chris thought he had lost it. He noted landmarks so that he would be able to find his way back. When he'd been a kid, his father had taken him on hunting and fishing trips in the Rockies, and he knew how to handle himself out in the wilderness without getting lost. He hurried for ten minutes down the trail. Then the vegetation opened up into a small meadow that sloped to a cliff overlooking the bay.

Chris paused at the edge of the clearing. Over near the cliff was a hut, with rock walls and a thatch roof which was mostly gone. At first, he assumed that he had stumbled upon someone's current dwelling. But then he remembered that no one lived on the island, and surmised that this must be an old brujo hut.

Suddenly the sound of a large animal crashing from the far side of the hut into the underbrush startled him. His instinct was to take off fast up the trail, but he held himself in check and watched to see if he could spot the animal. Silence now. A deer must have been sleeping in the hut and been frightened by the approaching human monster's noises or odor.

"Hola!" Chris shouted out, just to make sure it hadn't been a human he had sent running away in fright.

No response. He walked over toward the hut, around the left side, and up to the face of the cliff. Looking down, he saw the bay below. The bushes were so thick on the steep slope that he couldn't see anything down there. But he knew from hunting deer when he was a boy that the deer could be fifteen feet away from him and he would never notice it.

The bay caught his eye again. He wanted to go down and spend a little time along its white sandy shore, with the crystal-clear water welcoming him for a swim. But then he remembered the brujo hut, and turned around. The darkness inside stared out at him through the doorless opening. He approached the hut cautiously and stuck his head inside, feeling his courage increasing as his interest rose.

119

His eyes adjusted. There was nothing at all in the hut except for a shovel. And signs of recent digging in the middle of the earthern floor. He suddenly remembered the two French women who had been accused of coming over to the island and digging for artifacts. This must have been their site. Chris slipped off his backpack and went inside.

The hole in the center of the hut was about two feet deep. He knelt in the damp dirt, hesitated a moment, then plunged his hands into the loose loam, remembering the thrill of the archeological discoveries he had made up in Mexico. As he sifted through the dirt, his heart pounded in his throat, his body fearing sudden capture or worse, but his mind determined to at least see what was in the grave.

Five minutes later he had unearthed six artifacts: two obsidian knives, and four small statues, one slightly larger than the rest. Then he came up with a human shoulder blade, and he froze with it in his hand. "God," he said, realizing what he was holding, feeling a shiver run through his body.

He tossed the bone aside, half-frightened of it, and decided to stop digging. But he noticed in the dim light something else and lifted it out of the dirt. It was smooth to the touch, cool and heavy. About six or seven inches long, and an inch or two thick, almost like an erect penis. He felt a sudden compulsion, a strange, greedy desire to possess these artifacts, to somehow get them back to the States. He stuffed them into his backpack, put it on, and headed out of the hut to hurry to the cayuco with his booty.

Three steps out of the hut, his left foot came down on a rock and slipped sideways off it. Chris screamed out in pain as his ankle received the full weight of his body. Ligaments and muscles tore away from the bone and he fell to the ground, grabbing frantically at his sprained ankle.

"Goddamn!" he cried out. "Please, no, not this, not here!"

He slipped off his backpack and struggled to his feet to see if he could walk. But the pain was excruciating, the injury too severe to push beyond. He had sprained this same ankle three times before in his life, and he knew he wouldn't be able to walk for at least a week.

He felt panic rising in him, almost as intense as the pain. There was no way he could crawl back to the cayuco. He couldn't swim to the mainland. He was trapped here on the island until they discovered him missing tomorrow when they came by the house. He could see the house across the water, and yearned to be over there away from this sinister island. A night here would be frightening; he didn't even want to consider it.

The volcano stared down at him. "You did this to me!" he shouted angrily at it. But he immediately pushed the thought aside. He didn't believe in occult forces; he knew that it was pure coincidence that he had sprained his ankle concurrently with picking up a few Indian artifacts. To start thinking superstitiously right now would be fatal to his nerve.

A slight movement of wind touched his hot face. The Xocomil was already beginning its daily course across the lake. Chris threw off his thoughts of brujo curses and looked down at the bay. It was a beautiful day. He knew he was stuck on the island until Ricardo and Enrique found him tomorrow, so he might as well make the best of it and enjoy the afternoon.

He took off his shirt to let the warm sunlight caress his shoulders and chest. Sure, his ankle was swollen up like crazy and hurt like hell. But he had food in his backpack for a couple of days if necessary, and his sleeping bag rolled on top of it. He even had a bottle of aguardiente, the native hard liquor which the brujos poured on sacrificial fires, swigging the remainder to bring the gods closer.

121

He uncapped the bottle and took a gulp. It was rot-gut alcohol but the burning down his throat felt good. After a few more slugs, Chris could feel the swirling power of the aguardiente rising from his stomach to his brain with a hot rush of lightness. The beauty of the view swept him away on a wave of euphoria.

"To Guatemala!" he said out loud, raising the bottle to the volcano in salute. "To the power of the gods!"

A few minutes later he had the artifacts out on the ground in front of where he was sitting. The three smaller deities sat staring up at him from where he had placed them, their Mayan features solemn and potent in the sunlight. The larger figure was located directly in front of him, and the two obsidian knives rested on the ground, by happenstance placed with their points aimed at his balls, which retracted as they seemed to sense the menace of the sacrificial blades.

Finally, there was the smooth phallic piece. Chris held it in his hands, and even slightly drunk, he could feel its power run through his fingers. It was a very lifelike jade penis, erect, with a dominating head. "Well, I wonder what they did with this," he said aloud, glancing at the volcano and imagining ceremonially dressed Mayan priests on the temple altar with a sacrificial virgin spread out before them. "Little hanky-panky with the young ladies before the big scene, perhaps?" The image brought on a rush of pure sexual urgency in his groin, and he glanced down at the sharp ceremonial knives with their fine, carved handles—and there was Magdalena in his imagination again, standing in her skin-tight bathing suit at the hot springs, her crossed eyes looking at him with obvious sexual interest.

Chris's own penis started to grow, and he touched the bulge under his Levi's with one hand as he held the jade phallus in the other. It seemed to him that something was trying to make a connection in his brain, but he was too inebriated to let it happen; all he felt was a sudden flash of energy, as he raised his eyes to stare at Caban.

122

"So what shall it be?" he said to the volcano. "Shall we conjure up a little spell today? How about a rattling of the earth's bones and then a parting of the water, with a chariot coming down to take me to the house over there. No, I think I'll be a bit more commercial—how about opening up the tunnel for a starter?"

Chris stuck the jade phallus into the dirt, standing it upright in front of him. He laughed drunkenly at his joke, at his mock ceremony. Then he realized he needed to pee. Standing up was difficult; any weight at all on his left ankle caused him agonizing pain.

He hopped on his right foot a few feet toward the cliff, leaned against a tree trunk, and pulled out his own phallic piece.

He was right in the middle of a long pee when it hit. His first sensation was that of being on a boat, of having to constantly adjust his weight to keep up with the rocking. Then his eyes registered what was happening. It looked as though both the water and the dry land were being shaken with waves, matched by a motion of the fluid in his inner ear which gave him the sensation of losing his balance. A low-frequency rumble penetrated his bones, and he finally realized consciously that the earth was shaking, convulsing. The volcano, he thought, oh God *no,* not the volcano!

He wasn't sure how long it lasted, but the earthquake seemed to go on for a very long time. Chris stared up at the volcano but it showed no sign of erupting. His awareness took in the tree he was leaning against as it shook its limbs, its leaves thrashing like a thousand hooked fish.

Then he was sitting down, his body still shaking even after the quake was over. For a few moments, he couldn't tell what was inward motion, and what was outside. But finally everything subsided.

A sense of peace rose up as if he had been vibrated by a gymnasium exercise machine and suddenly switched it off. Silence pervaded the island so deeply that when a heron came swooping down toward the bay, its wings cutting through the air noisily, Chris jumped in fear, half-expecting some primeval god to attack him for meddling in the affairs of brujos, for violating some ancient taboo.

He hopped over to the assortment of idols and grabbed them up, carrying them into the hut and throwing them back into the grave. He hesitated, however, when it came to the phallic jade piece. He didn't want to let go of it; he seemed unable to throw it into the hole and be done with it. His fingers gripped the smooth sensual stone as he hobbled out into the sunlight.

A sudden urge came over him as he looked at its green depths of color, felt its power; and he touched his lips to its surface as though he were kissing the foot of a deity, not with any sexual feeling, but with an overwhelming sense of awe and devotion.

He glanced up fearfully at the volcano as his lips left the cool jade, expecting something drastic to happen in response to his impulsive act. But nothing happened. He felt a wave of relief.

"Fuck it!" he shouted at himself, pulling his mind out of the trancelike state it had slipped into.

He threw the jade piece away from him far into the undergrowth, and spit at the taste of the stone lingering on his lips. Then he sat down, took a deep breath, and looked around warily. There, that was better. Everything seemed calm. The birds were starting to sing again. The Xocomil was cool on his face. Reality settled in on him, and he took a deep breath of the fresh-scented air.

He sat there, with no thoughts coming to his mind, for an hour, as if he had been jolted by what had just happened into the very meditative state that had eluded him through years of seeking enlightenment from a gaggle of gurus, from yogis to primal screamers, and TM and est advocates. Now, without warning, everything became serene, perfect, beautiful. There was no urge to move, to think about the past or the future. He had arrived. He felt in the presence of something so holy that all he could do was sit there, breathe, experience.

Then, as Chris watched with acceptant eyes, a great storm cloud blew up over Caban from the Pacific, riding the gusts of the Xocomil and quickly obliterating the sunlight. A chill came into the air. With a rapidness that seemed almost supernatural, the sky was totally covered with dark clouds, and with a massive electrical flash from horizon to horizon, the rain started.

He moved back under the protection of the thatch of the hut and sat transfixed as lightning flared across the blackened sky, painting the surface of the lake with a flat metallic sheen. The thunder exploded almost instantly after the flash of lightning with a celestrial whipcrack, shaking Chris to the bone, as though a barrage had been called down on him. The rain was like a waterfall, splattering against the dirt, knocking down the grass, drawing tiny fountains from the lake. And then, the rain dwindled and was gone, the lightning over, and the clouds blowing away to the east.

Chris sat there, listening to the thatched roof dripping water onto the ground in front of him, watching the clouds disappear overhead and the sun break through with a brilliant beauty that brought tears to his eyes. A sense of simple thankfulness welled up inside him, thankfulness at being alive at that magnificent moment, on this most beautiful of planets, on this most beautiful of islands, by this most beautiful of lakes.

The sun set and evening gave way to night. He ate a banana and munched on some nuts. Contemplated his swollen ankle. Dreamed of Michelle arriving in less than a week. Peeled an orange. Watched as the softness of the darkening sky gave way to the stark contrast of stars and blackness.

A bird cried out suddenly, as if it had been wounded. The solitary foreigner listened to the night noises and felt a sense of uneasiness start to seep into his contentment. He responded to his vague sense of anxiety by unrolling his sleeping bag, smoothing out the dirt in front of the brujo hut, taking off the boot on his right foot—the other boot having been removed long before—and climbing into the sack.

The stars above him, as he lay on his back and stared up, could have been the stars above Mill Valley just as easily as the stars above Guatemala. He felt himself drifting away, dreaming of familiar settings, of his home, of nights with Wendy that had been soft, cozy. And there was Michelle, coming running up the steps to spend the weekend with him. He closed his eyes, drifting, dreaming asleep.

But the island was not falling asleep around him. It was coming alive. Birds cried out more frequently, long hoots, sudden shrill screams, deep-throated, haunting caws. Small animals scuttled through the grass, nosing their way along in search of grubs and other nighttime feasts. A large, waddling animal much like its northern badger-cousin approached the sleeping human, sniffed the air within a foot of the man's head, froze, stared in bewilderment at the exotic smell, and then hurried away.

Finally, certain that the man was asleep, a figure moved from the shadows of a distant mango tree and slowly approached the hut. Having been caught in the act of digging for artifacts that afternoon, she had made her escape, running a good distance before pausing. She had waited patiently for the intruder to go away, while she watched the trail beyond to be sure he was alone. But then he had sprained his ankle, and the earthquake had hit, and she had turned her attention to the volcano, focusing her powers upon Caban to keep him calm.

Now, having watched the gringo fall asleep, she made her move, her silent Indian gait bringing her up to the hut: Magdalena.

She paused and looked down at the sleeping man, her expression mixing determination with a softer emotion. Then she went into the hut. Kneeling down in the darkness, she felt in the hole. She found several artifacts, but the one she was looking for was missing. She dug frantically, deeper and deeper.

126

Finally, she gave up. Whatever she was looking for wasn't there. She stood up, went outside, and started rummaging through the gringo's pack, hoping that he had pilfered the artifact. She glanced over at him while her hands were finishing their fruitless search, and her breath caught.

Chris was sleeping on his back, like a mummy. One of his bare arms was outstretched on the grass. A black scorpion, the deadly Central American variety, was crawling along his forearm, its lethal tail raised in readiness to strike.

Magdalena sat down very carefully beside Chris. She didn't try to brush the scorpion off the man's arm. She knew that the scorpion was the god of death and that she should not interfere, here at the brujo's hut. Her eyes fused on the deadly bug as it continued its ominous journey up the arm onto Chris's naked chest.

He stirred slightly. Magdalena tensed. The scorpion was poised, ready to sting. This man Christopher, she thought, had come to her in a dream. The gods had brought him here to her. They could take him now just as easily as they had brought him. A sudden move, a reflex to brush off the tickle now passing over his heart, and he would be a dead man in minutes.

Chris raised his arm, his hand ready to brush clumsily in his sleep. Magdalena knew she mustn't interfere; the gods were the decision-makers, she was just their vehicle. She could see the tail of the scorpion quivering, ready to make its lethal strike.

She acted with sudden swiftness just as Chris started to brush away the insect. She flipped the scorpion with a finger off onto the ground, and then jumped up and ground it to death with a stone, her breathing hot and angry, her body a tense force of determination.

So, she said to herself. So I kill the scorpion. She glanced up at the black presence of Caban. This was wrong, she muttered at him. You are wrong! Everything is changing, you do not know what you are doing. Everything is changing, everything. You must change too. I challenge you!

She suddenly felt a shudder shake her body, as if Caban had sent down his response and paralyzed her. She was just a solitary woman—with the gods born inside her but still a woman, not a heartless god. She pressed her hand against her heart and felt it beating frantically. She felt so vulnerable, so very small. The gods could crush her, they certainly would if she didn't do their bidding this Ilum K'inal.

She looked one final time for the missing artifact. She came upon Chris's wallet, opened it, and took out the picture of Michelle. Ix Chel. The beautiful girl stared back at her. Magdalena looked at the photograph and felt yet another shiver run through her body.

"Hola, Christopher!"

A faint shouting from up over the hill toward the ruins. Magdalena froze. They had come looking for him already. She bolted and ran through the night toward her cayuco.

chapter 10

Sitting with her eyes closed, Michelle could feel the vibration of the jet engines deep in her bones. It was all happening so quickly now, after all those days and weeks of waiting. Guatemala, she whispered to herself. Guatemala. Only six hours ago she had been leaving for the airport in San Francisco. It was a cold drizzly day, sunless. Her mother had been such a worry-wart. Don't do this, don't do that. And whatever you do, don't talk to any of those Mexican men, they're very different from men up here, promise me you'll be careful, and so on, right up to when Michelle had left the giant circular boarding room and entered the bowels of the jet.

Now all that was long gone. She opened her eyes and leaned over to look out the window.

"Still just water," the man beside her said. "Give it another ten minutes and we'll be over Guatemala."

He was a pleasant man in his forties. He lived in Guatemala City, worked for the embassy there, and had told Michelle the details that her father's letter had left out. She could indeed take a taxi to the hotel downtown that Chris had recommended for the night. But getting to the Lago Atitlan bus in the morning would involve a transfer that Chris hadn't mentioned, and the man had written out just what bus to catch from the hotel to the Atitlan bus depot.

Michelle had given a rueful inward sigh. Just like Daddy—a superb, generous inspiration . . . and one or two details overlooked that could mess it up thoroughly. That, along with a number of other things, was what had made him and her mother divorce, finally. But it seemed that there was always somebody ready to tidy up, to see to those overlooked items—like the embassy man.

"You know," he said now, "why don't you come and spend the night with my wife and me? We'd love to have you."

Well, you would, anyhow, Michelle thought. But she did not consider his evident sexual interest in her a threat. When she had first taken on the contours of a woman, the changed manner of older men toward her horrified her; but she both reasoned it out on her own, and with the help of talks with Wendy and her father, came to see that it was an inevitable part of growing up, that adult men and women almost always, at some level, appraised each other as sexual partners, rarely with any intention of doing anything about the results of the appraisal. This man, she decided, didn't have the hots for her so much as . . . well, call it the warms. That is, he knew that she was highly attractive, and responded to it—but in a safe way. "Well," she said, "if you're certain it wouldn't be any problem."

"None at all, and I can drop you off at the bus stop on my way to the embassy tomorrow morning."

"That sounds great!"

"Look, land!" he said from his window seat.

Michelle leaned over his lap to look down, her body rising out of her seat in a graceful arch. "God, there it is!" she said, excited. The lowlands were lush with farmland and banana plantations. And ahead, she could just make out the hazy outlines of towering mountains rising to the east. A pain invaded her womb and she contracted, sitting back down in her seat. Oh no, she thought. But

130

she knew it was inevitable, her period was due in a while, and it seemed to be starting now. She grabbed her purse and made her way back to the bathroom.

Blood over Guatemala, she thought to herself with a half-joking grin. Blood over Guatemala.

As the embassy man had predicted, his wife seemed pleased to have Michelle as an overnight guest, or at least the diplomatic training to make it appear so.

"That's a strange place you're going to," the man said at dinner. "In a while, it'll be a major tourist attraction—there's a man named McGrabbin who's putting up a first-class resort hotel—but right now it's awfully primitive. A lot of the Indians there haven't really changed much since the Conquest."

"I happen to think that's a good thing," Michelle said. "It's always seemed to me, oh, just rotten that what we call civilization comes in and wrecks the old ways of the people who've been living here for ages."

"Maybe," the man's wife, a sprightly, fortyish blonde, said, "but if I'd lived here then, I'd be a worn-out old hag at my age, and you—" She studied Michelle closely, but in a not-unfriendly way. "—you'd be sweating out each year until you were married, wondering if you'd be the annual sacrifice. I prefer our own times, I have to say."

The next morning, the embassy man took her to the hole-in-the-wall bus depot and bought her a one-way ticket to Lago Atitlan. They parted warmly, and Michelle climbed up into the old bus.

There was a strong, unpleasant smell inside. She took a window seat, which immediately proved to be uncomfortable. A man sat down beside her, grinning at her with yellow teeth. He was an Indian, perhaps thirty, dressed in ripped dirty pants and a wrinkled white shirt. He smelled of alcohol although it was only eight-thirty in the morning.

The bus took on more and more people, most of them Indians in native consume returning to the mountains after a night of buying in the city. Many of the women had babies on their backs, and sat upright and leaning forward so the babies wouldn't be squashed against the seat backs. The seats filled and still people kept getting on, standing in the aisles. Then the driver put the bus in gear and it lurched forward into the traffic of the city, horn honking and passengers swaying against each other.

Michelle felt claustrophobic. The man beside her kept pressing against her at every turn of the bus, giggling and eyeing her. She had seen two American men, college students probably, with long hair and casual clothes, sit down two seats ahead of her, and she wished she could escape this dirty, lecherous man and go sit with them, but that would probably be impossible in this crowd.

She wished she'd worn pants instead of a dress today; the Indian kept looking down at her bare knees and staring. When the bus would swerve, he would press against her again. An old Indian woman spoke to him harshly the third time he did this, but he just scowled back at her and shouted something in a strange language.

It took twenty minutes to clear the city. Michelle was aghast at the smoggy, ugly, monstrosity of a metropolis; she hadn't expected anything like this in Guatemala. Everything seemed to be in high gear and in complete confusion. And the stench of the diesel fumes was suffocating.

"Stop that!" she cried out, feeling a coarse hand sliding up her thigh under her skirt. She grabbed at the man's hand and yanked it away from her. The old woman hit at the man with her purse. He giggled and as soon as Michelle let go his hand he grabbed at her again, yanking her dress up and exposing her tanned skin.

Michelle stood up, crying, her face flushed, and pushed past him into the crowded aisle. He reached at her and grabbed her as she slipped by him. It was frightening for her, pushing past the crammed bodies, forcing her way frantically forward. But the people she came into contact with now were friendly, and bright smiles radiated from several of the women, who looked at Michelle's blonde hair and beautiful face with open awe.

Finally, she made it to the two Americans. They weren't Americans at all, actually; they were German and spoke hardly any English. But they understood her need to sit down with them, and she ended up pressed between their two slender male bodies. The stimulation was certainly sexually loaded, but somehow Michelle didn't feel threatened. They laughed as the bus jerked and swayed off into the countryside and the approaching mountains.

It was a long ride, and Michelle, step by step, relaxed and opened up her contracted bubble of awareness. The bus was filled with the same colorfully dressed Indians that she had seen in so many pictures. She hardly knew how to respond to being actually immersed in this culture so suddenly, surrounded by curious eyes and friendly smiles. Even the three men she could see from her seat were genuinely warm in their glances at her, with a shyness in their eyes which she found beautiful. No wonder all the books about Guatemala talked on and on about the loving, friendly natives—it was true.

A little girl, perhaps seven or eight, in the seat across the aisle from her, kept glancing at her and staring with amazement at Michelle's hair, her complexion, her clothes. The girl's lips were parted in admiration, almost worship. When Michelle smiled back at her, the girl lit up radiantly, as if someone very special had greeted her, a princess, perhaps.

Michelle felt the same way toward the girl, with her long black hair and her mysterious, fathomless dark eyes. They continued glancing shyly at each other while the bus worked its way up the steep grades and around the countless sharp curves as the mountains became more and more rugged, the towns farther and farther apart, the small patches of family gardens steeper and steeper against the sides of the ridges. And then there was the lake! The panorama of volcanos and blue water was so

133

much more than she had expected that she stared, her heart pounding.

The bus navigated the narrow road that cut down the jagged cliffs and canyons toward the lake a thousand feet below. Michelle felt frightened that the brakes on the ancient vehicle would give out and that they would all plunge to their deaths over one of the cliffs. But half an hour later the bus came roaring down the last steep descent and then hurried up the cobblestone street of Panahachel, sending Indians scampering out of its way. Then it stopped, and Michelle joined the mass exit.

As she stepped outside, the warm, scented fresh air reached her, and the heady atmosphere made her feel almost weightless. She looked with a sudden anxiety for her father's face amidst the small crowd of Indians waiting to greet the bus passengers. But she didn't see any Americans at all, and her heart contracted.

The two Germans were trying to get her to go with them, but she was determined to wait for her father, no matter how long it took, so they gave up, and went striding down the street with their backpacks.

An Indian was walking toward her as she started to lift her suitcase to the side of the road. He was so impressive in both his clothing and his physical appearance that she stopped and met his eyes, then glanced away, suddenly flooded with bashfulness.

He stared at her intently, then to her dismay, walked up to her. She felt suddenly and deeply threatened.

"Hello," he said in English. "You are Michelle."

She eyed him in alarm. He was remarkably handsome, but she sensed danger and looked away, searching frantically for her father.

"Christopher sent me for you," the Indian said.

She looked at him. "Where is he?"

"Here is a note," he said, and with a little flourish presented her with a folded paper that he had tucked into his colorful belt. She glanced down at his purple-and-

134

white-striped shorts and his muscled legs, and took the note.

"You are Enrique?" she said after reading it.

"At your service."

"Is my father injured seriously?"

"No, it is healing."

"Hurry, let's go, I want to see him," she said.

"Allow me to carry your suitcase."

"Oh, thank you. But it's heavy."

"It is nothing," he said. They started walking down the street. Her thoughts were on her father's sprained ankle, but at the same time she was overwhelmed by the flow of Indians walking past her, the kaleidoscope of beautiful costumes and friendly faces. She felt swept away by the charm of this young Indian walking beside her; the awareness of danger that had invaded her at his approach was totally gone.

Chris sat impatiently on a large driftwood stump beside the lake. The Xocomil was already blowing; it was early today. And Enrique was late returning with Michelle. Waves lapped at the shore, rustling the tiny pebbles with each small breaker. The boat creaked against the dock. It was going to be bad heading into the wind, even in Ricardo's inboard. The mailboat had left half an hour ago; it was far out into the lake, a toy boat now.

Where the hell were they? What was taking them so long? Chris fumed. Maybe the bus was late, maybe there was an accident. Maybe something happened in the city last night. He thought briefly and uneasily of the photo of Michelle that had somehow disappeared from his wallet. He knew he had had it before his trip to the island, and that it was gone a few days later when he went to look at it; but just when it had been lost—or taken—he could not be sure . . . He wished to hell that he'd gone in to pick her up, but with his ankle still swollen and painful—

There she was!

"Daddy!" she shouted, running toward him down the

beach, long hair flowing out behind her, strong legs carrying her into his arms. Chris stood up with his weight on his good foot and felt her body pressing against him, her breasts solid against his chest, her face flushed and laughing, looking up into his eyes, kissing him on the lips, and then hugging him again tightly.

Finally their embrace relaxed and Chris looked up. Enrique was staring at them, his expression cloudy, almost menacing. Michelle stepped back and looked at Chris appraisingly. "You're so tanned, so healthy," she said. "But what about your foot?"

"It's just sprained."

She knelt down, her fingers feeling his swollen, bruised ankle delicately. "God, it's so huge, does it hurt terribly?"

"It's starting to get better."

"Do you soak it?"

"I did a few times," he said, glancing again at Enrique, who was looking with concern at the lake.

Michelle stood up, more relaxed now, looking Chris in the eye, letting the love between them come into more calm focus. "I can hardly believe I'm really here," she said, looking from his face across the lake at the volcano. "This is paradise."

"I can't tell you how good it is to see you," he said quietly, his voice soft. "I really love you, kiddo."

"I love you," she whispered back.

With his arm around her waist, he turned and looked across the lake. "So how do you like it?"

"I'm so happy I could cry."

"We'd better get going, the wind's already picking up." He looked to Enrique. "Vamanos," he said. "Hay viento."

"No hay problema," Enrique said brusquely.

Chris detected an edge to Enrique's voice which hadn't been there the last few days. He seemed almost jealous of Michelle's demonstration of affection for her father; he was obviously enthralled by her. They walked toward the boat, Michelle between the two men. Chris stared at Caban, and found himself thinking suddenly of the hot springs house. He was still paying rent on it; he and Michelle could just go there and forget the Zacapula house and all the drama of that side of the lake.

But after several days of peace in Ricardo's house at the foot of the volcano, Chris knew he wanted Michelle to spend some time there also. It was such a tranquil location, and there was such a sense of adventure over there, she would love it. And Chris still hadn't made contact with Magdalena, and he hadn't let go of that desire. He had dreamed of her last night, another sexually involved dream that had burnt her image even deeper into his memory, as if he already knew her intimately, and shared a potent bond with her.

Enrique started the engine. Chris helped Michelle into the boat, and then tossed the lines from the dock, jumping in on his good foot with his arms outstretched for balance. He was getting to be a pro at hopping around on one foot, he told himself; it was like an athletic challenge.

The wind was blowing strongly. The waves were choppy and the boat cut through them, bobbing and dipping with neck-jolting force. Enrique was busy keeping the craft headed into the waves so that it wouldn't take one broadside and perhaps capsize. All three occupants had on life jackets, but if they went overboard the waves would probably drown them even so, the way they rolled by the white froth at their crests.

Michelle sat in the back with Chris next to her, watching Enrique standing at the wheel up front on the left, listening to the big Chrysler engine working away under its enclosure in the middle of the open deck.

"So what did you hear from Wendy?" Chris shouted.

"We had lunch together two days ago, no, three now," Michelle shouted back. "She said she loved it down here. Why did she leave so soon?"

"What did she tell you?"

"She didn't, she just changed the subject when I asked her. Did you two have a fight?"

137

"Kind of, I guess."

"That's too bad."

"We'll work it out," Chris said, feeling the warmth of his daughter's body against him, noticing how mature she was, how her sexuality struck him almost beyond what was allowable in their relationship. There seemed to be something different about her, a look in her eyes, something that reminded him of Magdalena—ah, probably the eye stuff, he concluded, registering the familiar sight of Michelle's corrective glasses. Still, it was a little disconcerting, the vague sense of Magdalena's presence, when he was actually with Michelle.

Suddenly the engine sputtered, caught again, and then coughed and died. The silence that the absence of the engine noise left was filled with the loud slap of the waves on the hull. Enrique left the controls after trying three times to start the engine, and scrambled back to check the twin gas cans in the rear of the boat.

"What the hell's wrong?" Chris asked.

"Nothing," Enrique said, sounding frightened.

"There's gas?"

"Plenty."

"Try it again."

Enrique hurried up to the controls. Michelle and Chris exchanged worried glances as the boat turned sideways to the waves and rocked dangerously as a big one rolled by, sending spray into their faces.

"Look, the volcano," Michelle said.

Chris turned his head with a sudden edge of panic. There it was again, that white smoke coming from Caban.

"Does it smoke like that all the time?" she asked.

"No," Chris said impatiently as Enrique tried without success to get the engine started. Another wave hit the boat and deluged them. Chris stood up and hopped to the front besides Enrique. Another wave splashed into the boat. Michelle gragged a bucket and started bailing out the water in the cockpit.

"Goddamnit, get it started!" Chris shouted, sensing

138

disaster, glancing again at Caban, feeling somehow an urgent anger at the volcano, as if this was all its fault. They were five or six miles from the nearest shore. With the waves like they were, it would be hell trying to swim at all. With the engine dead, the tenuous hold of civilization on the lake had vanished away, and Chris felt the chilling awareness of something monstrous, like an unseen predator, stalking him.

"Look out, let me try it," Chris said, pushing Enrique from the controls.

"Get away," Enrique said, refusing to give ground.

A wave crashed over the boat as it rolled too deeply into the low side of the last one. Michelle, in the act of throwing a bucketful of water overboard, was hit with the full impact of the water and knocked over the side of the boat. She let go of the bucket and grabbed at the gunwale, gasping for air through the spray. Her fingers gripped the aluminum fiercely, but her grip slipped and her body lurched forward as the next wave hit.

Hands grabbed at her body, ripping her dress down from her shoulders. Her head went underwater. The hands grabbed again at a leg, catching her at her knee, pulling her back toward the boat. Another wave washed over the side and Michelle felt herself dragged aboard. Her left breast banged against the aluminum, then she was safely down in the seat, gasping frantically for air.

She blinked away the water, a surge of energy coming into her now, a strange sense of power that seemed to come from outside her body. "Go try the engine," she shouted desperately. Chris, staring down at her to be certain she was all right, turned and hopped up to where Enrique was gazing in a dumb stupor at Michelle's bare breasts and wet hair.

"Move!" Chris ordered the Indian, and reached for the ignition key. A fleeting prayer rose from his unconscious, but it wasn't a Christian prayer, it was an image of Magdalena in his mind, vivid, pulsating through his system as his fingers turned the key.

The engine coughed. Sputtered. Died. "Come *on!*" Chris shouted. On the second try, it miraculously started. The boat surged forward and Enrique grabbed at the controls, turning it into the waves. Chris splashed back to Michelle. She was just sitting, her dress down to her waist, her hair a wet tangle over her breasts; her face was pale, and she was shaking.

"You okay?" Chris said, sitting beside her and taking her chin in his fingers, turning her head toward him to look in her eyes.

She broke out crying, and he held her against him while she sobbed, releasing the panic of near-death she had experienced. Chris felt her heart pounding against his chest. Knowing how close he had come to losing her, he pressed her against him to be sure that she was really still there, alive. Again Magdalena flashed through his mind, and it was almost as if he was holding both women at the same time, comforting them.

He suddenly remembered the volcano. He glanced toward the mountain, fearing what he might see. But there was not even a hint of smoke left at Caban's top.

Words came in an unbidden mumble to Chris's lips. He could hardly make them come out. "Itzam'na," he muttered. "Itzam'na. Thank you. Thank you."

"What?" Michelle asked, her voice husky.

"Oh, nothing. How are you, kiddo? That was a close call."

He realized they were holding hands tightly. "We should bail the water," she said.

Chris saw that the water was a foot deep in the back of the boat. He reached down for the bucket.

"Here, let me; your foot must hurt," she said, and took the bucket from him.

For the first time since the engine stopped, Chris became aware of his ankle. It was throbbing, but the chill of the water had numbed it. Michelle leaned over, dipped the bucket, and then threw the water overboard. She still had not noticed that her dress was down to her waist; she was obviously half in shock. Chris put his hands on her wet shoulders.

"Hey, kiddo," he said. "Give me that, let's get your clothes on."

She paused, turned to him, looked down at her nakedness, glanced with a quick turn of her head at Enrique, and found him looking back at her. He didn't seem handsome at all now; he looked menacing as he stared at her naked breasts, her exposed thighs. She pulled down the wet material, half-transparent but better than nothing, over her legs, and then pulled up the top of her dress. It was badly ripped but with a little trying she managed to get herself covered.

Chris was finishing up the bailing job, glancing at her regularly to see how she was doing, bothered by his own sense of sexual attraction to her. "You could change clothes," he suggested, remembering her suitcase up front.

"No, this will be okay for now, I wouldn't undress anyway . . . in front of him."

"But you're all wet."

"It doesn't matter. You said in your letter that we have a house; are we going right there?"

"Definitely."

"Then I'll wait. Would you hold me a minute? I'm shaking."

"Sure."

They huddled together against the wind and water; Chris could feel her warmth against him where their wet bodies touched. For a moment he forgot who she was; they were just intimately close, supporting each other, surviving. His fingers around her waist massaged her gently, lovingly, with a sexual tenderness. Then he had the sudden conviction he was touching Magdalena, and the realization made his fingers freeze. He sighed and patted Michelle paternally, upset by his momentary lapse of awareness of who she was.

"Daddy?"

"Hmm?"

"The volcano, it looks so—so big."

"Yeah, it's a big one all right."

"The smoke's gone."

"Yep."

"Does it ever explode?"

"The volcano? No, not for a thousand years."

"Good."

"Look, you see that island there? Our house is right behind it."

"You mean, *on* the volcano?"

"Don't worry, it's not going to erupt."

Suddenly Michelle bent over double from a violent pain in her groin. She put her head down between her legs, her fists pressed against her stomach. It felt as though her insides were being ripped out. Then the pang passed as suddenly as it had come.

"Hey," Chris said anxiously, bending over with her, "what's wrong?"

She turned her head toward him, her face pale but composed. "It's just my period, I guess."

"Well we're almost there. Just hold out a little longer and we'll be at the house."

The boat plowed through the waves, its engines roaring powerfully. Minutes passed, then the island slipped by to the right. Chris stared at it, remembering his accident there. It seemed like a long time ago but it was less than a week since he had sprained his ankle. He glanced up at the volcano, remembering the smoke that had once again appeared from its top. So strange . . . and no one had felt the earthquake he had experienced that afternoon on the sacred island. It was confusing. But except for those experiences, and this near-disaster on the lake, everything was so perfect that Chris didn't want to focus on the uncanny moments; he wanted to stay with the beautiful hours and days of tranquillity he had had, and that he wanted to share now with Michelle.

chapter 11

Fifteen minutes later, father and daughter made their way along the narrow pier to dry ground, Chris hopping ahead of Michelle. Enrique carried the suitcase, and then gave Chris a strong shoulder to lean on to help him up the beach and then across the fifty feet of lawn to the front patio of the spacious house.

Michelle was shivering from the chill, but she took in the beauty of the small estate enthusiastically, exclaiming at its loveliness. Enrique, needing to depart quickly to get to the resort before the wind and waves were too extreme, excused himself, promising to come tomorrow and take Michelle over to Zacapula for a sightseeing excursion.

The living room was floored with red ornamental tile, covered with large throw rugs in the traditional Guatemalan hand-knotted style; the furniture was mainly solid antique pieces from Spain; and on the walls hung a number of fine paintings of Mayan subjects by an old friend of Ricardo's. One was a temple scene with blue-painted priests standing proudly at an altar with a lithe black-haired girl being brought up the steep steps. It was the only painting that Chris didn't like, but Michelle paused admiringly in front of it as she entered the house.

"I'll put on some water for coffee or tea," he said. "Here, I'll show you your bedroom first."

He led her down the tiled hallway. There were two bedrooms on the right, and one on the left, which was to be Michelle's. The bedroom furniture was heavy and Spanish also, and the room felt comfortable and secure. Chris put Michelle's suitcase on a low table, and hopped back down the hallway to put on tea at the gas stove. By the time he had done this and returned, he was out of breath, his mind awhirl with confused thoughts of Enrique, the boat ride, and the mysterious smoke that both he and Michelle had seen. Her door was ajar and he hopped in without thinking to knock. He found her in just her underpants, changing into dry clothes.

"Oh, excuse me," he said, turning to go.

"Don't be silly, Daddy, it doesn't matter."

"You're cut," he said, glancing back at her.

"It's just a scratch," she said, looking down at her left breast, which had a red streak across it just below the nipple.

"Do you want a Band-Aid?" he said.

"No."

"You probably should put some iodine on it."

"Do you have any?"

"I'll check the first-aid kit in the bathroom," he said, and started to hop out for it.

"No, wait, Daddy! You're too tired, hopping like that. I'll get it."

She went past him, her young body striking against the whiteness of the cotton pants. Chris sat down in a chair, finally feeling his exhaustion. She returned a moment later with an iodine bottle, handed it to him, and stood waiting for him to doctor her as he used to when she was a little girl. He felt uncomfortable, dabbing at her maturing breast with the glass stopper. After being away from her for a few weeks, and being alone in this house, yearning for a female's presence for almost a week, Chris was alarmed and shamed to find himself so sexually sensitive to Michelle. He finished up his medical task quickly and put the stopper back in the bottle.

"There, you're all set."

"Thanks," she said, and went over to her suitcase. She took out a beautiful wipile that Chris had bought her for Christmas at an import store in San Francisco, and slipped it over her head. Chris experienced another slippage in his mind, half-expecting Magdalena's face to emerge from the wipile. Michelle smiled a sheepish, almost seductive smile as she noticed Chris watching her dress. "Don't tell mommy I didn't wear a bra down here," she said. "She's been impossible; it's getting worse all the time. Sometimes I wish I could just live with you, Daddy. I don't like George at all."

"Well, you know I'd love that. You can choose for yourself."

"I wouldn't want to hurt Mommy's feelings, but it's getting too much for me to take. All we do is fight all the time." She slipped on a pair of tight pants, zipping them up with a wiggling action of her hips so that she could get the zipper up. Chris stood up and hopped into his bedroom to change his wet clothes and try to sort out his confused feelings.

He felt proud enough to have been the owner of the estate as he gave Michelle a tour half an hour later. They both had hot tea in their stomachs and dry clothes on their backs, and everything was taking on a warm paradisal glow. The Xocomil swept across the lake below them, blowing their hair with its brisk currents and heightening their sense of adventure.

"He's a pretty fine guy," Chris said, talking of Ricardo. "Sort of a good fairy to these Indians, it seems. Maybe we'll get a tour of the resort, I haven't been over yet because of my sprained ankle."

"How is it feeling?"

"A little sore." He hopped with a hand on her shoulder across the patio to the lawn. "Those are mango trees there. You can see the mangos are still green; they'll be ripe in a few weeks. Maybe we should just play hooky from California for a few more weeks. It seems a shame to have to take off just when the mangos are getting ripe."

"I could stay down here forever," she sighed. "And all those trees look like avocado."

"Two acres of them. There's oranges, papaya, pineapple, guava; you name it, I've got it. No bananas, though; we're a little too high up for good bananas. But that means that we're out of the tropical heat and humidity too."

"You really did find a paradise, Daddy."

"Yep."

They cooked dinner together, as they often had back home on weekends, and their mood was cheerful and intimate, as the chicken, delivered earlier that day by an Indian, cooked in the oven, and vegetables steamed on top of the stove. Chris opened a bottle of wine and as they clinked glasses, intoned: "To Guatemala; may we stay here forever."

"To us," Michelle added. "May we stay as happy and as close as this forever!"

The dusk deepened into night. Michelle set the table out on the back veranda, amidst a beautiful cactus garden that nestled against the beginning slope of the volcano. Pathways meandered around volcanic boulders and an assortment of cacti, trees, shrubs, and a proliferation of flowers in bloom.

They ate by the light of two tall red candles. The Xocomil had died down for the night, and the sound of crickets mingled with the lapping of waves down on the beach.

"The whole town seems to be down on her," Chris was saying. "But she's no more a witch than you are; it's pure jealousy—that and outright manipulation of the Indians by the priest. And I suspect that Enrique has done his share of bad-mouthing her, too. But I tell you, she's really beautiful; she's so far beyond the rest of these people that they can't accept her. She has the best of the Indian qualities, and she's educated and world-wise too."

Michelle glanced at her father with a suspicious smile and took a sip of her second glass of wine. "It sounds like you're in love," she said softly.

"Well, I wouldn't say that. No, it's different. First of all, I've hardly spent any time with her. And second, she's not like any other woman I've ever known."

"I don't imagine so, unless you've been flirting with Mayan girls in San Francisco and not telling me."

"But besides Magdalena," Chris went on, feeling the alcohol expanding his dreams of the future into a semblance of reality, "I just love it down here, anyway. What would you think if I sold my house in Mill Valley?" he said, shooting her a glance.

"I have only one condition, if you want to move down here."

"What's that?"

"That I get to live here too."

He met her eyes and could see that she was serious. "I've really been thinking about it," he said. "I could teach you the rest of high school, and—"

He saw her expression suddenly change, her mouth drop open, and her eyes widen with fear as she stared at something behind him. Chris spun around in his chair to face whatever had appeared in the night.

"Hola, gringo."

The tall woman was standing ten feet behind him, half-hidden in the shadows, dressed in a simple western outfit, a white blouse and high-waisted brown slacks. Her hair was long and fluffy, and her stance casual but poised.

"Hello," Chris said, his voice shaking slightly with the inner shock of her appearance.

"I do hope I'm not disturbing anything," Magdalena said. "I would have phoned but, of course, you have no facilities out here in no-man's-land."

"Well, uh, come on over. God, you scared us."

She walked toward them, extending her hand to Chris with a regal air but at the same time disarming him with a winning smile. "I realize that there was no way to make

147

an appearance without causing you some shock. I'm very sorry. I wanted to arrive before dark, but that wasn't possible." Her fingers held his and she stood by his side.

"Oh, uh, this is my daughter, Michelle. Michelle, this is Magdalena."

"Hello, Michelle," Magdalena said. "I do hope I'm not disturbing your dinner. Go right ahead."

"We were just finishing," Michelle said. "But there's plenty more, would you like some?"

"Actually, I am hungry, if there is enough. I'm sorry to intrude, but I wanted to stop by and see how you are enjoying the house. I heard that you arrived today."

"You've talked with your father, then?" Chris cut in.

"Of course not. He hasn't talked to me for three years."

Michelle stood up. "There are vegetables left, and some chicken," she said graciously, having recovered from the initial shock and pleased to have company.

"Anything will be fine," Magdalena responded with equal warmth. Michelle left for the kitchen.

"Please sit down," Chris offered, gesturing toward one of the other two chairs at the table. "I'm glad you've come; I left a message with the hotel. Did you get it?"

"No, but I know what had happened, so I didn't except you."

"How did you know?"

"Very little goes on in the town without my knowing it," she said, sitting down. "How is your ankle?"

"Oh, it's sore. Swollen."

"Perhaps I can help it later on."

"Help it?"

They met each other's eyes, Chris looking into her strong right one, feeling a sudden sense of intimacy now that they were alone. "So," she said, "we meet again."

"I was wondering if you were ever going to appear," he said.

"Things have been very, very difficult in town. And I knew you would be here for at least a week, so I have been trying to make headway with certain problems." She

148

gave him a sharp look and went on, "You are somewhat of a liar, I've discovered. The article you're writing; you didn't mention that to me."

"Well maybe I'm not writing one," he said. "Tell me, does your father know you're visiting me tonight?"

"Of course not."

"Well, anyway . . . listen, I'm glad you came."

Now they were looking at each other more openly. Chris smiled through his uncertainty, wanting to make contact with her. She sighed. "Thank you," she whispered across the table to him. "I want you to know that I am your friend."

"Well, I think you know I feel the same way."

"Your friendship is like a jewel among—among many deep disillusionments." Her voice sounded sincere enough to win Chris completely over.

"Well you're welcome here any time, really."

"Thank you. Your daughter, she is even more beautiful than her picture. It is good she is here. But, oh, Christopher, you are living in the lion's den here—staying in Ricardo's house, surrounded by his world! He is a very dangerous man and I am afraid he has fooled you, lulled you into a false sense of security. He is under my brother's power now, and the two of them mean nothing but danger for you and Michelle."

"Now what the hell does *that* mean?" Chris's stomach churned at her words.

Magdalena's strong eye held him pinned a moment, then her gaze softened and became social as she looked up and watched Michelle walking toward her from the kitchen with a plate of food. As the plate was put down in front of her she said a soft thank you, and began to eat almost ravenously. Michelle sat down, then stood up again. "Oh, wine," she said. "I'll get you a glass."

Magdalena watched the girl hurrying off. Chris watched the expression on the bruja's face and felt a sudden apprehension. When Magdalena turned her head back to face him, her eyes were focused in unison, and the fused

149

vision seemed to penetrate Chris and reveal him to her without any defenses.

"She is very special," Magdalena whispered.

"What do you mean by that?" he asked uneasily.

She gave him a level stare and did not answer his question directly. "I have something for you." She reached into her shirt pocket and produced a small photograph, handing it to Chris across the table, their fingers touching in the exchange. It was the photograph of Michelle that had disappeared from his wallet.

"How the *hell* did you get this?"

"I was on the island that night," she said evenly. "And I didn't want the picture to fall into Enrique's hands. I feared he could use it against Michelle. Now I give it back to you. Keep it safe, or destroy it. And Christopher, I must ask for your help tomorrow."

"My help?"

"We can talk later," she said as Michelle approached.

Michelle sat down and poured Magdalena a glass of red wine, eyeing her, fascinated by her crossed eyes—Chris hadn't mentioned anything about that. But Michelle had noticed it immediately, and now had removed her glasses and let her left eye have its freedom too, wondering what this dark, beautiful woman's reaction would be. At first Magdalena didn't look directly at Michelle's face, but watched her pour the wine, then picked up the glass.

"To the future," Magdalena said. "Not as we would have it unfold, but as Itzam'na knows it must."

They all drank the toast.

"Ah, very good wine," Magdalena said lightly, changing abruptly to a social mood. "The Republic of Chile makes excellent table wines, don't you think? Perhaps comparable to California."

"Who is Itzam'na?" Michelle asked.

Magdalena looked at her full in the eyes then, and the woman's expression again became grave as she noticed the crossed eyes of the American girl. "Itzam'na," she

150

said, holding the "m" a long time as if savoring the sound, "Itzam'na is the god beyond all the gods. He is to Caban what Caban is to us."

"Caban?"

"Has your father not told you already about Caban? Caban is the god of the volcano up there. We are sitting at the foot of the god of the Quitapul and your father has not even told you?"

At that moment, Michelle found herself looking into the strange woman's eyes. They were fused, staring at her in unison. Michelle felt something pulsate through her, like an electric shock, and her eyes fused also. The sensation was intense; Michelle found herself suddenly faint. Then Magdalena looked away from her, up at the black presence of the volcano.

"Cavan and I have been arguing recently," she said, glancing at Chris. "Like all gods who dabble in human affairs, he is not completely free of his own selfish desires. He is like a willful boy who has much to learn. Itzam'na is not a dominating father. But when his wrath is finally raised, the world shudders."

"What about the earthquake last week?" Chris asked.

Magdalena slowly turned her head toward him, and her eyes were again crossed, giving her an eerie expression that she seemed to accentuate with raised eyebrows. "What about it?"

"Did you feel it, damn it!"

"Of course."

"But no one in town did."

"They have no idea what is going on, that is obvious."

"Well what is going on?"

"I have no clear idea myself. But I certainly felt the earth shake. You and Caban, you seem to have much in common; he listens when you speak."

"What earthquake?" Michelle insisted.

"Just a little shake last week," Chris explained, not wanting to scare her, wishing now that he hadn't asked

151

about the quake. "More wine?" he asked Magdalena, filling her half-empty glass and glancing warily into her strong eye.

A short while later they moved inside. The air was getting cooler and Chris lit a fire. Magdalena and Michelle busied themselves in the kitchen making coffee. Chris could hear them talking casually about the coffee plantations on the volcano over toward Zacapula. Magdalena was asking Michelle questions also, about her school, her mother, her social life in California. To his surprise, he heard her talking about a visit she had made to California just last year. It was somehow disconcerting to him to think of Magdalena in San Francisco, moving easily in the contemporary world—the combination of Indian bruja and urbane traveler in one person was unsettling, even alarming, to contemplate.

When she came in with a cup of coffee for him, Chris was sitting with his hands to the fire, vainly trying to drive out a chill that was not physical. Michelle was busy washing dishes, and Magdalena bent down to him and gave him a light kiss on the cheek as she handed him his cup.

"From the slopes of Caban to you," she said. "The finest coffee in the world."

He took the cup but said nothing in response. She sat on the sofa with its burgundy plush pillows and sipped from her own cup, ignoring Chris's wtihdrawn mood.

"What do you need me for?" he finally said to her. "It sounds like you can take care of yourself perfectly well on your own."

"You are angry with me," she said.

"No. I just don't like the games you play."

"Neither do I."

"Well cut it out. Be straight with me."

"I am doing my best."

"What did you mean, you were on the island with me that night?"

152

"That is a simple statement of fact. There is no game there."

"Well I didn't see you. What were you doing?"

"I was looking for something."

"Why didn't you show yourself?"

"I didn't know if you were alone. And also there are certain rituals I must conform to when on the island. One of them restricted my dealings with you."

"Now you're playing games with me again."

The sound of running water in the kitchen stopped. Magdalena looked in that direction. "I was wondering if you would like to visit the island with me tomorrow morning," she said. "You could be of great help to me."

"How?"

Michelle appeared in the doorway, holding her cup. She felt as though she were intruding, but she didn't want to stay in the kitchen. The two were whispering together by the fire, and she felt slightly left out, jealous of this new woman, and also a little afraid of her.

"We were just talking about going to the sacred island you perhaps saw out in the lake," Magdalena said to her welcomingly. "Would you like to go for a canoe ride tomorrow, early in the morning?"

Michelle walked over to the fire and stood with her back to it, warming herself, sipping her coffee. "That sounds exciting," she said, feeling somehow a heavy emotion in the air that made her uncertain how to respond. She tried to meet Chris's eyes but he was staring into the fire.

"Won't Ricardo and Enrique object?" he said to Magdalena, not taking his eyes from the glowing embers.

"They will be busy at the resort site all day tomorrow. So we can explore the ruins without any worry of being discovered."

"Isn't it allowed to visit the island?" Michelle asked.

"There are regulations," Magdalena explained, "silly tribal rules."

"I don't think you should drink a full cup of coffee," Chris interjected, speaking to Michelle. "You need to get to bed soon. It's been a long day for you."

Michelle sensed that Chris wanted her off to bed so he could spend time alone with Magdalena. She eyed the woman sitting on the sofa, imagined her father making love with her as he did with Wendy. Somehow it wasn't the same; somehow this woman didn't strike Michelle as sexy at all. Yet she certainly was sexy in appearance and bearing . . . but that wasn't what Michelle felt in the air. She felt something that pulled at her invisibly, as if she could see it only with her left eye, and right now she was seeing through her dominant right eye.

"I guess I am tired," she conceded. She put her cup down on a table and walked over to Chris, bending over him and kissing him on the forehead.

" 'Night, kiddo," he said. "I'll work out the details and see if we'll go tomorrow morning. Get a good sleep. You have everything you need?"

"Sure," she said. "Wake me up early, okay?"

"Sweet dreams."

She suddenly felt the need to touch him again: her hand squeezed his shoulder, he tilted his head up to her, and she kissed him on the lips. "I love you," she whispered.

"Hey, me too. Welcome to Guatemala!"

She started for the bedroom, smiling to Magdalena, who nodded an unspoken good night.

Michelle walked down the hallway, which was lit with a tall candle at the far end, near the bathroom. Her tennis shoes squeaked on the large ceramic tiles with each step. She peed and brushed her teeth in the primitive but adequate bathroom—noticing that her period had not yet started, in spite of the pangs she had felt in the plane yesterday and on the lake this afternoon—and then went to her room, lit by its own flickering candle.

She slipped the wipile over her head, took off her jeans,

154

and felt the cut under her breast. In the candlelight, she could see a brownish smear where Chris had administered the iodine. Her memory took her back to the boat ride. She reflected on how she had somehow known she wouldn't drown.

She climbed between the sheets with the candle still lit. From the living room she could hear soft voices conversing. She waited a few minutes to see if Chris would come in and say good night. When he didn't, she got back out of bed. Her urge to spy on the two pushed her down the hallway silently on bare feet.

After a brief pause while the girl made her exit, the two remaining in the living room glanced at each other, adjusting to the more intimate situation. Chris sighed, thinking of Michelle. Magdalena shifted her position on the sofa.

"Why don't you come sit up here?" she said in Spanish. "You are too far away."

He hesitated, then stood up and hopped over to her. Sitting down, he crossed his leg to bring the injured foot up. Magdalena reached over and touched the swollen ankle, and mumbled something in Quitapul while her fingers maintained contact with his skin.

"What was that all about?" Chris asked in Spanish.

"Just a little spell to help you heal," she said with a sly smile. "I hope you don't mind. It would be helpful if you could walk tomorrow."

"Well it's going to take more than a little mumbo jumbo to take that swelling down and heal those ligaments."

"Perhaps. In any case," she said, letting her fingers drift up from his ankle to his knee, where her hand came to rest, "I do hope you will come with me early in the morning."

"What for? Tell me what's happening and then I'll decide."

She sighed. Chris looked at her face and saw fatigue.

155

"I cannot tell you how trying this week has been," she said softly, her Spanish flowing easily off her tongue, but her tone betraying how tired she was.

"Tell me, why don't you?"

"It is the same everywhere. Offered the chance to be free and independent, or slaves and looked after, people almost always choose slavery. It is no different in Zacapula."

"We chose freedom in the United States," Chris said.

"That was a special case. You certainly didn't offer any of that freedom to the Indians, did you?"

"Well, no, the whole thing wouldn't have been possible if we hadn't taken the land away from the Indians in the first place. I sometimes think that what's happening up there now is nothing more than our karma catching up with us."

"You have spoken the truth."

"But everywhere these days, in every country, freedom's being lost. I'm an old-fashioned freedom-fighter, you know. I can't stand to see what's happening up there, how everybody's turning to the Fascist way out—nationalism and war, egotism and control."

"That was what I noticed when I was there last. But I was tempted to stay in your country nonetheless. It is still the most free; it is still where the most hope lies because of that freedom."

"But most of the people are running headlong into being totally controlled. The computer is the new Secret Service. Worse than that, people actually want to give up their own mental powers to computers, in the home, everywhere. Convenience is going to do us in up there. We'd sell our souls to computers if they'd do our work for us, let us phase out brainwork and get even lazier."

"It is good you see such things," she said.

"I can't help it. I'm a teacher—or at least I was. And I have to face the fact that kids watch an average of five hours of television a day. God, I hate televisions! They suck energy, that's what they do. If one's on in a house, the whole house takes on a weird atmosphere. I can't stand it. That's why I'm down here. No televisions, no computers."

"But also no freedom. If the Quitapul get their treasure back, what will they do with their money?"

"Certainly not buy televisions and computers."

"Christopher! That's exactly where it will end up. You must see that. It drives me frantic but it is true. Everyone everywhere has his weaknesses. And television preys on those weaknesses. Of not wanting to make an effort. Of wanting to sit blankly and stare, to plug into a machine, for what? There is certainly education and entertainment on television. But there is also something insidious. And my people here, they want to plug in to modern civilization, I am certain of that. I have traveled a great deal. The priests controlled through fear and promises of a future paradise. Now, the television controls through hypnotism and promises of consumer paradise. It makes me sick!" she said angrily.

"But the Quitapul, they—"

"You know nothing of the Quitapul. Why do you think they worship Ricardo. Because he offers them everything they don't have in modern civilization. I tell you, there is something sinister going on everywhere. There is a cancer of the body and a cancer of the mind and a cancer of the soul—there is one cancerous growth and it is consuming the human race. What can I do against it? I am ready to give up. Even Caban—especially Caban—has been seduced by this current sickness. I was born to be the Chosen One, to lead my people to a new era this Ilum K'inal. But they will not follow me; they chose to follow Enrique. My mission here on earth is failing. But I have one last hope."

"What's that?"

She leaned against him softly, her fingers leaving his knee and stroking up his thigh. "You," she whispered affectionately.

Chris laughed a self-conscious laugh. "Me?"

"I wish we could just go to bed," she said.

"We can."

"I'm so tired; I have done everything possible in the village. They will not listen to me. They want the gold; they want the material power! What I offer them is nothing compared to the material power they lust after. It is like a man who is focused not on his heart, on love, but on his genitals. Better to have your genitals cut off than to lose your heart!"

"I'd rather keep both," Chris said.

"Then you had better be careful!"

She stood up and walked over to the window, looking out into the moonlit night at the shadowy help of Caban's presence. Chris watched her, feeling a lightness in his body that was both sexual and something else, like a free-flowing energy entering his nervous system, opening up new areas in him.

She turned and faced him, the light from the fire and the light from the kerosene lamp highlighting her face and slender body. She suddenly looked frail to Chris, small and vulnerable.

"Come over here," he said. "I don't want to stand on one foot and I want to touch you."

She looked at him with both eyes focused in unison. "I wish more than anything in the world that you and I could flee this place and be together," she said, and walked over to him. Sitting down, she nestled against him, her head against his chest. He put his arms around her, his fingers feeling the solid reality of her body.

"We could leave tomorrow," he said. "We could go anywhere."

"But everywhere," she started, and then had to finish her sentence through sobs. "Everywhere it is the same. Everywhere people are making the same choice."

"What choice is that?"

"To die," she said.

"Everyone dies."

"No! The spirit can live on. But people are letting their

spirits die now. All I can do is cry tonight; my energy is gone, my people are gone."

Chris held her while she sobbed against him, releasing a flood of despair, loneliness, tears. His sexual energy was growing while he held her, and when she started to recover, he felt her fingers reaching for him, under his shirt, with clinging intensity.

She raised her head and he wiped the tear-streaked cheeks and eyes gently, feeling her face, exploring her with touch, sensing that he knew her from some other time; some vague past memories strove to reach clarity but were lost in the fog of the past. He bent over lightly and kissed her salty lips. Her fingers clutched at him as she arched her body against his.

Chris lost all notion of who he was. He felt himself starting to glow inside; a white energy field seemed to radiate from her body, and his only desire was to move deeper and deeper into that energy. With a long stroke of his right hand he brought his fingers up her leg and pressed against her womb.

She broke the kiss, sighed, and gasped for air. She pushed herself back from him, as if some immense thought had struck her. "But everything is not lost," she whispered. "Tomorrow, we will go to the island. Promise me you will help me."

"What can I do?"

Her fingers slowly reached for his erect penis under his Levi's, and traced its bulging shape on the material, giving Chris a flood of ecstasy. "The jade phallus," she whispered. "I must have the jade phallus or Enrique cannot be stopped."

"That artifact, at the brujo hut?"

"Yes! Where is it?"

"I threw it in the bushes."

"I have looked for hour upon hour. I cannot find it. Your power must be used; only you can find it. Please!"

"Why do you think I can find it?"

"I know you can! You are a man of power."

"Don't start on that again."

"You made the earth shake!"

"Bullshit," he said. But there was no power in his attempt to push away her words; they were penetrating him too deeply, as if at some level what she was saying was true, only he didn't want to admit it.

"Tomorrow morning you must use your power. You must find the phallic stone. Everything depends on that. If I have it, there is hope. If not, who can say what will happen?"

"What's so important about that ridiculous penis?"

"Everything! It is crucial to the ceremonies I must perform for Ilum K'inal."

"What ceremonies?"

"I assure you, they are for good. They must be done, there is no choice. It is the only way to reach Caban, and Caban is the only way to reach the Quitapul, and through the Quitapul, we can reach the rest of the world."

"You've got a savior complex," Chris said, feeling her fingers still gently massaging his penis.

"No," she countered, "I am simply fulfilling what I was born to do. We are all equally born to fulfill our purpose. But few are aware of that."

"And what is yours?"

"I am in touch with my purpose, but I cannot know beforehand what that purpose is."

"So you're acting in the dark?"

"There is no other way. Come, let's go to bed. I'm so tired."

"But how can you trust your purpose. What if it's of the Devil, like the priest says? If you don't know what you're doing—"

She looked up at him, her eyes still fused in a common focus, but looking frightened nonetheless, like a little girl's. "I have only two choices. To act or not to act. I know that Enrique's energy is negative. I am counteracting him. I must have faith. I accept the power that has been given to me, that moves through me. That is all I know. I am here for a purpose, because this is where it is happening."

"And what's happening?"

"Caban requires a sacrifice of me. I am the Chosen One; if I do not comply with the ancient texts, then he will punish all of us. Caban requires blood. He wants a return to the old ways. I refuse, I feel there is a new power entering the world, and I challenge Caban to open up to it. If he does, there is hope. If he does not . . . I can't think of that. But this is what is happening."

"And you have to have the phallus?"

"Yes."

"But I can't even walk."

"Tomorrow your foot will be healed."

"So you can work miracles too?"

"I have worked this one."

"Well I'll have to see it to believe it."

"Let's go to bed," she said.

"Tell me one thing. Is it safe for Michelle, over there?"

"No one is safe anywhere."

"Answer my question!"

"If we find the phallus and I am successful, all will be well. But both of you are involved; there is no running away."

"We can leave tomorrow."

"No! Both of you would be dead. You saw what happened when you came over."

"What happened?"

"Michelle nearly drowned."

"How do you know that! You talked to Enrique."

"I'm too tired for this."

"Are you telling me that you—"

"I saw her go overboard, I felt it. I felt the energy in your stomach as you grabbed her, I have your strength. And I am drained to my limits from starting the engine. Yes, Christopher, yes."

"Who tried to drown us?"

"I don't know, that is the mystery."

"So we're poor little humans caught up in some giant supernatural drama of the gods?"

"Please," she cried out. "I'm so tired. Take me to bed." She stood up weakly. He hopped to his feet, and they made their way down the hallway into the bedroom. Chris went into the bathroom to pee. When he came back, she was under the covers, her clothes a small pile on a chair beside the massive bed. He undressed and slipped in beside her.

They lay side by side a long moment. He thought that she had fallen asleep. But then she sighed. "I have been wanting so deeply to be like this with you," she whispered. "But now I am so tired."

"It's okay."

"Put your hand on my stomach."

He reached over and touched her soft skin, rising and falling as she breathed. "Feel the energy," she said. "It is for you as well as for me."

Chris felt as if he had been plugged into an electric circuit, but it was more than that, it was a wave of energy invading his body, a white light shattering his concepts of reality, his notions of his limited being. He felt himself merging with the woman beside him; it was not sexual in a genital sense, but an all-pervading sexuality in his brain and body, an ecstatic flooding of energy and light.

Then it changed, and he felt a darkness coming over him, as if the energy had reversed itself and was now draining him of his life-force, pulling his very soul out of him. He tried to remove his hand but couldn't.

Without warning there was a gigantic explosion in his brain, mixing the darkness and the light into something that was so immense that Chris could not contain it and remain conscious. He slipped into sleep instantly.

chapter 12

Michelle awoke the next morning in a sweat. The sheet was wrapped around her body, and she remembered a vague, hazy dream, but it slipped away almost instantly. All she was left with was a shaky, panicky feeling and a clammy, sweaty body. At first she thought she was in her bedroom back home, but the faint morning light showed blank white walls and a window with a strange brightly colored curtain. She untangled herself, yanking at the sheet angrily when it didn't immediately release her. Although she didn't remember removing her underpants when she had sneaked back from eavesdropping the night before, she found herself naked as she stood up, her feet chilled by the tile, and walked over to the window to look out.

The lake. Placid, glassy, calm. And the island, looking much closer than she'd remembered. It was very early. She hadn't expected Guatemala to be this cold; she had goosebumps on her arms and legs. Last night she had felt them growing on her like this, when she was standing in the hallway listening to the soft voices talking in Spanish. It had been frustrating as well as scary, hiding there in the dark, that strange woman's voice evoking first angry, then confused, then pleading tones from her father. Michelle had understood hardly anything from the conversation—her classroom Spanish was of little use down here. But she had felt a weird energy coming from that room, and her gut reaction had been to suspect Magdalena of trying to do something to Chris.

The sudden knocking on her door made her jump and raise her hands to cover her breasts, as if someone was going to burst in on her. Enrique was there in her mind, opening the door—*that* had been the dream. God, it had been something; he had been chasing her up a mountain, she had run into a cave, and he had cornered her, wrestled her to the ground roughly but with a fervor that was sexually overwhelming, enticing . . . and he had tied her hands behind her, started to do something to her, something that wouldn't come to memory . . .

"Michelle, are you awake?"

It was her father's voice, whispering. "Yes, just a minute." She quickly put on her jeans without bothering with underpants. As she slipped the wipile over her head she called, "Come on in," and the door opened. Chris walked in. Not limping, she noticed immediately—noticed he was focused on it too as he walked, putting weight on the foot and wincing in anticipated pain, but not seeming to feel any.

"Your foot," she said.

"It's healed," he said in a half-whisper. "Listen, I think we should talk."

"Where's Magdalena?"

"Still asleep."

"You slept with her," Michelle said bluntly.

"Yes. Just slept. Nothing else. She's really tired. I need to talk with you." He sat down on her bed and she joined him.

"Let me see your foot. It can't be healed overnight."

"That's what we have to talk about. Magdalena. She worked some kind of spell and goddamnit, *my foot healed overnight*. Something's really heavy down here, I'm wondering if we should catch the mailboat and go back to Panahachel, or maybe back to Guatemala City."

164

"Daddy she really did heal you, didn't she? God, it's scary—look, the swelling's all gone; she really did it."

"Yeah."

"She's spooky."

"Why don't you put your glasses on? No, wait! Look at me—that's it, you're just the same as her!"

"As who?"

"Sometimes Magdalena's eyes get just like yours. Tell me, what do you think, what do you feel—should we leave here?"

"No!" Michelle said, not sure why her answer was so emphatic. "I just got here; please, no. I want to go over to the island this morning—isn't that what we're doing?"

"If you want to. But I want to tell you, Magdalena is very different from normal people. I'm starting to believe she does have powers that—well, she healed my ankle. But here's the thing; she's all involved in some Easter rite that's coming up, she's crazy if you ask me, and—"

"Well, why are you spending time with her if she's—"

"I want *you* to tell *me*. Do you believe in, um, occult powers; you know, people able to read other people's minds, control what happens? I want to know what you think, it's important."

"Yes," she said.

"Yes what?"

"Those powers exist, Daddy, and it's nothing to be afraid of really."

"Why do you say that?"

"Because . . . because sometimes I think I have them too. Sometimes everything gets very strange and—don't laugh at me."

"Believe me, I'm not laughing."

"Sometimes I think I'm crazy, Daddy."

"You never told me anything."

"I've tried to but you wouldn't listen."

"Tell me what?"

"There's just all sorts of different levels of everything—and sometimes I slip and feel strange things."

"What do you feel now; should we leave here? Concentrate. Use your intuition. What do you feel?"

"I want to go to the island."

"Why?"

"I don't know."

"What if you were in danger here?"

"Just being alive these days is dangerous, Daddy. The bomb could go off at any moment, the earthquake could hit and California could . . . Are you afraid we might drown or something?"

"Yeah. Or something."

"I feel really good; I don't feel any danger."

"So you want to go?"

"Yes."

"You could stay here while Magdalena and I—"

"No way. Enrique might came around and I don't think I want to be alone with him. Besides, I want to go to the island."

"It's a sacred island."

"You told me."

"Okay then. I'll wake her up."

"Daddy?"

Neither of them could remember when they had taken each other's hand, but they were holding hands. "Yeah, kiddo?"

"She healed you, Daddy."

"I know."

"That's a spiritual thing; the energy has to be good for someone to heal. I don't think you should be afraid of her. I think we should respect her. Healing is a gift of God."

"It's a gift from somewhere."

"The Devil can't heal," she said.

"Are you sure?"

"Well . . . I never thought about it."

"Me either."

"Do you love her?"

"Magdalena? I—I guess I do. But it's not like any—"

"You've never loved a healer before, Daddy."

"No. No, I guess not. Well. I'll wake her up."

She was awake, sitting upright on the bed, her long legs crossed, Indian-style. Chris found himself looking at her nakedness with a mixture of sexual and spiritual excitement. She should be Ix Chel, the fertility goddess she had mentioned at their first meeting, he said to himself. He turned around. Michelle was standing in the doorway staring at the meditating figure. He looked back to Magdalena and her eyes opened, crossed. For a moment no one spoke or moved. Chris had a sensation of the three of them being in one of the great cathedrals, with a hush pervading the air. A vulnerability which was so intense that the slightest movement or sound might cause irreparable damage to something essential.

Then Michelle whispered. "You look so beautiful."

Magdalena made no response. The two women were looking at each other. And then Chris noticed—Michelle's gaze, like Magdalena's, was cross-eyed. "You forgot your glasses," he said.

"No, I don't want to wear them today," she said with certainty. She had thought about it; it was not an oversight.

Magdalena moved, slipping gracefully off the bed, her nakedness appearing natural, the clothes she slipped into unnecessary. "So we're off to the island?" she asked in English.

"Yes," Chris said, glancing at Michelle.

"We should be going, then. I feel rested; it was a good sleep. We should take some fruit, perhaps. I noticed you have a cayuco at the dock; can we use that?"

Twenty minutes later they were on the water. An early mist hung over the island; a chill was in the air. Magdalena sat in the back of the cayuco, rowing with experienced strength while Chris and Michelle sat side by side in the forward seat, staring ahead as the island approached. The sun was still not up across the lake, but a deepening red colored the sky above Panahachel in the far distance.

Chris felt a mixture of adventure, excitement, and foreboding. The conversation with Magdalena was still on his mind, as were the feelings he had experienced before drifting off to sleep—and the miraculous healing of his ankle. It all threatened his early-morning calm with a hidden sense of lurking danger.

Michelle was leaning slightly against him, with a childlike tenderness in her gesture of affection. These two women, Chris found himself thinking as the cayuco skimmed along through the glassy water, they are like two halves of my fantasy world. And I'm in between and I'm goddamned confused. Here I am in a dugout canoe with a witch doctor rowing me and my daughter to a sacred island, to look for a jade penis that is supposedly crucial to the well-being of the human race. That's the stuff romantic tales are made of, not real, everyday life. Who's in charge here, anyway? Will the real creator of the universe please step forward? There are a few questions that need to be answered.

"Daddy?"

"Yeah, kiddo?"

"Did you come over to this side of the lake with Wendy?"

"No."

"Oh, look! The sun's coming up."

"Hurakán," Magdalena said. "The heart of the heavens."

Chris stared as the great glowing ball of fire began to reveal itself from behind the eastern mountain, just to the right of the island and far in the distance. At first he could look at it straight on, but soon it was too intense, soon it demanded the ultimate human gesture—to avert the eyes, to look down in the presence of Hurakán. He humbles us all, Chris thought, no one can face the sun god. As he felt the energy of the heat and light on his forehead, he realized as he never had before that the sun's power could indeed be used to power mankind's life. It was such a striking power, felt deeply. He closed his eyes and let the energy pulse through his eyes, down his optic nerves, and directly into his brain—a massage from the heavens. Hurakán, yet another god. Chris thought of Itzam'na, who was beyond all the pantheon of visible gods. Itzam'na, he caught himself thinking, lapsing again into half-acceptance of the myth, Itzam'na be with us, there's no telling when we might need you again, old man.

They approached the bay Chris had overlooked from the brujo hut a week ago. It was as fine when approached by water as when seen from the land, especially when the lake was so crystal-clear and smooth early in the morning, reflecting the greens and browns of the island, the blue of the sky, patches of white puffy cloud—

A large heron rose in flight from a tree on the cliff. Magdalena stopped rowing. The bird flew over their heads, making a strained, upset cry, wings flapping the air with loud buffeting sounds. It was headed for the mainland, for the volcano.

"A guardian spirit," Magdalena muttered.

"Your guardian spirit?" Chris asked.

"No. My brother's."

"Ah."

"High clouds. Early Xocomil today," she said, continuing to row, bringing the cayuco into the small bay, across its still shallow waters, and then rowing strenuously at the last moment, sending the cayuco grating onto the sandy shore. She stepped out with bare feet and gave the boat another push, so the gringos wouldn't have to get their feet wet.

"God, this is paradise," Michelle said, looking around. Chris returned her eager smile, and then she went running down the beach. The two older people stood watching her.

169

"I'm sure glad she made it down," Chris said.

"She is a special being. You have done well with her; she has not had her spirit broken."

"I imagined it's had some bends and bruises," Chris said. "But she's always stayed free inside."

"She is very important. You must help her however you can, Christopher."

"It's good to be back here on the island; it feels different over here."

"Your ankle, is it good enough for walking?"

"Can you heal anything you want to?"

"No, I cannot heal anything at all. Itzam'na healed you. I am simply a vehicle, I can do nothing on my own."

"I don't know what to think anymore," he said.

"That is good."

"Well I don't like it."

"Don't fight it. No one can comprehend reality."

"Well someone has to."

"We can only do what needs doing at the time. Right now we need to find the jade phallus. Everything depends on it."

"Everything for you, maybe. Just leave Michelle and me out of your generalizations, okay?"

"That is impossible. You are here. First I dreamed of you and your daughter, many times. Then you appeared. This is what is real, Christopher. Can you visualize the phallus?"

Christopher in fact suddenly did have an image in his mind. He felt a contact with the jade piece, an impulse to start walking, heading across the beach to the trail up the cliff.

At the same moment, Michelle was hurrying along the top of the cliff. Without her corrective lenses, everything seemed multidimensional to her. The island felt magical; she could hardly contain her energy. She felt as light as air, running under giant mango trees, then through a patch of sweet-smelling pines, and suddenly emerging into a small meadow of sunlight and tall grass.

There was a hut in the distance. She headed for it, feeling drawn to it excitedly. But the exposed root of a mango tree tripped her, and she fell, rolling off the trail a few feet over the bank.

She lay where she had fallen, breathing heavily, not hurt, feeling warm and tingly in her body, bright and clear in her head. She stared up at the sky, at high clouds passing overhead. She could project herself up into the cloud when she looked away from it with her right eye and let her left eye glance at it. The sensation was ecstatic, she suddenly felt perfectly relaxed, as if she was at the exact right place at the exact right time, in a magical point of stillness and peace.

But, ugh! There was something ruining her feelings, something under her back digging into her. She rolled off the object and pushed it away. But wait. It wasn't just a rock. It was green. Smooth. Oh my God, she thought. Her vision fused; her eyes looked in unison at the thing. It was a stone penis.

Her fingers reached out and touched it tentatively, as if it might somehow be alive and react to her touch. It was cold from the night air. She took it in her hands carefully, amazed.

"Michelle!"

Her father's voice, calling for her. At first she wanted to run and show him what she had found. But a sudden possessive urge gripped her. She wanted this for herself, she didn't want them to take it away from her. She felt it had come to her and she should keep it. And certainly, her father wouldn't let her keep something like this, something so lifelike, so—

"Michelle, where are you?"

She stood up quickly, sticking the phallus into her jeans pocket. But it was too long, the tip stuck out. She started giggling as she looked down at the head of the erect green penis protruding from her pocket; it was so funny! But then she controlled her giggles, found where her daypack had fallen off when she fell down the bank, and stuffed the jade piece down under her sweater. With the pack in place on her back, she stepped up onto the trail, dusting herself off.

"Up here, Daddy!"

She walked back down the trail toward them. There they were, walking up along the edge of the cliff under the mango trees. She felt differently toward them now that she had a secret. And she enjoyed the sensation; it made everything even more intense, more exciting. As Chris came up to her, she glanced first at him, then at Magdalena, afraid at first that they might notice in her expression that she had a secret. But she felt a wave of energy surge through her, giving her the feeling of having a magic barrier that they couldn't break through to her inner world.

"You shouldn't run around up here alone," Chris said.

"Why not?"

He glanced at Magdalena. "Well, up here is the sacred burial ground of the brujos. It's special, we should let Magdalena give us a tour. She's offered to take you up the hill over to the ruins."

"Aren't you coming?"

"I'll be over in a few minutes. I'm going to look for something I lost the last time I was here."

"How long will you be? I can help you look," Michelle said, uncertain whether she wanted to go off alone with the Indian woman.

"It shouldn't take me very long."

Magdalena started walking along the trail. Michelle looked to Chris apprehensively, but he smiled in reassurance. "They're beautiful ruins," he said. "I'll meet you on the main temple."

"What are you looking for, Daddy?"

"Oh, nothing, just an artifact I want to find to show Magdalena."

"Can't she use her powers to find it?"

"No, she says she can't."

"I want to help you look."

"No, go with Magdalena," he said, using a tone of authority which left no room for argument. Michelle gave him a hurt look and then went hurrying after Magdalena.

chapter 13

The sun was just peeping over the trees along the top of the ridge, sending yellow shafts of light through the branches into the dark shadows of the hill. By the time Michelle caught up with Magdalena, they were well into the trees. When she looked back toward her father, he was out of sight.

The tall Indian maintained her swift pace for ten minutes, while the younger girl tried to keep up with her. Then they topped the hill and paused. Michelle was out of breath. "It's beautiful," she said.

Magdalena looked very closely at Michelle, as if she were looking at her for the first time, her strong eye moving over her body while her wandering eye stared at what it would elsewhere. "And you," the Indian said finally. "You are beautiful also, even more than I dreamed."

Michelle found herself blushing, feeling exposed, vulnerable. "My hair's a mess," she said, running her fingers through the thick tangle of blonde curls.

"Please, you don't need to be afraid of me," Magdalena said in a low, soft voice. "Let's be friends. Come, I'll show you the ruins."

She started down the trail, with Michelle at her heels. Five minutes later they came to a clearing, a beautiful little meadow with a small stream running through it.

And there were the ruins. Magdalena didn't pause until she was at the foot of the main temple.

"Can we go up?" Michelle asked.

"Of course."

"I—I'm kind of scared. Are you sure it's okay?"

"Yes. I understand." Magdalena took the girl's hand and they started climbing the steep steps. Michelle could feel the damp sogginess of the deep blue-green moss under her tennis shoes, and she had a momentary flash of recall of damp grass back home, that morning when the cat . . . But there was no time for anything but hard climbing for several minutes, until they reached the top.

"God," Michelle whispered, breathless. "It's so high up here. And look at the volcano!"

But Magdalena was busy with something else, inspecting the altar, wiping her finger along its surface. Michelle remembered such altars from photographs—and also, it seemed to her dimly, from somewhere else. She felt a jolt run through her as her eyes fused their vision fixed on the stone altar, and on the pool of thick, dark-red liquid Magdalena was inspecting.

"What's that?" Michelle whispered.

"Someone did a sacrifice here, late last night," Magdalena said, her eyes scanning the surrounding area with sharp swiftness.

"That's *blood*," Michelle said.

"Chicken blood."

"How do you know it's chicken blood and not—"

"Quiet!" Magdalena said sharply, cutting off Michelle's voice, suddenly shrill with anxiety. "Sit down, come over here. Face the volcano."

Michelle walked around the altar with Magdalena. Her mind brought back her joking words in the plane, "Blood over Guatemala, blood over Guatemala."

Magdalena was sitting on the top step of the temple. She took Michelle's hand as she joined her. The volcano seemed to be brooding, with a layer of mist shrouding its head in dark clouds which the sunlight had not yet penetrated. Michelle was bursting with a question she felt she must ask. "Do you—does anybody—still sacrifice, you know, sacrifice people up here?"

The question hung in the morning air.

"That has been forbidden since the Spanish arrived," Magdalena said, her voice vague, distant.

"You're a Mayan?"

"Of the Quitapul tribe, yes."

"Daddy said you're part American."

"American? Of course I'm an American. All of us born on this continent are Americans. You and I, we are sisters of the same blood, blood comes of the spirit. What you feel is what you are."

"What I feel right now is scared, up here."

Magdalena put her arm around Michelle's shoulder, but Michelle felt her fear grow, not lessen. "This is where the power resides," Magdalena said. "Open yourself, feel the energy come into you from Caban. Don't be afraid, I am with you. Open yourself."

Michelle felt her vertigo increase frighteningly, and she jumped up, throwing off Magdalena's arm. She backed up until her legs touched the altar. Her breath came hoarsely through her open mouth, her head shaking, jaw slack, eyes rolling. She saw Magdalena stand up facing her, backdropped by the volcano, and the juxtaposition created an almost visible force field emanating from the volcano, vibrating lines of power that went through Magdalena's body and came out of her eyes, which were focused on a spot in Michelle's chest.

Michelle's heart seemed to stop, and the scream rising up from her depths froze in her throat. Magdalena reached forward and put her hand over the girl's eyes. Michelle slowly started to sag into darkness as she fainted. Her body was caught in the Indian's strong arms and lifted onto the altar, laid out upon the cold stone.

Reaching into her pouch, Magdalena produced a small gourd. She uncorked the gourd and took a sip. Then she pulled up Michelle's wipile, exposing her stomach and breasts. Pouring a small amount of the liquid into her palm, Magdalena rubbed it into the skin of the girl's chest, and then paused with her hand over the solar plexus, mumbling in Quitapul as her right eye watched the girl's face and her left eye looked directly up at the volcano.

"This heart," Magdalena then said in Quitapul. "This heart is mine! Feel it beating, Caban. This heart is my heart. Feel our hearts beating, Caban!"

Suddenly a beating of wings startled Magdalena from her trance as the giant heron swooped over the canyon. She glanced up and, without a second's hesitation, jumped onto the altar, covering the girl's body with her own to hide it from the bird.

Moments passed. Silence. Magdalena could feel Michelle's heart beating against her own breast, and the girl's breath warm against the bruja's cheek. "Itzam'na!" she muttered.

Then she slipped off the altar and took another sip of the harsh-tasting liquid. She mumbled something in Quitapul and poured some of the liquid directly onto the girl's face and neck. Michelle started to come to. Magdalena pulled down her wipile, noticing the cut under the left breast as she did so.

The girl's eyes flickered and then opened. She stared, her vision focused directly into Magdalena's right eye. For a long moment neither of them spoke. Then Magdalena took her hand and helped her sit up.

"You seem to have fainted," she said.

Michelle blinked at the brightness of the sunlight. Everything seemed to be swirling in front of her, swirling in two directions at once, toward the middle of her focus of vision.

"Do you feel better?" Magdalena said, jolting Michelle's vision out of its dizziness. "Are you ready to walk down?"

"Down?" Michelle said vaguely. "Down. Yes. Down."

"Good. Take my hand."

Slowly they started down the steps. Michelle put all her attention into making her body perform the task at hand, and the descent took on an almost regal atmosphere, as if the two women were royalty descending from the throne. There was a sensation in Michell's stomach, and in her womb, that remained from her experience on the pyramid, an energy which lingered and felt very good. But as far as what had actually happened up there, her mind was a blank. Something about chicken blood, and fainting, that was all she could remember.

When they reached the level of ground it was a tremendous relief to Michelle. Magdalena took her over to the small stream and told her to drink. The water was cool and refreshing, bringing the girl back to her senses.

"Splash some on your face," Magdalena said.

"Ah," the girl responded, laughing at the chilling feel of the water, inhaling through her nose and feeling the cold tingle rush through her head.

"Do you faint often?" Magdalena asked.

"Faint? No."

"It must have been the climb up. And also, there are powers. You are very vulnerable to them. Listen to me."

"I am."

"We should not play games with each other."

They sat on the grass beside the stream, the warm sunlight shining on their backs. "You scare me," Michelle said.

"I know. It cannot be helped."

"You have the power."

"Yes."

"You are not afraid to die."

"No."

"I know about the power."

"What about it?"

"Just that it's there. And that it scares me."

Magdalena smiled a big-sister's smile, as if she were

talking with Michelle about sexual coming-of-age. "It is good that you are down here," she said. "I can help you understand."

"What happened up there?"

"Caban felt you. Caban is a great force."

"I feel like I almost died," Michelle whispered.

"Yes. But it was not yet your time. When the time comes, you will know it, you will open up and welcome it. But until then, you must fight with all your might to stay alive."

"What about you?" Michelle asked.

"What about me?"

"What is going to happen to you?"

Magdalena turned and glanced at Caban, who stared down on the two women from above the tip of the temple. Then she dabbed her hand in the water, and stared at the hole ten feet away where the water disappeared into the earth. "You and I," she said, "whatever happens, we are sisters. We are doing a beautiful dance together which will never end. This I know. Beyond that, the future is nothing, only the present. But I know one thing which you are still learning."

"Tell me."

"There is no time."

"Tell me!"

"It is the heart that counts. You are in confusion. You have your sexual center as your focus of attention: this is how it was with me when I was your age. It nearly killed me; it nearly caused a great tragedy for my people. The sexual center, the will, the lust for sacrifice—these three must be balanced by the heart or disaster comes. And you and I, we bring great disaster with us if we succumb."

"But I feel my heart."

"No, that is not your heart."

"It is too, you don't know," Michelle said defensively.

"Whatever happens, know that I will be with you if you will open your heart to me."

Michelle looked into her eyes for the first time during the conversation. But she felt a force pulling her into the other woman, threatening her very identity, as if Magdalena would rush into her body and take her over if she didn't resist with all her might.

"There you two are!"

It was Christopher, hurrying down the trail toward them, out of breath.

Magdalena touched Michelle's forehead. "Drink some water. Relax," she said, her voice quiet, soft, mothering. "Enjoy what you have here, now." She stood up and walked quickly to meet Chris.

"It's not there, somebody found it and took it," he said urgently. "I know where it was, I went right to the spot. The bushes were all smashed around the spot. Someone found it."

"You're certain?" Magdalena said, her face losing the temporary calm it had achieved, talking to Michelle, and becoming anxious.

"I'm *damned* sure," Chris said. He walked over to the stream and knelt down, sticking his face into the small pool. Then he glanced up at Michelle. "Hi, kiddo, how you doing?"

"Fine."

"Quite a set of ruins," he said, wiping his face with the cuff of his shirt.

"What were you looking for, Daddy; what did it look like?"

"Um, just a carved piece of jade."

"Why's it so important?"

"Magdalena needs it."

"Oh."

Michelle glanced at the other woman, who was standing lost in thought a few yards away. The jade piece; I've got what they're looking for, she thought. Her first impulse was to save the day, to hand the phallus to Chris triumphantly. But as she eyed Magdalena, an impulse came over her to keep the special artifact that the bruja

181

needed so badly. Somehow, Michelle felt she wanted that power over Magdalena, that with the jade phallus she wouldn't be vulnerable to Magdalena's overpowering presence. There was a feeling of power, of security, in controlling something, even if she didn't know what that something was aside from a striking likeness to a man's erect penis. Maybe tomorrow she would give up the phallus, but for now it would remain her secret. She glanced over to where she had left her daypack at the foot of the temple.

Chris seemed to think of her daypack at the same time, and started walking toward it. The sandwiches and fruit were in it. Michelle jumped up and ran ahead of him picking it up and walking back to the stream with it. "Anyone hungry?" she asked, opening it and taking out the food, then closing it up again.

They ate hungrily, sitting beside the stream. Michelle finished first, and started playing in the water, piling stones to form a dam across the stream about ten feet from where it ran down into that dark mysterious hole.

Chris made himself calm down after his disappointment. He had been thrilled by the sense of clairvoyance he had experienced in knowing where to find the jade piece; he had been led directly to the spot. And then, finding it gone! Even now, he sensed somehow the phallus's presence, but he had lost any feeliing of its location.

"Do you suppose Enrique found it?" he asked.

Magdalena sighed resignedly. "That is all that could have happened."

"So what happens now?"

"There is another way," she said.

"Good."

"But you will have to help."

"Me?"

"Tomorrow night. Perhaps you would have some time free tomorrow night?"

"Sounds like you want to make a date," he said, smiling slightly and relaxing.

"Exactly," she said, and leaned over to him and kissed him on the lips.

Michelle had been listening in on the conversation, but it had been in Spanish and she felt excluded. A feeling of resentment grew in her toward Magdalena. She was always in control, she was manipulating Chris, and Michelle didn't like it one bit. She was glad she had the phallus; it served Magdalena right.

Magdalena broke off the kiss and said in clear English, glancing to Michelle to include her, "We are sitting just twenty feet from where the tunnel once opened into the depths of Caban," she said. "Who can guess where it was?"

Michelle was intensely curious about the tunnel; her father had told her all about it. But she didn't want to play Magdalena's game; she didn't even look around her as Chris was doing; she put all her attention on the stone-and-dirt dam she was building across the two-foot stream. She had it half-finished; she wanted to dam the whole stream up and stop it from running down into that hole for a few minutes. She didn't know why; it was just a challenge to her.

Chris was inspecting the temple area with new eyes, searching for any sign of where the tunnel might have been. He guessed that the tunnel was either related to that hole where the water ran down into the ground, or somehow buried at the foot of the main temple, or maybe in the cliff behind him. He turned around and glanced there. Then he looked at Magdalena. He was still caught up in the lingering kiss she had given him, and he leaned to her and gave her one in return before guessing. Her lips were warm, full of soft energy, and he felt his penis rising against his Levi's.

"Guess," she said, breaking off the kiss.

"Must be down that hole," he said.

Magdalena stood up. Chris watched her, his sexual desire more urgent than his interest in the tunnel. She walked over to the hole. "The stream has always run

183

down this hole, and yes, it does run into the tunnel, or so the tradition says. But you see, it goes through a very narrow crack for at least a hundred feet; no one could enter the tunnel through there. No, the entrance was over there."

She started walking toward the cliff behind them. Chris followed her. The face of the cliff was overgrown with moss, ferns, and tenacious bushes that grew all the way up its height.

"Hey, look, someone was digging here," he said excitedly, noticing a pile of chipped rock and a two-foot indention into the cliff.

"Yes," she said. "A long time ago."

"Why doesn't Ricardo come over here with some dynamite and find the opening?"

"I assure you, he would if he could."

"Why can't he?"

She sat down on a small boulder among a pile of similar rocks which had once been part of the cliff. "My father has money, equipment. He even has my brother to play brujo for him. Together they are very powerful. But he knows also that Caban is not to be violated. He has learned from experience that there are limits which he must accept or suffer disaster. No, there is only one way the tunnel will open up."

"Magic," Chris said disdainfully.

"It is very complex, Christopher."

"But you really expect this cliff to just open up?"

"Anything is possible."

"Well, there are limits even to magic."

"Itzam'na closed off the tunnel. He can open it again."

"You really believe that?"

"It is all up to Caban."

"How?"

"He was punished by Itzam'na. Now he is to have another chance to exercise his power. The question is, has he learned his lesson."

"Well has he?"

184

"No one knows."

"Not even Caban himself?"

"Who can say. Caban is like you, like me. The human brain does not really control the human being. Caban does not know himself what he will do, that is how I feel. Who can say what is meant to happen. No one can comprehend Itzam'na."

"So Itzam'na is God?"

"Itzam'na is a word to label the forces which are beyond us."

"Tell me just one thing. Are these forces good, or evil?"

"I have told you, I don't know. All I know is that Ilum K'inal is approaching in three days. You are here as I dreamed. Your daughter is here. But the phallic stone is missing. Tomorrow night we will try to counter that loss. I know nothing else. We should head back, the wind will be blowing."

She started to stand up, but Chris grabbed her arm, with a rising sense of anxiety at her words. "Wait a minute," he insisted. "What is this plan you have? I get a feeling you have Michelle involved in your plans. Tell me the truth right now!"

Magdalena glanced to where Michelle was finishing up her dam. Then her arm registered the pain of the man's grip. "Please, you're hurting me," she said.

He let go his grip but he was determined, and Magdalena sensed almost a violent edge to him right then. "Tell me," he ordered.

She hesitated. The stillness of the meadow seemed to underscore her uncertainty. Only the gurgling of the water running down into the lost tunnel gave an impression of time going by. And then that gurgling seemed to fade, to die. Michelle's dam was complete and the water was backing up into the meadow, not running down the hole anymore. Magdalena took a deep breath and sighed.

"I will tell you the tradition," she said. "You cannot escape in any case. Ricardo will never let you leave until Ilum K'inal is finished. And besides, you must know if we are to perform the ceremony tomorrow night.

"You see, in essence the entire tradition of the Quitapul is rooted in evil. It is rooted in the desire of man and gods to gain tremendous power. And there is only one way to gain that power."

"What is that?"

"Through the life-force of living beings. Through sacrifice. Caban is not human. He has no heart. Do you understand?"

"Keep talking."

"This temple. That altar up there. Caban once gained the power of the heart."

"Through heart sacrifice?"

"Yes!" she said angrily. "Yes, and Itzam'na punished him. Now, Caban is to be given another chance. The Quitapul are to be given another chance. My people and Caban, they are one, you must understand. It is the Quitapul who are being given another chance. But they are still not in touch with their hearts; they want the power of Caban in order to destroy, to conquer, not to nurture. I am so angry with them!"

She stood up. "What is happening here." she said. "It is happening all over the world. There are days where humans choose. They are choosing in Zacapula right now. They are choosing in the United States. I am half-Indian, half-white, I feel both sides, and it is the same."

"But what can we do?" Chris said, standing up beside her.

"For the Quitapul, you and I can perform the ceremony tomorrow night. For your country, who can say. But something must be done. Caban and your nuclear reactors, they are the same. They tap the power of the planet. But who are we to dare to tap that power? Humans are greedy, they want all the power! But power is not everything. What about the heart, what about love, what about the spirit?"

She spun around and faced Chris. "I can tell, you still

186

do not believe, even after all you have been shown. You are a stupid gringo. Go climb the temple, quickly."

"Why?"

"I feel you must. Please. Go now, we must leave soon."

"Just climb it?"

"Yes, go to the top, let Caban feel your presence, let him know you are here at this moment. Quickly, while the water is still dammed. He is vulnerable now. Go! Then we must leave."

Chris felt confused, and more than a little frightened about going up onto that pyramid again. But he felt Magdalena's urgency, and started toward the temple.

"Where are you going, Daddy?" Michelle shouted from the dam.

"Quick hike to the top, then we'll take off," he said.

He started up the steps, his hiking boots squishing moss underfoot with each strong upward step. His head cleared of its anxiety and confusion as he climbed, and when he reached the top he felt light, full of energy, somehow triumphant. He stared at the volcano as if he were its equal, with nothing to fear.

He turned and looked back down. Just as he did so, Magdalena turned her head and looked toward the trail that went up the east hill. Sighting something, she instantly broke into a run across the meadow, heading toward the trail.

"Hey!" Chris shouted at her.

But she didn't respond; she just kept on running until she disappeared into the trees to the west. Chris started down the steps, going as fast as he could. What the hell's the matter? he wondered. When he reached the ground, breathless, he found out. Three men appeared at the edge of the clearing. He started protectively toward Michelle, but one of the Indians raised a rifle and fired a warning in the air. Chris froze. The rifle was aimed at his head. The other two Indians started walking quickly toward Michelle.

"Put down that gun!" Chris ordered in Spanish. But the Indian ignored his demand, and came walking toward him with the rifle still ready.

Enrique came running down the trail; he too was holding a rifle. He sauntered over to where Michelle and Chris were being held, and hand-signaled the Indians to lower their guns.

"So," he said, "you have violated the rules."

Chris, realizing that they hadn't seen Magdalena escape, spoke with forced casualness. "I just wanted to show Michelle the ruins; there's no harm in that," he said apologetically.

Enrique did not appear to be really upset. He stood with the butt of his rifle on the ground, eyeing Michelle.

"No harm, perhaps, but you should have had me bring you here. Ricardo will be angry."

"It was just a quick decision this morning," Chris said, glancing at Michelle, hoping she would realize that Magdalena's presence on the island shouldn't be revealed.

"The temple is so beautiful," she said in an appealing tone, smiling winningly at Enrique.

"Have you been to the top?"

"Yes, someone sacrificed a chicken up there."

Enrique showed a slight reaction to the statement, and Chris detected it.

"Are you certain?" Enrique said.

"Go up and see for yourself," Chris suggested, wanting to play for time so that Magdalena could make good her escape.

Enrique looked to Michelle. "Would you like to go up again for an official tour?" he said.

Michelle glanced to Chris for guidance, and Chris nodded his approval.

"Thank you," she said formally. With her backpack in place, she joined Enrique in the climb up. He started talking about the ancient Mayans, about the great civilization of the Quitapul, about the vast treasure of gold and precious gems and artifacts buried somewhere nearby, deep in the earth.

Fifteen minutes to the cayuco, Chris was figuring, then at least half an hour to row back to the volcano. If Enrique could be stalled here for an hour, everything would be okay. Michelle was doing her part, but Chris wasn't certain she was doing it for Magdalena. She seemed to be enthralled by Enrique. The Indian was, after all, very handsome. He had shattered the serene scene down in the meadow with his appearance, and had replaced it with an intensity, a male vitality, that any lively girl would respond to.

Chris noticed that the small lake Michelle created had backed up thirty feet, flooding a quarter of the meadow. It was nearly to the brim of the dam now; the stream would be running down the hole again. He decided to go back up the temple to be near enough to the couple ahead of him to overhear their conversation.

Three-quarters of the way up, he paused, winded, and sat down on a step to catch his breath. He could hear Enrique's voice talking, and Michelle's light, cheerful laugh punctuating the Indian's comments. Across from him, Chris could see the cliff staring back at him.

"My God!" he muttered, staring in disbelief. Fifteen feet behind where the three Indian guards were sitting casually smoking cigarettes was an opening in the cliff! It looked as though the rock had opened up along a natural fault line that ran at an angle down the face of the cliff. The bottom of the fault had widened into a triangle about six feet at the bottom, tapering to a close ten feet higher up.

Chris stood up with a jolt. It had happened! The goddamned mountain had opened up, just like that. He looked up at Michelle and Enrique, standing beside the altar talking. What would happen now? Enrique and Ricardo would get all the gold, the Quitapul would be wealthy beyond their wildest dreams—and with the money, the town of Zacapula would be transformed, everything would—

His glance back at the cliff stopped his flow of thoughts. The entrance to the tunnel. Where was it? His eyes scanned the entire cliff's surface. Nothing. No opening. It was gone!

He sat down, shaking, his mind a blank confusion. Michelle and Enrique were starting down. They walked past him, leaving a trail of small-talk in the air. He stood and started up the rest of the steps to the top. When he reached the altar, there was Caban staring down at him. He sat on the altar and stared back, his mind shaken and confused, his world somehow held together only by the presence of this giant volcano filling his sight. A sense of calm suddenly flowed into his agitated body. His shaking stopped. For a moment he experienced himself looking from the volcano down at himself sitting on the altar on top of the pyramid. From the volcano he was no more than a tiny, indistinct figure, insignificant and very slight.

chapter 14

"You built this dam?" Enrique asked Michelle as they left the pyramid and walked along the stream.

Michelle was proud of her achievement. "Yes," she said. They sat down beside the little lake a few feet from the dam. Enrique glanced at her with those dark eyes of his and smiled. She returned his smile bashfully, captivated by his presence. Ever since he had appeared ten minutes ago, she felt an excitement in her body. Enrique was obviously interested in her.

"You do everything so well," he said. "Did you help row over here?"

"No, Magdalena did all the—"

She stopped, but it was too late.

"Magdalena?" he said, a sudden anger flaring in his voice.

"I meant Daddy—"

"Magdalena brought you over, I should have guessed!" He turned to the three Indians and shouted to them in Quitapul. They jumped up, one of them running back up the trail to the east, the other two heading up the trail Magdalena had taken back to the cayuco. Enrique jumped to his feet.

"Wait!" she shouted at him. "Call them back. Don't!"

But it was too late to stop anything now. Enrique went

running across the meadow, his feet splashing in the flooded water, and then headed up the trail to the west.

"What's happening?" Christopher called down from the temple.

"They're going after Magdalena!"

"Goddamnit!" he muttered, and started hurrying down. Michelle stood up, panicked, guilty, helpless. When Chris came running over to her, she couldn't meet his eyes. "It just slipped out," she stammered." I knew not to say anything about her, but I was talking about coming across in the cayuco and—"

"Stay here," he ordered, and went running up the trail after Enrique, the adrenaline pumping through his system giving him renewed strength for the chase.

He was halfway up the trail when a shot rang out, crashing at his eardrums. In his imagination, Chris saw Magdalena slump in the cayuco, blood spattering, Enrique standing with his rifle watching his sister dying out in the lake, finally eliminated from the Quitapul march toward destiny.

He started running again, up and over the ridge, down the overgrown trail, and at last out into the clearing. Enrique was running toward him. Way out on the lake was Magdalena in the cayuco. Still rowing, not shot, alive!

"Come on, come with me, hurry," Enrique ordered, hot with anger, wet with perspiration.

The other Indians were coming at a dead run. Chris hesitated. The barrel of Enrique's rifle jabbed into his ribs. He glared at the enraged man, but saw instantly that Enrique was crazed with anger, that he might even shoot if crossed. Chris started running back up the trail, with Enrique ahead and the three other Indians behind.

Ten minutes later they were in the clearing of the temples; Michelle was roughly ordered to join them; then they were heading for the boat on the other side of the island. Chris's chest was pounding, his boots hurting from the running. But the manic pace didn't cease—Enrique was clearly after his sister with a vengeance. Chris thought of falling, of faking a sprained ankle so that he could slow down the Indians. But he felt that he might just be left behind, and he wanted to be on the scene when Enrique caught up with Magdalena.

Minutes later, they were at the boat. Enrique roughly lifted Michelle inside, and then turned to Chris.

"Stop this, you're crazy!" Chris shouted at him.

"Get in! I should have known she was here when I noticed your ankle healed. Hop aboard!"

"You're going to shoot me if I don't?"

"I'll leave you here and return for you."

"Why did you shoot at her? All she did was row us over."

"Get in!"

Chris stared him down, man to man, holding his own against the hot-tempered Indian. Enrique broke the stare and jumped aboard, ready to leave Chris behind. Chris jumped in behind him and sat down beside Michelle, as the engine coughed and started, and they headed away from shore.

"I'm sorry," she cried. "I didn't mean to."

"It's okay, don't worry."

"What's he going to do? He's acting crazy; why's he so upset?" she asked.

They were zooming around the tip of the island. Chris stood up and walked to the front of the half-enclosed cabin. The Xocomil was just starting to blow, and choppy waves slapped against the hull of the boat. Chris stood beside Enrique while the Indian steered directly toward Magdalena in her tiny cayuco.

"Why don't you leave her alone?" Chris shouted over the noise of the engine.

When Enrique didn't respond, he grabbed at his arm. A rifle barrel poked into his back. He backed off, stood silently watching the cayuco getting closer and closer as the speedboat raced toward it across the lake. Enrique

193

held his bearing for a collision, then at the last moment veered off to the right, missing the cayuco by only a few feet. He spun around in a sharp turn and headed back, cutting the engine and coming broadside against the canoe, bumping it roughly.

Magdalena sat impassively, staring with disdain at her brother. Enrique blurted out a challenge to her in Quitapul. She responded in a voice that was superior, powerful, regal. When Enrique shouted back at her, his voice was cracking, angry, somehow losing power.

She started rowing away. He shouted at her but she ignored him completely. He shouted again, then raised his rifle and fired before Chris could jump to stop him.

The resonating boom made Chris's knees go weak. But as he watched, Magdalena continued to row, unhurt. Enrique had aimed at the rear of her cayuco, blowing a hole in the wood into which water was rushing.

Enrique worked the lever of the .30/.30 and threw another cartridge into the firing chamber. Chris made a move toward him and felt the rifle barrel behind him jab at his ribs again. Another shot from Enrique's gun and the entire back end of the cayuco was shattered. Water flooded the small boat and Magdalena stood up, slipped off her pants, and dove into the water.

Michelle, numbed by the rifle discharges, stood up. Enrique aimed at the water ahead of Magdalena and fired. Michelle ran at Enrique and grabbed his rifle from his hands, catching both him and the three guards completely by surprise. She threw the rifle overboard. Enrique raised his hand to hit her, but stopped himself. Chris lunged at him but two of the guards grabbed his arms from behind and pinned him.

The laugh that came out of Enrique's mouth was coarse, harsh.

"Go pick her up, damn you!" Michelle shouted at him.

The third Indian had his rifle aimed at Michelle's back; Enrique waved it away. "She deserves to swim," he said with a snarl. "She deserves much worse."

194

"Give her a ride to shore, it's over half a mile, she—"

"She could swim across this lake if she needed to. She broke the rules. Let her swim."

"You're horrible," Michelle scowled.

"I am only doing my duty. That woman, she is evil."

"No she isn't!"

"You are an ignorant girl, you know nothing."

"I know more than you think," Michelle fired back at him.

"Then you should have known better than to have gone to the island with a woman who works for the Devil."

"Cut the bullshit," Chris put in. "If you're not going to give her a ride, take us back to the house right now."

"No, Ricardo wants to see you," Enrique said, and gestured for the Indians to release Chris.

"You're a bigger idiot than I thought," he muttered.

Enrique met his stare for a moment, but then looked away, at Magdalena, as he started the engine, pushed the forward lever, and gunned the engine into action.

Chris and Michelle sat down without speaking. A tense silence matched the high whine of the inboard as it cut through the early roughness of the Xocomil. Chris tried to regain some sanity, some perspective on what had happened. No one had been hurt. Enrique hadn't done anything but scare his sister; he seemed afraid actually to harm her in spite of his hatred for her.

Michelle sat holding her daypack tightly in her lap. "Daddy, are we in trouble?"

"No," he said.

"He was horrible to treat his sister that way! He thinks he's so tough, with his guns and these bullies of his."

"He's a real punk."

"Will we have to leave now?"

Chris thought a moment, trying to integrate the deep contact he had made with Caban on the temple with this sudden eruption of violence. "I don't know," he said. "Do you want to?"

"No."

"This place is getting too dangerous for us. We really should leave tomorrow and go back to Panahachel."

Michelle gazed at him and suddenly her eyes fused to a common focus. Chris felt his stomach contract, the same way it did when Magdalena looked at him like that.

"Your eyes," he said.

"I know. It happens sometimes. Daddy, I don't want to leave. Magdalena needs us."

"It's too dangerous for you around here."

"That doesn't matter."

"We're not responsible for her. She can leave if she wants to," he said.

"Daddy, I can feel it. We should stay here. Please?"

"We'll see."

The half-finished resort, with its stone walls incomplete and its roof mostly missing, looked like a ruin as the boat approached it. When Enrique cut the engine at the dock, the sound of hammers and chisels splitting stone rang out. Chris jumped onto the dock and strode down its length to the shore, where Ricardo was walking quickly to meet him. He approached Chris with a relaxed, welcoming smile, his hand outstretched in greeting.

"There you are," he said when he was ten feet from Chris, with Enrique close on Chris's heels.

"They were over at the island," Enrique put in, "with Magdalena."

"This idiot of a son of yours almost killed her," Chris said hotly, not accepting Ricardo's hand. "You should train him a little better before you let him go around with a loaded gun."

"You haven't been seeing that daughter of mine again, after all I told you about her, have you?" Ricardo countered.

"It's a free world," Chris said.

"So where is she now?"

Michelle arrived. "He made her swim to shore; he sank her cayuco!" she said hotly.

"Well then. It's been quite a morning. Anyone hungry?"

"What do you want with us?" Chris asked. "We want to go back to the house."

"I'm sorry, it's been an upsetting time," he said, and then turned to Enrique. "It sounds like you've been a little overzealous again. Damn it! Wipe that grin off your face. Get over to the north quad and check on the work in number eleven."

Enrique sulked away.

"You'll have to forgive him if he gets a touch feisty. It's just the way he is," Ricardo said to Chris.

"Well, it was too much. He has no right to go around playing tough like that."

"You have no right to trespass and violate his tribal rules, remember that. *You* caused the problem."

"There wasn't any problem until he arrived," Chris argued.

"Well, come inside and at least have a tour of the resort while you're here. Your ankle seems to have gotten better awfully fast."

"It has," Chris said.

Ricardo raised his eyebrows inquiringly, but said nothing. He turned to lead them up the steps of the front lawns to the resort. He seemed calm on the surface, maintaining his control, but underneath, Chris could tell, he was fuming at the incident, and afraid even to consider the healing of Chris's ankle. "So is everything going fine over at the house?" he asked. "I assume this is your daughter."

"Oh, I guess you didn't get introduced. Michelle, this is Ricardo."

"Hello," she said, still tense.

"Please, let's relax. I'm very sorry about Enrique; I assure you it won't happen again. But do promise not to go against the tribal laws, then everything will go much better all around. The times are touchy here these days, as you know. Enrique is hardly himself. He spends most of his time recently in tribal meetings with the Quitapul priests; it's going to his head a little, I'm afraid. But it will blow over in a few days."

"Blow over or explode," Chris said.

"Now, I hope you're not listening seriously to either Magdalena or Enrique when it comes to Ilum K'inal. They both have too much Quitapul blood in them; they believe fairy tales as if they were real."

"Who's to say what's real?" Chris said, starting to relax but still edgy.

"Indeed," Ricardo said, smiling at Michelle who was walking silently beside her father. "Well—let's agree to look at this as past history. You see that main room up ahead to the right? That's going to be the ballroom. And up to the left on the second floor, the luxury suites overlooking the lake and the volcano."

"Very impressive," Chris said. "Must be costing you a pretty penny to build this."

"Actually, it's going up quite reasonably. And I have investors. Money is no problem."

"And when the tunnel opens up and you have all that treasure, you'll have no problems at all," Chris put in.

"Ah yes," Ricardo said patiently. "The treasure. The Indians have dreamed of their lost treasure so long, they actually seem to believe a miracle will happen this Easter. Well, I for one don't believe in it. Mind you, I'm certainly not going to *refuse* to believe if I see that tunnel open with my own two eyes. But you see, these Indians are so childlike. And anything my daughter has told you, you'd do best to treat as delusions of grandeur. I don't like to say it, but she's been diagnosed as psychotic—she's had a problem for years, and from what I hear, I'm afraid it's getting worse. A tragedy."

"I don't think there's anything wrong with her," Michelle said hotly. "It's Enrique who has something wrong with him."

"Indians," Ricardo said. "They're different from us.

198

There's no denying that. In any case, what do you think of the construction?"

"Excellent masonry," Chris admitted, looking around as they entered a massive ballroom, the two-story roof still not on but the stone walls nearly complete. There were at least twenty Indians working at once, carrying rock to the work sites, chiseling stone, placing the finished pieces in their proper niches. The workers stared at Chris with curiosity and at his beautiful blonde daughter in awe, with an edge of sexual excitement that bothered him.

"How is your article coming along?" Ricardo asked.

"I'm just waiting to see what happens at Ilum K'inal," Chris replied, "to see if the tunnel opens up, you know."

"Well, I hope you aren't holding your breath. The Indians are all worked up about it in town, but if nothing happens, it will be just as well."

They walked through the ballroom and on into smaller rooms, with piles of rubble in corners and paths through the masoners' work areas. "If it actually does happen," Chris went on, "won't that give you a lot of headaches? I mean, if that gold really is down there, it's going to be a gigantic security problem for you in a few days."

"If in fact the Quitapul are right and I'm wrong, I assure you we're prepared to handle anything."

"Oh?"

"In here," Ricardo said, leading the way through a massive inner doorway, "is where we will store the treasure if it does come our way. This is Enrique's room."

Chris and Michelle followed Ricardo into a circular, domed room, with impeccable masonry work. The ceiling rose to twenty feet in the center of the dome; directly below the center was an altar similar to that up on the temple at the island. Two kerosene lamps lit the room with an eerie yellow glow.

"What the hell's this place?" Chris asked, briefly startled at the way his voice echoed in the room. He glanced around at the carpets on the floor, a table with various herbs and gourds on the other side of the altar.

"Enrique wanted his own ceremonial room, so I said sure, why not?" Ricardo said lightly.

"What kind of ceremonies?" Chris asked.

"You know, Quitapul rites. And ceremonies of protection. He performed one for you, for instance, to safeguard you during your stay."

Michelle walked up to the altar, touched the cold stone tentatively. She could feel an energy in the room which struck her powerfully, as if it were a magic place. "Do you kill chickens here?" she asked.

He looked at her, gazing at the full length of her body with appreciation. In the cold, tomblike room, Michelle felt his eyes and a chill ran through her body, half of revulsion, half somehow of satisfaction. "You'll have to talk with Enrique about what he does. I stay clear of this room when he and his tribal priests are doing their voodoo in here."

The two men continued talking and drifted out of the room. Michelle lingered, feeling a sense of power, an attraction to the room which was almost physical, that started as an urge to masturbate and then radiated through her body as an aching for some kind of greater release.

She walked over to the altar again and touched it with the palm of her left hand. The stone seemed hot. And at the same time she felt faint. Her eyes went out of focus, her skin became sweaty. She thought of the phallic stone. She wanted to take it out of her daypack, to feel it, to play with it.

Ricardo and Chris were gone, their voices slight echoes some distance away. Alone in the ceremonial room, Michelle gave in to her desire to lie down on the altar, just to see what it felt like. She had experienced the same desire up on the temple with Enrique, but of course had not yielded to it in his presence.

She listened. There was no one nearby. She couldn't even hear Ricardo and Chris; they must have gone outside the building. She took off her daypack, placed it carefully beside the altar, then jumped up onto the stone slab.

Lying there, letting her eyes go out of focus as she looked up at the domed ceiling, she felt a sudden sense of peace flood over her.

Suddenly she became aware of him, standing just outside the range of her vision. Her hands froze, and she twisted her head to look. Enrique was standing watching, backlighted by the lamps so that she couldn't make out his expression.

He took two steps toward her and stood beside the altar. Michelle felt a wave of energy emanating from him, pulling him toward her. Nothing was said. Her face flushed with something beyond embarrassment. He was standing over her now, his breathing loud in the room. Dreams flooded her, exquisite sensations of yielding, giving herself to this man, letting him—.

"There you are!"

Her father's voice. Boots tramping loudly across the stone floor. Michelle pulled her hands out of her pants. Oh God, she thought, we're caught!

Chris was aghast at finding his daughter on the altar, her hands in her jeans in an obviously erotic gesture, Enrique standing ready to join in. Emotions shook Chris's body, a flush of red anger came over him; without thinking he took a swing at Enrique and hit him squarely on the chin, knocking him away from the altar. As Michelle sat up, he gave her a loud slap across the cheek.

"What the hell's going on here?" he growled.

He yanked her off the altar. Enrique was getting to his feet. Chris was so angry that he would have hit him again if Ricardo hadn't appeared.

"What's the matter?" Ricardo asked, his mature presence helping to relax the tension.

"Ask your idiot son here!" Chris shouted, and then pulled Michelle out of the room.

"I'm sorry, Daddy."

"You'd better be."

"I don't know what came over me."

"That goddamned Indian is what came over you!" he said, and headed across the ballroom and out of the building.

A few minutes later, Ricardo and Enrique came walking down to the boat dock where Chris and Michelle were waiting. The Xocomil was picking up and it was past time to be headed back to the house. Ricardo came up to the Americans, but Enrique sulked a few feet away.

"I'm sorry about the upset. Enrique certainly didn't mean any harm," Ricardo said, turning to his son as if giving him a cue.

"I'm sorry," Enrique muttered flatly.

"Take us back to the house, okay?" Chris asked. "This whole day's screwed up."

"Of course. I'll take you myself," Ricardo said smoothly. "Oh, but there is one thing," he added. Turning to Enrique, he gave him a Quitapul order; Enrique hurried off. "I can't have Magdalena over on my property bothering you any more, so I'm going to assign a man to stay in the outbuilding beyond the avocado orchard from now on for your protection. There's no telling what Magdalena might do next. She's out to interfere both with the resort here and with Enrique's plans for Ilum K'inal. We can't be too careful; she's about crazy these days."

"I don't want any guard around the house," Chris said.

"I must insist."

"Then we won't stay there."

"I'm afraid," Ricardo said slowly and firmly, "that a change in plans right now would not be possible."

"Then I'll leave tomorrow, for Panahachel," Chris said uneasily.

"But you must stay for the holidays."

"I don't have to do *anything*," Chris said. "Now—"

"Please, I have enough problems right now—I can't send my boat to Panahachel tomorrow. Don't run away; we need a journalist here to report if anything in fact does happen on Ilum K'inal. You're my guests. Don't leave just because my daughter has frightened you."

"She hasn't frightened me," Chris retorted.

"Seduced you, then."

"She hasn't done anything."

"Well I intend to keep it that way. Benito will stay in the back house, you won't even know he's there. This is how it must be. I insist."

Chris hesitated a moment, and then agreed. It was clear enough from Ricardo's manner that he considered it a settled issue; Chris shied away from dwelling on what might happen if he persisted in wanting to leave. Ricardo chose to keep him and Michelle here, and that, it seemed, was that.

But why?

chapter 15

Benito was actually a friendly, companionable Indian. On the boat ride over to the house, Chris met his eyes several times, and felt a definite flow of goodwill from the man. He was about forty, small but siney, with close-cropped black hair and a wide, sincere face. The rifle that rested in his lap seemed out of place.

Ricardo brought the boat professionally up to the dock. "Please," he said as Chris and Michelle stepped out, "don't let all this ruin your stay here. I'm sorry that Magdalena's antics are getting in the way of your vacation. I want the next few days before Easter to be happy, relaxed ones for you, and I'm sure they will be. We have everything under control. Father Morales is working with the Indians and assures me that there will be no more problems. So enjoy yourselves."

Chris stared down at the aging powerhouse of a man, wondering if his impression that Ricardo was deliberately preventing their departure for some reason of his own was in fact correct. His concern now did seem genuine. Maybe it was just that he would consider it bad luck if the first two guests at his resort, even before its official opening, went away unhappy. "Okay," he said, "but I want to talk to Magdalena again."

Ricardo sighed. "Not a good idea, not at all."

"I mean it. Either you arrange for her to come here by tomorrow morning, or I go looking for her. Benito'll be on hand to see that she doesn't do us or your property any harm, if that's what you're afraid of."

Ricardo scowled, then forced a smile. "I'll see what I can do. I can see that a journalist has to get a lot of local color for a piece like you're writing, and I'll admit Magdalena's colorful, whatever else she is. Peace to you both!"

The boat zoomed away from the dock, and Benito retired to the outbuilding beyond the avocado orchard, out of sight of the house.

The wind blew strong all afternoon. Chris and Michelle sat inside and sipped hot drinks. Silence seemed to suit the mood of the day, after all the crazy developments of the morning. Michelle sat with a novel in her lap, half-lost in drifting romantic images and blank spaces of pure physical sensations. The early morning trip to the island seemed like a dream, hardly reality at all. All she wanted to remember was the expansive lightness she had felt after being on the temple with Magdalena, and the moments of mounting bliss on the altar in the dome room with Enrique. There was another memory which gave her a good feeling inside, as she remembered jumping up and grabbing Enrique's rifle from him and putting him in his place. Somehow they were equal now; she wasn't afraid of him —there were doors ajar that she hoped would continue to open wider.

No clouds came this afternoon; the sun remained bright and the air warm and scented. Around four o'clock, Benito knocked on the front door, announcing the man who brought provisions along the trail from town. He had fresh fish and vegetables, cheese and eggs. Michelle took over in the kitchen, eager to cook up a meal. Chris, still mulling over the happenings of the last twenty-four hours, returned to the living room with a glass of cream sherry, sipping the sweet wine and trying to detach himself enough from the actual events to gain a reasonable perspective on them. Still, Magdalena continued to intrude into his thoughts as an emotional force which dominated his mind and increased his desire to see her again.

When he rejoined Michelle in the kitchen, she had the fish breaded and ready to be cooked. A quiche dish was cooking in the oven, and water was boiling for the vegetables. Chris stood behind her and put his arms softly around her waist. "How's it coming, kiddo?"

She leaned back against his chest, and he brought his chin down to touch the top of her head. "Fifteen minutes," she said, "and counting."

"Smells terrific."

"I'm really sorry about what happened," she said.

"To Magdalena?"

"No, I meant at the resort."

"Oh."

"Did you hurt your hand when you hit him?"

"No, not much. How's your cheek?"

She turned around in his arms and held him close to her. "This morning was weird," she whispered, her head turned sideways against his chest, listening to his heart beat.

"Guatemala seems to be like that. A totally different world from up north."

"Do you think she'll sneak over here tonight?" she asked.

"Magdalena? I don't know."

"Do you want her to?"

"I'm not sure what I want."

Michelle stood back from him, her arms still around him but the top of her body arched backward. "Do you really think people can sell their souls to the Devil?" she asked.

"Of course not. There isn't any Devil in the first place."

"I think there is."

"Come on now."

"I feel forces, Daddy. What made me do what I was doing in the dome room? I felt something taking me over."

Chris met her stare. She had her glasses on and both her eyes were looking at him, searching his eyes for an

207

answer now that more memories of the day were coming to her, foggy memories of being on the temple with Magdalena, of seeing her face set against the volcano's heights.

"I think that what you felt was sexual energy," Chris said tentatively. "I mean, you're growing up; you're feeling all that wild rush of creative energy that comes with maturity. Down here, those feelings might get all caught up in the Quitapul energies. They seem to be kind of perverted deep down, you know. Sacrificing virgins and all that junk."

"It's not junk."

"Well whatever it is, it's not right. If there is a Devil, he was behind that kind of atrocity. But I think that the best thing for us to do is just relax, enjoy ourselves like Ricardo suggested, and have a good holiday."

"Are you hungry?"

"Starving," he said. "Need any help?"

"You could set the table, and uncork a bottle of wine," she said, returning his smile.

They sat out on the veranda eating dinner. The wind was gone, the stars out, the moon not yet up. They couldn't see the little one-room house where Benito was, but they could feel his presence. Chris half-expected Magdalena to come to them in spite of the guard. But dinner was finished, the wine bottle nearly empty, and still no magical bruja appeared.

Michelle was secretly relieved. The presence of the jade phallus in her bedroom made her uncomfortable about the thought of meeting Magdalena. The woman was too dominating—Michelle felt it would be fine with her if she never saw Magdalena again. But when she thought of the bruja's brother, she was aware of other feelings. There was something about him, regardless of his brutish behavior—perhaps even partly because of it—that made him immensely attractive to her, on levels which she didn't understand at all but which she wanted to find out more about.

When dinner was over, Michelle made coffee while

Chris washed the dishes. He watched the coffee dripping down through the cloth filter and remembered Magdalena making him coffee last night, telling him she needed his help, healing his ankle. And there had been that strong vision he had experienced, of the tunnel opening up. Something was starting to gel in his mind; he was beginning to grasp something that had eluded him for years.

They went into the living room with their cups of coffee and sat together on the wicker sofa that faced the large picture window overlooking the lake. The moon was showing itself as an orange glow along the horizon. It slowly rose into full view, hovering large over the water, sending a rippling reflection up to the boat dock from far across the water.

"This is paradise," Michelle whispered. "I feel so peaceful suddenly."

"Yeah," Chris replied softly.

"It's as if time doesn't matter anymore."

"I know what you mean."

"I feel like I can be myself down here, Daddy."

"Me too."

"But it's horrible, that man with his gun out there."

"Don't worry, Magdalena's too smart to get caught."

"And she has powers," Michelle said. "She could put a spell on him. She could put a spell on all of us."

"Why do you say that?"

"Do you feel under a spell, Daddy?"

"That's a good question."

"Well, do you?"

He met her stare. "I'll tell you something," he said. "I'm beginning to think I've been under a spell all my life, and I'm finally getting clear of it. I'm finally seeing things the way they really are."

"And how is that, tell me."

"Well—when I was your age, I really felt that there was something real behind all the myths, the spiritual beliefs. My dreams, they were as real as waking reality, you know. That's why I started smoking grass, and got into taking psychedelics for a while. There was something more real there than the world I was supposed to grow up into. And when I started studying anthropology and mythology, it all seemed to make sense. The primitives were in touch with a reality that we had lost, that the scientific age had tried to destroy."

"I feel that too, Daddy."

"But every direction I turned, all the gurus and all the psychedelics and all the books—and the hopes failed me. Your mom was just dipping her toes into the psychedelic revolution when we got together. She got pregnant. We got married. And something happened."

"I know, I came along and ruined your life."

"Don't say that! You know that isn't true. But in taking on a family, I thought I had to let go of other things. I tried to. But I just couldn't.

"Well I'm glad," she said. "You and Mommy, you're so different; you're two opposite extremes."

"So now, I've given into the pull to drop teaching and take off to Guatemala. Just for the hell of it. But you know, there's something happening down here. And I can't help it, I feel involved. I can close my eyes and see Magdalena; it's as if she's always with me."

"It's weird, but I feel that too!" Michelle exclaimed. "She's scary."

"I think she's so real it's hard for us to see her at all," Chris said.

The moon was higher in the sky, obliterating all but the strongest stars. The conversation dwindled into silence; the mood was quiet. Michelle felt sleepy, and curled up on her side of the sofa with Chris's lap as a pillow. He stared into the moonlight. Time passed; Michelle snoozed off. The moon rose higher. Chris sat without thinking, lost in a meditative trance.

Michelle stirred and Chris looked down at her. The expression on her face was contorted, her breathing agitated in her sleep. He could see her eyes moving rapidly under her lids, indicating that a dream was going on.

"Ah," she said in a guttural tone.

"Hey, what's going on?" Chris asked her.

"Aghh!"

Chris hesitated. He recalled hypnosis work he had done in dream therapy classes, and knew how to go ahead with Michelle now, if he wanted to. But did he have the right to do such a thing to his daughter?

He put aside the shamed sense that he was overpowered by his need to see Magdalena through Michelle's eyes, and told himself that the dream might be the key to the disturbing influences she had been feeling all day. "Tell me, you can talk while you dream, tell me what's happening," he whispered intently. "What do you see?"

"She's in a small hut," Michelle whispered. "There is a pool of water in the hut. And—steam, hot steam, coming out of the mountain. She's alone. Naked, sweating. There is, there is—aghh!"

"What?"

Michelle's eye lids were tightly shut, her breath halting. "She's staring at me, she's grinning at me!"

"Who is?"

"Magdalena! She's laughing, she's—she's turning into the Devil, oh God! Her face, it's horrible, she's laughing like the Devil, like she's finally realized something, like she knows what she's doing."

"And what is that?"

"I don't know. But she's looking right at me, she's going to get me!"

"Don't be afraid; move with it," Chris said.

But Michelle's eyes were fluttering, opening. She gasped for air as if she had just surfaced from a deep dive. Her body was limp, her skin hot and clammy.

"Oh Daddy!" she cried out, and grabbed onto him while she sobbed against his chest.

Chris held her close. It seemed to him that somehow the dream was continuing within his own mind now. It had hit him directly, and he felt that he could almost contact Magdalena himself; he could see her naked body sit-

211

ting cross-legged on a pad of boughs in the little stone hut against a mountain. The steam was intense, billowing out from the cliff behind her that was the back of the hut. And she was looking right at him. But she wasn't the Devil, she was . . . some new god, he felt, some creature that was alive but somehow a mythical being at the same time, drawing him to her like a magnet, pulling him into the devastating ecstasy of a giant orgasmic energy pool . . .

"I feel it," Michelle cried out. "I feel it, she's got you under her spell, Daddy; she wants something, she wants to do something to us; it's horrible!"

Chris felt the vision slipping from him; he felt Magdalena's presence fading. Now he saw the moon above the lake. Michelle was curled up against him like a little child, her sobbing over, her body starting to recover from its dream attack. She took a deep shaking breath, and then exhaled, sitting up beside him, waking up completely. Her eyes stared out blankly to the lake, and for a few minutes they sat in silence.

"That was so strange," she finally said. "I hardly remember what happened; all my dreams, they come and then they disappear. But Daddy, why did she become the Devil. It scared me; I don't ever want to see her again!"

"In dreams, kiddo, anything can happen. It doesn't mean that she's the Devil; it means that you're projecting the Devil—something inside you that you don't admit to —onto her. Or something like that."

"I'm so sleepy."

"Why don't you go to bed? It's been a long day."

"Will you come in with me for a minute?"

"Sure."

They walked down the hallway and into her bedroom. She sat down on her bed and pulled the wipile up over her head, then stood up and slipped off her jeans and tennis shoes. Chris stood uncomfortably, again feeling the sexual energy rise inside him and threaten his identity as a father. She slipped into bed and he sat down beside her on the covers.

"How's your cut?" he asked.

She pulled the blankets down and showed him. He looked at her breasts. When he looked up into her face ... there was Magdalena! Smiling to him, there in the bed in place of Michelle, her body beckoning him to join her, her lips parted, waiting to be kissed. Chris felt himself yielding, bending over her, kissing her.

But when his lips touched Michelle's, they recognized his daughter; he caught himself before the kiss became passionate, and sat upright on the bed, gasping.

"Good night, Daddy. I'm so sleepy."

He pulled the blankets up over her breasts, kissed her on the forehead, and left the room.

She lay there for a few moments after the door closed. Her body was suddenly wide-awake. His kiss had felt ... as if he were Enrique. And although she was physically exhausted, something in her was alert.

She rolled her head and looked out the window. The moon was shining in, throwing a bright patch of light on the floor, illuminating her daypack. Her heart caught in her throat as she remembered the phallic piece. She waited, listening to make sure Chris wasn't returning. Then she slipped out of bed, padded barefoot across the tiles, and opened the pack. She took out the sweater and felt for the cold stone. Her fingers pulled back from its touch, then went in again, found it, grabbed it, and pulled it out into the open.

In bed again, she held the phallus in her hand on her stomach while she lay on her back. She found herself remembering Barry, then forgetting about him entirely as she felt the weight of the stone against her. She ran her fingertip along the long smooth surface, up to the tip, thinking of sperm, of God's sperm, entering the Virgin Mary.

In her grip, the jade seemed to turn soft; she thought of the phallus ejaculating God's sperm. Or was it the Devil's? She froze, her fingers pulling away from the jade. The heavy phallus rested on her stomach, nestled in her

213

pubic hair and reaching up to her navel. Radiant energy seemed to be coming from the jade, penetrating her, vibrating her pelvic bone, stimulating her clitoris, sending shock waves through her uterus. She felt a sudden, sharp pang, as she had on the plane and on her first trip across the lake. She sensed dimly that those pains had not been forecasting her period—they had been a signal, a greeting and a warning. And whatever had sent that signal to her womb was closer, stronger . . .

She felt pinned down by the phallus, unable to move. What if this was the Devil's penis? Suddenly she couldn't tell if it was outside resting on her body, or inside her vagina. Her consciousness was fading; she was drifting away, falling asleep, the jade absorbing the warmth of her body, becoming the same temperature, rising and falling as she breathed.

chapter 16

Chris returned to the living room. The moon was high in the eastern sky. His mind was buzzing with confused thoughts. What was Magdalena doing, anyway? Had she caused him to mistake her for Michelle just then, or was it all his own mind's doing?

His ears picked up the night sounds outside. Crickets chirping their monotone mantras; an owl hooting with the same hoot as barn owls in California; and that strange eerie whistle of some night bird that started out low and then slid up high in pitch, like the first part of an appreciative male whistle, but missing the final downward ending.

What must Magdalena have been like, as a girl? he wondered. With her crossed eyes, and being half-gringo, she must have had a hard time of it, being set apart from all the other kids. A heavy cross to bear.

Tomorrow would be Good Friday. Easter was already almost here. Jesus trudging his way up to the top of the hill, expecting God to save him at the last moment, expecting his Father to miraculously turn the death scene into the day of transcendence. But no, no miracle for Jesus. He had hung up on the cross waiting for the great occult flash of salvation from mortality. Finally he had given up. Father, Father, why hast thou forsaken me?

Goddamnit, I'm dying up here, save me! And the Roman had come over with his sword and stabbed the sacrificial lamb in the heart with a swift jab through the ribs.

And all these half-starving Indians, waiting for the miracle to come to their town, waiting for Easter when the tunnel would open up, when their variation on the tomb scene would happen, an angel opening up the tunnel. Would there be any angel? Was that who they expected Magdalena to be? Where was the truth in it all? The Christian myth was like any other primitive tale, except that it was too close to home for people to look at clearly.

But that wasn't true, Chris thought. The Christian myth had transformed the Old Testament and Greek myths, adding new dimensions to human consciousness. And perhaps that was what was happening here in this primitive tribe, perhaps there was some new myth being born.

He was growing sleepy at last. There was still no sign of Magdalena. He realized he had been listening with part of his mind alert for sounds outside—but listening more with dread for the sound of a rifle shot than for soft footsteps. But surely, if Magdalena had the power to heal a sprained ankle, she could protect herself if she wanted to. Chris wondered what the true extent of her powers was. Even Jesus had possessed limited powers, or at least had chosen not to use any greater ones he might have had.

Chris stood up and walked down the hallway to check on Michelle. She was sleeping like a baby, curled up in the fetal position. He looked down at her face, wondered what she was dreaming now. His little girl, almost grown up, but still needing his protection. He stood over her, waiting to see if that weird hallucination of Magdalena would occur again; he wanted to be ready for it this time, to see what it really was. But nothing happened, and he walked quietly out and shut the door.

He wasn't feeling sleepy anymore, and walked outside through his bedroom onto the side patio that faced the avocado orchard. The moon was bright on his face; he could feel its power. Everything down here seemed to have power, he reflected. Was he just starting to take on the superstitions of the Indians, or was it true, was the planet and all its surface manifestations really caught up in the world of the gods?

He walked down through the grove of avocados, through the haunting shadows created by the giant branches and the moon. He looked carefully in every direction, feeling that his vision was starting to play too many games with him, not wanting to be caught by surprise if another hallucination appeared. He knew what he was fearing: He was afraid that Magdalena would suddenly appear, and he wouldn't know if she was a vision or the real thing. Out here in the orchard, it was getting spooky. He decided to cut short his walk and—

"Freeze!" a deep voice ordered in Spanish, jolting Chris out of his thoughts. A man emerged from behind a tree trunk with a rifle, and Chris automatically raised his hands.

"It's you," the man said.

"Benito?"

"What are you doing out here?"

Chris let his hands come down. " You scared me," he said.

"It is dangerous, this time of night."

"I couldn't sleep."

"You should go back to bed," the Indian said, his voice softening, but still showing signs of nervousness and fatigue.

"You too."

"I have my job to do," he said.

Chris walked over to him, feeling a need for company. Perhaps he could relax the Indian, send him to sleep. "You are on the lookout for Magdalena," Chris said.

"Yes."

"Come on, let's go sit on the lawn; it's too dark here."

Benito hesitated, then accepted the offer. They walked out into the moonlight and sat on the stone wall that bordered the lawn where it dropped down to the beach.

217

"A beautiful night," Chris said after a moment's silence.

"Sí pues."

"You have a family back in town?"

"Por supuesto."

"Do you know Magdalena?"

"Sí pues."

"You are about her age."

"We went to school together until they sent her away."

"What was she like, as a little girl?" Chris asekd.

"She had the Devil in her, even then!"

"Why do you say that?"

"Everybody knew it."

"How could they tell?"

"Things she did."

"Like what?" Chris pressed him.

Benito pulled out a pack of cigarettes, offered Chris one, and lit up when Chris declined. He inhaled deeply and then blew the smoke out into the night air, in the direction of the ghostlike Caban over his left shoulder. "She put spells on people," he said.

"What kind of spells?"

"Sickness. Death. Many children died."

"Children die, Benito, with or without curses."

"No, she did these things; that is why they sent her away to Quetzaltenango to school. And there were other things."

"Tell me," Chris insisted.

Benito looked him in the eye. He had soft eyes, hardly the eyes of a killer he was meant to be if he caught Magdalena. But there was fear in them also as he thought of the bruja. "What is she to you?" he asked.

"I like her," Chris answered.

"She has put a spell on you. I will protect you from her."

"No, you don't understand. It's no spell. People can be attracted to people without it being a spell."

"Not to such as her. Anyone can tell that she is of the Devil except those under her spell—they cannot tell."

"You're wrong, Benito!"

"No, my friend, you are wrong. You don't know about her; you don't know what she does."

"Tell me."

"Shameful things."

"Like what?"

"She tried to seduce her brother," Benito said. "She tried to get him under her spell so he would do the work of the Devil also."

"Enrique?"

"She is an evil woman; if she wasn't the Special One, she would have been killed long ago, stoned to death as is the custom for people such as her, who turn against God and work for the Evil One. But no one could touch her; she was born the Special One."

"Well what if she shows up tonight?"

"Everything is different now," Benito said.

"How so?"

"Enrique has been fighting for years, trying to gain the powers of the Special One; they should be his. Since she is not fulfilling her role, Enrique is next in line, and we must have a Special One or the Ilum K'inal ceremonies will fail."

"What kind of ceremonies?"

"To regain the power of Caban!"

"So Enrique has gained the powers now, is that what you're saying?"

"Yes, it has happened."

"How can you be so sure?"

"It is what everyone talks about," Benito insisted.

"If Magdalena shows up, what are you going to do?"

"My orders are to shoot."

"Would you really do that?"

"My sister. She killed my sister!"

"How?"

"A curse!" Benito said, and stood up suddenly. "Listen, we talk too much. Go back to bed."

"You too."

"I stay up all night."

"She's not coming, anyway," Chris said.

"We will see."

"Would you like a little aguardiente?"

"No," Benito said, and walked away into the shadows.

Chris sat there, feeling tired, drained. The image of a little girl, cross-eyed and persecuted, came into his mind. She was running down a street with her arms up over her head, while other children ran after her, throwing stones.

Chris stood up and walked up into the house, bothered by the whiteness of the moonlight. Everything looked two-dimensional, flat, unreal, without depth or color. He poured himself a glass of cream sherry and drank it down like water, the sweetness satisfying him temporarily.

Michelle was still asleep. He kissed her on the cheek softly. "Good night, kiddo," he whispered, and then went to his own bedroom and undressed, crawling under the sheets.

He fell quickly asleep. The tension in his body started to ease. As he drifted off, the image of Magdalena was in his mind, and it was a soothing image, unthreatening, protective. He went deeply into blank sleep, and then slowly started to rise up into dreams.

He was sitting on the temple, with the first rays of sunlight striking him. There was a lush feeling in the air, a feeling of eternal spring. The energy of the sun entered his eyes, penetrated down to his heart, to his solar plexus, setting his entire body vibrating with ecstatic light.

He looked at Caban, then at the cliff in front of him to the east, then back to the sun. The ultimate god. The supreme male. The energy source. The closest physical manifestation of Itzam'na.

Something was happening with the volcano. Chris turned his head expecting to see smoke, or even lava flowing out from Caban. But instead, a gigantic jade penis was rising up into the morning sky, like the erection of a dog, a giant animal of some kind.

A strange wet sound struck his ears, and Chris turned

back to the cliff. It seemed to be transformed; the bushes and moss were pubic hair, and the cave was starting to open up in the pubic hair, a vagina beckoning him, parting for him like a woman, as though Magdalena had become the mountain and was opening up to him. He stood up and went running urgently down the temple toward the cliff.

He approached the cliff; he found the jade phallus in his hands, aimed at the opening. And as he entered the shadow of the cliff he felt the warmth of the insides of the volcano, the black heat of a woman. As soon as he pushed the phallus into the opening, his arms started to be sucked in also, and then his whole body, absorbed into the warm, slick interior of the volcano.

Blackness, slippery effortless movement down, down into the female insides of the volcano. "Caban, Caban!" Chris kept repeating, the name now sounding feminine to him.

Down deeper, infinitely deep, black, hot—but the blackness was becoming bright somehow, a black light emanating from the center of the volcano. And then there it was, the heart of Caban, radiating golden energy, alive somehow, pumping lava blood and pulling Chris closer and closer to it until he merged suddenly with a blinding flash of light, obliterated in a euphoric, orgasmic explosion.

Total weightlessness. Floating in the bliss of the female god. But now something else. Now a reversal of energy. A sense of being pushed out, a forced evacuation of the womb. Being sent out of the Garden, up through the tunnel, pressured outward until suddenly something gives way.

Blinding sunlight, the opposite of the light in the womb. Chris stands outside the tunnel, and it closes itself, becoming more and more solid, less and less feminine, turning back to stone. Chris walks through the sunlight, looking up at Caban, knowing now that Caban has a female heart hidden away.

And then nothing.

Another dream. A ground squirrel looking up, seeing a hawk ready to dive, diving now, hitting another squirrel from behind without warning, carrying it away. The squirrel still alive hides in his hole, in the darkness. But he knows he has to come out, to go on with his life, even though at any moment a hawk could catch him unaware and end his life with those deadly talons.

Running back outside in the sunlight. Wham! Hit from behind with a flash of white light, an explosion that obliterates the life center of the squirrel, liberates the life-force into its infinite potential.

And Chris, asleep, expanding infinitely, letting go. His heart glowing, gigantic, turning into a pulsing planet, spinning through black space, radiating energy like the sun, pumping life-force like the heart of the volcano.

Chris woke up. He was not sure if the light shining softly on the window curtain was the moon or dawn. As he watched, the light grew brighter. Another sunrise on planet Earth. He got out of bed, dressed, and went outside to watch. As the sun peeked up behind the far horizon across the still-sleeping lake, Chris smiled at himself. I'm a pagan at heart, he admitted, feeling flushed with adoration at the sunrise.

He turned around and stared up at the mist-enshrouded volcano. "And I know your secret," he said at Caban. "You're a tough male on the outside, but inside you're feminine, and so am I. It's the twist of the new reality. You and I are a hundred percent male. But at the same time, we're a hundred percent female. It's a two-hundred percent universe, and it's time people accept the fact. The either-or way of thinking is on its way out. There's got to be an alternative. Good or Evil, God or the Devil, live or die, on or off, up or down. There's got to be a third possibility, that's all I can say. Mind or genitals, reason or passion. There's got to be a merger or we're done for."

Caban, however, stared down at Chris without an ounce

of female softness or heart. He felt the power of the volcano as totally male, lacking an essential quality.

So that's it, he thought. That's what this is all about. Caban is out of touch with his heart; he's unbalanced. Going for power. That's what all the sacrifices of the Mayan were about—the heartless god needing human hearts; female hearts. Needing them desperately because it lacked its own. But goddamnit, Caban! You've got your heart down there, but you don't admit it to yourself. Because if you did that, if you got in touch with your heart, you'd have to give up your lust for power and dominion . . .

"Daddy, there you are!"

Michelle came running down the lawn, wearing her swim top and light gray cords, barefoot in the grassy dampness.

She sat down beside him on the stone wall, the sun now risen above the far mountains, radiating white-hot energy onto the Guatemalan world below.

"She didn't come, did she?" Michelle asked, her arm casually around him.

"Magdalena? No."

"Beautiful day," she said, taking a deep breath of fresh air. "How'd you sleep?"

"Lot of dreams," Chris said.

"Me too. Want some breakfast?"

"Sure, sounds good."

"I hope Enrique comes by."

"Oh?"

"He said he'd take me on a tour of the town."

"I don't know if that's safe. The town looks quiet enough, but there's all that stuff Ricardo was talking about."

"Well at least for a boat ride."

They walked up to the kitchen, squeezed fresh orange juice, cut open a beautiful papaya, and put on some oats for hot cereal.

"Listen, do you hear that?" Michelle said.

223

Chris cocked his ear. "Yes. Speedboat. How'd you know he was coming?" he said. "You psychic these days?"

"Of course," she said, smiling.

"Well I'm not going to have you going off with that madman."

"Come on, Daddy, just for a little fun." She jumped up. "I'll go wave him down at least," she said, and went running out of the house.

Chris sat with his breakfast and his uneasiness about Enrique. But the morning felt empty of negative energy; his dreams seemed to have purged him of the anxieties of the day before. Let the girl enjoy herself a little, he thought. This is what she came down for, to vacation and explore Guatemala. A visit to Zacapula would be all right; Chris would accompany them and see what was going on in the town as it prepared for Easter. After all, he was supposed to be writing an article on the celebrations.

Michelle ran across the lawn as the inboard came zooming across the smooth aquamarine surface of the lake, the sound of the engine cutting like a twentieth-century knife through the primitive silence of the morning. By the time the boat was at the dock, she was there to catch the line Enrique threw to her.

He stood in a blue windbreaker and form-fitting swimming trunks, smiling a broad grin. "Good morning, beautiful one!" he shouted to her, as full of the morning's energy as she was.

"I'm glad you came," she shouted back.

He cut the engine. "Would you like to go for a picnic?" he asked in his Mayan-accented English.

Michelle quickly glanced up to the house, spying her father at the kitchen window watching. Then she looked back to Enrique: "Yes, definitely. Where?"

"The island," he said.

"Oh?"

"Can you come?"

She went running up to ask Chris.

"Please," she pleaded with him a moment later. "It's perfectly safe."

"No, it's not a good idea." Chris resisted.

"We'll only be gone a couple of hours."

Enrique appeared in the doorway. Chris was struck by his casual, relaxed countenance, his gentlemanly stance. "May she come?" he asked politely, as if he had never had any conflict with Chris the day before. "I thought she might like to do some water skiing; I've brought the skis."

"Where are you planning on going?" Chris hesitated. Today, Enrique seemed very different from the gun-wielding berserker of yesterday—and, after all, he had not hurt Magdalena, had he? And that business in the ceremonial room at the resort . . . well, that had been Michelle's doing, really—at the most, Enrique had *looked* as if he might be reacting to it, as who wouldn't. Whatever had come over Michelle there, it might do her some good to get outdoors and indulge in some strenuous exercise; a good, fatiguing workout might leave her too tired for moods and fantasies.

"Just to the bay over at the island," he said. "For a couple of hours of sunbathing. There will be no problems."

"Well," Chris said. "As long as it's just a couple of hours. Do you have a life jacket for her?"

"Of course," Enrique replied.

"Okay then, but just for a couple of hours."

"Ricardo will be over to see you soon," Enrique said as he turned to leave with Michelle.

"Oh?" Chris asked. "Well, good. Have fun, Michelle."

"Thanks, Daddy. Don't worry, we'll be back soon, I promise."

"Do you want to ski over?" Enrique asked as they hurried side by side down the lawn.

"Oh, yes, that would be excellent."

At the dock she slipped down her cords while he stood

225

in the boat with the ski line in his hand, captivated by her unveiling. She glanced at the young man as she stepped out of her pants, saw the look in his eye, and smiled back. She knew that look; it marked a vulnerable spot that exposed a man, which gave her at least some control over him, some edge in the relationship that she could use to keep from being pushed around. He wanted her, that gave her the upper hand with him, and she was glad to have it. He excited her, but at the same time, she was a little scared to be going off with him.

"Which do you want, the doubles or the singles?" he asked.

"The single," she said. She had spent several summers at Lake Tahoe skiing, and felt sure of her ability.

He slipped the single ski onto the dock and she untied the boat, giving it a push away. This is more like a normal vacation, she thought. Like two vacations in one—skiing, and with a real Mayan. The day before had been so strange, she hoped that today would be more normal. She had awoken with that jade phallus in the bed with her, with no memory of how it had gotten there. Her memory was bothering her lately. Anyway, the phallus was hidden under her mattress, and today was going to be a day of fun, with Enrique to play with in the sun.

Chris stood at the window again, watching his beautiful little girl in her slight bikini jumping into the water from the pier with her ski, gasping at the coolness of the morning lake. Then she was ready, up, and away across the water. Chris felt like the lake, calm on the surface, but strangely dark and uncertain deep down, as if he expected a sea monster in his unconscious to surface suddenly and change the placid morning into another nightmarish Guatemalan day.

He made himself a cup of coffee and threw off his anxieties. Enrique was a strange character when he dealt with his native customs and problems, but until yesterday, he had been very helpful in getting Chris settled into the house, and in going to pick up Michelle with him. Forgive and forget, and hope that the rest of the vacation goes smoothly, he told himself.

Still, as he sat on the patio, watching Michelle make a final circle out in the lake and then head for the hidden cove over at the island, Chris found himself worrying. Michelle was so virginal in some ways, still a little girl; but he was sure she could handle herself, and Enrique knew that if he tried anything funny with her Chris would do him in. The day seemed so innocent, idyllic. But he knew what devious energies ran under the surface of this lake's serenity, and try as he might, he couldn't shake the subsurface sense of danger even in this most peaceful of situations. He would just have to wait impatiently until they came back.

Just as Michelle was disappearing into the cove, an outboard cayuco came putt-putting into view from Zacapula. Ricardo approached the dock with an air of casualness, tied up, and came walking up the lawn. Even he seemed more relaxed today than usual. As if the whole occult thing had blown over and everyone was friendly, content, happy.

Ricardo shook Chris's hand in greeting, his face clean-shaven and his hair blown by the boat trip. He was wearing Levi's, a red-and-white-striped cowboy shirt, and tennis shoes instead of his boots.

"Beautiful day!" he intoned in his booming voice.

"How about coffee?"

"Sounds great. Enrique come by?"

"He's off with Michelle. He'd better behave himself," Chris put in as they walked into the house together.

"Don't worry about the boy; basically he's a fine kid. It's just when he gets worked up about this Ilum K'inal thing that he gets out of hand."

"So how's Easter looking?"

"Perfect, everything's under control now."

"The tunnel going to open up?"

227

"Enrique thinks so. He's sure now that nothing can stop him."

They were in the kitchen, waiting for the water on the stove to heat up. "How can he be so sure?"

Ricardo eyed Chris with a stare that betrayed deep emotions. "Magdalena is out of the picture," he said.

"What?"

"She no longer threatens Ilum K'inal."

"Why, what happened?" Chris insisted, his blood pressure shooting up suddenly.

"We decided to act last night. We have her under arrest."

"What the hell for?"

"Various crimes. Father Morales invoked a church edict against the practice of witchcraft."

"Get serious."

"It is very serious," Ricardo said sincerely. "You seem to forget that she is my daughter. It has been extremely painful for me to see her humiliated before her people. But she could no longer be allowed to disturb the peace of the town."

"So you throw her in jail!"

"Christopher, it was the only way, I assure you. She had been captured by the Indian authorities while trying to cast a spell on several men, to get them to help her in her sabotage. She was brought before the tribal leaders on charges which wouldn't even make sense to you. She was accused of refusing to fulfill her ordained role as leader of the tribe this Ilum K'inal, and the sentence was death. We had to act to save her!"

"So where is she now; I want to see her."

"She's safe in the church prison room, under Father Morales' protection."

"Protection? It sounds more like the Inquisition to me. I wouldn't put it past Morales to put her to the stake as a witch."

"Personally, I don't trust the man either. But the guards

are my men. They obey me, not the padre. Don't worry, after Sunday it will be all over anyway; she will be tried and receive a short sentence and that'll be the end of it."

"I'll bet!"

chapter 17

The boat was a powerful one, and it pulled her almost effortlessly over the water. Michelle's legs felt the slight beat of tiny waves under the ski as she zoomed out to one side, the spray shooting up behind her like a translucent tail. She could see Enrique looking back at her regularly. Finally her legs were trembling from the skiing, and she signaled for him to head for the island.

He sped into the small bay. Michelle, skimming along the surface of the smooth lagoon, leaned to the left and cut toward the beach. She held the rope until she was close in and then let go, free-skiing the last thirty feet. Then with arms outstretched, she slowed down and sank in four feet of water, kicking off the ski and pushing it ahead of her as she swam to shore.

The boat came roaring up toward the beach. Enrique cut the engine and let it drift to shore, grating up onto the sand just enough to take hold. He stood in back, pulling in the towline. She waded over to him and gave the boat a final push to set it firmly on the beach.

Smiling up at him, she thanked him for the skiing. He looked down at her, his eyes taking in her strong, slender legs, half-submerged in the clear water, her tight, rounded belly above her bikini bottom, her blossoming breasts held in place with the twin terry-cloth cups.

"You ski with magnificence," he said.

She stared at him intently, searching for his deeper aspects. But she couldn't penetrate him. His eager grin seemed to be a façade, hiding something which he was determined she would not discover. She felt a twinge of apprehension, almost as if a memory, or a premonition, had risen close to the surface of her consciousness, only to sink from the weight of its . . . of its what? She couldn't focus clear on her intuitive flash. Frustrated, she turned and waded to shore, the tiny grains of quartz tingling against her feet.

He quickly followed her, carrying a sheet of foot-loomed Quitapul material and a basket of food. She was walking ahead up the beach with long, lazy steps, still puzzled by the vague anxiety evoked by looking into the Indian's dark, youthful, and somehow ominous eyes.

"How about here?" he said.

She turned around. "It doesn't matter to me."

He spread out the colorful sheet on the sand, just beyond the shade of a large, broad-leafed mango tree at the top of the beach. Michelle sat down and stared for a moment up the cliff, thinking about the jade phallus, remembering with a sudden clarity the previous morning when she arrived here with Magdalena. It seemed as though that whole episode had been a dream. But she had woken up with that phallus in bed with her this morning, warm and shocking to her, as if she had discovered the dismembered penis of a god, still rigid from who knew what superhuman desire.

She glanced across the lake to the volcano. She wished the house was visible from here. That would have made her feet more secure, here with this wild young man who ran around with armed guards and shot at his sister. But now, he was friendly, contained. As long as she kept up her defenses she would be okay, she concluded. She lay down on her back with her knees up, eyes closed to the morning sun.

Pulsing redness shot from her eyes up her optic nerves

232

into her brain, just as the science teacher had described it last week. Just a week ago, she thought, I was in class back in Mill Valley with my friends. If they could see me now, alone on this beautiful isolated beach with this beautiful, powerful Indian! This Indian who is also part American, although it hardly showed in anything but his command of English.

"A little wine?" he suggested.

She opened her eyes. He was working with a corkscrew at a bottle, and—pop!—off came the cork. He had two glasses on the material. "Very formal," Michelle said, feeling somehow manipulated, reaching for the wine.

He handed it to her, expecting her to inspect the label as his father's women often did. But instead, she took a long swig straight from the bottle, wiped her mouth with the back of her hand, and handed it back to him. "Pretty good stuff," she said. And it was. The taste was rich, authoritative, seeming to blend several different flavors smoothly, catching something of the glow of the sun in its ruby depths. Once or twice her father had had her to dinner and served a wine that came close to this, and she knew it was top quality. That was the trouble—it was a fine wine, for a special occasion. It seemed to her that it was best not to let Enrique make whatever impression he had meant to make, and to treat it as she would the jug stuff that was passed from hand to hand at a picnic back home.

"The best," he said, taken a little aback by her unceremonious guzzling. "Don't you want it in a glass, though?"

"No, it's better right out of the bottle; that's how we drink it back home. Would you do me a favor?"

"Of course."

"Would you get my pants out of the boat?"

"Your pants?"

"I've something in the pocket that I want."

"Certainly," he said, jumping up and running down to the beach. She watched his strong legs, his wide, muscular shoulders, his head of close-cropped black hair. He's a

233

big challenge, she thought. He's up to something, I can sense it. And I'm going to outsmart him, not give him a single chance to try anything with me. Funny, though, it's not like he wants to jump on me; he's not interested in me the way Barry is. But he definitely is after something.

Enrique came running back, his body athletic but somehow tight, too muscular for much flexibility, she thought. As if he's tensed against something all the time, ready to strike out, given the chance. She remembered him with his rifle yesterday morning. He had been crazy with anger, but controlled. That was it; he was exploding with anger inside, but he controlled that anger so that it was masked as a friendly, positive energy. But what was it, really? She felt that she wanted to find out, that he needed someone to help him with his feeling. It was so horrible, to be so turned against one's own sister. She must have done something very bad to him to make him hate her so.

Michelle let her corduroys rest in her lap while they drank more wine. The alcohol gave both of them a slight buzz. She found herself relaxing inside, letting the warmth of the sun stimulate her skin, letting the presence of this beautiful Indian beside her stimulate her also, flushing her body with luxuriant, catlike sensations. She lay on her back again and stretched, releasing a long, sensuous yawn. She could feel Enrique's eyes on her and she liked that. She felt that he would come under her power quickly, be eager to please her, willing to let himself be controlled in order to gain her acceptance.

"This is certainly paradise," she said.

"What were you doing over here with Magdalena yesterday?" he asked, his voice cautiously casual.

"Oh, Daddy was looking for some silly jade thing," she said without thinking. But when she glanced at him, he was looking back with intensity.

"Jade? Did he find it?"

"Uh, no."

"I knew that; I had a dream last night."

"Oh?"

234

"The jade piece Magdalena is searching for—I have known for weeks now that I had nothing to fear. My dreams assured me that it would come into my possession, that Caban would help me."

"What's so important about some jade piece; what is it anyway?"

"You do not know?"

"Daddy wouldn't tell me."

"The jade piece," he said, "is essential for the Ilum K'inal ceremonies. It is essential for the opening up of the tunnel. The greatest brujo for hundreds of years found it up on the volcano, and it was buried in his hut up there on the cliff. Magdalena tried to steal it, but Caban was watching. I was certain it would come to me effortlessly, and so it shall."

"How can you be so sure?" Michelle asked, feeling a tightness in her stomach.

"I have dreamed it! And my dreams, they come true. Always! I dreamed your father, and he came. I dreamed you, and you came."

"You're kidding," she said. But her interest was up. "Do you mean that?"

He looked at her, and for a moment the façade broke down, and she saw a frightened truth in his eyes. She saw something that made her shudder, as if she had found something as important to her as the jade piece was to him—some missing link in her psyche, some key to the strange experiences she was always having. Now Enrique turned away, avoiding her eyes. "It is true," he said. "And last night, Caban told me in a dream that the jade piece is safe and will be given to me by a friend, a very special friend, at the proper time."

"What does this jade piece look like, anyway?" she asked, afraid of the question but just adequately loosened by the alcohol to ask it.

"It is a stone with great power," he said.

"What kind of power?"

"Power from the gods. Masculine power."

"How big is it?"

"Oh," he said, and raised his two hands in the air six inches apart, "about this long."

"What is it, come on, tell me."

"You guess," he said.

"Okay," she answered, responding to the challenge, sitting up cross-legged and facing him where he was lying on his back. "It's six inches long. Is it narrow or thick? Give me a few clues."

"Narrow."

"Round or square?"

"Round."

"Huh," she said, glancing down at the man's hidden penis under his bathing suit, noticing its large bulge. "It's masculine, six inches long, round and narrow. Does it represent something physical?"

"Sí pues."

"Uh, a part of the human body perhaps?"

"Sí," he said, and she could see his penis getting slightly longer under the material of his bathing suit.

"And it's masculine."

"Definitely," he said, and a slight grin broke through his sober exterior, a boyish giggle that evoked one from Michelle too, as his penis grew even longer, almost frightening in its size, so much larger than Barry's.

"And does it serve some particular function?" she asked.

He glanced at her, caught her looking down at his penis, and met her eyes as they looked up to him. "A definite function, yes," he said.

"And does this function give a man pleasure, or is it simply performed as a matter of necessity?"

"Oh, pleasure. Pleasure," he said, his eyes closed again, his erect penis flat against his body, almost pushing its head up beyond the top of his elastic waistband. Michelle felt light-headed suddenly, daring, out of control. She reached forward and touched his erection with a finger, maintaining a slight pressure against the heated organ. "Could it just possibly be *this* particular part of the male body?" she said, her voice trembling slightly.

"You win the prize," he said, luxuriating at her touch.

"Well what are you going to do with a jade penis?"

She could feel him contract at the question. His penis started to lose its pulsing hardness, softening so that her finger could make a slight indentation in it. "We need it as part of the ceremony, that is all," he said, his voice flat, hard, defensive.

"Well you've got to tell me what you're going to do with it," she insisted. "Come on, don't be a spoilsport, Enrique. God, it isn't like I don't know what penises are for."

His eyes shot open with a flash of sudden anger and accusation. "What do you mean?"

She reacted, taking her finger from his wilting erection. "Nothing, I just mean that I'm old enough to know what penises are for, that's all."

He sat up with a sharp contraction of his stomach muscles. "Tell me something," he said. "I want to know the truth. Are you one of those girls who makes love with everybody?"

"No!"

"You're lying to me. I want to know. I don't care; I'm just curious. I want to know the truth, it is important."

"Well, I haven't done it."

"You American girls, you do it all the time."

"We do not!"

"I can tell, you've done it."

"No I haven't. And it's none of your business anyway."

"So you won't tell me the truth? Listen, you think I want to do it with you. But I am not that kind of man. Down here we have different standards; there is respect for girls."

"Well it's the same up north."

"So you haven't done it yet?"

She looked at him intently, gravely. "No," she said.

"Why haven't you?"

"Because—because I just haven't felt it was the right time—I haven't met the right boy—I don't know why, I just haven't."

"Well good," he said, and lay back down.

Michelle sat there a few moments, confused. The conversation had been in his control; she hadn't held her ground. And what bothered her most was that she couldn't understand what it was he was up to. These Indians, she thought. They're spooky. But to hell with it all, I'm going to just enjoy myself. I didn't come down here to be all confused and upset all the time.

She reached into her pants pocket and took out her small zip-purse. Inside it was her glasses case, and she removed them and put them away. Then she took out a booklet of matches and a hand-rolled joint. Striking a match, she lit up and inhaled, feeling her liberated eyes staring into different aspects of the sky overhead, her liberated brain moving into different aspects of the universe inside.

"What's that?" Enrique asked, opening his eyes at the pungent smell of the joint.

"Your turn to guess," she retorted.

"Marijuana."

"Home-grown in my home town. Here," she said, handing the joint to him.

He took it, inhaled the smoke expertly to test its quality, and then made an "Mmmmm" sound as he held his breath and handed the joint back to her. "Very good," he said, keeping most of his breath held in.

"Do people smoke it down here much?"

"Of course. The older people do not like it, but the brujos have used it forever. It is only now that many of the young people are smoking it, and not for the old reasons, either."

"What were the old reasons?"

"Spells."

"Really?"

"I have used it at times; it is very potent when combined with certain incantations."

"And what are the new reasons for smoking it?"

"It liberates you from the old ways; it lets you see everything differently. That is why most people do not want it to be smoked. It is dangerous to have it down here; you shouldn't smoke it around anyone."

"Are you going to report me to the authorities?"

He was taking his turn inhaling again, and he glanced at her with his head back. "I am the authorities," he said.

"Well then. What are you going to do with me?"

"That all depends. Your eyes—your eyes!"

Michelle saw his immediate agitation as he noticed her wandering left eye. "So?" she said. "That's the way they are. I just took off my glasses."

"You should leave them on."

"No."

"You look like my sister with your eyes like that. I don't like it."

Michelle felt her head swirling from the cannabis; the sensation was euphoric and she let her mind flow where it wanted to. "Your sister," she said. "Tell me about her."

There was a silence. Michelle put out the half-smoked joint in the sand. It was potent marijuana; she didn't want to float away completely, or Enrique might—might . . .

"She wasn't nice to me," Enrique said suddenly, his voice whining, boyish.

Michelle, lost in watching a cloud overhead, felt his words penetrate her. She glanced at him. He was lying with his eyes closed, his body tense, remembering something that made his face contort with pain. "How wasn't she nice to you?" she said.

His breathing caught with a choking gasp. "She wanted me to join her," he said, talking as if under hypnosis.

His breathing caught again, as he fought back emotions. Michelle let her hand come gently down on his stomach. "Join her in what?" she asked, her voice soft, encouraging.

"She—she tried to lure me in, to put a spell on me. She wanted me for the Devil."

"How did you know?"

"I could tell!"

"How old were you?"

"Twelve."

"What happened?"

"She, she had me. I went with her."

"Where?"

"Up to the steam house on the volcano."

"What is happening? Tell me," she said, as his body jerked in remembrance of the past.

"We're sitting in the steam room. It's hot. I haven't seen her for several years. She has returned from Europe and seems changed; everyone hopes that she is changed, that she is going to take her position as the Chosen One now. She is so beautiful. She sits and takes off her wipile and smiles at me. She tells me to take off my shirt."

He stopped talking. Michelle saw his penis rising again. She had a sudden urge to take off her top and did so, freeing her breasts to the sunlight.

"She is so beautiful, her breasts, her body, she takes off her skirt and she is glistening with sweat."

"What then?"

"She helps me off with my clothes, and when she finds me hard, she touches me."

"What happens next?"

"Ah, aahhh! It feels so good. I have dreamed about this feeling, but it is the first time I have had a girl touch me. She tells me not to be afraid, that together we will be anything we desire, that Caban is with us and all we can do is follow him. But I'm scared; I feel danger. She is looking at me suddenly with her eyes not crossed, and her fingers go down to my balls and I know it! I know

240

what she is going to do, she is going to cut them off, I know it!"

"No," Michelle said. "No, she wouldn't do that, no."

"Yes! I jump up, and start running before she can catch me. I run down the hill naked, as fast as I can, hurting myself on the rocks, but she doesn't catch me. I escape and tell Ricardo. But he doesn't believe me. I was so scared, I was afraid she would come and get me. I slept with a pistol of Ricardo's with me, and whenever I saw her, I wouldn't talk to her ever again. She's horrible, horrible!" A groan of pleasure mixed with inner anguish came out of his mouth, and he reached up and grabbed at Michelle, pulling her down on him roughly.

They were breathless, urgent, her lips came up to his and kissed with slippery abandon as his hands pushed into her bikini bottom, yanking the material down from her. They both kicked off their suits. Michelle felt white flashes of energy as she lay back down on him, her breasts against his heaving chest, his penis thrusting against her pubic lips, pushing, pushing, she could feel it coming, almost feel him inside her before he really was, feel his phallus penetrating—

"No!" he shouted, and with a violent convulsion threw her off him. "No!"

She lay there stunned, aching for him, starting to cry. He gasped for air, put his shorts back on and stood up. "Don't you ever do that!" he muttered. "You have the Devil in you too!"

He walked away, leaving Michelle with her tears, her aching for satisfaction, her feeling of deep rejection. She sat up, reached for her bikini bottom, put it on, and stood up, starting after him across the sand. He was walking up toward the trail. She ran after him and pulled him to a stop. "What's wrong? Please tell me," she pleaded.

His look pinned her. The passion was gone from his face, and so was his friendly façade. He looked older, and his eyes were menacing, powerful, penetrating to her

241

heart. "There are things that are sacred," he said, his voice slow, low, frightening.

"But—"

"Say nothing. You are on the sacred island. You are in the presence of Caban. You are Ix Chel. Say nothing!"

He seemed almost visibly to swell with power; Michelle felt totally vulnerable, as if he would strike her dead if she spoke—and it would be justified, she found herself thinking. He was a brujo; she suddenly saw a quality in his eyes, in his very being, that overwhelmed her. "You have the phallus," he said.

She nodded, offering no resistance to him, as if he had gained control over her, as if she had yielded to him.

"I dreamed it, I knew," he said, his voice triumphant. "The power has come to me. You will keep the phallus. Tomorrow night I will come for you. You are to tell no one."

She nodded again.

"Come with me," he ordered. "We have ceremonies to attend to at the temple. It is time Caban knew that it is you who has come. Hurry."

He started walking up the trail. Michelle followed mindlessly. She felt no fear, no expectation, just a growing conviction of being involved in something that made perfect sense. Of flowing toward a moment she had unconsciously felt coming for years.

chapter 18

The outboard motor sputtered to life as Ricardo gave a yank on the starter rope. "I still think you're making a mistake!" he shouted.

Chris jumped down into the large cayuco, pushed the boat away from the dock, and sat down in front, cross-legged on one of the flotation pads. He said nothing in response to Ricardo's final objection.

The boat headed toward Zacapula, moving smoothly through the still-glassy water. Chris could feel a hard knot of psychic muscle inside him, the kind of fierce inner strength that comes when a close relative or loved one has been endangered or abused. He was going to see Magdalena and that was that! Ricardo had at first resisted with his usual easy assumption of superiority, knowing that Chris couldn't actually make him do anything. But there had been a ferocious, cold determination in Chris's insistence that had overridden Ricardo's opposition.

Chris kept glancing back toward the island, hoping to sight the inboard returning to the house. He felt acutely uncomfortable, leaving Michelle with only a note saying he was in town and to join him if the Xocomil hadn't started. But there was no alternative. He had to head for town now if he was to see Magdalena today; otherwise the water would be too rough for the return trip, and he didn't want to have to walk the two hours around the volcano trail.

The scent of lush vegetation and shoreline reeds was strong and invigorating. When they arrived at Zacapula, there was the usual gathering of women washing clothes down by the rocks, but there were no nets out being mended today, and Chris detected even from the water a sense of suspense over the town, of anxious waiting and tense anticipation.

"I wish to hell this whole Ilum K'inal thing had never come up," Ricardo said, breaking the silence between the two men as he came up against the boat dock.

"Didn't you have any power over what holidays they celebrate?" Chris said.

"There are certain things the Quitapul let no outsiders interfere with, and one of them is their calendar. No, this Easter is the year of Ilum K'inal, the Indians have been awaiting this year for hundreds of years. It's a damn shame if you ask me, how these poor natives get caught up in superstitions in the first place."

"You could at least have brought your kids up free of—"

"Listen, Barker," Ricardo growled at him fiercely, "I did everything I damn well could! Who could have guessed it would all end up this way? You seem to blame me."

"You're the head man in this town."

"You talk economics, that's true. But there's so many undercurrents I didn't even know existed until recently. All the brujo stuff was tolerable until Ilum K'inal started coming on, and my kids got thrown into the spotlight."

"Well, you could just ship them off, then," Chris said, feeling hesitant about walking into the town to the jail. "You could just load Magdalena and Enrique into your boat and take off this morning for Panahachel. Nothing's stopping you."

Ricardo stared at Chris from his sitting position in the back of the cayuco. "You tourists, you think there's easy

244

solutions to everything down here. But you don't see that this is Quitapul country—we outsiders can help out; we can try to turn the natives in positive directions. But if you interfere with their religious life too much, you're a dead man. It's happened more'n a few times while I've been here, gringos found dead. What do I do? I have 'em buried quietly, and that's the end of it. And if I tried to take Magdalena out of that jail today, I would be a dead man and that would be the end of me. Same goes for you. So go on and pay Magdalena a visit. But you'd better keep in mind that heroics will get you dead quick."

He stood up abruptly and stepped onto the dock with a heave of exertion. Chris saw the extra effort he had to make, and realized the Ricardo was aging, that he was in his fifties and trying to perform as though he were still his son's age.

The main street was busy as usual, but Chris received hostile stares from the Indians, while Ricardo got only curt gestures of greeting rather than the effusive signs of paternal respect Chris expected. Ricardo, a dweller here for thirty years, was still an outsider, and today, probably even more of an outsider than ever before, with his daughter locked up as a traitor. But there was Enrique, of course, the leader, who should redound to Ricardo's credit as a father. Strange, Chris pondered as they walked up the steep main street and turned left to head up to the church, strange how fate made the leaders of the Quitapul half-gringo. Of course, the Indians of many American tribes had in their tradition the great white saviors who would bring them a new era of wealth and victory. Perhaps it made perfect sense that Ricardo's half-breed children would be the best-suited for carrying through the Ilum K'inal magic. After all, the pure-blooded brujos had failed.

The main marketplace, a square with women sitting on the ground on blankets, their small piles of produce laid out in front of them, was on the right, halfway up the hill to the buildings of the church. Vegetables, fruits, teas,

245

herbs, and the rest were spread out like an organic patchwork quilt, and for a moment Chris was aware only of the colorful bazaar, serving the needs of this community—just, he thought with an inward grin, like Safeway up north. But then he came to the butcher stalls, with hanging parts of pigs and cows, covered with flies, for sale; no not Safeway, after all.

"Father Morales has been wanting to come visit you," Ricardo said as they walked up on the hill, "but he's been very busy with the Indians lately."

"I'll bet."

"He does his best."

"His best to what?" Chris asked scornfully.

"To teach these damned Indians something about Christian love! You're so quick to judge, Barker."

"So where's the jail where this loving man of God is holding a witch for trial?"

"Inside the churchyard."

"Figures."

The hostile stares continued to push at Chris's nerves as he walked through the eddying crowd of Indians who glanced at him as though he were an unwelcome complication to the morning. At the church gate, the human flow was conjested. Chris could hear shouts coming from beyond the high adobe walls. Quitapul voices, angry and harsh to the ear, created a growing din as Ricardo pushed his way through the Indians.

"What's all the shouting about?" Chris asked, tensing even further at the anger of the voices ahead of him.

"I warned you not to come see her!" Ricardo yelled back to him.

In the courtyard, two hundred feet square, a mass of Indians stood mumbling in small groups to the left and the right, pressing toward the far corner where a small adobe house sat against the wall. Eight guards with rifles kept the Indians back thirty feet from the little jailhouse. But a continual barrage of stones was being thrown over the guards, chipping off chunks of plaster from the walls, banging on the corrugated tin roof.

Ricardo shouted orders and the townspeople parted to let him and Chris through the front line. A temporary lessening of noise followed Ricardo's appearance. He talked with a guard, whom Chris recognized as one of the three men who had accompanied Enrique to the island yesterday.

"The padre is with her now," Ricardo explained to Chris. "We have to wait."

There was a tense, menacing edge to the waiting; the crowd milled and was evidently putting off rock-throwing only until Ricardo would be gone. Chris felt the intense hatred of these people toward Magdalena, and it wasn't a clean hatred; it was muddled, confused, with fear just under the surface of anger on the faces of the men and women now staring at Chris and Ricardo. Damn superstitions! Chris thought. Damn priests of all types who play on people's fears until they're like this, a crazy mob of frightened aggressors, trying to kill on the outside what they really fear inside themselves. Ugly world! Maybe western civilization would be a step up for these people. But shit, no. Now we have nuclear bombs as the wicked witch, and who can throw stones at the Pentagon?

"Listen," Ricardo said, breaking Chris out of his numb trance, "I've decided to get Magdalena out of here tomorrow night, before Ilum K'inal. If the tunnel doesn't open up, there's going to be hell to pay if she's still here; I can see that. So when you talk to her, tell her to be ready, around midnight tomorrow night."

"Why don't you tell her yourself?"

"We don't speak."

"Well, that's a fucked-up situation between a father and a daughter."

"You don't know anything about her, Barker. You don't know how she's turned against me."

"Against you what way?" Chris asked.

"Listen, she thinks she's some kind of savior; she's a psychiatric case. I'm not about to let anybody, even my daughter, stop honest progress in this town."

The priest emerged from the jailhouse, hurrying out with a stooped, agitated gait. "It's no use," he said to Ricardo. "She won't even speak to me. She's gone into some demonic trance."

"Thanks for trying. Maybe Chris here can get through to her."

Chris met Morales' eyes. He was shaken by their intensity, and suddenly unsure of his long-held opposition to the priest and what he and his kind stood for. There was power, raw power, unleashed and prowling down here—he had felt it, seen it so many times now. Call it Caban, call it the Devil, call it the dark side of the psyche —did the names matter, after all? And if they didn't, how was Morales any more or less right or wrong about it than Chris or Magdalena? At least, Morales was keeping the power and prestige of the Church between Magdalena and the crowd who wanted to kill her, so he was for the moment an ally.

"Come on," Ricardo said. "Let's get this over with." He led Chris past the mute priest and over to the heavy wooden door. The guard gave it a shove and it opened on creaking hinges. The crowd shouted Quitapul phrases that struck like stones. This is too much like a movie set, Chris told himself, trying to find some lighter aspect to the situation. But it didn't work. As soon as the door closed behind him with a thud, and the relative darkness invaded his vision, his perspective was shattered and he stood there, blinking at the darkness.

A single grilled opening in the ceiling gave the room what light it had. At first all he could see was the foot-square patch of light on the dirt floor. The energy in the small room was unnerving, and he felt his flesh creep as he sensed the unseen presence of the bruja.

"Hello, gringo."

The low voice came from behind him to his right. His

248

eyes were starting to adjust; he could see a form sitting in the corner. "Magdalena," he said.

"You came."

He walked over to her. "Yeah."

"Please, sit down."

He sat cross-legged in front of her. He could see her better now. Her face was dark with emotion, her lips full and parted, her eyes fused on him with intense probing. "Well," he said, trying to be casual. "You've got yourself in a pretty tight little situation here."

She shrugged her shoulders. But he could see the desperation in her eyes. "I know," she said. "I made a final attempt to talk with some of the people. And here I am. They do not want what I offer; they want the treasure!"

"I guess it's human instinct," Chris said.

"Then the humans will soon be as extinct as the dinosaurs."

"Listen, is there anything I can do?"

She reached out and touched his hand with her fingers. "You could give me a kiss—unless you're afraid I'll put a spell on you."

He leaned forward and their lips met. She was, he sensed, so hungry for human contact that the embrace was like fire; her need was immense. And it did not stop with sexual need; she groaned and pressed herself against him as tears welled up and coursed down her cheeks and onto his hands as he clutched her face strongly, kissing her salty, wet lips.

"It's been so horrible," she sobbed. "I have lost everything. My power is gone; the gods are against me. It is the end."

"Don't say that."

"If only I could escape!"

"There must be a way."

"The last of my followers, they have been taken. There is no one to help me."

"I can help."

"Where is Michelle?"

249

"Um, back at the house," he lied, not wanting to admit she was with Enrique.

"Listen to me. Whatever you do, don't let her out of your sight once you return to the house. And tomorrow, don't allow her to go anyplace. Don't let Enrique spend time with her or all is lost."

"What does that mean?"

"I can't explain to you now. But I have faith. I do not believe the gods want me to die. I have faith. And as for you and your daughter—everything depends on Caban."

"I thought you were finished relying on things like that," Chris said.

"It is so complex. But I feel forces at work. Something will happen. Think of me tonight, gringo."

"They're going to take you out of here tomorrow at midnight so you'll be safe," he said.

"Anything could happen by then," she responded.

The door grated open. Bright sunlight flooded the middle of the room. "Come on," Ricardo shouted. "Time's up."

Magdalena kissed Chris on the lips. "Meditate on me," she whispered anxiously. "Let me come to you."

"I'll come see you tomorrow."

"No! Stay with your daughter. Don't bring her to town."

"Why not?"

"Come on out, Barker," Ricardo shouted impatiently.

He held her head in his hands, feeling suddenly that he might never see her again, realizing that somehow she was immensely important to him. "I'll do anything," he said.

"I know," she whispered back, and kissed him again.

"Barker!"

He stood up. They held each other for a moment. And then he walked out into the blinding sunlight, blinking numbly at the mob outside.

chapter 19

Michelle sat on the end of the pier where Enrique had left her. The breeze was blowing down from the volcano against her back and the sun was shining on her back, too, giving her a warm but not hot sensation on her skin. Time went by. The sound of the speedboat had long since died away around the bend toward the resort.

She expected Chris to come down from the house at any moment, but more and more time passed as she sat, and still he didn't come. Maybe he was taking a nap. She thought of walking up to the house but the sunlight was so soothing and she was so relaxed that she didn't want to move. She didn't know how much time had gone by, because just before getting into the boat to come back from the island, Enrique had suggested smoking the rest of the joint, and she was very spaced.

As the breeze turned into a stronger wind, the fog in her mind lifted slightly, as it always did with marijuana, but for some reason it wouldn't lift all the way this time. She was aware of a remaining haze that lingered after the grass should have eased up, giving her back her normal mind. She tried to think about the morning on the island; she felt that there was something she had to remember. But the whole trip with Enrique was blurry, and everytime she tried to think about it, she felt a countering impulse to float into the space inside her head, to enjoy the present and let go of everything in the past.

She stood suddenly and dove into the lake, hoping the swim would clear her mind, knowing that there was something she needed to think about. But as she stroked through the cool water, the numbness remained. Her body felt slack, almost too relaxed for swimming. A memory flickered as she rolled onto her back and did a lazy frog-kick. She remembered being on her back, looking up at Enrique, and then looking with her wandering left eye at the volcano, feeling a sudden realization, a sudden realization of, um, of— The memory drifted away.

She headed back to the dock, still swimming on her back, sinking into a vague enjoyment of the swim. What was that? A sound in the water, a low, rumbling, penetrating vibration. She thought suddenly of the volcano—an image jumped to her mind of it exploding. She stopped swimming, trod water, bringing her head high enough so her ears were exposed to the air. But there was no sound of an eruption, and no visible sign of one.

Ah, a boat! Coming from Zacapula. She could tell it wasn't Enrique in the speedboat; it was a cayuco with an outboard on back, with two people in it, still indistinct in the distance. She started stroking strongly for shore. By the time she was climbing up onto the dock the boat was much closer and—Daddy!

She stood on the dock and waved, and he waved back. He was with Ricardo; they had been gone all this time. As they approached, she felt a wave of apprehension sweep over her. There was something that she was afraid he might find out. What was it? Damned marijuana, ruining her memory. Oh, that was probably it; she didn't want him to know she was stoned. That must be it. She could remember now that nothing had happened with Enrique; well, they had kissed, something had almost happened; she remembered it with a hot flash, how they had made love on the beach. But he stopped before they had really

252

done it; he had, um, she thought, struggling to keep the memory going. But it was dissolving into nothingness.

To camouflage her grassed-out state, she decided to act tired, sleepy, ready for a nap. Chris got out of the boat and Ricardo putt-putted away. She could detect tension between the two men.

"Hi, Daddy."

"Hey, kiddo, everything okay?"

"Sure. You were in town?"

"Yeah. How was the skiing?"

They were off the dock now, walking side by side across the beach to the lawn. "It was fun. We just lay around in the sun and came back. I'm sleepy from the sun."

"What was Enrique like today?"

"Just fine."

"Well I don't want you seeing him again."

"What?"

"They've locked Magdalena up. Enrique was behind the whole thing. He's got the town hating her; it's really ugly."

"She's *locked up*?"

"In jail. I don't know what's going to happen. But you're not going to see Enrique again until this is all cleared up."

Somehow, his words made her feel a wave of relief. Not see Enrique again ... "Okay," she said, searching the wreckage of her memory for something, anything, but finding nothing along the shore of her unconscious except the sexual bits of driftwood scattered here and there.

"You're sure everything went okay?" he said, pulling her to a stop and looking in her eyes.

"Everything's fine, Daddy."

"You seem a little strange."

"We drank some wine."

"He didn't try anything with you?"

"Daddy, I can take care of myself."

"Not with men like him. Are you sure you're not holding anything back from me? Did he fool around with any ceremonies?"

"No."

"I don't like the sound of that 'no'."

"Daddy, I'm just sleepy."

"Well watch it, we're not playing games down here, this is serious and Enrique's dangerous."

"All right, whatever you say," she said, just wanting to fade away.

"I don't know what's going to happen around here the next couple of days," he said. "But I know one thing. Until Easter's over, you're not going out of my sight, okay?"

"Okay. I'm so tired, can I go take a nap?"

"Give me a hug first, would you?" he asked.

She stepped up and put her arms around him. But there was a strange lack of emotion, of feeling, in her; she felt numb to the core, as if she were asleep.

"I'm sorry if I'm acting strange," Chris said, holding her tight. "But seeing Magdalena in jail—it's getting so weird down here, I hope to God nothing happens to her. I wish I could do something, but the most important thing is that I stay with you."

She held him a moment longer but her thoughts were only of bed, of sleep. He let go of her and kissed her lightly, gently on the forehead. "I love you, kiddo," he said.

"Me too, Daddy. See you in a while. I'm so sleepy."

"If I'm sleeping when you wake up, don't go walking around anywhere."

"Okay."

He watched her walking across the lawn into the house. She seemed so slight in her bikini, with her pants over one arm. So young, her developing sexuality conflicting with her childish vulnerability. She's holding something back, he said to himself. Goddamn Enrique, if he did anything to her, I'll kill him!

254

He walked up to the house and poured himself a double shot of tequila, squeezing a couple of oranges into the tall glass to dilute it. Sitting out on the front patio, he drank quickly, wanting to blunt the raw edge of reality that was jabbing him. The feeling of Magdalena's body against his as he had left her in the jail still remained, a permanent imprint which the alcohol intensified, as if she were still with him, the taste of her salty lips in his mouth, the feel of her fingers on his skin—his yearning for her increased as the tequila took effect.

Heroic images exploded in his mind. He could see himself riding up to the jailhouse on a horse, firing pistols, chasing off the Indians who were persecuting her, shooting every guard in sight, breaking her out, and riding away with her behind him on the horse, her breath hot on his neck.

But quickly the euphoric rush of alcohol turned into depression. He found himself sitting on the veranda feeling helpless, hopeless, pathetic in his inability to save the woman. If Michelle weren't here, he told himself, he'd find some solution for Magdalena. But he was responsible for his daughter and had to put his energy into protecting her. That was what Magdalena had stressed, and Chris felt for that there was indeed danger surrounding them, aimed at Michelle.

And Michelle was acting so weird, almost as if she were under some kind of—some kind of spell! The thought struck him with the force of a blow to the gut. How could he have let her go off with that goddamned brujo—and what if he had the sacrificial phallus? What if he had used it on Michelle!

"Goddamn, this is fucked-up!" Chris blurted, standing up and going inside to make himself another drink. He squeezed the oranges ferociously as he loosely plotted a course of action. Probably Enrique hadn't done anything with the phallus today. On the way back from Zacapula, Ricardo had told him what he knew about that artifact, that it was to be used only when everything was ready for

Ilum K'inal, and certainly, Ricardo had said, the Quitapul priests had some poor Mayan girl picked out for the ceremony. It was a horrible idea but it was certainly better than cutting her heart out the way they used to, at least there was some progress there.

Well, Chris thought as he finished off his second drink, at least he would make sure nobody touched his own daughter with any ceremonial notions the next few days. Let Enrique stick his jade penis up some Mayan princess, it was probably an honor the girls had lined up to try for. But the thought of anyone trying anything like that with his daughter made Chris explode inside.

He walked down the lawn, dizzy from the alcohol but determined. If he could catch Benito asleep and get his rifle, then he would have the upper hand here at the house. He could protect Michelle no matter what happened. As he hurried through the avocado grove, he feared that Benito would catch him off guard as he had last night, and spoil his plans. But he made it through the grove to the boulders beyond.

From the highest boulder, he looked down on the little house set back against the volcano in its own small cove beside the lake. No sign of Benito. The door to the house was open, the padlock resting on a wooden bench out front. Chris sneaked down along the trail into the clearing, his boots noisy in the dry mango leaves.

He was at the door now, peering into the darkness. There was Benito asleep on a mat on the floor. Where was the rifle—there it was! In the corner leaning against the wall. Chris started for it, glancing at Benito, and then making his move for the gun. But he tripped over something in the darkness and fell. Quickly he was on his feet again, grabbing the gun, working the lever to throw a shell into the firing chamber. He turned around to get Benito covered, but just then he was hit hard in the gut. Benito swung again and hit a little higher, knocking the wind out of Chris's drunken body. He went limp and fell to the floor.

"Idioto!" Benito shouted hoarsely at him, standing over him with the rifle.

Chris gasped for breath. "Don't shoot," he said feebly in English.

"Estas borracho,"—you're drunk—Benito said with disgust.

"Don't shoot," Chris said, this time in Spanish.

"Stand up!"

Chris managed to get to his feet after first failing and falling back down to the floor. "Listen," he said, "I was drinking, I don't know what I was doing. I'm sorry, I just got mad at you hanging around with that gun, so I decided to take it away from you."

"Get outside," Benito ordered, pushing him in the back with the rifle barrel as they walked out into the sunlight.

"Man, my head hurts," Chris said, stumbling, blinking at the brightness.

"You're crazy," Benito grumbled

"I said I was sorry. Look, I really need to lie down. I'm sorry I got drunk and bothered you."

"Go to the house. Where is the girl?"

"She's sleeping," Chris said.

"Go back to the house. And don't you ever come back here again. You stay at the house!"

"Hey, I promise. I'm sorry, I was drinking."

"Well, then, don't drink anymore."

"I won't. But stop pointing that thing at me. It makes me nervous."

"Don't tell me what to do. They'll shoot me if I don't do my job—don't tell me what to do."

"Okay, okay. I'm heading to the house. See you."

Benito stood there with his gun still aimed at the gringo, and Chris could see the fear mixed with the Indian's anger. If Chris had succeeded in disarming him, had locked him up in the room as he'd planned and been on the loose with the rifle, what would they have done to Benito?

Benito watched the gringo disappear into the avocado

257

grove, then quickly went running up the trail between the two large boulders behind the hut. The trail took him to the top of the forty-foot-high outcropping of volcanic rock above the estate. From there he could see the pier and the entire grounds of the house. But more importantly, at this time of day, he could see the trail that wound along the edge of the lake from Zacapula, where Magdalena would have to come if she traveled by foot. He had been told yesterday of the plan to arrest the bruja, so she was probably in jail by now. But Benito knew he had better not take any chances; he would not sleep anymore. He would stand guard, drink coffee all night, and stay alert in case Magdalena was still on the loose, trying to get at the gringo and his daughter.

From his vantage point, he watched Chris cross the lawn and enter the house. The sound of the toilet flushing reached his ears a few minutes later. Then silence. The Xocomil was blowing stronger by the minute; there would be no boats the rest of the afternoon. Anyone approaching the house would have to come by the trail along the edge of the volcano.

Two days to go . . . He brought out and went over once again the thoughts that were in the minds of all the Indians of Zacapula. Two days, and then that poor girl in there . . . Would Enrique really be able to fulfill the prophecies? Benito knew he himself would never be able to do such a thing. But Enrique was different; Benito had watched Enrique kill three men just a month ago, after the uprising. Enrique had simply taken his pistol out of his holster, aimed point-blank at the rebels, and fired a bullet into each of their heads. They had been Magdalena's closest friends. Benito had jumped with shock at the sound of the pistol, and then felt sick to his stomach at the sight of the ruined heads. Surely a man such as Enrique, a brujo with the power and the nerve, would be able to do the ancient heart sacrifice also.

Magdalena was another story. It was she who had been destined to lead the Ilum K'inal ceremonies this year, and it would have been her fate to perform the sacrifice. Not the phallus sacrifice that would open the tunnel, but the heart sacrifice that would ensure that Caban would leave his own heart open to the Quitapul. Would a woman be able to do such a thing?

Yes, Benito concluded. *That* woman would have the nerve to cut out the blonde virgin's heart, just as her brother would. Magdalena had been a sweet, angelic child. But she had had that other dark side. She would take a great deal of abuse about being cross-eyed, about being the daughter of a gringo. But when her patience was gone, she would retaliate with a fiery attack. She had been a real fighter at the age of four and five. But then she had become more and more subtle, and children had become more and more afraid of what she could do to them with her powers.

She had been so subtle that there was never any evidence to be found against her when someone was struck by a curse. But everyone knew she was the one with the power. When Rubita broke her leg, right after picking a fight with Magdalena, the broken leg had been caused by a curse, everyone was certain of that. And Julia, falling sick so suddenly with a fever after losing her temper in school and calling Magdalena names on the playground, calling her the Devil—everyone knew Magdalena had put a curse on her and made her sick. The tribal council had met to consider what to do; Julia's mother had gone to them pleading for action against Magdalena. But there was nothing the tribal council could do against the Chosen One.

And then, the very next week, while rowing her cayuco in the bay, Julia's mother had capsized and drowned. The town was frightened of the little girl's power now, and Ricardo had sent her away quickly to Quetzaltenango to a boarding school so that there would not be further trouble.

And there hadn't been further trouble. Enrique had taken on the role of Chosen One and the hopes for Ilum

259

K'inal had started to grow as Enrique talked about the treasure to the townspeople. Only when Magdalena had returned home from school one summer, and tried to seduce her very own brother, had trouble started again, and talk about the Devil of Zacapula arisen. Ricardo had again sent his daughter away, this time to España, and Enrique had continued to be trained by the priests to do his duties as the Chosen One.

But this last year since she had returned, everything had been chaos. Sometimes Benito wished he had been born in one of the other tribes along the lake. The other tribes had no tradition of Ilum K'inal. They had no buried treasure to dream of; they had no Chosen Ones. They lived calm, happy lives. They had no Magdalenas to frighten them, and they weren't having to face the return of the heart sacrifices of the ancients. Only Zacapula, of all the towns on the lake, was going crazy this Easter.

The afternoon passed with no signs of humans. Benito went down to his house several times for food and coffee, knowing he could leave his watch on the trail for fifteen or twenty minutes and not be negligent, that it would take someone at least an hour to cross the visible section of the trail. But still, he felt acutely uneasy, he would be glad when this Ilum K'inal event was over. Whether or not the tunnel opened up and Caban gave his treasure to the Quitapul, Benito would be happy, because he would be back with his family in town, with his wife and seven children. He did not like guns, he did not like violence.

The gold, everyone wanted the gold, to see Zacapula wealthy, to bring the Quitapul all the riches they saw in magazines, that they saw in Guatemala City when they visited the great capital. But, Benito wondered as the sun sloped toward the volcano's top, was all the gold in the world worth what was going to happen to that poor gringa girl down in that house?

Benito knew he sided with the girl, because he had a daughter her age who—that was it, that was the frightening part of all this. Once the Quitapul started performing heart sacrifices, would Caban be satisfied with just one heart? Would he not want more and more? Would he not end up wanting the heart of Benito's eldest daughter also? Perhaps Magdalena and her followers had been right all along in their insistence that Ilum K'inal not be performed, that the ceremonies never be allowed to take place in Zacapula. But everyone knew that Magdalena had her own schemes, that her fight to stop Ilum K'inal was just her devious way of regaining the power that Enrique had taken from her while she was gone.

The sun disappeared behind the volcano. Benito sat in the shadow of Caban, contemplating what it meant to have been born a Quitapul, the last tribe of the Mayas to hold onto the lost powers, the only tribe now in a position to gain untold power, both in money and in the unseen realms that Caban controlled. The wind died down. Everything became calm, cool.

There was the gringo, walking across the lawn in the dying light; now sitting on the dock alone, cross-legged, facing Zacapula. Time went by, perhaps half an hour, and the gringo maintained his silent vigil, sitting as still as an Indian would sit, meditating on who could guess what? Benito had no idea what a gringo would be thinking, sitting down there on the pier this evening. Did he know what was to be the fate of his daughter, could he feel that something devastating was about to happen to him? Benito watched him walk through the dusk back to the house.

He looked closely along the trail, realizing he hadn't been watching very often the last half-hour. But there was no one there. Time passed. Darkness deepened. Benito's eyes adjusted and he continued his vigil. For half an hour he had only starlight to look by, and it was difficult. But then the moon started to bring a slight glow of light to the east.

Candlelight in the house. Benito wished he could be down there with the gringo; he even considered helping the poor man and his daughter escape. But of course that

261

would be impossible. Benito would not sacrifice his family for another man's family; life was simply not that way. What would be a tragedy for the gringos would be victory for the Quitapul. The designs of power were clear; they had brought the gringo and his daughter down for this very event. What would happen would happen.

Fingers gripped his neck. He tried to scream, to fight back, but he was instantly limp as hard fingers found the pressure points and his consciousness flickered out, as if a psychic blanket had been drawn over him. He was dragged down from the high rock and left in some bushes like a discarded rag doll.

chapter 20

Chris sat in the living room watching the moon rise over the lake. After his sleep he was feeling better. Michelle was sleeping again after getting up briefly for something to eat. She had a slight fever and seemed drained. He hoped she hadn't picked up any bugs from the food.

He sipped the glass of orange juice he had just squeezed after his meditation down on the pier. It had been so clear, his vision of Magdalena, as if she had been with him in person instead of locked up two miles away. But then suddenly she had disappeared from his mind, just when he felt he could almost reach out and touch her.

It would be nice to have some grass to smoke, he found himself thinking. He had given up marijuana years ago, but right now he wanted something to knock him a few notches down into oblivion for the rest of the night; he felt wide-awake, as if he would be up the whole night.

Fingers grabbed him around the neck. His heart leapt in his throat; a scream formed but could not come out. He felt the white-hot energy in the fingers, pressing at his life-force. It was over. He was going to die. There was the certainty of death in the grip on his neck. But the fingers failed to follow through. Instead, they slowly eased their grasp. Chris, in a state of shock, felt something else on the nape of his neck. Something hot, wet; a woman's lips.

"Hello, gringo," she said.

He spun around. "Jesus, it's you!"

Her eyes were crossed, and she emanated an almost visible energy. She bent down and kissed his tense lips. "Where is Michelle?" she asked.

"Asleep. She's feeling a little sick."

Magdalena looked worried. "A fever?" she asked.

"Yes."

"Enrique's work. She will sleep through the night. He will have no need for her until tomorrow."

"What do you mean; what's he done?"

"He was with her today. You lied to me, I felt it."

"What did you feel?"

"I always know it when he is at work. He has put a simple spell on her, nothing more. He wants her semiconscious when she is not with him. I imagine she has been sleeping."

"Yes. Listen, how'd you get out?"

She walked around the sofa to him and they pressed their bodies together. "The power came to me," she said. "I knew it would."

"What happened?"

"We need to go," she said, her right eye looking at him, her left eye wandering off to the side intently, looking also.

"I can't go anywhere; I won't leave Michelle," Chris insisted.

"Tonight you must leave her. Everything is happening tonight. You must come with me or all is lost."

"No, I'll wake her up and we can take her with us. Where are we going? Why don't we try to get away from here tonight?"

"No, you do not understand. If she is moved, Enrique would know of it, he would feel it. He has worked a spell on her. You should never have let her go with him."

264

"I know."

"But it is good that you did; he had to begin the ceremonies today with her."

"What do you mean, with her?"

"He would have taken her by force if you had resisted. There can be no delay in the ceremonies."

"He'd take her over my dead body," Chris said hotly.

"No, he needs you also; you will not be killed. But this is all in the past. If we can succeed tonight, my powers will be with me and he will be lost."

"What do you want me to do?"

"Come up to the steam hut with me on the volcano."

"What about Benito?"

She smiled thinly, and glanced at her extended fingers. "I have seen to Benito. Do not worry for him; I used these with care, and he will wake in due time. You can help me carry him to the hut; we can lock him up in there for the night."

"I won't leave Michelle, not if you say Enrique's planning something with her."

"Christopher, if you do not come with me, she will be a dead girl!"

"What the hell do you mean?"

"We must perform a ceremony with Caban, now, or all is lost and Enrique will have his way."

"What kind of ceremony?"

"It is a beautiful ceremony. Come, they will check my jail at midnight, perhaps, and find me gone. We have only three or four hours."

"How did you escape?"

"I felt you on the dock, meditating on me. I will never be able to thank you for those moments when you focused your energy toward me. Suddenly the power returned and I was free."

"How?"

"It is impossible to describe. I was suddenly moved two feet through the wall and found myself on the outside. I hurried off and no one noticed. The power is with us, Christopher! But we must hurry. First, though, let me see Michelle."

They went down the hallway to the girl's room. She was sleeping. Magdalena knelt down beside her, put her hand on her forehead, and mumbled something in Quitapul. Then she pulled down the sheet, exposing the girl's rising and falling breasts. Taking a gourd out of her pouch, she rubbed a small amount of liquid over the heart. Chris scented a strong odor, like rancid eucalyptus. He felt his trust reach out to this woman, working over his daughter; a prayer almost formed on his lips. Then she was done, pulling the covers back over Michelle, standing up and hurrying out the door.

Moments later they were running single file up the trail in the darkness. The moon was up and Chris followed Magdalena's tall body until she paused abruptly. "Help me carry him," she said.

The body, limp and lifeless, felt dead to Chris as he lifted it, and a sudden fear of Magdalena swept through him. But then he saw the Indian's chest heave as they carried him down the trail. The man was alive. They lugged him into the little house and put him down. "We should remember to let him go later, or Enrique will have him shot for failing in his duty," Magdalena said as they padlocked the door. "He is a good man. I do not want him harmed by all this."

She took the rifle with her as they went running back up the trail. Chris felt his energy high, and the running gave him a much-needed release of tension. Caban loomed above them as they hurried up his lower slopes. The trail zigzagged up higher and higher, until they were approaching a small canyon. Magdalena led the way down into the dark gorge without hesitation.

A stream ran with tinkling purity, and they paused to drink the cold water. "Where this stream comes out, we will stop," she said.

Chris looked up the canyon, then back down to where the house was just a toy on the lake's edge. "If you knew that Enrique was planning something with Michelle, why didn't you warn me?" he asked, giving voice to the thoughts that had been growing in his mind as they hiked up the trail.

"If I had the phallus, everything would be different now," she said. "You and Michelle—from the time she was born, she has been marked for Ilum K'inal."

"That's bullshit," Chris said.

"Everything has gone according to plan, except for Enrique gaining the phallus. And tonight we will counteract him anyway and his power will fail. There is a ceremony that you and I will perform with Michelle on Ilum K'inal, which will bring about the blossoming of a new era."

"What does Enrique have planned for Michelle? Tell me!"

"He will never do it now."

"Tell me!"

"Very well. Then we must hurry. The tradition says that on this Ilum K'inal a blonde-haired virgin is to sacrifice her virginity to the jade phallus, and then the tunnel will open to the treasure. Then a heart sacrifice must be made to ensure Caban of the unending devotion of the Quitapul."

"You've *got* to be kidding."

"I have fought it for years! Enrique, he usurped my power while I was away. But you and I, her father and her sister in the spirit, we can perform a ceremony with Caban which will bring his heart from Enrique, back to me. Come, there is no time to lose."

"This is insane!" Chris shouted at her, but she was already running up the trail.

Ten minutes later they came upon a stone hut. A tiny stream ran out the open door. Steam swirled upward in a billowing fog from the opening. The hut was built against the side of the volcano, on a small ledge at the end of the box canyon. The rock under Chris's feet was a solid lava flow.

"Come inside," Magdalena said.

Chris's eyes were just starting to adjust to the darkness of the hut's interior when Magdalena struck a match and lit a kerosene lamp. In the soft light he could see a pool where the cold water emerged from the side of the volcano, a deep pool five feet across. The steam was billowing out of a small tunnel a couple of feet to the left of the pool, down low. Chris felt his body start to perspire in the humid heat.

Over in the left-hand corner was a reed pad on top of a pile of boughs. Magdalena turned and looked at him, smiled softly, and pulled her wipile up over her head. "Undress. This is where we will do the ceremony," she said, untying the belt that held her skirt up. "Caban knows me here; this is his temple. Only brujos come here, for anyone else it is death to step foot in this hut."

"So I'm a dead man?" Chris said, unbuttoning his shirt.

"No," she replied, stepping out of her skirt into nakedness. "You are a gringo brujo. Caban will listen and see; his power must not go to the Quitapul. His power is beyond them; it must merge with the gringo world. That is where it is needed!"

"What kind of power?" Chris asked, sitting down and pulling off his boots, glancing up at her physical beauty and feeling the direct power of her sexual presence.

"The heart sacrifice has been understood by the Mayans only in terms of the old age. They have tapped Caban's powers through offering him the hearts, the spiritual essence, of human virgins. Caban cannot resist. But there is another heart sacrifice which he also cannot resist, which can tap immense powers from his source in Itzam'na. It is the only hope."

"Hope for what?" Chris said, standing up to unbutton his Levi's, responding to her as if already half-hypnotized into joining in her plans.

268

"Hope for . . . I have no idea what is coming. All I know is that I was born into a new energy. Michelle was born into the new energy. What can we do but trust? Here, let me do that; it is important."

She took his hands away from his pants very gently, and they stood a moment looking at each other. Instead of a seductive smile, she suddenly showed a deep uncertainty as she searched his eyes. Chris saw her slender, naked body as fragile, vulnerable. Her breasts heaved with a swift intake of air.

"You're remarkable," he whispered. "I can't even explain to you what I feel."

"We feel it together," she murmured, and with trembling fingers unbuttoned his Levi's.

"Huiscoyol paxte arroyan ajonjoli," she murmured, taking his half-distended phallus in her hands reverently. She stroked the head lightly, smoothly, bringing him into full erection. Then she bent forward and delicately touched his penis with her lips. "Caban!" she whispered. "Feel this, Caban. Feel this and understand. I have come with what I promised."

She slowly stood up again, released his penis and went over to close the door. The intensity of the wet heat increased instantly. She returned to him and for a moment pressed her body against his, her breasts to his chest, her belly against his penis. "May the gods be with us," she whispered almost unaudibly. She led him by the hand to the soft bed. They sat down facing each other, cross-legged. Chris watched her close her eyes; her lips trembled as if with inner thoughts.

"Close your eyes," she said softly.

With his eyes shut, Chris became acutely aware of his body, of the sweat pouring out of his skin, of the steam entering his lungs with every breath. And that steam—it seemed as though he were inhaling some ultra-strong marijuana; it seemed to expand in his lungs like hashish, to blank out his mind with flashes of bright light.

Suddenly everything went black inside. Chris started to

contract, but then in the middle of that vast blackness he sensed something, something coming at him, penetrating him, something exhilarating, overpowering. His physical boundaries were expanding, his notion of who he was dissolving, fading . . .

He found himself in a new body, a female body. Her body! He was certain of it. He opened his eyes and found himself staring at his own body across from him, its eyes open also, staring at him. Eyelids closed again and he felt his awareness sinking down through her body, down into her chest. Her heart was beating with great pumping thrusts, like a male organ constantly, effortlessly ejaculating

Then he sensed her breasts and his eyesight seemed to be opening up into a strange visual world that felt emotions, nipples that detected the heart across from her, and then with a sudden erection of their own, felt Caban's heart deep inside the earth, sensed its presence, felt a responsive flowing of heart energy from Caban into her heart.

Down deeper still, into her belly, encountering an energy swirl of willpower, the center of her being, a bright, blinding center of power! Chris wanted to stay in the swirl forever but he felt himself moving through a womb-world that would not hold him, that pushed him out, squeezed him through the tight band of cervical muscles and then into her hot, fleshy vaginal passage. Then he slipped into consciousness.

His eyes snapped open. She was looking at him with both eyes focused, and he met her stare, for a moment losing any sense of which were her eyes and which were his. But then his eyes dropped down from hers as if pulled by some outside force. Her chest rose softly as he looked at her breasts. They seemed like twin volcanoes to him, the heart inside pumping red blood like the volcano's red lava. And inside that flat stomach, the womb. The repository of the human egg. The beginning of a universe. His eyes closed again without forethought.

Fingers touched him lightly, explored his half-erect penis, then found his balls and cupped them like precious gems. "Caban," she whispered intensely. "Caban, feel this, feel your testicles, Caban. Those testicles I would not give you long ago. Feel now, allow this to come to pass. Let go, Caban!"

· The hot energy moving through her fingers into his balls flowed into his penis, his own red lava flooding him till he was full and hard. "Caban!" she said again.

Suddenly Chris felt the presence of the volcano there with him in the hut, a totally frightening entity of energy that made him want to bolt and run from the hut before Caban could take over his body, take over his identity.

Hard fingers gripped his penis as the idea of escape ran through his system.

"No!" she said. "You must stay. We are among the gods. Touch me. Let Caban touch me!"

With one hand still gripping his erection, her other hand took Chris's fingers and brought them toward her body, guiding them between her legs until he felt her opening, felt the hot wetness of her. With his fingers slightly inside her, they remained motionless. Chris felt he was floating, felt a liquid current flowing between them between their procreative centers, the intensity rising, building, threatening—

"Come with me," Magdalena said suddenly, jolting him. She took his hand away from her and pulled him forcefully to his feet. He was dizzy, barely conscious. She led him quickly to the pool. "Step in, now!" she insisted.

The shock of the cold water revived him. "All the way," she said. "Quickly."

She joined him. Held both his hands in hers. He was turning numb now. "I will tell you something," she whispered. "We are sitting in the water of Caban. I was here years ago with my brother. Enrique. I felt the power coming to me then, as now. But it was different, it was different!"

Chris closed his eyes and immediately felt himself starting to spin backward, a powerful force pulling him through inner space. Her words seemed far away, as if propelling him further and further into unknown territory.

"Caban was talking to me," she was saying. "I knew what he required for me to gain full power over my people. I could hear him talking then, but now he is silent. He was telling me of a new age, where women would rule as men had for centuries past. All I had to do was perform one ceremony, with my brother, and the tunnel would open for me and I would gain immense power! Enrique sat there as you are now, all I had to do was put him one step further into trance. Wait until he was completely numb in the water—and then slice off his testicles with my obsidian knife—and Caban would surge, the energy of the male released into my power!"

Chris was spinning, spinning, losing consciousness. Volcanic energy blasted through his nervous system. Everything was gone; there was only the energy of the volcano, taking him over, obliterating his consciousness.

"But there is something more!" Magdalena said, her voice penetrating his spinning being. "There is something beyond blood sacrifice! Listen, Caban, I am challenging you now. Risk what you know. Let go the heart sacrifice, let go your craving for young boys also—you have had us giving you our vital parts for too long. I will not! There is something more."

Her hands grabbed Chris and pulled him up. "Get out of the water quickly," she said with urgency. "He is taking you, don't let him take you! If he takes you I have no choice, it will be your balls given to a female Caban and there will be no difference from the old days—your blood flowing into his water—no!"

She pulled his numb body out of the pool. Chris felt the heat of the steam eroding the power of the spinning inside him, hitting him like a womb-embrace after the cold water.

Then they were sitting on the pad again, facing each

272

other. "Christopher, listen to me," she said. "Caban, listen!"

Chris could hear her words only vaguely when she said his name, but when she called Caban, something inside him reacted, made contact, awoke.

"Focus, Caban. We are here together. This is where the power has led us to—not your old ways, but this new way. Feel the energy alive in my heart, not dying with a final gushing gasp on the altar. Feel the energy alive in your balls, the energy returning after countless thousands of numb years. I feel the egg dropping, dropping. I feel your sperm flowing, flowing. Lie down, you stupid blind mountain! Abandon the blinding brightness of your power. There is something else, coming now, Caban, coming now!"

Chris felt himself falling onto his back, the energy moving out the top of his head with a searing heat, then circling and returning up through his feet, up his legs, into his balls like red fire. He opened his eyes. Magdalena was on her back, her eyes rolled up in her head. Without thought he sat up, feeling pulled toward her, into her.

Then she sat up, slowly, seemingly in a deep trance, looking at him as if recognizing him for the first time. "Itzam'na," she muttered, her lips trembling. "Come into me, now!"

chapter 21

Michelle stirred slightly, the sound almost reaching her in her sleep. But she drifted off once again, her dreams overriding the increasingly loud droning sound outside in the night. Moments passed. The sound came closer, and then suddenly stopped. She opened her eyes at the silence, blinking at the pale moonlight coming through the window.

Listening, she heard a distant sound. Her body tensed.

"Daddy? Are you awake?" she called out in a throaty whisper.

More silence. Then—voices outside, she was sure she heard voices!

"Daddy!"

A squeak. The front door opening. Footsteps, quick on the tile floor. More than one person. Michelle froze, unable even to sit up. Footsteps coming up the hallway, going into Chris's room. She was sweating, her heart racing. Someone was after them. But no sounds from Chris's bedroom. The footsteps coming toward her.

The door opened and she screamed out. "Daddy, help!"

Two men came running at her, and she found strength suddenly to sit up and fight them.

"Don't be afraid," one of the men said.

"Enrique?"

"They've taken your father away," he said, coming up to her bed, his face tense. "Did you see who took him?"

"No one took him, he's—"

"He's gone," Enrique said hotly. "Magdalena escaped from jail and she's taken your father. Come with me, we have to work quickly."

The other Indian was staring at her with wide eyes. She realized he was staring at her naked breasts, and she grabbed at the sheet, pulling it up to cover her. "Why would they want Daddy?" she asked.

"To use him. Get dressed, we must perform a counter-ceremony. Will you help me help your father?"

"Help him? Of course."

"Hurry up, then. We'll be waiting outside."

He gestured to the other Indian, a young man in traditional Quitapul dress like Enrique's, and they both left the room. Michelle sat there a moment, trying to wake up, trying to make sure she wasn't just dreaming. She got out of bed, and the cool tiles on her feet helped her gain a slight grip on reality. Magdalena had Chris. Something had to be done. Enrique wanted to help.

The door banged open and Enrique walked in, looking at her body, clad only in underpants. "And bring the jade phallus. We don't need it, but I want to have it in my possession, now that Magdalena is loose. You do have it, don't you?"

"Yes."

"Hurry then."

The door closed. Michelle slipped on her wipile and a pair of jeans, stepped into her sandals, and then reached under her mattress for the jade phallus. There it was, cold stone in her hand. She hurried out into the dark hallway. "I'm ready," she said.

"You have it?"

"Yes. Here." She handed the stone to him and in the act suddenly felt faint, dizzy. A different reality seemed to be trying to break through to her.

Enrique took her firmly by the arm and led her out into

276

the moonlight. "Where do you think she took him?" she asked as they hurried across the dewy lawn.

"Up to the sweat house on the volcano," he said.

"Then let's go up after them."

"Impossible."

"Why?"

"She's got Benito's rifle; she'd shoot up before we were halfway there. Get into the boat; there's no time to lose."

She stepped off the dock into the waiting speedboat. A moment later they were motoring across the moonlit lake, Michelle and four Indians. "What will she do to him?" she shouted, standing beside Enrique at the controls.

"If we perform the proper ceremony in time, she won't be able to touch him," he said. "But you must be a brave girl."

"What can I do?"

"Help me with the ceremony."

"I'll do anything."

"You have power; you can use it to help me, to help your father."

"Anything, just tell me what to do."

"I'm not sure exactly what ceremony she will choose, but there is a ceremony which will protect your father against her, and take her power from her."

Fifteen minutes later they pulled up to the resort dock. Ricardo was standing there with a half-dozen armed Indians. "She's nowhere in town," the older man said, shaken.

"She's been to the house, overpowered Benito, and taken Christopher to the sweat house," Enrique said with a dominating tone, walking quickly with Michelle past the small group.

Ricardo caught up with him. "What are you going to do?"

"There is a ceremony."

"Which one?" Ricardo asked hesitantly, glancing at the girl.

"Don't worry, as long as we have Michelle, little harm

277

can be done. Let Magdalena do what she wants; it is only helping us now."

"Wait a minute!" Ricardo ordered his son.

Enrique turned around, a belligerent look on his face. "What is it, old man? There is no time to waste in small talk."

"Go do your brujo ceremonies, I don't care. But leave this girl out of your plans. She's been through enough already; this isn't her world. You have no right to involve her in your ugly little games. I'm taking her back to the house."

"Keep your hands off her!" Enrique snarled.

"I've had my fill of this. You can go on with your ceremonies, but leave this girl out of them."

"This girl *is* the ceremony."

Ricardo had his hand on Michelle's arm. He spun around to face Enrique. "What did you say?"

"How dumb can you be, old man?"

"You don't mean you're planning on—"

"My plans are my own business! Let the girl go and get out of the way, or I'll have you taken off."

"Now you listen here," Ricardo fired at him. "I run this town and don't you forget it."

Enrique stared hard at his father, then turned to the dozen guards standing nearby and gave an order in Quitapul. The guards started toward Ricardo. Ricardo shouted a counter-order. The men paused momentarily. Enrique shouted at them again, and they acted, grabbing Ricardo and, despite his shouts, dragging him away.

Michelle, confused, upset, even in her trancelike condition, asked Enrique why they were being mean to Ricardo.

"The old man has gone soft," he said mockingly. "He will spend the night in the guardhouse. Come with me. We must be quick or there will be no stopping Magdalena."

He took Michelle tightly by the arm and hurried up the

278

stone steps into the vastness of the interior of the resort building. Torches lit the way. Michelle felt excitement, mixed with a numb, blissful state. They went into the inner room, with the high-domed ceiling and the stone altar. Enrique shouted tersely at the guards and they left the room, closing the massive wooden door behind them with a thud.

Candles flickered from niches in the circular walls. Michelle stared at the altar, feeling urgent emotions struggling to reach her. She was drawn to the altar, walking over and running her fingers along its smooth surface. Images, memories, dreams flooded her mind, but it was as if a thin membrane kept her from feeling them directly.

"Now it is time to relax and focus," Enrique said, his words echoing against the stone walls. "Come sit with me."

He led the way to a mattress covered with a beautiful native blanket, and they sat down facing each other. "Breathe deeply, relax," he said, and closed his eyes. She did as he ordered, her chest still heaving from the excitement and exertion. After a few moments, she started to slow down. She could hear herself breathing. Enrique breathing. Those were the only sounds in the room. No, she could hear a fly buzzing too.

"This is very serious," Enrique finally said, opening his eyes. "There is no time to prepare you gently; we must plunge into the ceremony. Because we have the jade phallus, Magdalena will be using your father directly. This is not a time for you to be weak."

"I can do anything," she said.

"Then do exactly what I say, without hesitation. Take off your wipile and come over here."

He stood up; so did she. She hesitated a moment, drawing a sharp look of disapproval from him, then did as ordered, bringing her wipile up over her head and following him to the altar. With her skin exposed, she felt a sudden chill course down her body.

"This is a simple blood ceremony," he said, pushing her to sit on the altar. "You, his daughter, and me, Magdalena's brother, we will have the necessary power between us. You simply have to take a little pain, it will be nothing."

He reached into the pouch attached to his belt and produced a razor-sharp obsidian knife. Michelle gasped, having seen pictures of such knives, six inches long, black, glistening glass from the volcano—the ancient Mayans had cut out virgins' hearts with that kind of knife!

"Give me your hand," he said.

Slowly she extended her right hand to him. He took it, mumbled in Quitapul, and with a swift jab punctured her middle finger near the tip. Blood appeared instantly. He did the same to his finger, and then pressed the bleeding cuts together.

"That's all there is to it?" Michelle asked.

"That is to prepare us to work together."

"Oh," she said feeling slightly faint.

"This is no time to be a delicate little girl. I will not damage you."

"Do anything you want, as long as it will help Daddy."

"Good."

His finger, with blood dripping from it, reached out and touched her right nipple, then her left, leaving a wet red imprint on each. "Magdalena is violating your father sexually, I can feel it. You must trust me. You remember on the island today, I could have had you if I wanted to. I am not going to threaten your virginity, that would be disastrous. But we must be blunt. Take off your jeans and sit down on the altar."

She did as ordered, unsnapping them and slipping them off.

"The underpants also."

She removed her underpants, and the cold stone raised gooseflesh on her naked legs. He reached into his pouch and felt around, coming out with a gourd, a cup, and a small stone figure. "Hold this," he said, handing the artifact to her. "It is our power against Magdalena's. If we counter her directly, we can regain the power she has taken from me."

He joined her on the altar, sitting cross-legged, facing her. "Take the stone and place it inside you," he said. "Just a little way, easily. But we must have its power in you, down there."

"Are you sure?"

"Stop talking, do it!"

She reached down between her legs and touched the stone artifact to her labia. There were moist and the stone figurine slipped slightly inside her. Enrique watched her perform the intimate female gesture, his eyes engrossed in her movements. Then he started untying the belt that held up his shorts, and in a moment had his penis freed from the clothing, upright, fully erect. He's going to do it to me now, Michelle found herself thinking. But he didn't. Instead, he handed her the obsidian knife.

"Here, cut me," he said.

"What?"

Then she saw what he meant. He was holding his erection out toward her. "Cut here, we must have phallic blood."

"No, I couldn't do that!"

"*Cut*, or your father will suffer much worse. There is no time to hesitate."

She trembled; the glassy obsidian knife cold in her fingers. Then, without pausing to think, she reached out and sliced the foreskin with one quick motion.

Blood flowed. Enrique, showing no signs of pain, held the cup under his penis while the blood ran in a tiny stream into it. They sat in rapt silence a moment and then he said, "Press over the cut now, hold it."

She did as ordered, watching in dreamlike fascination as he uncorked the gourd and poured some of the contents into the blood. "Now I must do it to you," he said. "Just a small amount."

281

He picked up the knife and before she could think about stopping him, he sliced at her nipple so that a red spring of blood opened up on it. He held the cup against her breast under the cut as the blood ran down. There was another moment of painful silence. He removed the cup and stirred the mixture with his finger. Blood ran down in a tiny rivulet from her breast to her stomach and thigh. Enrique took his finger out of the mixture and stuck the finger between her legs into her opening, touching the stone figurine with his blood-covered fingertip.

He stirred the mixture once again, her vaginal juices joining the other ingredients.

"Now drink this," he ordered, handing her the cup.

She gasped.

"I said drink it, *now!*"

He started chanting in a strange nasal voice, the Quitapul words sounding guttural. Her dizziness increased and she felt almost on the point of losing consciousness. Enrique's eyes closed and he moved deeper into his own trance with the chanting.

She sat holding the cup another moment. Then quickly, she put the cup to her mouth and downed the contents, gasping for breath when she was done, her eyes bulging from the vile taste and texture of the thick liquid as it went down her throat.

The chanting grew in intensity, penetrating her bones, radiating, echoing, filling her entire universe with its energy. The room seemed to be taking on an ominous yellow glow, separate from the flickering candles. Michelle dropped the cup and closed her eyes. Her other hand was still holding Enrique's penis tightly.

Energy surged in her stomach, flared up in a giant inner explosion. The stone figurine grew hotter, began to radiate a strange energy into her womb. She felt a rush of euphoria flash through her body. Her tight grip on his penis slowly started to ease, until the limp fingers released it as her body slumped back on the altar, unconscious.

Enrique's voice chanted on in Quitapul, his tone more and more relaxed, confident, triumphant.

chapter 22

Slowly, Chris started to bring himself to wakefulness. He had passed out on top of her. He opened his eyes and raised himself up. Memories flashed, memories of total sexual fulfillment, beyond anything he had ever dreamed. Caban had come into him, had become one with him, and together the two males had exploded into Magdalena with such force that the volcano had shuddered, the steam had suddenly ceased, and the water had turned hot in the pool.

Chris looked down at Magdalena's face, expecting to see her blissfully asleep. But instead, her eyes were staring blankly upward. For a moment he feared she was dead. Then she blinked a slow, single blink. And he could feel her breathing now against his belly.

"Magdalena," he whispered.

She didn't respond. Her stare remained fixated.

"Hey," he said, rolling off her. "Wake up; it must be late. I've got to get back to Michelle."

The bruja remained in her trance. Chris, frightened by her zombie state, stood up and walked over to the pool of water to cup some in his hands and wake her up with a cold splash. But the water scalded his hands when he dipped them into it. He jumped back.

He heard a low mumbling. Magdalena had started

chanting in Quitapul. It sounded like a funeral chant to Chris. He hurried over to her. "Magdalena," he said urgently. "Say something I can understand; what's wrong?"

Her eyes were frightening, rolling wildly in her head. At the sound of his words, her right eye started to focus on him and she stared up with anguish.

"Todo el mundo está perdido," she murmured. "Everything is now lost."

"Why do you say that? I thought the ceremony—"

"Something happened? Enrique, your daughter. They have done something together that has destroyed everything."

"No, she wouldn't do anything."

"She has!" Magdalena said, life coming back into her naked body. She sad upright, staring at Chris with a penetrating but ghostlike gaze. "Right when I had the power of Caban turned toward the light, they pulled him back into redness, back into blood!"

"But you said Michelle would be all right if I left her," he shouted. "You said—"

"I was certain the power was with me! The power came to me, freed me. I was certain that we would be victorious."

Chris was frantically pulling up his pants. "Well I'm getting down there to see what's happened," he said.

"No, don't go. We can perform another ceremony, perhaps I can—"

"Bullshit to that, I'm going down," he said, sitting down to pull on his boots. "Are you coming?"

She seemed to be regaining full consciousness, but her spirit was limp. "It was all lost," she said, as if to herself. "I have no power. Enrique has won. It is all lost."

Chris stood up and grabbed the rifle. "Well, maybe for you, but I'm gettng down there and take care of my daughter."

"They will be waiting for you; you will be captured."

"I'll take my chances. I'm not going to just sit up here and let them have Michelle!"

286

Magdalena sighed, stood up, and reached for her skirt. "I·will come also. They can have me now; there is nothing more to fight for."

"So what happened to make it all go wrong?" Chris asked, watching her cover herself, wrapping the material of the skirt around her slender body and then tying it in place with the long red sash, her body that had so recently been a rich sexual universe now seeming skinny, frail, sexless.

"Caban," she answered. "Caban has made his choice. My mission has failed. Perhaps we can save your daughter. But I doubt it. Caban has made his choice, and he has chosen the old ways."

"Well as long as I'm alive, Caban isn't doing anything with my daughter."

"We will be captured."

"We have a chance."

"Whatever you want. Nothing matters now, anyway. Caban has chosen darkness, and we will live and die in darkness."

"Hey, cut the melodrama; let's get on the move," he retorted, impatient and angry.

He opened the door and stepped outside. The moon was almost gone behind the mountain. Hours had passed since they had entered the hut. He started down the trail, with Magdalena following him a few yards behind. The rifle felt solid in his grip and his energy was like iron in his muscles, pushing him down the volcano toward Michelle.

The moon was gone from sight when they arrived at the rock outcropping above the house. There was no boat at the dock. Perhaps Magdalena was wrong about everything. Chris had expected to see Enrique's boat there, but it was gone. Then the thought struck him. Of course the boat wouldn't be there; they had taken Michelle away. Goddamn!

He pushed on down the trail recklessly, the rifle cocked and ready to shoot anyone who got in his way. They approached Benito's house cautiously. But everything was as they had left it. The lock was in place. Benito seemed asleep on the floor. Chris turned to Magdalena. Her expression had changed during the run down the mountain. A softness had come over her. But it was a softness of defeat. Chris felt she had yielded her fighting edge completely; she was just flowing with whatever happened, rather than trying to make anything happen anymore.

They headed for the house, running through the avocado grove. As they neared the edge of the orchard, he pulled her to a stop beside him. "Listen," he whispered, "it looks like you were wrong; it looks like everything's okay here. But why don't I go ahead? If they catch me, you'll be free to act."

"Yes," she whispered back.

"I'll call if all's clear."

"Go carefully."

Chris took off through the shadowy orchard, his heart pounding, his throat dry with exertion and dread. When he came upon the expanse of lawn between him and his bedroom door, he paused, listening. His breathing was loud and his heart pounded in his ears. He could see the faint white hint of coming dawn to the east. Morning birds were just starting to chirp from their tree roosts.

He made his break across the lawn, running quickly to the bedroom door. Pausing again, he listened for sounds inside. But everything was quiet. Oh God, he said to himself. Let her be in her bed. Just let us get out of here, please!

He turned the knob on the door, gave it a push, and went inside, expecting at any moment to feel hands grab at his neck from the darkness, or a bullet to crash into his back. Into the hallway. Still no one, nothing. His hopes were rising by the moment, a gigantic weight lifting from his heart. Magdalena had been wrong. She might have suffered some occult disaster, but Michelle hadn't been involved in it. She was going to be in her bed sleeping, just like when he'd left her. She had to be!

He made it to her door and pushed it open.

There she was! Sleeping like a baby in the early morning light. Chris almost wept for joy. He hurried over to her and reached down to touch her, to make sure his eyes weren't playing games with him. While coming down the mountain he had been assaulted with horrifying visions of Michelle on an altar, ravished, sacrificed. But here she was, untouched. He pulled down the sheet, still not believing until he saw, that indeed her breast was whole, that his monstrous visions were nothing more than nightmares he could now throw aside.

He went running back outside and shouted to Magdalena. "She's okay! Everything's all right, come on in."

Magdalena came running quickly from the darkness of the avocado grove. "She's still in the bed?" she asked, astounded.

"Yes, sleeping like a baby. Come look."

They hurried into the house and down the hallway. Chris led the way into Michelle's bedroom, and Magdalena was just through the door when it suddenly slapped shut behind them and two men with rifles stepped out from behind the door. A third appeared at the window. Chris turned and started to raise his own rifle, but he was too late; one of the Indians hit him violently in the abdomen with a gun butt, and he went down onto the floor, groaning and gasping for breath.

"Well well," the other Indian said to Magdalena. "Look at what we have here." He grabbed her by the arm and pushed her out of the room. Chris was dragged to his feet and pushed along behind her. They were taken into his bedroom. Regaining his breath, he struggled wildly against the Indians, and received a fist in his solar plexus. Magdalena shouted something in Quitapul at her captors, and the head Indian turned on her, slapping her across the face and pushing her roughly onto the bed. He ripped at her long skirt and pulled it off her, giving a coarse, victorious laugh, then shouting at her menacingly in Quitapul. He turned to one of the other Indians and handed him his rifle. Untying his belt, he stepped out of his shorts, releasing his throbbing erection. He jumped onto the conquered bruja, and forced himself into her with angry thrusts, grabbing at her breasts, kissing her with a rapist's anger. With a loud grunt he climaxed inside her and pulled himself out, grinning at his conquest.

He ordered her tied hand and foot. Then the other two Indians took their turns with her. Chris was then tied up also, and flung onto the bed beside Magdalena. The Indians left them lying together.

For a few minutes they lay face to face, both of them only half-conscious. Slowly Chris felt himself regaining awareness. He could hear Magdalena breathing, could make out her body beside him.

"Are you all right?" he said quietly.

"Yes."

"Goddamn them."

"They will burn in hell!" she said venomously.

"I couldn't do anything."

"I knew it was coming. I know those men; they are Enrique's best friends; they have hated me ever since he turned against me."

"They tied me so tight I don't think I can get loose."

"Relax. We can only accept our fate now."

"Like hell I will," Chris growled defiantly, struggling with the reeds that held his wrists, feeling them cut into his skin but not giving up hope of getting free.

"We have no choice," she told him. "There is more to life than the physical body. We are moving on to what is beyond. I know that the power is ultimately with me. But I accept that, for this lifetime, it is over."

"Ricardo can still save us," Chris said.

"That is stupid talk."

"He's got a good heart deep down."

"Ricardo is one of them," she said hotly.

The sound of a speedboat penetrated the walls of the house. "Do you hear that?" Chris said, excited. "That's

290

probably Ricardo now, coming to get us out of here."

"They will be coming for Michelle now. It is time for the ceremony to begin."

"You can't give up hope."

"Caban has made his choice; our only hope all along was with Caban."

"Then Caban can still save us!"

"I am sorry for you, Christopher. Before I die, I ask you for your forgiveness. Because I failed, you and your daughter must die. But this death, it is nothing; we have died many times before, you and I. We will die many times again. Please, forgive me for not succeeding with the Quitapul."

"Damn it, don't just give up!"

The speedboat came zooming up to the dock, and the engine was cut. Magdalena's eyes were looking at Chris, both the dominant one and the wandering one focused on him at once in an intent, fused gaze. He remembered the first time they had been alone together at the hot springs, and the fantasies he had conjured up around her. The reality was far more fantastic, and infinitely horrible. And the worst horror of all was that he had dragged Michelle into it. . . . He gave a groan of despair.

"Christopher," Magdalena said softly, "it is a time to be strong. Something that could have happened is not going to happen and that is indeed a tragedy. But the designs of power know better than we can ever guess. People live and people die, but there is something happening on this planet which will move to its conclusion."

"I'll tell you, Magdalena," Chris said with savage irony, "right now I couldn't care less about planetary conclusions. You and I and Michelle look as if *we're* just about concluded, and that's what's on my mind."

Magdalena ignored his sarcasm and went on almost dreamily, "The Quitapul have chosen the way of darkness. They are the end of the past. There is always something new."

Chris said impatiently, "There may be something new coming, but it doesn't seem like we'll be on hand to see it unless we can find a way to get out of this! What's happened to you? You've worked and fought for . . . for whatever the hell you were up to, for years. But now you just seem content to lie back and let the worst happen. This is one hell of a time to give up the fight."

"You keep on fighting, Christopher. That is your destiny. But me, I feel a relaxation coming over me, as if a burden has been taken from my shoulders. It has been worthwhile, just being one with you again after who knows how many lifetimes. I am content."

Footsteps came up the hallway toward the bedroom. Chris blinked at the brightness when the door opened. The figure in the doorway was Enrique.

"Well look at this," he said with a sneer. "The two partners of the Devil have been caught like rats." He strode over to the bed. "So, sister, you must admit that my plans are successful."

Magdalena glared up at him for a moment with hatred. Then she relaxed. Said nothing.

"Where is your power now?" he said mockingly to her. "What happened up at the steam hut? Did this gringo satisfy you enough to bring Caban under your spell?"

"Damn it, Enrique," Chris shouted at him, "untie us; stop this idiotic game you're playing!"

"As for you, gringo, there are final plans for you also; everything is working out perfectly."

"If you so much as touch Michelle, I'll—"

Enrique gave Chris a blow in the kidney that cut short his threat and left him moaning in pain.

"Dear brother," Magdalena said. "You should indeed be proud of yourself."

Her tone of voice was deceptively humble. "What are you talking about?" he grumbled, turning to leave.

"You have learned well the ways of the ancients."

"I have!"

"May you die into the same hell they now live in."

He scowled at her, but her crossed eyes were a threat to him even with her hands tied, and he hurried out of the room, shouting orders to the guards to bring the prisoners out and down to the boat.

chapter 23

The sun was just rising as Chris and Magdalena were pushed outside onto the lawn. They were taken down to the beach and kept waiting for fifteen minutes.

"What's he doing to her?" Chris asked Magdalena, knowing that the delay had something to do with Michelle.

But Magdalena did not respond. She seemed to be putting herself into a trance, gazing at Caban vacantly, breathing with deep rhythmic inhalations and then strong exhalations through her nose.

Suddenly, there was Michelle, walking out the living room door, wearing a long white gown, her long blonde hair brilliant in the light of the rising sun.

"Michelle!" Chris shouted to her.

She looked down the fifty feet to where he was being held prisoner by three guards. She smiled a vague, trance-like smile. "Hello, Daddy," she said calmly.

Enrique came hurrying out of the house. Michelle was walking toward Chris, but Enrique caught her by the arm and stopped her, told her to wait, and went ahead down to Chris and Magdalena. "Listen," he muttered at the gringo. "You say one word to her to disturb her, and you will be killed instantly, do you understand? I want you at the final ceremonies, but you are dispensable. I will kill you right now if you so much as look at her wrong."

"Tell me something?"

"What?"

"Where is Ricardo? I want to talk to him."

"He's in jail where he belongs."

"What?" Under what charges?"

"Attempting to interfere with tribal custom."

Michelle was walking down toward them, looking like an angel except for the vacant expression in her eyes. "Daddy, why are your hands tied?" she asked slowly, unemotionally.

Enrique spoke up instantly. "It is nothing; he and Magdalena still insist on stopping our ceremonies, so they must be detained for a while. Let's get started; the preliminary rites must begin soon."

Enrique took Michelle by the arm and escorted her down to the dock. Chris glanced at Magdalena, but she was deeper in her trance, of no use to him. This isn't the moment to act, he told himself. But soon there must come a moment when a chance opens up. Nothing can happen to Michelle; that isn't the way life unfolds.

He looked up at Caban as one of the guards grabbed him and pulled him toward the boat. The entire top half of the volcano was covered in a shroud of mist. Chris felt a surge of emotion inside him, as if he could suddenly feel a connection with Caban. But the emotion was vague, and it troubled him as much as it encouraged him about Caban's role in the drama of this nightmarish day.

The lake was glassy smooth. The speedboat cut across its surface, sending out a rippling wake on either side, one wave heading toward the volcano's shore, the other toward the sacred island. Chris tried to make contact with Michelle with his eyes, but she seemed to be in such a deep trance that she was emotionally numb, not really awake at all, like a sleep-walker. Anger swelled inside his chest. He struggled again with the wet reeds that held his wrists. But the more he struggled the more they cut into

296

his skin; he was already bleeding and the pain increased with each new attempt to get loose.

He gave up for the moment. His body was racked with pain from the bruises he had received and his head throbbed, but the worst pain of all was the agony of total powerlessness. He glanced at Magdalena. She was sitting on the floor beside him. She was looking at him with her strong eye, but he felt she was hardly conscious in that eye at all; she seemed lost gazing into the distance with her other eye. And when he met Michelle's eyes again, he felt the same thing. Her strong eye looked at him vaguely, but he sensed that she was mostly conscious in the wandering left eye. If only she would look at him with that eye!

With Enrique at the helm, the speedboat with its eight passengers closed the distance between itself and the resort. The very thought of the circular, domed ceremonial room brought a tight knot to Chris' stomach. A dozen men in Quitapul ceremonial dress stood on the beach awaiting the arrival of the boat.

"Michelle," he whispered.

She looked in his direction.

"Kiddo, hang in there, we'll get out of this. Try to wake up!"

A guard pushed Chris hard with the barrel of a rifle, and he fell silent. He thought, though, that he detected a slight response from Michelle, enough at least to give him hope that when it came time to act, she might come out of her trance and help him in the escape.

The boat put in at the dock, but only Michelle and two guards were allowed to debark. Chris stood up, insisting on going with her, and Enrique turned around and kicked him squarely in the balls, not hard enough to injure him severely, but hard enough to make him double up in pain while the boat zoomed off again—leaving Michelle in the hands of the tribal priests while he and Magdalena were taken around the point of the bay to the main dock at Zacapula.

By the time the boat was landing, Chris was recovered enough to hear the shouting of hostile, excited voices on shore. He glanced at Magdalena and found her staring at him with both her eyes focused intently. There was a lightness to her expression now, as if she had suddenly surfaced from her trance into a level of euphoria. The expression struck him deeply. A part of him felt itself yielding inside, joining her in a state of mind that had let go of . . . of life itself.

She gave him a faint, soft smile and then spoke in a gentle voice. "I'll always be with you," she whispered over the harsh outside sounds. "We are born so many times. I will see you again, my love. A Dios!"

Two guards pulled her to her feet and threw her up onto the pier. She landed hard, with her hands tied behind her, unable to block her fall onto the rough planks. Chris shuddered as he heard the sudden swelling of noise from the crowd on shore at the sight of her. Then he was being lifted himself and thrown onto the pier. He looked to the shore as he was raised to his feet by the guards.

The entire town, except for the priests who were now at the resort with Michelle, must have been there—standing along the beach, up the slope toward the main street, over on the rocks. Everywhere there was space, there was a Quitapul Indian. The color of their clothes was so vibrant that Chris felt a sudden psychedelic euphoria rush over him at the sight, as he was absorbed into the moving mass of brilliant reds, vibrating oranges, and shimmering blues.

Then Enrique, at the end of the pier, raised his hands and the crowd became silent, focused on his presence. He started talking in a commanding voice. Chris couldn't understand a word, but he had heard that same tone of voice before, that same haranguing, cajoling, manipulating voice that could control a mob of people, evoke the proper responses, elicit the desired action.

The result of his short speech was a general movement of the people on shore up the road toward the church.

The guards forced Chris and Magdalena down the long pier onto the shore. Magdalena walked off the pier of her own volition. Someone in the crowd threw a small stone, and it hit her hard on the arm. She acted as if nothing had happened. The guards pressed the Indians back, pushed rifle barrels at angry women who stood shouting insults in Quitapul at Magdalena as she was escorted, along with Chris and Enrique, up the road through the town.

It was a long march, and Chris felt his sanity endangered by the barrage of hostile voices, the constant shoving as the guards formed a small wedge to force the prisoners through the crowd. He found himself more and more certain that his end was coming at the end of this march. He knew he bore no similarity to Jesus; his death would mean nothing except to him and those close to him. But the sensation of being marched up the hill, with an angry, abusive mob surrounding him, made him feel suddenly that he *was* Jesus, that both he and Magdalena were being taken to be unjustly crucified.

The church square was packed with Indians. The guards shoved and threatened, opening a way for the three Special Ones to pass up to the foot of the church steps. The church itself loomed tall and ominous in front of them, and Chris found himself coldly convinced that no Christian God was going to help him. Somehow the adobe church in front of him seemed more pagan than the Indians themselves; there was a coldness coming from it which struck a final blow to his hope that his tradition would strike down this pagan atrocity.

Farther Morales appeared at the top of the steps. He started talking to the crowd urgently. Enrique went running up the steps and confronted him, arguing fiercely with him. Then the attention of both men was shifted as Ricardo was brought out of the jailhouse and up to the stairs where Chris and Magdalena were being held. Chris watched as father confronted daughter.

Ricardo's face was streaked with tears. He reached out

and touched Magdalena's face. She raised her head and looked up at him. Nothing was said. But in the midst of the frightening mob, Chris found himself moved almost to tears at the encounter. There was the love that had been missing all along, that might have prevented this tragedy from happening. But now, as the two looked each other in the eye, it was a shared look of forgiveness and acceptance, with no element of hope.

Loud shouting came again from the top of the steps. Father Morales was addressing the mob.

"What's he saying?" Chris asked Ricardo.

"He says . . . he says that Magdalena must be tried by church laws, that she will be burned at the stake if found to be a witch, but that the mob must now disperse."

The crowd wouldn't let the priest finish his speech. They shouted back at him until he gave up, looking sunken, dejected, defeated as he stood beside the dynamic young Enrique, who raised his arms again for silence. He spoke, and Ricardo translated for Chris.

"He is telling the crowd that they can have Magdalena, but that the two gringos are needed for the ceremonies," Ricardo said, his voice shaking. "Oh God, no, no, no!"

But it was too late. Enrique came running down the steps. When the priest shouted out a final time for order, a stone hit him in the stomach, and then another stone and another, and he crumpled. With a thrill of horror, Chris realized that the balance of power in this weird conflict had altered drastically. Morales, whatever his faults—his fanaticism, his hatred for Magdalena, his superstition—had been a force for some kind of recognizable justice and law. But now he was out of it, and everything was in the hands of these Indians—and their bloodthirsty gods.

Magdalena stood and started walking up the steps of her own volition.

"No!" Chris and Ricardo shouted out in unison, making a move toward her. Guards grabbed at them and held

300

them back while she began her long ascent. She was half-way up when a stone struck her. And then a hail of stones pelted her body.

Chris was grabbed by his tied hands and pulled away by two guards. His vision had blurred with shock, his spirit broken by the sight, and he was limp while the guards worked to get him clear of the crowd while the focus was still on Magdalena. For a hundred feet, he was dragged as dead weight. Then he struggled to his feet and was pushed brusquely ahead of the guards, along with Ricardo and Enrique, running away from the mob while they could.

They made it, breathless, to the boat, and jumped in. Enrique started the engine and they were off, away from the mob, safe. He stood at the helm with his jaw set, his eyes flaring with determined fire. Ricardo was collapsed on the deck, sobbing. Chris felt his stomach heaving, but could only gag; there was nothing in it to come up.

Magdalena! he cried out silently. Magdalena!

He eyed Enrique and rage erupted in him, a murderous blind rage that had him on his feet suddenly, running at Enrique even with his hands tied behind his back, determined to kill the man who had caused the stoning. But the guards were ready for him. He received two fists in his exposed stomach and went down onto the deck again.

Lying there, panting, Chris found himself looking at Ricardo. They lay there a long moment staring into each other's eyes. For the first time in his life, Chris felt the reality of all historical atrocities ever committed. He felt horror of the human race. He felt the total devastating reality of human insanity.

chapter 24

The burning incense sent a fine line of smoke up into the room. The center of the dome was white with smoke, and the sealed room was strongly scented with the aroma of the resinous ceremonial "pom."

Fourteen candles were burning on the wooden stand behind the altar. Earlier in the day, the Ah Kin, or high priest under Enrique, had entered the ceremonial dome and painted the altar sacrificial blue. A chicken had been sacrified to expel any enemy spirits or curses generated by the renegade bruja.

Now the door was locked from the inside. Michelle had been left alone, in a trance, while the Ah Kin and his assistants prepared Enrique. Now he was with her in the room, looking down at where she lay asleep on the mattress.

"Wake up, Ah K'aaba!" he said to her.

Her eyes fluttered, opened, gazed at the young man. He looked transformed. There was a bold black line circling his left eye and running down his left cheek. His face was smeared with blood, drying into a hard mask. His hair also was a clotted mop of blood. He was naked except for a white loincloth, and his body was painted a dark purple.

"It is time to prepare," he said, feeling the weight of

thousands of years of tradition and power pressing him into his own trance. "You are to be painted blue. Stand up, take off your clothes!"

She stared at him, her mind blank. His words slowly seeped into her mind. She stood up, her fear obliterated by the ceremonial reality surrounding her, hypnotizing her further into her role.

"Off!"

She reached down and slowly pulled the traditional white gown up from her legs, her middle, her breasts, and finally over her head while Enrique stood watching. Naked, she felt a sudden chill that made her shiver involuntarily. After the shiver came a warm afterflow, however, and she had a fleeting recollection of a summer evening in Mill Valley, stepping out of a swimming pool and standing naked with a towel.

She was jolted out of the reverie by a strange sensation on her left foot, as if a large tongue was licking her, wetting her skin, covering her with something sticky. She became aware of Enrique kneeling in front of her, a clay pot beside him and a paintbrush in his hand, applying blue paint to her body. He smeared the cool liquid over both her feet and then started working his way up her left leg, dipping the brush in the large pot after each two or three strokes.

"Spread your legs," he said. She moved her left foot to the side and he swabbed her inner thigh, almost to her pubic hair. Then he started up the right leg. Michelle found herself drifting into the sensory experience of the ritual, feeling nothing but the soft wet licking, almost a tingling, as the brush applied more and more paint to her body, covering her tanned legs with a blue coat of sacred emulsion. As Enrique performed his duty for her, the small silver-and-gold bells around his ankles and wrists jingled. Michelle closed her eyes. The sound was thrilling; the sensation of the brush reaching higher and higher up her right thigh was stimulating.

As he reached her pubic area and brushed between

her spread legs, she groaned involuntarily. He lingered over his work, passing the brush back and forth until her pubic hair was a thousand tiny blue curls, her body glistening. Then up higher, painting with more rapid strokes her stomach, her breasts, turning her around and painting her firm buttocks and slender back. "Close your eyes," he said, and painted her face. Only her hair, which he had pinned on top of her head, remained its natural color.

"Come over here," he said when he was done, leading her to the mat.

They sat down facing each other as they had the time before. He handed her a large goblet, made entirely of gold, with bas-reliefs of Mayan deities covering its outer surface. "Drink," he said.

It was sweet, like honey wine, with a strong alcoholic burn to it as it went down. She almost coughed up her first mouthful. "Drink more," he ordered, and she did, taking two more gulps. He drank next, deeply, thirstily, glancing avidly at her blue body. When the goblet was drained he stood up, walked to the candlestand, and returned with the obsidian knife. Without speaking a word he reached out and sliced the lower lobe of her left ear.

He caught the dripping blood in the palm of his hand, rubbed his hands together, and then rubbed the blood into his hair. The cut in her ear continued to drip blood in a red stream down onto her neck, her left shoulder, over her left breast and down her stomach, mixing with the blue to form a deep purple.

She stared at him, her right eye looking at this wild, painted Indian, her left eye taking in the flickering candles and the altar. He pulled her to her feet and placed a peaked headdress on her head, letting her blond hair fall down onto her now-dry shoulders and back. He picked up a small drum, and set up a slow, rhythmic beat; his voice joined in with a hypnotic chant.

She allowed herself to take in the sounds and the image of the Indian dancing slowly in front of her. "Join me," he said, and then closed his eyes, threw his head back, and let his voice resonate in the stone chamber until Michelle felt herself caught up in his music, her body moving also to the beat, swaying, undulating slowly. The words he was saying, repeating them over and over, echoed through her mind into long-lost tunnels . . . tunnels, black tunnels, deep inside her.

The music stopped but she continued swaying, the rhythm lingering in her body as she was led over to the altar. As she walked, her legs felt strange, as if they weren't her own legs, as if they were hollow. Her whole body felt hollow, a giant void, with the blue paint pressing on her hollowness and the air outside feeling solid, weighty.

She was on the altar now, on her back. Enrique was chanting again. Michelle felt his voice as if she were the one chanting, as if she knew the words before he said them, as if she were moving into his body, while her body became more and hollow, black, but somehow plugged up, blocked off, incomplete. There was a yearning growing within her as the Indian's voice droned on beside her, a yearning for something deep down in her hollowness. She could feel it now; it was bright, glowing, heavy. It was her center. At the end of the hollowness, the end of the tunnel of her body, was a great mound of glowing gold, her very essence.

Something touched her. Her eyes opened and looked up at Enrique standing at her side in the act of slicing his penis with the knife. He put the knife down and reached for the jade phallus. With slow, deliberate movements he smeared the jade phallus with blood from his own penis. She watched, lost in a deep trance of fascination, as the green stone became slippery with the red blood.

Her eyes closed. She felt herself floating, returning to her deep center, to the gold glowing center. Then starting up her hollowness, up through the blackness of her tunnel, moving with a compulsive yearning to emerge into

306

the outside light, but then coming against a blockage, a flexible but solid membrane which she could not break.

Something from the outside was trying to get in. Moving up and down against her, softly at first, then starting to push harder. Her legs opened wide as Enrique pushed the jade phallus into her sexual opening, pushing while he chanted louder and louder, faster and faster, building to a wild, powerful crescendo.

And then his chanting stopped short with a piercing cry as he thrust the jade beyond the barrier of her virginity and deep into her. She felt its presence; her glowing, golden center reverberated from the penetration, as if her hollowness were being destroyed. Enrique gave a piercing, victorious shout. The floor under him rumbled, stones fell from the ceiling around him, but he was overcome with his victory. He ignored the earth's shaking and pulled the jade phallus out of the girl and threw it away, feeling the rush of power take over his reason.

He wanted final victory for himself also, and he climbed up onto the altar on top of this blonde beauty. Michelle felt the jade slip out of her, and there was a strange hollowness again within her body. But the darkness suddenly became light. She felt herself again; the trance was gone. She was Michelle Barker from Mill Valley—and this wild Indian was on top of her, trying to rape her!

She screamed out at him, hit at him frantically. But he was a maniac now, forcing himself inside her.

"Get off, goddamn you!" she cried.

But he had her pinned and was now pushing with thrusts that hurt her, forcing his organ deep inside her. She felt a horror she had never imagined before as she experienced this man's penis starting to ejaculate unwanted sperm inside her womb. Her hatred was boundless, and she clawed at him with her fingernails, drawing blood on his cheeks and forehead. He growled and slapped her, and then pulled himself out of her with an excruciating yank that left her crying, sobbing hysterically, on the altar.

A strong earth tremor shook the room. A large stone fell just an inch from Michelle's head, crashing against the edge of the altar and smashing to the floor below. Enrique got up off her, tied up his loincloth, and pulled her to her feet.

As he looked around for his pouch and her gown, Michelle saw the obsidian knife on the candle-table and grabbed for it. He picked up her gown, and as he turned toward her, she lunged at him, knowing that if she didn't get him, that he would get her—cut out her heart. And her romantic notions of sacrifice were gone now; she wanted to live.

He was too fast for her. He saw the knife coming and dodged her jab, catching her arm in an iron grip that made her drop the knife and cry out in pain.

"You idiot!" he muttered, and slapped her hard across the face.

She stared at him, and again he suddenly had a fearful conviction that she wasn't Michelle but Magdalena. He threw the gown at her. Another shock hit and he grabbed her arm, pulling her toward the door.

chapter 25

Chris and Ricardo stood side by side, surrounded by eight armed guards, near the resort dock. Most of the townspeople had assembled outside the resort and were standing in muted silence waiting for the ceremony to end and Enrique to emerge. The earthquakes of the last few minutes had brought an end to any conversation. The crowd was in a radically different mood from what it had been in at the church, like a giant organism after orgasm, drained and numb after the stoning on the church steps.

Another earthquake shook the area. Stones toppled from the resort building's walls. One large piece fell from the top of the two-story main wall and rolled down the slope, scattering Indians all the way to the beach.

"I'm loose," Ricardo whispered in English.

"What will you do?"

Enrique appeared up at the building entrance, and a shout went up from the tense crowd. He had Michelle in his grip with one hand, and they paused at the top of the stairs.

"Goddamn him!" Chris cried out, seeing his daughter naked, painted blue, a spectacle on the outdoor pagan stage. Enrique had her gown in his other hand, and he shouted at two guards who came up and dressed her while he spoke to the crowd in Quitapul.

"I'll kill him," Chris muttered.

"That is my duty," Ricardo muttered back.

As Enrique started to address the crowd, Ricardo made his move, lunging at the nearest guard and grabbing his rifle from him. Before Enrique noticed what was happening, Ricardo raised the rifle, cocked it, and fired.

Enrique's head jerked as a splash of blood blossomed on his left temple. Screams rose from the Indians. Ricardo was jumped by two guards at once and knocked to the ground.

Chris stared as Enrique stumbled backward. But very quickly, Enrique recovered, standing straight while blue-painted tribal priests inspected his wound. It was a surface scratch, nothing more. Enrique held up his hands in triumph, and the mob responded with manic cheers.

Michelle suddenly bolted and ran, pushing her way past surprised guards. Chris lost sight of her in the crowd. "Michelle!" he shouted.

But she was caught and brought back. Enrique said a few ranting sentences to the crowd, grabbing Michelle by the arm and marched down the steps toward where Ricardo was being held by two guards, awaiting Enrique's deadly attention.

Chris yanked one more time at his tied hands, but it was no use, and the pain of the effort was intense. In any case, a guard held him tightly. When Enrique and Michelle were in sight again, walking across the grass toward the dock, Chris cried out to her, "Kiddo!" Her head turned in his direction and she recognized him.

"Daddy!"

Enrique pushed her roughly to two guards at the dock, and they bound her hands behind her. Then father confronted son. Enrique stood three feet in front of Ricardo.

"So you would have me dead," Enrique said.

"I would have you dead," Ricardo agreed stolidly.

"You idiot! Everything we have worked for, it is now ours. The tunnel has opened up, I am sure it has!"

"You let them kill your own sister."

"She had to die!"

"And so do you!"

Enrique slowly grinned, took a pistol from the guard standing beside him, and raised it to Ricardo's head.

"No!" Chris shouted.

There was an explosion that he took for the pistol's discharge. But Enrique, instead of pulling the trigger, spun around and stared up at the volcano, as did Chris, realizing that the shattering sound was not a gunshot. It was Caban!

Panic gripped the massed Quitapul natives as a giant cloud of ash billowed up from the volcano. A second explosion came like a thunderclap, shooting boulders hundreds of feet into the air, and sending up a massive dark cloud of ash which filled the sky, casting an ominous shadow over the lake.

Forgetting about Ricardo, Enrique grabbed Michelle and pushed her down the dock toward the boat. Chris found himself shoved and dragged there also; and along with four priests with rifles, they quickly set off for the island. Chris looked back and saw Ricardo being taken away under guard through the mute crowd.

The Xocomil was blowing. The boat rocked sharply as Enrique drove it toward the island, the engine revved to maximum in his panic to get to the island. Caban was demanding sacrifice! He had opened his heart and now he required his just reward. Enrique had expected there to be some time between the phallus ceremony and the heart sacrifice, but Caban's demand was obvious—the heart of the virgin now, or death to the Quitapul!

Ash rained down on the boat and its passengers as they crashed through the waves. Michelle was sobbing, but when Chris tried to move to comfort her, a guard pushed him roughly back into his corner in the back of the boat.

She raised her head and looked at him. There was his little girl again, out of the trance.

311

"Don't worry," Chris shouted to her over the noise of the engine. "We'll get out of this, I swear to God."

One of the priests stuck a rifle barrel to his throat threateningly, and he closed his mouth.

The Xocomil was whipping up the lake and blowing ash like black rain, the tiny cinders getting in eyes and darkening hair and clothing. Enrique drove the speedboat around to the eastern side of the island, where its mass broke the force of the wind, and rammed the boat up onto the beach with a loud grating.

Caban seemed to have relaxed, temporarily. As the guards hurried the captives up the trail to the ruins, Chris felt that very soon his moment would come to act. There were four guards to get the better of somehow, not to mention Enrique himself. But Chris, in his fever of rage and panic, felt he could handle any odds—no matter what, he would not let them do anything to Michelle!

Enrique felt his triumph nearly complete. If the tunnel were open when he arrived at the ruins, then he only had to perform the sacrifice and his power would be unbounded. Caban would be *his* force and nothing on the planet could stop him.

They ran down the trail into the canyon. The wind whipped cinders into their eyes. Michelle was half-carried by two guards twenty feet ahead of Chris, and he was escorted with a guard in front of him and a guard behind. Enrique ran on ahead with driving energy all the way down into the meadow, to meet his fate, to see if Caban had opened his heart and treasure to the Quitapul.

When Michelle and Chris were brought into the clearing, Enrique was nowhere in sight. Chris stopped, along with the priests, the four of whom forgot their responsibilities for a moment as they gaped at the sight in front of them. The same tunnel in the cliff that Chris had visualized before was there again. *It had happened.*

As the four guards stared at the opening, Michelle moved quickly up behind her father, back to back, and their fingers worked urgently to untie each other's bonds.

312

Chris's reed ropes wouldn't budge; the knots were too tight from hours of pulling at them. But Michelle's started to give, and then she was free.

A guard noticed her just as she grabbed at his rifle. Chris ran at him with his head down and butted him in the stomach. She had the rifle in her hands; she tried to work the lever action to cock it but couldn't. One of the guards grabbed it from her. Chris was pulled to his feet.

"Ajonjoli!"

It was Enrique, emerging from the tunnel, crying out his victory. He came running across the meadow, shouting. "The gold, the gold! A mountain of gold!" He arrived at the group breathless, his eyes wild with power. "Hurry, up the temple, there is no time to lose!"

"No!" Chris shouted at him.

"Shut up, gringo. Your time is coming. Up the steps quickly!"

Michelle struggled against the hands holding her on either side. "You can't do this!" she cried out.

But quickly the two guard-priests lifted her and started carrying her kicking body up the temple steps. Chris hesitated a moment, and then realized he had at least to stay beside her, not let them take her away from him. He ran up the steps behind her, with Enrique at his side, outdistancing him because his hands weren't tied behind him.

An earthquake hit the island. Stones were dislodged from the temple, and one rolled down the steps, dangerously close to the small band running up. "Caban, be patient!" Enrique called out. "Five minutes and all will be yours!"

Ahead of him, Michelle was suddenly hit with an epilepticlike fit, her body convulsing so violently that the guards had to put her down, sit her on a step until the spasms left her. Chris and Enrique stopped several steps below her, frightened by the energy attacking her body.

Then the seizure was over. She opened her eyes and stared at Enrique, her vision fused. Both men felt a tremor of terror run through them. Her eyes—they looked like Magdalena's eyes.

Michelle slowly stood up, turned around, and started walking up the steps. The two guard-priests followed her. Enrique hurried up behind them, his face ashen. Chris walked up also, something in him numb, hollow.

Michelle reached the top of the temple and without hesitation, slipped the ash-blackened gown up over her head. Chris reached the top, gasping for breath.

"No," he said. "No, Michelle."

But she turned her back on him and faced Caban. "I am ready," she whispered.

"Get her on the altar," Enrique ordered the priests. "Hurry or Caban will speak again."

Hands reached for Michelle. Chris exploded at the guards, growling, attacking them with his teeth like a rabid animal. But it was of no use; he was seized and overcome.

"Gringo," Enrique muttered. "It will be your balls when I am done with her."

Chris had no energy left, no breath in his lungs. His heart was pounding from overexertion and his knees felt ready to crumple under him if the guard holding him from behind let go.

Michelle turned and looked at her father, then directly at Enrique. She placed herself on the stone altar without being forced. Her breasts arched to the sky, her head rolled back on the curved stone. A priest grabbed her ankles, another grabbed her wrists.

Enrique reached into his pouch and brought out the sacrificial knife. He began chanting in Quitapul. There was a responsive rumble from the volcano towering over them, a deep, vibrating sound that increased in volume as Enrique chanted. Then an explosion blasted up from Caban's depths, shooting red-hot lava high into the blackened sky.

Michelle rolled her head and looked at Enrique. Her mind flashed back to the cat killing the mouse, remembering the calm, determined, guilt-free expression in the cat's eyes. But Enrique lacked that quality; there was nothing sacred in his eyes; they were glassed over with his blind lust for power. Her right eye looked into his eyes and her left eye stared at the shining obsidian knife in his hand.

Enrique muttered the final words of the ancient ceremony and then took a deep breath. With the knife in his hand, ready to slit open the young girl's chest, between the ribs as he had been instructed, he met her stare as tradition dictated he must before making the incision. He would open her so that he could reach in, grab the still-beating heart, and raise it up in sacrifice to Caban.

But Michelle rolled her head toward Caban. An electric blast shattered her being into a billion colored shards that shot away from her center into infinity, and then instantly seemed sucked back toward her center—coming together not as Michelle, but as Magdalena! And the voice of Magdalena cried out at the volcano just as Enrique raised the knife in the air to cut.

The powerful cry of the victim was lost in a vaster noise, as a blinding explosion blew the entire top off the volcano, shooting white-hot lava hundreds of feet into the air. The sound was deafening and the ensuing quake so strong that Enrique dropped the obsidian knife, staggered back from the altar. The Indians stared in dumb, frozen shock. Michelle jumped free of the altar, grabbed the knife, took Chris's arm, and started down the steps with him. Another explosion flashed like a nuclear bomb atop Caban. Enrique came running down. All three reached the base of the temple together. Michelle and Chris ran toward the boat. Enrique suddenly froze in his tracks, looking at the tunnel opening. Red-hot lava was pouring out in great gushes, like an artery pumping its blood out of the body. The lava flowing across the meadow, heating the stream into steam, burning everything in its path.

Michelle slashed at Chris's bonds, and suddenly his hands were free. They ran without looking back, up the trail, through the ash-filled darkness. Chris stumbled as they headed down the other side, wrenching his ankle again. Michelle helped him to his feet. Behind them, another explosion from the volcano made the earth shudder.

They made it to the boat. The Xocomil was a fury, the lake a raging demon. "Hurry, get in!" Michelle cried out. "Here come Enrique and the guards."

Chris scrambled into the boat, Michelle pushed it out into the waves and jumped in. Mercifully, the engine started at the first pull, and Chris put the boat in reverse, backing into the lake. By the time he had it in forward gear and was speeding out into the rampaging wind and water, Enrique was at the beach, aiming, firing.

The first bullet struck the back of the boat and splintered wood, ripping a hole high up and not doing any harm. The second bullet smashed into the mahogany dashboard inches from Chris's body. But the boat roared ahead, and they were soon out of range. Michelle stood aft, ignored by Chris as he struggled to keep the boat afloat in the raging storm. They had no chance; they would capsize at any moment.

Michelle, as she stood facing the violent, glowing mountain behind them, raised her arms. When she shouted, her voice wasn't that of a fourteen-year-old girl from Mill Valley. It was the voice of a bruja from Zacapula.

"Hear me, Xocomil! Listen to me! Cease!"

Chris couldn't hear her over the roar of the engine and the howl of the wind. But he felt the wind suddenly lose its power, felt the waves slacken their savage pounding at the boat. For the first time that day, he felt the warm rush of hope. It was one thing to fight to survive; it was something else entirely to expect to.

Twenty minutes later they were in the middle of the lake, headed for Panahachel. Behind them, the volcano still spewed lava down on the helpless town of Zacapula, destroying the last bastion of Mayan power. Chris glanced at his daughter, standing beside him.

"Goddamn, we made it!" he said. "We're going to make it out of here, back to the States!"

She returned his smile. "Back to the States, yes," she said.

Chris grinned and attended to navigating the boat. Michelle stared at him a moment, and then turned to look back to Zacapula. Her crossed eyes fused at the sight of the devastated town, and for a fleeting minute the eyes were those of Magdalena, surfacing to see the end of the Quitapul. Then the power and the personality of the bruja receded, and the eyes were once again those of a girl, unaware of the Other her being now harbored.

MYSTERY...SUSPENSE...ESPIONAGE

THE GOLD CREW
*by Thomas N Scortia
& Frank M Robinson*   (B83 522 $2 95)
The most dangerous test the world has ever known is now
taking place aboard the mammoth nuclear sub *Alaska*
Human beings, unpredictable in moments of crisis, are
being put under the ultimate stress On patrol out of contact with the outside world the crew is deliberately being
led to believe that the U S S R has attacked the U S.A
Will the crew follow standing orders and fire the *Alaska's*
missiles in retaliation? Now the fate of the world depends
on what's going on in the minds of the men of THE GOLD
CREW

__ THE OFFICERS' WIVES
by Thomas Fleming   (A90-920 $3 95)
This is a book you will never forget It is about the U S
Army the huge unwieldy organism on which much of the
nation's survival depends It is about Americans trying to
live personal lives to cling to touchstones of faith and
hope in the grip of the blind blunderous history of the last
25 years It is about marriage the illusions and hopes that
people bring to it the struggle to maintain and renew com-
mitment

__ THE HAMLET ULTIMATUM
by Leonard Sanders   (B83-461 $2 95)
World takeover is HAMLET's goal! The mysterious terrorist
group has already sabotaged all the computer networks it
requires, even that of the C I.A. Now the group is ready for
its ultimatum to the U S government Surrender or watch
the entire Northeast burn in a nuclear disaster Only ex-
agent Loomis can stop them And only Loomis and his
team have the courage to oppose the President and fight
the world they want to save

WARNER BOOKS PROUDLY PRESENTS

A BAD MAN
by Stanley Elkin (95-539 $2 75)
"A very funny book   The prose dialogue and imagery are brilliant   The laughs alternate with the philosophy and sometimes merge with it " —*The Saturday Review*

BOSWELL
by Stanley Elkin (95-538 $2 75)
Boswell wrestled with the Angel of Death and suddenly realized that everybody dies With that realization he begins an odyssey of the ego searching out VIP's and prostrating himself before them BOSWELL "crackles with gusto and imaginative fertility " —*Book Week*

THE DICK GIBSON SHOW
by Stanley Elkin (95-540 $2 75)
Like *The Great Gatsby,* he wants life to live up to myth He is the perpetual apprentice whetting his skills and adopting names and accents to suit geography Elkin's "prose is alive with its wealth of detail and specifically American metaphors   compulsively readable and exhilarating."
—*The Library Journal*

CRIERS AND KIBITZERS, KIBITZERS AND CRIERS
by Stanley Elkin (91 543, $2 50)
"An air of mysterious joy hangs over these stories," says *Life* magazine Yet the *New York Times Review of Books* reports that "Bedeviling with his witchcraft the poor souls he has conjured and set into action, Stanley Elkin involves his spirits sometimes in the dread machineries of allegory and fantasy "

Mystery...Intrigue...Suspense

FLETCH AND THE WIDOW BRADLEY
by Gregory Mcdonald   (B90-922 $2.95)
Fletch has got *some* trouble! Body trouble with an executive dead in
Switzerland His ashes shipped home prove it Or do they? Job trouble
When Fletch's career is ruined for the mistake no reporter should make
Woman trouble with a wily widow and her suspect sister in-law From
Alaska to Mexico, Fletch the laid-back muckraker covers it all!

FLETCH'S MOXIE
by Gregory Mcdonald   (B90-923, $3.25)
Fletch has got plenty of Moxie And she's just beautiful Moxie's a hot
movie star She's got a dad who's one of the roaring legends of Hollywood
She's dead center in a case that begins with a sensational on-camera
murder and explodes in race riots and police raids. Most of all, she's got
problems. Because she's the number one suspect!

To order use the coupon below If you prefer to use your
own stationery please include complete title as well as
book number and price Allow 4 weeks for delivery